EVERYONE LOVES A LINDSEY!

Winner of the *Romantic Times* Award for
Best Historical Romance Author

Johanna Lindsey

New York Times Bestselling Author of

Captive Bride	*Paradise Wild*
Fires of Winter	*So Speaks the Heart*
Glorious Angel	*A Gentle Feuding*
Heart of Thunder	*Tender is the Storm*
Brave the Wild Wind	*Love Only Once*
When Love Awaits	*Hearts Aflame*
A Heart So Wild	*Secret Fire*
A Pirate's Love	and now . . .

"Her stories prove that love is timeless. Ms. Lindsey sustains the sensuality of her story from cover to cover. You can almost smell the flowers, feel the wind, and touch the hero."

Romantic Times

"The stories are fast moving and well written, with the characters revealing themselves to us through lively dialogue."

Chicago Sun-Times

"Congratulations, Johanna! We look forward to more of the same!"

Affaire de Coeur

Tender Rebel

Johanna Lindsey

AVON BOOKS  NEW YORK

TENDER REBEL is an original publication of Avon Books. This work has never before appeared in book form. This work is a novel. Any similarity to actual persons or events is purely coincidental.

AVON BOOKS
A division of
The Hearst Corporation
105 Madison Avenue
New York, New York 10016

Copyright © 1988 by Johanna Lindsey
Published by arrangement with the author
Library of Congress Catalog Card Number: 87-91458
ISBN: 0-380-75086-4

First Avon Books Printing: June 1988

*This book is dedicated with love
to all my readers,
with special thanks to those who wanted
Uncle Tony to have his own story.*

Chapter One

England, 1818

"*A*re ye scared, hinny?"

Roslynn Chadwick turned away from the coach window and the passing scenery she had been staring at for the last hour without actually seeing. Scared? She was alone in the world now with no guardian, no family worth mentioning. She was on her way to an uncertain future and leaving behind all that was familiar to her. Scared? She was terrified.

But Nettie MacDonald wasn't to know that, not if Roslynn could help it. Nettie was too uneasy herself, had been ever since they'd crossed the English border yesterday morning, though she too tried to hide it by turning querulous, as was her way. Nettie had been all chipper and cheer before that, even while crossing the Lowlands, which she disdained. A Highlander all her life, and that was forty-two years' worth, Nettie never thought the day would come when she would be forced to leave her beloved Highlands, let alone cross the border into England. England! But Nettie wouldn't be left behind, no, not dear Nettie.

Roslynn managed a smile for Nettie's benefit, and even a bit of a twinkle in her hazel eyes to reassure her abigail. "Och, and what've I to be scared of, Nettie? Didna we manage to sneak off in the dead of night wi' none the wiser? Geordie'll be searching Aberdeen and Edinburgh for weeks and weeks and never guess we've absconded to London.''

"That he will." Nettie spared herself a pleased smile for their success so far, forgetting for the moment her fear and dislike of the English. Her dislike of Geordie Cameron went much deeper. "And I hope that devil chokes on his spleen when he realizes ye've escaped his foul plans, that I do. I didna like Duncan, bless him, making ye promise what ye had tae, but he knew what was best fer ye. And dinna be thinking I'm sae fashed I didna hear ye fergetting yer proper English, lass, that Duncan brought that fine snobbish tutor tae be teaching ye. Ye'll no' be fergetting it, especially now we're here among the devil's kin.''

Roslynn grinned when this last was delivered in Nettie's most scolding tone, and couldn't resist teasing a bit more. "When I see an Englishmon will be soon enough for me to be remembering my proper English. You wouldna deny me this wee bit of time left when I dinna have to be thinking about every word I say, would you now?''

"Humph! 'Tis only when ye're that upset that ye ferget anymore, and well I ken it.''

Of course Nettie knew it. Nettie knew Roslynn better than herself sometimes. And if Roslynn wasn't in a temper, which was when she most often forgot herself and lapsed into the Scottish brogue she had picked up from Gramp and Nettie, she was still upset, and with reason. But not enough to forget the proper English that had been drummed into her by her tutor. Roslynn sighed.

"I hope the trunks got there, or we'll be in a fine pickle.'' They had both left with only one change of clothes, to further outwit her cousin Geordie, just in case someone saw them leave and told him.

"That's the least of yer worries, lass. Sure and it saved time bringing that London modiste tae Cameron Hall tae be making ye all those bonny dresses, sae ye dinna have tae be fitted when we get there. Duncan, bless him, thought of everything, even sending the trunks ahead, one by one, sae Geordie wouldna suspect anything if he was watching."

And Nettie had thought it was such a lark, sneaking off in the middle of the night as they had, with their skirts hiked up and wearing old breeches underneath so in the moonlight they might pass for men. Truth be known, Roslynn had thought so too. In fact, that was the only part of this madness she had enjoyed. They had ridden to the nearest town where the pre-arranged coach and driver were waiting, and had had to wait several hours to be sure they weren't followed before they actually set off on this journey. But all the stealth and bother had been necessary to outwit Geordie Cameron. At least Gramp had made Roslynn believe it was necessary.

And Roslynn could believe it after seeing Geordie's face when Gramp's will was read. After all, Geordie was Duncan Cameron's great-nephew, his youngest brother's grandson, and his only male relative still living. Geordie had every right to assume some of Duncan's great wealth would be left to him, if only a small part. But Duncan had left his entire estate to Roslynn, his only grandchild: Cameron Hall, the mills, the countless other businesses, everything. And Geordie had been hard put not to fly into a rage.

"He shouldna have been sae surprised," Nettie had said after Geordie left the day of the reading. "He knew Duncan hated him, that he blamed him fer yer dear mother's death. Why, 'tis why he was courting ye sae diligently all these years. He knew Duncan'd leave it all tae ye. And 'tis why we've nae time tae lose, now Duncan's gone.''

No, there was no time to lose. Roslynn knew it when Geordie once more asked her to marry him after the will was read, and she once more refused. She and Nettie had left that very night, with no time to grieve, no time to regret the promise she had made to her grandfather. But she had done her grieving in the last two months, when they had known Duncan's time was finally up. And it had been a blessing in fact, his death, for he had been wasting away these last seven years and suffering with the pain, and it was only his Scot's stubbornness that had let him linger this long. No, she couldn't be sorry Gramp's suffering was finally over. But oh, how she would miss that dear old man who had been both mother and father to her all these years.

''Ye'll no' grieve fer me, lassie,'' he'd told her weeks before he died. ''I forbid it. Ye've given me too many years, too many wasted years, and I'll no' have ye giving even one day more once I'm gone. Ye'll promise me that too.''

One more promise to the old man she loved, the man who had raised her and bullied her and loved her ever since his daughter had returned to him tugging along a six-year-old Roslynn in her wake. What did one more promise matter when she'd already given him the fateful one that had her in such trepidation now? And then there had been no time for grieving anyway, so she had at least fulfilled that promise.

Nettie scowled as she watched Roslynn turn her eyes back to the window and knew she was thinking of Duncan Cameron again. ''Gramp'' she had disrespectfully called him from the day her mother had first brought her to Cameron Hall to stay, and that

just to get his goat. How the little imp had loved
nettling the fierce old Scot, and how he had delighted
in every bit of teasing and mischief she served him.
They would both miss him, but there were too many
other things to think of now.

"We're coming tae the inn finally," Nettie observed from her seat facing the front of the coach.

Roslynn leaned forward and turned to the side to
see out the window in the same direction, and the
setting sun caught her full in the face, touching her
hair and making it appear like a sunset itself. Pretty
hair, the lass had, red-gold like Janet's, her mother.
Nettie's own hair was black as coal, and her eyes were
the dull green of a loch shadowed by tall oaks. Roslynn had Janet's eyes too, that greenish-gray color that
was saved from being nondescript by the golden flecks
that were so brightly noticeable. Come to that, everything about her was a lot like Janet Cameron before
she had gone away with her Englishman. In fact, there
was nothing at all of Roslynn's father in her, that self-
same Englishman who had stolen Janet's heart and
turned her into a shadow of herself after the tragic
accident that killed him. Perhaps it was just as well
Janet had died a year afterward, for she had never
been the same. And Roslynn, thank God, had her
grandfather to lean on then. A seven-year-old child,
with both parents gone, was fortunately adaptable,
especially with an old Scot to dote on her every whim.

*Och, I'm as bad as the lass, tae be thinking about
the dead when 'tis the future that's sae in doubt.*

"Let's hope the beds are at least softer than last
night," Roslynn commented as the coach stopped before the country inn. "That is the *only* thing that has
me eager to get to London. I know Frances will have
comfortable beds waiting for us."

"Ye mean ye'll no' be glad tae see yer best friend after all these years?"

Roslynn glanced at Nettie with surprise. "Well, of course, there's that. Of course there is. I can't wait to see her again. But the circumstances won't allow a pleasant reunion, will they? I mean, with no time to lose, how much actual visiting will I get to have with Frances? Oh, drat Geordie anyway," she added with a scowl that drew her titian brows closer together. "If it weren't for him—"

"Ye wouldna have made nae promises, and we wouldna be here now, and it does nae good tae be bewailing it, now, does it?" Nettie retorted.

Roslynn grinned. "Who was bewailing what last night when she lay in a hard bed that wasn't fit for bedbugs, let alone a tired body?"

Nettie snorted, refusing to answer that reminder, and shooed Roslynn out of the coach as soon as the driver opened the door and held up his hand for her. Roslynn's chuckle carried back to her abigail as she walked ahead, still thinking about it, and Nettie snorted again, this time to herself.

Ye're no' sae auld that ye canna stand a few nights' discomfort, Nettie, lass, she thought, watching Roslynn's bouncy step that in fact made her feel twice her age at the moment. *The bed can be made of stone and ye'll no' say one word tonight, or ye'll never hear the end of it from the wee lassie.*

But then Nettie grinned, shaking her head. A bit of teasing was just what Roslynn needed to be doing to get her mind off the future. *That bed can be soft as down, but ye better say 'tis full of rocks, lass. 'Tis been too long since ye've heard her laugh and seen the mischief in her eyes. She needs tae tease, that she does.*

As Roslynn approached the inn, she barely noticed the sixteen-year-old lad standing on a stool lighting the lamp above the door, but he unfortunately noticed her. Hearing the husky chuckle that was so different from any sound of humor he'd ever heard before, he glanced over his shoulder, then nearly fell off the stool, he was so boggled by the sight of her. Lit up like a flame, she was, in the reddish glow of the setting sun that streaked across the yard, and getting closer by the second, until he could make out every feature of her heart-shaped face, from the finely molded cheekbones and small tapered nose to the firm little chin and generous, full lips. And then she passed through the door, and his head craned around it to follow her inside, until a sharp *humph* snapped his head back around and he stared at the stern-faced abigail looking up at him, his cheeks flushing hotly.

But Nettie took pity on the lad and didn't dress him down as she usually did anyone caught gawking at her Roslynn. It happened wherever they went, for Lady Roslynn Chadwick had that effect on the male species, and no age seemed to be immune, from small tykes to old men, and everything in breeches in between. And this was the lass to be turned loose on London.

Chapter Two

"*A*nd you wondered who his tailor is?" the Honorable William Fairfax snickered aside to his young friend. "Told you his tailor had nothing to do with it, didn't I? You want to turn yourself out in a reasonable facsimile, best take up the gloves. He's been at it for more'n a dozen years, so I hear."

William's young friend, Cully, flinched at the sound of leather connecting with solid flesh again, but squinted his eyes open this time. He had closed them tight a few minutes ago when the first dribble of blood had appeared from an abused nose. He shuddered now, for that same abused nose was gushing blood, and so was the swollen mouth below it, and so was a split brow above it.

"No taste for it, Cully?" William grinned, eyeing his friend's green pallor. "Imagine his partner don't either, not today leastways." He chuckled here, thinking that funny. "Now if Knighton would just climb in the ring with him, we might have something to wager on. He trained him, you know. 'Course, Knighton ain't come out ahead in the last ten years, so I hear, though he does give the lord a better showing. But then Malory's winded now, so that'd even the odds some."

But as they watched along with a few dozen other gentlemen surrounding the boxing ring, Sir Anthony Malory relaxed his stance and turned to glower at the owner of the sporting hall. "Blister it, Knighton, I told you he wasn't ready yet. He hasn't healed from the last time.''

John Knighton shrugged, though there was a definite spark of humor in his dark eyes as he gazed back at the disgusted pugilist he considered a friend. ''I didn't hear any other takers, my lord, did you? Maybe if you let someone else win for a change, you'd find more partners to choose from for your exercise.''

There were a good many chuckles over that remark. Everyone there knew it had been a decade since Malory had lost a match or let anyone get the better of him even in a few rounds of sparring. He was in superb condition, muscles honed to perfection, but it was his skill in the ring that made him so remarkable—and unchallenged. The promoters, Knighton among them, would give their eyeteeth to get him in the ring for a professional fight. But to a rakehell like Malory, boxing was no more than a means of exercise to keep him fit and counteract the life of dissipation he enjoyed. His thrice-weekly visits to Knighton's Hall were treated in the same vein as his morning rides in the park, simply for his own pleasure.

Half the gentlemen there were pugilists as well, awaiting their turn to exercise in the ring. Some, like the Honorable Fairfax, just dropped by to watch the experts work out, though occasionally there was the opportunity to do a little gambling if any serious challenges were issued. A few others who were present were Malory's cronies; they frequently showed up to watch him demolish the sparring partners Knighton had the misfortune to provide, being wise enough themselves never to get in the ring with him.

One of them ribbed Anthony now. Nearly of the same height, but more on the lean side, Lord Amherst was a devil-may-care fellow whose gray eyes were more often than not crinkled with humor. The same age, but fair where Anthony was dark, he often shared the same interests, mainly women, gambling, and women.

"The only way you'll get someone to put his heart into it, Malory, is if you cuckold some young Corinthian your size and force him to issue the challenge."

"With my luck, George," Malory shot back, "he'd call for pistols instead, and what fun is that?"

George Amherst laughed at the dry tone, for if not everyone knew that Anthony was unbeatable in the ring, they did know he was nonpareil on the dueling field. He was even known to quite nonchalantly ask his challengers on what luckless part of their anatomy they would like to receive their wound of honor, which naturally set the poor fellows trembling in their boots, if they weren't already.

As far as George knew, Anthony had never actually killed anyone in a duel, since nearly all his were fought over women, rake that he was, and he firmly believed there wasn't a woman born worth dying over—well, that was excluding those in his family, of course. Malory was devilish touchy about his family. He might be a bachelor, confirmed positively, but with three older brothers with offspring aplenty, he didn't lack for nieces and nephews to dote on.

"Looking for competition, Tony? You should have sent your man round to find me. You know I'm always happy to oblige you."

George swung around sharply, disbelieving his ears at the sound of a voice he hadn't heard in more than ten years. And then his brows shot up incredulously, for he hadn't been mistaken. Standing in the doorway was James Malory, older certainly, but looking every bit as dangerous as he ever had ten years ago when he had been London's most notorious rakehell. Big, blond, and still handsome too, by God! Incredible!

And then George swung back to see how Anthony was taking this unexpected appearance. The two brothers had been close before, being only a year apart in age and inclined toward the same interests, though James was assuredly the wilder of the two— at least he had been. But then James had disappeared, and for some reason or other that the family never spoke of, the other brothers had disowned him, Anthony included, and wouldn't even mention his name. As close as George was to Anthony all these years since, and he liked to think they were best friends, Anthony had never once confided what it was that James had done to be ousted from the family.

But to George's surprise, Anthony was showing no signs of his formidable temper. In fact, no emotion whatever crossed his handsome countenance for those in the hall to remark on. You had to know him well to recognize that gleam in his cobalt-blue eyes for what it was: pleasure, not fury.

And yet when he spoke, you'd have thought he was addressing his worst enemy. "James, what the bloody hell are you still doing in London? You were to sail this morning!"

James did no more than offer a bored shrug. "Change of plans, thanks to Jeremy's newfound stubbornness. Since he's met the rest of the family, he's become impossible to handle. I swear he's been taking lessons from Regan in manipulation, for he managed somehow or other to talk me into letting him finish his schooling here, though I'm deuced if I know exactly how he did it."

Anthony wanted to laugh at James' expression of bafflement at being outmaneuvered by a seventeen-

year-old whelp who looked more Anthony's son than
James', and he would have if James hadn't slipped
the name Regan into his explanation. The name always rubbed Anthony on the raw, as it did Jason and
Edward, their older brothers, and James knew it,
which was why he used ''Regan'' instead of ''Reggie,'' as the rest of the family called Regina Eden.
But as far back as Anthony could remember, James
had had to be different, going his own way and doing
as he bloody well pleased, and to hell with the consequences.

As James had spoken, he had walked forward, casually slipping out of his coat to reveal the sort of
loose-sleeved shirt that he preferred when captaining
the *Maiden Anne*. Since he gave every appearance of
being about to oblige Anthony in the ring, Anthony
refrained from taking him to task over his ''Regan,''
which would have started their usual argument and
likely jeopardized a little friendly sparring.

''Does this mean you'll be staying as well?'' Anthony asked as James handed over his coat to George
and accepted the gloves a grinning John Knighton
helped him into.

''Only long enough to get the youngun settled and
togged up, I think, at least for now. Though Connie
has pointed out that the only reason we were willing
to set ourselves down in the islands was to give Jeremy a home.''

Anthony couldn't help laughing this time. ''Two
old sea dogs playing mother. God, I wish I could've
seen it.''

''I wouldn't talk, Tony,'' James said, unperturbed
by the taunting. ''You played mother yourself each
summer for six years, didn't you?''

''Father,'' Anthony corrected. ''Or more like big

brother, which is neither here nor there. I'm surprised you didn't marry like Jason did, just to give Jeremy a mother. 'Course, with Conrad Sharp willing to help you raise the lad, I suppose you didn't think it necessary.''

James leaped up into the ring. ''That's my best friend you're disparaging.''

Anthony bowed slightly. ''Point taken. So who gets the dear boy while you and Connie are deciding whether to come home for good?''

James' right connected solidly with Anthony's midsection just before he said, ''You do.''

While Anthony doubled over, absorbing the punch as well as the answer, the wagers began flying about the room. At last there was someone who looked as if he just might be able to beat the unbeatable Lord Malory. Malory was taller by a few inches, but the other bloke was brawnier, and looked quite capable of wiping the floor with anyone in the room, Malory included. And they were going to be privileged to see it. Only a few there realized these two were brothers.

As soon as Anthony was able to draw breath, he scowled at James for the surprise punch, but as to his revelation, he simply said, ''Me? How'd I get so lucky?''

''You're the lad's choice. You're his bloody idol, don't you know—next to me, of course.''

''Of course,'' Anthony replied and took James equally by surprise with an uppercut that staggered James back several paces. As James flexed his jaw, Anthony added, ''I'll be glad to have him, as long as you realize I won't curtail my activities as I did for Reggie.''

They circled each other now, both getting in another punch before James replied, ''Don't expect you to, lad, when I didn't. It's different when you've got a boy underfoot. Hell and fire, he's been wenching since he was fourteen.''

Anthony burst into laughter at that, unfortunately letting down his guard to receive a ringing blow to the side of his head. But he was quick enough to counteract with an upper to James' middle that lifted him a good five inches off the floor, amazingly done, since James was a good thirty pounds heavier in solid muscle.

Anthony stood back, allowing his brother a moment to catch his breath. When James glanced up, still bent over, he was grinning.

''Do we really want to take aches and pains to bed tonight, Tony?''

Anthony's teeth flashed in accordance. ''Not when something softer can be found, and I assure you, something softer can be found.'' He came forward to throw an arm around his brother's shoulder.

''Then you'll take the lad until school starts?''

''Love to, but good God, I can see I'll get a fair amount of ribbing from it. Anyone who looks at Jeremy will think he's mine.''

''That's why he wants you.'' James grinned, flashing his own set of pearly whites. ''He's got a devilish sense of humor. Now about tonight. I know a couple of wenches—''

''Wenches, indeed. You were a pirate too long, Captain Hawke. Now I know a couple of ladies . . .''

Chapter Three

"*B*ut I don't understand, Ros," Lady Frances leaned forward to say. "Why would you want to tie yourself to a man when you don't have to? I mean, if you were already in love, that'd be different. But you're talking about marrying someone you haven't even met yet."

"Frances, if I hadn't promised, do you really think I'd do it?" Roslynn asked.

"Well, I should certainly hope not—but who's to know if you don't keep the promise? I mean, your grandfather's dead and—" Frances broke off at the look on her friend's face. "Forget I said that."

"I will."

"Oh, I just think it's such a shame!" Frances sighed with emphasis.

Lady Frances Grenfell was a striking woman by any standards. On the tiny side, she was not exactly beautiful but was, however, very handsome with her blond hair and dark brown eyes. At one time she had been the most cheerful, effervescent girl Roslynn had ever known, but that was before her disappointing marriage to Henry Grenfell seven years ago. Now she was demure, matronly even, yet she did still have her moments that could remind Roslynn of the happy girl she had once been.

"You're as independent now as anyone could ever ask to be," Frances continued determinedly. "With more money than you know what to do with, and not a soul to tell you what to do. It took me seven years and living with a man I didn't love for five of them to get to where you are now, and still I have a mother who nags if she hears of me doing the slightest thing she doesn't approve of. Even as a widow living alone with my son, I still have someone to answer to. But you, Roslynn, you have no one at all to worry about, and yet you must give yourself over to some man who will delight in putting a harness on your freedom as Lord Henry did to me. And I know you don't want to do it. I know that very well.''

''It doesn't matter what I want, Frances. It's what I have to do.''

''But why?'' Frances cried in exasperation. ''That's what I want to know. And don't just say again because you promised your grandfather you would. Tell me why he made you make such a promise. If it was so important to him, he had ample time to have married you off himself.''

''Well, as to that,'' Roslynn replied, ''there was no one I wanted to marry. And Gramp wouldn't have forced me on someone I didn't want.''

''In all these years? No one at all?''

''Och, I hate the way you say *all these years,* Frances, I really do. Dinna remind me how difficult it's going to be for me.''

Frances' brown eyes widened. ''Difficult?'' She nearly laughed. ''Posh! If ever there was going to be anything so easy, it's getting you married. You'll have so many hopefuls, you won't know what to do with them all. And your age, m'dear, won't matter one little jot. Good God, don't you know how incredibly lovely you are? And if that weren't enough, you've got a fortune that would make a banker positively drool.''

''I'm twenty-five years old, Frances!'' Roslynn said

in such a way that she might as well have said one hundred.

Frances grinned. "So am I, and I don't consider that ancient, thank you."

"It's different when you're a widow. You've been married. No one would think anything of you marrying again."

"No, they won't, because I never will."

Roslynn frowned at the interruption. "But the *ton* will take one look at me on the marriage block next to all those young debutantes and laugh their heads off."

Frances smiled. "Honestly, Ros—"

"It's true. Hell's teeth, I'd laugh myself to see a twenty-five-year-old spinster making a fool of herself." Roslynn snorted.

"Now stop it. I tell you—I *swear* to you, your age won't matter."

Roslynn couldn't believe it, much as she wanted to. She hid it well, but she was very close to tears. This was the very reason she was so terrified of putting herself forward in search of a husband. She was going to make a fool of herself, and that was something she couldn't bear.

"They'll think something's terribly wrong with me because I didn't marry before now, Fran. You know they're bound to. It's human nature."

"They'll understand perfectly when they hear you've spent the past six years nursing your grandfather, and they'll commend you for it. Now, not another word about your age. That is the least of your worries. And you have quite managed to avoid answering my question, haven't you?"

Roslynn chuckled at the stern look on her friend's face, a warm, husky sound that was uniquely her own.

She and Nettie had arrived at the town house on South Audley Street late last night, so late that there had been no time for the two old friends to talk until this morning. And it was an old friendship, one that had survived twelve years with only one visit in the last ten, and that was when Frances had brought her son, Timmy, to the Highlands for a holiday four years ago.

Roslynn had other women friends in Scotland, but none as close as Frances, and none to whom she felt free to confide all her secrets. They had met when they were thirteen, when Gramp had carted her off to school in England to "ladify" her, since he swore she was turning into a wee hoyden with no sense a-tall of her station—which was certainly true, for all that, but not very fair as far as she was concerned at the time.

Roslynn had lasted two years at school before she was kicked out and carted back to Cameron Hall for "incorrigible behavior." Gramp didn't scold. Fact was he had missed her too much and was glad to have her back. But he enticed one of the fine teachers away from the school to continue Roslynn's education, and there wasn't any mischief terrible enough to make Miss Beechham quit; Gramp was paying her too much.

But during those two years in England, Frances and Roslynn had been inseparable. And if she hadn't had her own coming out when she turned eighteen, she had shared Frances' through their letters. Through Frances, she knew what it was like to fall in love. Through Frances, she also knew what it was like to have a husband you didn't love. And although she never had any children of her own, there wasn't a single thing she didn't know about them, at least about a son, because Frances had shared every phase of Timmy's development with her.

Roslynn had shared everything too in her letters over the years, though her life in the Highlands had been singularly lacking in excitement. But she hadn't wanted to worry Frances these last months with Gramp's fears, so she hadn't told her about Geordie. And how to tell her now? How to make her understand that this was not just an old man's senility to scoff at, but a very real and dangerous situation?

Roslynn decided to start at the beginning. "Frances, do you remember my telling you that my mother drowned in Loch Etive when I was seven?"

"Yes, a year after your father died, wasn't it?" Frances said gently, patting her hand.

Roslynn nodded, trying not to remember how desolate she had been from both deaths. "Gramp always blamed his grandnephew, Geordie, for my mother's death. Geordie was a mean child, you see, always hurting animals and causing accidents that he could laugh over. He was only eleven at the time, but he'd already caused one of our grooms to break a leg, our cook to be severely burned, and one horse to be put down, and no telling what he'd done at his own home that we never heard about. His father was my mother's cousin, and when he came to visit, he always brought Geordie. And the day my mother drowned, they'd been visiting a week already."

"But how could he have caused your mother to drown?"

"There was never any proof, Frances. The boat she took out was assumed to have overturned, and she was too constricted in her heavy clothing, it being winter, to be able to swim to shore."

"What was she doing out on the loch in winter?"

"She had grown up on the loch. It was second nature to her to be in the water. She loved it, swam
every day in the summer, and did all her visiting that
could be done up and down the shore, both sides of
the loch. If she could row herself, she'd have nothing
to do with a carriage or a horse, no matter the
weather. And she had her own little rowboat that was
easy for her to handle. We both did, though I was
never allowed to take mine out alone. But anyway, as
good a swimmer as she was, she didn't make it out
that day."

"There was no one to help?"

"No one saw it happen. She'd planned to cross the
loch that day, so likely the boat went down too far in
the middle. It was several days later when one of the
crofters happened to mention to Gramp that he'd seen
Geordie down by where the boats were kept, earlier
in the week. If Geordie weren't such a little devil for
causing accidents, Gramp would never have thought
anything of it. But the fact was, Geordie had taken
my mother's death near as bad as I did, which was
most surprising since he had never really liked my
mother or me."

"So your grandfather thought Geordie had tampered with her boat?"

Roslynn nodded. "Something that would have
caused a slow leak. It would have been just the sort
of thing Geordie would have laughed over, to have
someone get a dousing and lose a good boat. If he
did do it, I don't think it was any more than a nasty
prank, one gone awry. I don't think he meant to *kill*
anyone, just get them wet and mad. He couldn't have
known that my mother wouldn't have been rowing
near shore. It wasn't often she crossed the loch."

"But still . . ."

"Yes, still." Roslynn sighed. "But Gramp could never prove it, and so what could he do? The boat was never found to show it'd been tampered with. Gramp never trusted Geordie after that, never let him come to the Hall but that he put one of the servants to following him. He *hated* him, Frances, deep down, yet without telling his father what he suspected, he couldn't deny him his home. But he swore Geordie would never get anything out of him, and he was emphatic about that. When Geordie's father died, he left him only a small inheritance. Gramp knew Geordie resented him having so much, while Geordie's side of the family had so little, but that came with Gramp being the oldest son and inheriting the Cameron wealth. And Gramp knew for certain Geordie wanted the money when he asked me to marry him."

"You do yourself a disservice there, Ros. You don't have only money to recommend you."

Roslynn waved that aside. "The fact was that Geordie had never liked me, Frances, even as we got older, and the feeling was more than mutual. He resented me, you see, being Gramp's closest relative. It wasn't until his father died and he learned how little was left him that he did a turnabout and became Mister Charming to me."

"But you turned him down." Frances pointed out the obvious.

"Of course I turned him down. I'm not a stupid looby who can't see through false flattery when it's poured on with such ruthlessness. But he didn't give up. He continued to pretend a great love for me even while I could see the cold hatred in his icy blue eyes."

"Very well, now I have all that, I still don't see why you have to rush onto the marriage block."

"With Gramp gone, I've got no protection. I

wouldn't need protection but for Geordie. He's asked me to marry him too many times, you see. He's made it clear in every way he wants the Cameron wealth, and he'll do anything to get it.''

''But what can he do?''

Roslynn snorted in disgust. ''I thought nothing. But Gramp was wiser.''

Frances gasped. ''The money wouldn't go to Geordie if anything happened to you, would it?''

''No, Gramp made sure of that. The thing is, Geordie can force me to marry him if he can get his hands on me. There are ways, drugging or beating, or even an unscrupulous parson, and there'd be no signing of the marriage contract that Gramp had drawn up for me. Geordie would have control of everything if he could manage it, and as I said, it would only take his getting his hands on me. Once I'm his wife, he'd have no use for me, would he? In fact, he daren't keep me around to tell all that he'd done.''

Frances shivered, despite the warm summer night. ''You're not making this up, are you?''

''I wish I was, Frances, I really do. Gramp always hoped Geordie would marry, but he never did. Gramp knew he had just been biding his time, waiting for the day I'd be left alone with no one to protest very loudly if he forced me to marry him. And he's too big for me to fight, even if I am right handy with a dirk and keep one in my boot.''

''You don't!''

''Oh, I do. Gramp made sure I knew how to use it too. But what help would a little dirk be if Geordie hired help to abduct me? Now you know why I had to leave Scotland so quickly, why I'm here.''

''And why you want a husband.''

''Yes, that too. Once I'm married, there's nothing

Geordie can do. Gramp made me promise I'd marry, and quickly. He planned everything, even my escape. Geordie will search Scotland first before he looks for me here, so I have a little time to choose someone, but not much.''

''Dash it all, it's not fair, none of it,'' Frances said with feeling. ''How can you fall in love in such a rush?''

Roslynn grinned, remembering Gramp's stern admonishment. ''Protect yerself first, lassie, wi' a ring on yer finger. Ye can find love later.'' And how she had blushed, understanding exactly what he'd meant. But he had also conceded. ''Of course, if love falls into yer lap, dinna be pushing it off. Hold fast and dinna let go, fer it could work, and then ye'll have nae need tae be looking fer it later.''

Gramp had had other advice too, about whom she should consider. ''They say a rake makes a dandy husband, that's if a bonny lass can catch his heart—no' his eye, mind ye—his heart. He's sowed his oats, ye see, more than sowed them, plowed the whole field, sae tae speak. Sae when he settles down, he's ready tae do just that.''

''They also say, once a rake, always a rake,'' Roslynn had been compelled to point out. This bit of advice from Gramp she hadn't been at all thrilled with.

''Who says sae? If that's sae, then the heart hasna been caught. Ye catch the heart, lassie, and ye'll be glad of it, ye will. But I'm no' talking 'bout the young hellions, nae, nae. Ye want tae find a mon wi' enough years on him tae ken he's had his wild days aplenty and doesna need more. But ye dinna want him jaded either. Be careful of that.''

''And how do you tell the difference?''

"If he still has feeling. If ye can excite him—och, never mind those blushes, lassie. Ye'll be exciting more young bloods then ye'll ken what tae do wi', and enough rakes as well, sae ye'll have plenty tae choose from."

"But I don't want a rake," she had insisted.

"Ye will," Duncan predicted. "Happens they're the ones the lassies canna resist. Just make sure ye get the ring afore ye allow—"

"Gramp!"

He snorted at her exclamation. "If I dinna tell ye, who will? Ye need tae ken how tae handle such a mon."

"With the back of my hand, that's how."

He chuckled. "Now, hinny, ye're no' being open-minded about this," he cajoled her. "If the mon attracts ye and sets yer heart tae fluttering, are ye going tae ignore him simply because he's a rake?"

"Yes!"

"But I tell ye they make the best husbands!" He had turned to shouting in the face of her stubbornness. "And I want the best mon fer ye, even if ye willna have much time tae find him."

"How in the blue blazes do you know, Gramp? Just tell me that, if you can." She wasn't angry, just flustered. Gramp didn't know she already had knowledge of rakes through Frances, and as far as she was concerned, they were to be avoided like the plague.

"I was one myself, and dinna look sae surprised. I'd had sixteen years of plowing the fields afore I met and married yer grandmother, and I was faithful tae the lass until the day she died."

An exception. One exception. Certainly not enough for Roslynn to change her mind about that particular breed of gentleman. But she didn't tell Duncan that.

She let him think he had made his point. Still, this was one part of his advice she wouldn't follow and so made no promises about.

To Frances and her question about love, Roslynn shrugged. "If it doesn't happen right off, then it doesn't. You managed to live through it."

Frances frowned. "I had no choice."

"I'm sorry. I shouldn't have reminded you of that. But as for me, show me a fine-looking fellow who isn't too much of a skirt-chaser and he'll do nicely. If I think I can like him, that should suffice." And then she grinned. "After all, I have my grandfather's permission, suggestion even, to find love later if I don't get it in my marriage."

"He . . . would you?"

Roslynn chuckled at her friend's shocked countenance. "Let me find the husband before I start thinking about the lover. Just cross your fingers for me that they turn out to be one and the same."

Chapter Four

"*W*ell, youngun? What boring bit of nonsense have you to impart? Will it do?" Anthony leaned casually against the doorjamb, watching Jeremy survey his new room with obvious delight.

"Hell's bells, Uncle Tony, I—"

"Stop right there." Anthony put on his most unnerving scowl for the lad's benefit. "You can uncle my brothers to death if you like, but a simple Tony will do here, thank you."

Jeremy smiled widely, not at all intimidated. "It's great, Tony, it really is. The room, the house, you. I can't thank you en—"

"Then don't, please," Anthony cut in quickly. "And before you go on with this bloody hero worship, be apprised I'm going to thoroughly debauch you, dear boy. Serve your father right for entrusting you in my care."

"You promise?"

Anthony had to constrain the short bark of laughter. The lad had taken him seriously. "No, I do not. Good God, d'you think I want Jason down my throat? He's going to go through the roof as it is when he learns James turned you over to me instead of him. No, I'll introduce you to the type of female your father has forgotten exists."

"Like Regan?"

Anthony's scowl was quite real this time. "We'll get on, you and I, as long as I never hear that name. Blister it, you're as bad as your father—"

"Now, I can't let you speak poorly of my father, Uncle Tony," Jeremy interrupted quite seriously.

Anthony stepped forward and tossed the lad's coal-black hair, so like his own. "Understand me, puppy. I love your father. Always have. But I'll run him through the coals anytime I feel the urge to. He was my brother before he was your father, after all, and he doesn't need defending by the likes of you. So keep your hackles down. I never meant anything by it."

Jeremy chuckled, mollified. "Rega—Reggie said you weren't happy unless you were arguing with your brothers."

"Did she? Well, that puss always has been a know-it-all," Anthony replied fondly. "And speaking of the lady, she sent round a note today. Seems she's in town without her viscount for a change and in need of an escort for some ball tonight. How would you like the chore?"

"Me? D'you mean it?" Jeremy asked excitedly.

"I don't see why not. She knows I can't abide such affairs and wouldn't have asked me if someone else were available. But Edward's taken his brood up to Haverston for the week to visit Jason, and Derek's up there too, so that unfortunately leaves you and me the only Malorys in town she can prevail upon—unless, of course, we foist the chore on your father. That's if we could find him in time. He might be laying his pallet here for the week, but he mentioned something about looking up an old friend—"

"Sarah," Jeremy supplied, blue eyes twinkling. "She works in a tavern down—"

"Spare me the details."

"You wouldn't catch him going to a ball anyway, even for his favorite niece. But I'd love to. I even have the clothes for it. And I know how to dance, I really do. Connie taught me.''

Anthony nearly choked on that one. "Did he? Who led, you or he?''

Jeremy grinned. "A little of both, but I've had practice with the wenches since, and they haven't complained.''

Anthony wasn't about to ask what other forms of practice the lad had been at, for he could well imagine. Too much association with his father's unsavory friends, obviously. Whatever was he going to do with such a charming scamp? But he would have to do something, for Jeremy was sadly lacking in the social graces, thanks to his father. A gentleman pirate—well, retired pirate—and a disreputable rake, yours truly— fine examples to choose from. Perhaps he ought to turn the lad over to his cousins when they returned to London and see if they could teach him the rudiments.

"I'm sure Reggie'll be delighted to dance with you, youngun, but call *her* a wench and she's libel to box your ears. And she knows you well enough now, so she'll be glad to have you for the evening. I understand she's rather fond of you.''

"Aye, she took right to me the day we abducted her.''

"Must you remind me of that? And it was only after she knew who you were that she took to you, dear boy. Good God, for James to go to so much trouble to even the score with the viscount, then to find Reggie had married him.''

"Well, that changed everything.''

"Of course it did. But he shouldn't have dragged you along in this quest for vengeance anyway.''

"It was a matter of honor.''

"Ah, so you know about honor, do you?" Anthony said dryly. "Then there's hope for you, I suppose . . . if we can manage to remove 'wenches' from your vocabulary, that is."

Jeremy blushed slightly. It wasn't his fault he had spent the first years of his life in a tavern until his father discovered his existence and took him in hand. Connie, James' first mate and best friend, was always on him about his speech; now here was another one determined to correct him.

"Perhaps I'm not good enough to escort—"

"There you go taking what I say to heart again." Anthony shook his head at the boy. "Would I have suggested you escort *my* favorite niece if I didn't think you were capable?"

Jeremy was frowning now, but for a different reason. "I can't do it. Hell's bells, what was I even thinking of? Of course I can't. If it was anyone else— no, I just can't."

"What the devil are you mumbling about?"

Jeremy stared at him intently. "I can't take her to no ball if I'm to be her only protection. What if someone like you bothers her?"

"Like *me*?" Anthony wasn't sure whether he wanted to laugh or strangle the whelp.

"You know what I mean, Tony, someone who doesn't take well to a 'no' when he hears it. Not that I wouldn't gullet anyone who dared—"

"But who's to take a seventeen-year-old seriously?" Anthony finished with a scowl. "Damnation, I can't tolerate those bloody affairs! Never could, never will. But you're quite right. I suppose we'll have to compromise. You escort her, and I'll keep an eye on her, too. The Crandal ballroom fronts a garden, I believe, so I ought to manage it without actually making an appearance. That should satisfy even her overprotective husband. Does that suit you, young Galahad?''

''Aye, as long as I know you're there and can step in if she has any real trouble. But hell's bells, Tony, won't you be bored stuck out in the garden all night?''

''Assuredly, but I suppose I can suffer it for one evening. You don't know what the alternative is should I actually show up at one of these affairs, and don't ask. It's the bane of my life, but it's the life I choose, so I've no complaints.''

And with that cryptic remark, Anthony left Jeremy to settle into his new quarters.

Chapter Five

"Well, m'dear, do you believe me now?" Frances whispered, coming up behind Roslynn, who stood in a circle of admirers, none of whom had left her alone since she arrived at this ball, the third such affair in as many days.

The question was innocent enough, if anyone had heard, but no one had. Though the eyes of the gentlemen present returned continuously to Roslynn in her teal satin gown, their attention was momentarily engaged by a friendly argument about some race that was supposed to take place tomorrow. *She* had started the argument, which seemed the thing to do since it broke up the previous argument about who was to dance with her next. She was quite tired of dancing, especially with Lord Bradley, who must have the biggest feet this side of the Scottish border.

Fortunately, or unfortunately in Roslynn's case, she didn't need to ask Frances to explain her question. Frances had asked it once too often in the last days, quite thrilled that she had been right about Roslynn's reception by the *ton* and Roslynn had been wrong. She was rubbing it in good, taking Roslynn's success personally, as if it were her own.

"I believe you." Roslynn sighed, hoping this would be the last time she would have to say it. "Honest to God, I do. But however am I to make a choice from so many?"

Frances pulled her back a few steps to admonish her. "You don't *have* to choose any of them. Heavens, you've only just begun the hunt. There are other eligibles you haven't met yet. You're not going to jump into this blindly, now are you?''

''No, no, of course not. I don't intend to marry a *complete* stranger. Well, he will be one to me in actuality, but I mean to learn everything I can about him first. I believe in knowing my quarry as well as possible to avoid mistakes.''

''Quarry indeed.'' Frances rolled her eyes dramatically. ''Is that how you're looking at this?''

Roslynn sighed again. ''Oh, I don't know, Frances. It just seems so cold-blooded, no matter how you look at it, especially when no one I've met yet has tickled my interest even a wee bit. I'm going to *buy* myself a husband. There's no nicer way of putting it. And it doesn't look as if I'm going to particularly like the fellow if this is all I have to choose from. But as long as he meets the other criteria—''

''Posh!'' Frances admonished sternly. ''You're giving up when you've only just begun the search. What's happened to depress you so?''

Roslynn grimaced. ''They're all so *young*, Frances. Gilbert Tyrwhitt can't be more than twenty, and Neville Baldwin not much older. The earl is my age, and Lord Bradley is only a few years older, though *he* acts as if he should never have been let out of the schoolroom. Those other two are no better. Damnation, they make me feel so ancient. But Gramp did warn me. He said I should look to an older man, but where are they? And if you tell me they're all married already, I think I'll scream.''

Frances laughed. ''Ros, you're just rushing it. There are a number of distinguished gentlemen here, widowers, and some confirmed bachelors who I'm sure will reconsider that status once they meet you.

But I'll no doubt have to point them out to you, because they're probably intimidated by these young bucks dancing attendance on you and feel the competition's too stiff. After all, you are a smashing success. If you want an older man, you'll have to give the poor fellow some encouragement, let him know that you're interested—well, you know what I mean."

"Hell's teeth, Frances, you don't have to blush. I've no problem with being forward if I have to. I'm even prepared to state my case and do the proposing myself. Now don't raise your eyebrows at me. You know I mean it, and I'll do it if I have to."

"You know very well you'd be too embarrassed to be that bold."

"Under normal circumstances, perhaps. But under these circumstances, I haven't much choice. I've no time to be wasting on a proper courtship, and certainly no time to be sitting around waiting for the right man to come along. So point out the more experienced eligibles, and I'll tell you which ones I want to be introduced to. I've quite had enough of these young bloods."

"So be it," Frances replied and looked casually about the room. "There, by the musicians, that tall one. I can't think of his name offhand, but I understand he's a widower with two children—no, three, I think it is. He must be forty-one or -two, and is a very likable sort from what I hear. Has a big estate up in Kent where the children are, but he prefers town life. Is he more what you had in mind?"

Roslynn grinned at Frances' inept attempt at sarcasm. "Oh, he's not bad, not bad a-tall. I like that silver at the temples. If I can't have love, I must insist on pleasant-looking, and he is, don't you think? Yes, he'll do for a start. Now who else?"

Frances gave her a disgusted look, for she certainly
felt as if *she* were at a market selecting choice goods,
even if Roslynn didn't. It was all so unsavory, the
logical and businesslike way Ros was approaching
this. But then wasn't that really the way it was, only
most women had a father or a guardian to handle the
particulars, while they concerned themselves merely
with the happy fantasies of love evermore, or in the
unfortunate cases, love nevermore. Ros didn't have
anyone to deal with the realities of marriage for her,
so she had to make all the arrangements herself, including the financial settlements.

More in the spirit of the thing now since to fight it
was so useless, Frances pointed out another gentleman, and another; after an hour, Roslynn had met
them all and had narrowed down a new list of possibles, this one much more acceptable agewise. But
the young blades still wouldn't leave her alone and
insisted on dance after dance. Although her popular-
ity relieved a good deal of her anxiety, a very great
deal of it actually, it was becoming a bit of a nuisance
too.

Having lived so long in seclusion with her grandfather and the servants known to her for most of her
life, Roslynn had had very little traffic with gentlemen. The males of her acquaintance were used to her,
and those she didn't know she very properly didn't
take notice of. Unlike Nettie, who took in everything
at a glance and was well aware of Roslynn's effect on
the male gender, Roslynn was too circumspect when
out and about to pay attention to what went on around
her. It was not surprising that she had put so little
store in her looks, which had never seemed very out-
of-the-ordinary to her, and so much store in her age,
which seemed inappropriate for her purpose, and had

counted solely on her status as an heiress to win her
a husband quickly.

She had assumed, given her advanced age in comparison with all the other girls out on their first season, that she would have to settle for the second or
third sons with no prospects, or even a gambling
rogue, a lord who was down and out and heavily
mortgaged. And even if there would be a marriage
contract that would leave the control of the bulk of
her fortune in her hands, she would be generous. She
could afford to be generous. She was so rich it was
embarrassing.

But she had had to reevaluate her situation after the
first party Frances took her to. She had quickly found
that all sorts of gentlemen were interested in her, and
the extent of her wealth wasn't even known yet. Of
course, her gowns and jewels spoke for themselves,
but really, that wealthy earl had already called on her
at South Audley Street, and so had the obnoxious Lord
Bradley. The older men on her new list were not pau-
pers either, and all had seemed extremely flattered by
her interest in them. But would they be willing to
marry her? Well, that remained to be seen. Her priority now was to find out more about each of them.
She wanted no nasty habits or surprises revealed *after*
she was married.

What she was in need of at this point was a confidant and adviser, someone who had known these men
for a number of years and could help her whittle down
her list. Frances had simply been too sheltered and
reclusive since her widowhood to be of any help in a
thorough character analysis. She knew no men personally other than her late husband's friends, none of
whom she would recommend for consideration. The
men she had introduced to Roslynn tonight were mere

acquaintances about whom she had only the vaguest knowledge.

A good gossip might help, but that was so unreliable, and old gossip tended to be forgotten in lieu of new, so that wouldn't serve her purpose anyway. If only Roslynn had other friends in London, but Frances was her one and only.

It never occurred to either woman that Roslynn could hire someone to find out anything she wanted to know about her candidates. And even if it had occurred to them, they wouldn't know how to go about finding such a person. But then that would have been too simple, and Roslynn had expected from the beginning that this husband-hunting business would be difficult. She expected to agonize over it, simply because she knew she couldn't afford the time necessary to make a cautious decision.

At least she was making progress tonight, slow but helpful. Sir Artemus Shadwell, her silver-templed widower, had braved her pack of randy bucks, as she was beginning to think of them because of their overzealous pursuit, and stolen her away for a dance. Unfortunately, it wasn't a dance conducive to conversation, and the most she was able to learn from him was that with five children from his first marriage (och, but Frances was way off there!), he wasn't at all interested in starting a new family if he ever married again. How he could avoid it, she'd like to know, but so he said.

That was too bad, because if Roslynn was determined to get anything out of the husband she eventually decided on, it was children. That was the only thing about getting married she was looking forward to. She wanted children, not many, but some, two or three or four, and that was definite. Nor was this something she could wait on either, not at her age. If she was going to have a family, it had to be started immediately. That would have to be understood. There would be no "Maybes" or "We'll sees" about it.

But she needn't write Sir Artemus off her list yet. After all, he wasn't aware that he was one of her "possibles," so he couldn't have considered her question about children serious. And a man's mind could be changed. If she knew anything about men, it was that.

After their dance he took her back to Frances, who was standing by the refreshment table with a young woman Roslynn hadn't met yet. But a waltz began immediately, and Roslynn noticed the persistent Lord Bradley making a beeline toward her. She groaned audibly. It was too much. She was *not* going to get her feet mashed up again by that clumsy fellow.

"What's wrong now, Roslynn?" Frances inquired, hearing her.

"Nothing—och, everything," she answered, exasperated and then quite determined, without the least thought for the stranger who hadn't yet been introduced to her. "I'm not going to dance with that looby Bradley again, Frances. I swear I'm not. I'll faint first, which will embarrass you, so you must excuse me while I go hide this one out."

And with a pleased chuckle for the one decision she had been able to make with ease, she gave both ladies a conspiratorial grin and disappeared into the crowd, leaving them to explain to the persistent Bradley how his quarry could simply vanish.

Quickly making her way to one of several open French doors that led out onto a terrace, Roslynn ducked outside but went no further. Pressed up against the wall beside the door, she spared a quick glance to make sure she wouldn't be observed by anyone taking advantage of the lovely moonlit garden that spread out over a large lawn beyond the flat stone terrace, but thankfully she saw no one. She then twisted and bent over at the waist to peek around the door to make sure her escape was successful. And it was. She was just in time to see Lord Bradley leaving Frances, quite obviously disappointed.

It was shameful, but she couldn't dredge up even the slightest pang of remorse. In fact, she continued to watch Lord Bradley just to make certain he wouldn't think to look outside for her when he couldn't find her on the dance floor. She would have to rush to another hiding place then, and she could see herself crouching ridiculously behind flower beds in the garden, but looking no more ridiculous than she did at the moment, she realized belatedly and spared another nervous glance behind her to make sure the garden was still deserted. It was, as far as she could see. After spying on Lord Bradley for a few moments longer, she finally saw him ask someone else to dance.

Roslynn straightened then with a sigh, silently congratulating herself on saving her feet for the time being. She should have escaped to the garden sooner. The fresh air was welcome, a balm to her muddled thoughts so filled with the complexity her life had become. She could use a few minutes alone, to simply think of nothing, to let it all drain away on the gentle strains of the waltz coming through the open doorways.

Soft gold light spread across the stone terrace in rectangular patches from each doorway and window facing the lawn. A few chairs and tables were scattered about but were too noticeable from inside, so Roslynn wisely avoided them.

She spotted a bench tucked under a tree just on the edge of the terrace where it blended into the lawn, or at least the legs of what looked like a bench. The light reached only that far, what with one low-hanging branch bending toward the house, almost like a shielding curtain. The rest of the area was darkly shadowed because of the thick tree limbs, the moonlight unable to penetrate either. How perfect. She could tuck her feet up on the seat and be almost invisible if someone should come outside. Invisible would be nice for a change.

It was only a few dozen feet away, but still Roslynn ran toward this unexpected haven, hoping in those few seconds she wouldn't be spotted through one of the windows. She actually had a moment's anxiety that she wouldn't reach the safe shadows in time. Their importance was absurd. She was desirous of only a few minutes' respite. She wouldn't crumble if her wish weren't granted. She couldn't stay away long anyway, or Frances would worry.

But none of that seemed to matter next to her anxiety. The silly bench had become essential for a purely emotional need. And then abruptly everything she was feeling froze. She had reached no haven at all. The bench, *her* bench, was already occupied.

She stood there in a pool of light, staring blankly at what had seemed no more than a dark shadow from a dozen feet away but was revealed now to be a man's black-clad leg, just one leg, bent over the backrest of the bench at the corner of it, his foot planted firmly on the seat that *she* had intended to become invisible on. Her eyes traveled upward, discovering the bent knee, seeing finally that he was bracing one hip on the edge of the backrest, half sitting, half standing, no doubt comfortably. She looked higher and saw the forearms casually resting on the bent knee, the hands lax, palms down, fingers long and graceful, details clear only because they were lighter in color next to the black of his trousers. Higher still were wide shoulders relaxed, bent forward, and the contrasting, lighter shade at his neck of a white cravat, loosely tied. She finally looked at his face but could see nothing of his features even at this close distance, just a gray blur defined by dark hair.

He was totally in shadow, where she had meant to be. He was nothing but shades of black and gray to her, but he was there, real, silent. Her feelings melted with a vengeance. She felt violated, angry beyond reason. She knew he could see her clearly in the light from the house, and where that light didn't reach, there was the silvery moonlight. He had probably been able to see her looking utterly ridiculous peeking around the door into the ballroom, like a little child in a game of hide-and-seek. And he said nothing. He hadn't moved. He simply looked at her.

Her skin burned with the shame of it. Her anger soared that he was playing mute, as if he were still invisible to her. He could have put her at ease. A gentleman would have said something to make her believe she had been noticed only now, at this moment, even if it weren't true.

The continued silence tugged on her instinct to flee, but it was too much, not knowing who he was, while he could easily recognize her. To meet new men at some later date, and she surely would, and have to constantly wonder if one of them was this man, the one who would be silently laughing at her. One more worry to add to her others. It just wouldn't do.

She steeled herself to demand who he was, prepared to insist, even prepared to forcefully drag him out into the light if she had to—she was that angry. The words weren't necessary, were actually forgotten. A light appeared in an upstairs room, near enough to the window to cast down a beam of gold that filtered through the upper tree limbs at an angle. It was selective, that beam of light. Where it broke through the leaves above, it touched only certain parts of the man's upper body, his hands, a shoulder clad in black velvet—his face.

Roslynn was simply not prepared. The breath sucked right out of her. For several long moments her mind became such a blank, she couldn't have remembered her own name if asked.

There was a wide mouth gently turned at the corners, a strong, arrogant line of jaw. The nose was chiseled sharply, aquiline, proud. The skin was darkly tanned, swarthy, yet still a sharp contrast to the ebony hair that crowned his head in thick waves. The eyes— God protect the innocent from such eyes—were purest blue, heavy-lidded, with the barest suggestion of a slant. They were exotic, hypnotic, framed by black lashes and slashing brows. They were assessing, probing, boldly sensual—warm, too warm.

It was her weakness from lack of air that jolted Roslynn back to her senses. She breathed in deeply, slowly, and exhaled on a sigh. It simply wasn't fair. Gramp had warned her. She didn't have to be told. She knew. He was one of them, one of the "not to be considered." He was too ruthlessly handsome not to be.

Her earlier annoyance was forgotten. A new irritation took hold. She had the strangest urge to hit him for being what he was. Why him? Why did the one

man who took her breath away have to be the only
type of man unacceptable to her?

"You are staring, sir." Where had that come from,
when the rest of her thoughts were so chaotic?

"I know," he said simply, his smile deepening.

He refrained from pointing out that she was staring
too. He was enjoying himself too much just watching
her. Words were unnecessary, an intrusion, even
though her husky voice rubbed over his skin like a
caress.

Anthony Malory was purely fascinated. He had
seen her before she came outside. He had been keeping his eye on Reggie through the nearest window,
and then she came into his line of vision. He hadn't
seen her face then, just her slim back sheathed in teal
satin—and her hair. The glorious red-gold color
caught his interest immediately. When she moved out
of sight before he had gotten a better look at her, he
actually stood up, prepared to brave the masses just
this once, the urge to see the face that went with that
hair overpowering.

But she came outside. He relaxed back against the
bench, patient now. With the light behind her, he still
couldn't make out her features clearly, but he would.
She wasn't going anywhere until he did.

And then he simply watched her antics in hiding
beside the door, and bending over to peek back inside. The shapely derrière she presented to him
brought a grin to his lips. *Oh, sweetheart, you can't
know the invitation you're offering.*

He almost chuckled aloud, but it was as if she had
read his thoughts. She straightened, glancing across
the terrace. When she stared in his direction, he
thought he was discovered. And then she managed to
shock him, coming toward him, *running* toward him,

flashing into a patch of bright light, making him doubt his sight with the breathtaking loveliness of her face finally revealed to him, disappearing into the shadows briefly before she reached the patch of light directly in front of the bench. She stopped there, looking now as shocked as he was, only his surprise waned quickly when he realized she hadn't been running to him, hadn't known he was even there. But she did now.

It was amusing, the emotions that flitted over her flawless features. Shock, curiosity, then pink-tinged embarrassment, but no fear. With intense, gold-flecked eyes, she started on his leg and worked her way up. He wondered how much of him she could actually see. Not much probably, standing in the light as she was, but he had no inclination to reveal himself just yet.

On one level he was amazed that she hadn't run off immediately, or fainted, or done some other silly thing that a previously sheltered young debutante was likely to do when presented with a strange man lurking in the shadows. Unconsciously, he sought a reason that she should react differently from all the other inno-cents he staunchly avoided. When it came to him, it was another shock. She wasn't that young, not too young for him anyway. She wasn't off limits, then.

That knowledge worked on Anthony's system im-mediately. Where before he had simply appreciated her beauty like a connoisseur, now he registered that he needn't be damned to only look, he could also touch. And then the light came on upstairs, and she was staring at him with a new look, obvious fasci-nation, and he was never so glad in his life that women found him appealing to the senses.

It was suddenly imperative for him to ask, "Who guards you?"

Roslynn was startled to hear his voice again after the long silence; she knew very well she should have walked away after their first brief words had brought no more. Only she had stood fast, unable to take her eyes off him, not caring that she was staring, that he was too.

"Guards me?"

"Yes. Who do you belong to?"

"Oh. No one."

Anthony smiled, amused. "Perhaps I should rephrase my question?"

"No, I understood. So did you. My grandfather recently died, you see. I lived with him. Now I have no one."

"Then have me."

The soft words tripped her heart. Oh, what she wouldn't do to have him. But she was almost certain he didn't mean what she wanted him to mean, but what she should be embarrassed over hearing instead. But she wasn't embarrassed. It was something she would expect a man like him to say. They were never sincere, Frances had told her. And they loved to say shocking things to enhance their image of being dissipated and unprincipled.

Still, she had to ask. She couldn't help herself. "Would you marry me, then?"

"Marry?"

She had managed to discompose him. She almost laughed at his look of horror.

"I don't mince words, sir, though I'm not usually *that* forward. But considering what you said to me, my question was perfectly in order. So I may assume you are not husband material?"

"Good God, no!"

"You needn't be *that* emphatic," she said, disappointment just barely discernible in her tone. "I didn't think you were."

He wasn't so pleased himself now, drawing his own conclusions. "You're not going to dash my hopes this soon, are you, sweetheart? Tell me you're not seeking matrimony along with the masses."

"Oh, but I am, most definitely. It's why I've come to London."

"Don't they all."

"I beg your pardon."

He smiled at her again, and it had the strangest effect on her, sort of like melting into honey. "You're not married yet, are you." He wasn't asking, but clarifying it in her mind as well as his. He leaned forward and caught at her hand, gently tugging her closer. "What name goes with such loveliness?"

What name? What name? Her mind was filled with gloveless fingers lightly gripping her own. Warm, strong. Gooseflesh rushed up her bare arm. Her shins bumped the edge of the bench next to his foot, but she didn't feel it. He had brought her into the shadows.

"You do have one, don't you?" he persisted.

A clean, masculine scent assailed Roslynn's nostrils. "What?"

He chuckled, delighted with her confusion. "My dear girl, a name. We all of us must bear one, good or bad. Mine is Anthony Malory, Tony to my intimates. Now do confess yours."

She closed her eyes. It was the only way she could think. "Ros—Roslynn."

She heard his tongue click. "No wonder you want to marry, Ros Roslynn. You simply want to change your name."

Her eyes snapped open to be dazzled by his smile.

He was only teasing. It was nice that he felt free to. The other men she had met recently were too busy trying to make a good impression on her to be at ease in her presence.

She returned his smile. "Roslynn Chadwick, to be precise."

"A name you should keep, sweetheart . . . at least until after we become much better acquainted. And we will, you know. Shall I tell you how?"

She laughed, the husky sound jolting him to his socks. "Ah, you're trying to shock me again, but it won't do. I'm too old to blush, and I've been warned about men like you."

"Like me?"

"A rake."

"Guilty." He gave a mock sigh.

"A master of seduction."

"I should hope so."

She chuckled, and again this was no silly giggle or simper to irritate the senses, but a warm, rich sound that made him want . . . he dared not. This was one woman he didn't want to risk scaring off. She might not be innocent in years, but he didn't know yet whether she was experienced otherwise.

That fateful upstairs light that had started Roslynn on the path to confusion was suddenly put out. Panic was instantaneous. It didn't matter that she had enjoyed his company. It didn't matter that she had felt perfectly at ease with him. They were now enshrouded in darkness, and he was a rake, and she couldn't afford to be seduced.

"I must go."

"Not yet."

"No, I really must."

She tried to pull her hand away, but his grip tightened. His other hand found her cheek, fingertips softly caressing, and something unfurled in her belly. She had to make him understand.

"I—I mun thank you, Mr. Malory." She slipped into the brogue without realizing it, half her mind on his touch, half on her increasing panic. "You've taken my mind off my worries for a spell, but dinna add to them now. It's a husband I'm needing, no' a lover, and you dinna qualify . . . more's the pity."

She got her release, simply because she had managed to surprise him once again.

Anthony watched her passing in and out of the different shades of light before she disappeared inside, and again he had that ridiculous urge to go after her. He didn't. A slow smile started and widened. "More's the pity," she had said with such poignant regret. The little miss didn't know it, but she had sealed her own fate with those words.

Chapter Six

"You've been watching a master at work, Connie."

"Seemed more like a comedy of errors to me," the tall redhead replied. "Opportunity lost is opportunity lost, no matter how you look at it."

Anthony laughed as the two joined him under the tree. "Spying on me, brother?"

James leaned forward to casually rest his forearms on the back of the bench and flashed Anthony a grin. "Truth to tell, I couldn't resist. Was afraid it was going to get embarrassing, though."

"Not bloody likely. I just met her."

"And lost her." Conrad Sharp turned the screw.

Anthony shot the first mate a quelling look as he came around and propped a foot on the opposite end of the bench, but it wasn't effective in the dark.

"Now, Connie, you can't fault him there," James said. "She did throw him quite a turn, appealing to the goodness of his heart and in such a quaint Scottish brogue. And here I thought the lad's halo was perpetually tarnished."

"A lass like that could polish any halo," Conrad replied.

"Yes, she was rather stunning, wasn't she?"

Anthony had heard enough. "And unavailable."

James chuckled. "Staked a claim, have you, lad? Careful, or I might take that as a challenge."

Anthony's blood ran cold. It had been sport in their younger days to compete for the same woman, those days when they had prowled London together. And every outcome had been a simple matter of which brother had managed to get to the lady first. But the years and overindulgence had tempered Anthony's libido. It was no longer do or die. Or at least it hadn't been, until tonight.

But James, well, he simply didn't know James anymore. Most of their lives they had been close, exceedingly close. It had always been them against the other two brothers, who were a good ten years older. But that was before James had thought it would be a lark to try his hand at pirating on the high seas.

For ten years he had seen James only on rare occasions, the last time ending in a rift that caused all three brothers to disown him—after they had soundly thrashed him for taking Reggie pirating that summer. But now James was reinstated. He had given up pirating. Now he was even likely to return to England for good. And *right* now, Anthony didn't know if he was serious or not about challenging him over Roslynn Chadwick.

At that moment he saw her again, through the window, and noticed that James did too. "Blister it, James, what are you doing here anyway?"

The older brother by one year straightened to his full height, which was a tad shorter than Anthony's. To look at them was not to know they were brothers. James was blond and green-eyed, the marks of a Malory, and stockier in build. It was only Anthony, Regina, Edward's daughter Amy, and now Jeremy who bore the black hair and cobalt-blue eyes of their grandmother, rumored to have had gypsy blood flowing in her veins.

"If you had been a little more informative in that note you left for me, I wouldn't have had to ruin my evening by coming here," James replied. "And now that you've reminded me of it, I've a bone to pick with you, brother. What the devil can you be thinking of, to let that scamp of mine escort Regan anywhere?''

Anthony gritted his teeth over the name Regan. ''Is that why you showed up?''

''That was all you saw fit to inform me about. You couldn't scribble a few more words to let me know you would be here as well, could you?''

Anthony spared a glance around the garden. ''If you can call my hiding in the shadows being here, well, then, I guess I am.''

''Don't be obnoxious, puppy,'' Conrad joined in. ''Until you've had one of your own, you don't know what it's like worrying about what they're up to.''

''What could the poor boy possibly get up to with two such diligent fathers hounding him? And besides, much as I would have liked to ignore it, Jeremy was the one who pointed out that he might not be up to scratch in protecting her. That's why I've been dragged along.''

''You misunderstand, Tony. It wasn't who was going to protect Regan from the masses that had me worried. It was who was going to protect her from her escort.''

Five seconds passed while Anthony wondered how much animosity he would elicit by laughing at this point. ''She's his cousin, for God's sake!''

''You think he gives a bloody damn?''

''You're serious, aren't you?'' Anthony ventured.

''He's infatuated with her,'' was all James returned.

''Be that as it may, you are overlooking the 'infatuatee.' She'd have him begging for mercy in less than a minute if he even looked at her wrong. I thought you knew our niece better than that, old boy.''

"Aye, I know she can hold her own. But I know my son too, and he isn't easily discouraged."

"Need I remind you this is a seventeen-year-old boy we're talking about?"

"Need I remind you what *you* were like when you were seventeen?" James countered.

Anthony grinned finally. "Point taken. Very well, I'll not only keep an eye on her, I'll keep one on him too."

"That's *if* he can keep his eyes off the Scot," Conrad interjected.

"Then by all means stay," Anthony replied tightly. "There is no reason we can't all three keep this vigil. After all, it's such a pleasant way to spend an evening."

James smiled. "I do believe that's his way of telling us to run along, Connie. Come on, let's leave the poor boy to his pining. You never know. She might even venture forth again and make this chaperoning business more to his liking." Here he chuckled. "It won't be otherwise. He wouldn't brave that den of vultures any more than I would, even for her."

James was wrong on both counts.

Chapter Seven

"Well, what's he doing here? That's what I want to know. Lady Crandal doesn't approve of his sort. She'd never have invited him."

"Sir Anthony doesn't need an invite, m'dear. That one does as he pleases."

"But he's always had the decency to stay away from our parties."

"Decency?" A brief laugh. "There's no decency about it. He simply can't abide these affairs. And it's no wonder. There probably isn't a lady here who wouldn't like to reform that particular rake."

"There's nothing funny about it, Lenore. He shows up, and half the women in the room fall in love with him. I've seen it happen before. That's why a hostess wouldn't dream of inviting him to her party if she wants it to go smoothly. He causes too much of a stir."

"But it does give us something to talk about for months thereafter. Admit it. He does make a delicious subject, doesn't he?"

"That's easy for you to say, Lenore." This from another lady, clearly distressed. "You don't have a daughter out this season. My God, look at my Jane over there. She can't take her eyes off him. I just know she'll never accept Percy now. She can be *so* difficult."

"There's no harm in looking, Alice. You need only tell your girl a few stories about him and she'll be properly horrified and glad he didn't notice her."

"But what's he *doing* here? I still want to know." The question was repeated more sharply.

"Probably keeping an eye on his son," Lenore offered the ladies smugly.

"His *what?*"

"Take a look at the boy dancing with Sarah Lordes. Now, if he isn't the mirror image of Sir Anthony, then they ought to do away with mirrors."

"Good Lord, another Malory bastard! That family really ought to be more circumspect."

"Well, the marquis acknowledged his. I wonder if Sir Anthony will do the same."

"This is priceless! However could they have kept him a secret this long?"

"Must have been hidden away until now. But it appears the Malorys are going to be full of surprises this season. I understand the third brother is back."

"Third brother?" This from a new party. "But there are only three."

"Where have you been, Lidia?" Lenore said cattily. "There are four, and the third is the black sheep."

"But I thought Sir Anthony was that."

"Being the youngest, he's only a close second. Oh, I could tell you stories about the other one. He's been gone for years and years, but no one knows where or why."

"Then it's no wonder I didn't know he existed," Lidia replied stiffly in self-defense.

"Hello again."

Roslynn was annoyed by the untimely interruption, but at least it wasn't one of her young admirers. Fortunately, most of them had retired to the card room for a while, leaving her free to become better acquainted with the gentlemen on her new list. But instead of seeking one out, she had gotten sidetracked by the numerous conversations that erupted when Anthony Malory had stepped into the ballroom.

Roslynn had unobtrusively settled herself behind one group of older ladies and made no bones about eavesdropping. There was no use denying it. She found the subject under discussion infinitely fascinating and listened avidly to every word. But now someone wanted to engage her in conversation, and there was no help for it.

She glanced at Lady Eden, yet still tried to keep one ear tuned in on the older ladies in front of her. "Tired of dancing so soon?"

The younger woman was amused, recognizing inattentiveness when she encountered it. She was further amused when she overheard several remarks nearby and realized the reason for Roslynn's distraction.

"Everyone knows I rarely dance except with my husband, but he wasn't able to join me tonight."

"That's nice."

Regina Eden rolled her eyes, smiled, and hooked her arm through Roslynn's. "Come along, m'dear. It's devilish hot in this spot. Let's move along, shall we?"

Roslynn sighed as she was forcefully dragged away. Lady Eden was certainly pushy for such a young woman. Roslynn had been surprised, in fact, to learn that she was married and had a child already, when she didn't look as though she was very long out of the schoolroom. She was the lady with Frances earlier whom Roslynn hadn't stayed long enough to meet, but Frances had taken care of the introductions upon her return from the garden. At the time she had still been pretty shaken from her encounter with Malory.

In fact, she couldn't remember the conversation she had had with Lady Eden then, if she had even had one.

Lady Eden stopped near the refreshment tables. Unfortunately, Roslynn now had a clear view of the subject on everyone's lips. He hadn't really come inside the ballroom. With an air of nonchalance, he stood in the doorway to the garden, one shoulder braced against the frame, arms crossed over his chest, eyes slowly scanning the room—until they lit on her. There they stayed, and he flashed that smile that made her feel like warming honey.

Seeing him in the light, seeing *all* of him in the light, was an experience of the senses. He had a body you couldn't help but admire for its pure symmetry. Wide shoulders, narrow waist, lean hips, and long legs. Yes, he was tall. She hadn't noticed it in the garden. And he fairly reeked of sensuality. She *had* noticed that before.

The cut of his evening clothes was impeccable, though he looked almost sinister in black. But black complemented him. She couldn't imagine him wearing the bright colors of a dandy. That would draw even more attention to him, yet he commanded everyone's attention anyway, just by appearing.

"He *is* devilish handsome, isn't he?"

Roslynn started, realizing she had been caught staring at him. But then it would be unusual if she weren't, for *everyone* was staring at him.

She glanced at Lady Eden and gave a careless shrug. "Do you think so?"

"Oh, most definitely. His brothers are terribly good-looking too, but I've always thought Tony was the handsomest of the lot."

Roslynn wasn't sure if she liked that "Tony" from

this beautiful young woman with the midnight hair and vivid blue eyes that glittered with humor. What had he said? "Tony to my intimates."

"I take it you know him well?"

Regina grinned engagingly. "I know the whole family very well."

Roslynn found herself blushing, which was something she so rarely did. She was relieved with that answer but annoyed with herself for how sharp her question had sounded. If the viscountess was well acquainted with the Malorys, then she was the last person Roslynn wanted to be aware of her interest in Sir Anthony. She ought not to be interested at all. She ought to introduce a new topic. She couldn't.

"He's awfully old, isn't he?"

"Well, if you think thirty-five is old—"

"Only thirty-five?"

Regina had to suppress her urge to laugh. The woman was determined to find something wrong with Tony, but heaven knew what that could be. It was obvious he had made another conquest without even trying. Or was he trying? It was really too bad of him to stare like that. If she weren't standing here with Lady Roslynn, the poor woman would be quite undone by what the gossips would make of his interest in her.

Yes, it really was too bad of him, because nothing would come of it. Nothing ever did. And she rather liked Lady Roslynn. She wouldn't like to see her get hurt.

"He's a confirmed bachelor," Regina felt compelled to warn her. "With three older brothers, there's never been any reason for him to marry, you see."

"You don't have to wrap it up prettily. I know he's a rake."

"He prefers 'connoisseur of women.' "

"Then he likes to wrap it up prettily too."

Regina laughed. Oh, she did like this woman. Roslynn might be feigning an indifference toward Tony, but she was refreshingly straightforward otherwise.

Roslynn stole another glance at Sir Anthony. She felt silly for having called him Mr. Malory, but how was she to have known then that he was a member of the peerage? The eldest brother the Marquis of Haverston, the second an earl, the third the black sheep of the family, and Anthony a close second. Oh, she had heard much about him tonight. Why couldn't she learn as much about her potential "possibles"?

"He doesn't dance?" Roslynn heard herself asking and wondered why she couldn't leave it alone.

"Oh, he does, beautifully, but he doesn't dare ask anyone here. If he did, he'd have to dance with a few dozen other women too, just to throw the vultures off the scent. But Tony wouldn't go through so much bother just to dance with the lady of his choice. That's why he can't tolerate these affairs. They force him to discretion when the word isn't even in his vocabulary."

"Is he really so notorious that just to be seen dancing with him would fairly ruin a girl?"

"I have seen it happen, and it's a shame really, because he's not *that* much of a womanizer. Not that he ever lacks for female companionship. But he's not out to seduce the whole of London either."

"Just his fair share?"

Regina noted the grin and realized Roslynn was amused by Anthony's reputation rather than scandalized. Perhaps she wasn't interested after all. Or perhaps she wisely sensed that it was hopeless.

"Gossips can be cruel, m'dear." Regina leaned

closer to whisper. "In fact, I don't dare leave your side. He *is* misbehaving, staring at you like that."

Roslynn avoided the other woman's eyes. "He could be looking at you."

"Of course he isn't. But as long as no one here is quite sure which of us he's ogling, you're safe."

"Ah, there you are, Ros." Frances joined them. "Lord Grahame was just asking for you. He claims you promised him a waltz."

"So I did." Roslynn sighed. It was time to forget Anthony Malory and get back to work. "I just hope the fellow can loosen up and be a little more revealing this time."

Too late, she realized how that must have sounded to Lady Eden, but Regina simply smiled. "It's all right, m'dear. Frances has told me something of your situation. You might be amused to know I had the exact same problem when I was looking for a husband. But unlike yours, my choice had to be approved by my family, which only made it exceedingly difficult because, to them, no one was good enough for me. Thank God my Nicholas compromised me, or I still might be looking for a husband."

It was Frances who appeared shocked. "But I thought you had been promised to him!"

"That was the general assumption after the announcement was made, but the fact was, he had abducted me, thinking I was his current mistress, and that little mistake got out. Oh, he brought me home immediately upon realizing his mistake, but the damage was done. And he came kicking and protesting to the altar, confirmed bachelor that he was. Yet he has settled nicely into marriage. It just goes to show that if someone seems unsuitable in all respects, they might turn out to be the best choice after all. You just never know.''

The last was said for Roslynn's benefit, but she forced herself to disregard it. Her chore was hard enough without adding to it the unsuitables. She wasn't going to end up with a bad penny on the off chance that he could be reformed. A gambler she was not.

With that resolve firmly set in her mind, she went off in search of Lord Grahame.

Chapter Eight

If an order had been placed, the weather that morning couldn't have been more perfect. It nearly tripled the amount of riders who were generally found in Hyde Park at such an early hour. Afternoons were the time for promenading, when every conceivable type of carriage could be seen making slow progress along the countrylike lanes. Mornings were reserved for the exercising of stock and body, when one didn't usually encounter one's acquaintances and so was not forced to stop repeatedly for conversation, as would happen in the afternoon.

Anthony Malory was resigned to giving up his customary hard gallop through the park that morning in favor of a brisk trot. Not that Reggie wasn't game, but he doubted her frisky mare could keep up with his powerful stallion, and since she insisted on joining him, he was forced to keep to her pace.

After last night, he had his suspicions as to why she had invited herself along, and he wasn't sure he wanted to discuss the lady. But when Reggie slowed and reigned in, waving James and Jeremy on, he knew there would be no help for it. The little darling could be uncomfortably persevering at times.

"When I asked to ride with you this morning, I rather thought we would be alone," Regina began with just the faintest degree of annoyance in her tone. "Jeremy I could understand wanting to come along with us, but Uncle James? He rarely rises before noon."

Actually, Anthony had pulled brother and nephew out of bed, browbeating and cajoling them into joining him. That ploy hadn't worked, however, to keep Reggie from her purpose. And blast James. He knew very well the only reason he was along was to keep the conversation impersonal, but there he trotted off, flashing Anthony an amused grin.

Anthony shrugged innocently. "What can I say? James has changed his habits considerably since he became a father. Hasn't that scoundrel you married done the same?"

"Famous! Why is it you always attack Nicholas when your own behavior has been less than exemplary?" And she jumped right into it. "She's half Scot, you know."

He didn't bother to ask who, but said indifferently, "Is she?"

"They're known for terrible tempers."

"All right, puss." He sighed. "What's on your mind that you feel obliged to warn me?"

Her brow wrinkled, blue eyes probing blue eyes of a like shade. "Are you interested in her, Tony?"

"Have I died and don't know it?"

She laughed, unable to help it. "Yes, I suppose that was a silly question. Of course you're interested—you and a few dozen others. I guess my next question should be, are you going to do anything about it?"

"That, my girl, is none of your business."

His tone was gentle but firm, and Regina's frown was back. "I know. But I thought you should learn a little something about her before you make up your mind to pursue her."

"Is this to be a full history?" he asked dryly.

"Don't be difficult, Tony. She's come to London to get married."

"I've already been told that appalling news by the lady herself."

"You mean you've talked to her? When?"

"If you must know, last night in the garden."

She gasped. "You didn't—"

"I didn't."

Regina let out a sigh, but it was only temporary relief. If knowing Lady Roslynn was actively seeking marriage didn't put him off, the poor woman was doomed.

"Perhaps you don't realize how serious she is, Tony. She means to be married by the end of the month. No, you needn't raise your brows. It's not that. In fact, she might as well be sixteen for all the experience she has had of men."

"Now *that* I won't believe."

"There, you see? You don't know anything about her, and yet you're contemplating disrupting her life. The truth is, that life has been extremely sheltered until now. She's been tucked away with her grandfather in the Highlands ever since her parents died, and apparently these past years have been spent nursing him, which is why she hasn't considered marriage until now. Were you aware of that?"

"Our talk was brief, Reggie."

She noted his irritation but pressed on. "Her father was an earl of some consequence. You know Uncle Jason won't like it—"

Anthony interrupted this warning. "Much as I hate to be on big brother's blacklist, I'm not answerable to him, puss."

"There's still more to it, Tony. She's an heiress. Her grandfather was ridiculously wealthy, and he's left it all to Lady Roslynn. That little piece of news isn't common knowledge yet, but you can imagine what will happen if she isn't married before that happens.''

"Every scoundrel in London will crawl out from under his rock to pursue her," Anthony answered tightly.

"Exactly. But fortunately, she already has several gentlemen picked out for consideration. As I understand it, it's just a matter now of learning what she can about them before she chooses one. In fact, I'm to ask Nicholas what he knows about them.''

"Since you know so much, miss, tell me what the bloody rush is.''

Oh, he was definitely interested, enough not to care that his irritation was now plainly showing. It gave Regina pause simply because it was so unique. Never had she seen him stirred up over a woman before. There were just too many for him to choose from for one in particular to mean overmuch to him. She might have to rearrange her own thinking on the matter.

Hesitantly, she offered, "It has something to do with a deathbed promise Lady Roslynn made to her grandfather, the rush, and the reason she's actively looking for a husband. According to her friend Frances Grenfell, she probably wouldn't marry at all if not for that promise. I mean, you don't see a situation like hers very often, a woman so beautiful, so rich, and answerable to no one but herself.''

It was indeed a unique situation, but Anthony didn't consider it at the moment, the Grenfell name causing unease. "How close a friend is she to Frances Grenfell?''

He threw Regina off the track with that question. "Why?''

"Lady Frances was one of George's youthful mistakes, though that's not to be repeated, puss.''

"No, of course not," she said in one breath, and then in the next, "You mean good old George, your best friend, the one who always teased me so outrageously? *That* George?"

He grinned at her surprise. "One and the same, and you haven't answered my question."

"Well, I don't see that it matters, but they're as close as two friends could be. They met in school and never lost touch with each other."

"Which means bloody confidences and all that," he fairly growled.

Damnation! Anthony could still hear her husky voice confessing, "I've been warned about men like you." He had thought she was teasing, but now he knew where the warnings must have come from and how damning they probably were. She hadn't been teasing at all. She would be on her guard against him no matter what, always remembering what had happened to her friend. He was suddenly of a mind to soundly thrash George Amherst for his youthful indiscretion. Bloody rotten hell!

Seeing his black scowl, Regina was reluctant to say what she knew needed saying, but no one else would dare be so bold with him, so she had to. "You know, Tony, unless you're willing to take the big step yourself, which would shock the whole of London but absolutely delight the family, you really ought to leave the lady alone."

He suddenly laughed. "For God's sake, puss, when did you become my conscience?"

She flushed at that. "Well, it's devilish unfair, you know. I doubt there's a woman alive you couldn't seduce if you set your mind to it."

"You exaggerate my abilities."

"Bother that," she retorted. "I've seen you turn

on the charm, Tony, and it's utterly devastating when you do. But I rather like Roslynn Chadwick. Only she has a promise to fulfill that's important to her, and for whatever reason, there's a time limit on it. If you interfere, there's liable to be trouble, not to mention hurt.''

Anthony smiled at her fondly. "Your concern is commendable for someone you've just met, Reggie, but a bit premature, don't you think? And besides, she's not some ninnyhammer without a lick of sense. She's independent and answerable to no one but herself. You said so yourself. So don't you think she's old enough, and mature enough, to fend off a rakehell like me if she wants to?''

"That word *want* scares me to death," she groaned, only to hear him laugh again.

"You talked to her for a considerable time last night. Did she happen to mention me?''

Good Lord! That he should ask such a question proved he was most definitely serious, even after everything she had told him.

"If you must know, you were about the only topic we discussed, but that's not unusual, since just about everyone there last night was discussing you. In fact, I'm quite sure she heard an earful from the gossips before I got hold of her.''

"Did you paint a pretty picture for me, puss?''

"I tried, but she wasn't buying it. And yet I suppose you'll be delighted to know that however much she feigned indifference, her interest was as plain to recognize as yours is.'' The smile that remark elicited nearly blinded her. "Oh, dear. I shouldn't have told you that, but since I did, I must also tell you that regardless of her interest, she still went off to better her acquaintance with the gentlemen she is considering for marriage. You might have made an impression, but it hasn't changed her plans in the least.''

Regina could see that nothing she said was going to discourage him, and she had said all she could. She might as well have saved her breath. She had never tried to interfere in his love life before, and now she saw how pointless it was to try this once. He was going to do as he pleased, just as he always did. God knew, Uncle Jason had tried for years and years to curb Tony's hedonism without success. What had made her think she would have any better luck?

She realized suddenly how utterly foolish she had been. Here she had been trying to change the very qualities that she had always found most endearing in Anthony. He was a charming rake. That was what he was and what made him her favorite uncle. If he left countless broken hearts behind, it was only because women couldn't help falling in love with him, although he never took any of his affairs seriously. But he did give pleasure and happiness too. That counted for a lot.

''I hope you're not going to be angry with me for putting my nose in where it doesn't belong.'' She gave him the smile he could never resist.

''It's such a pretty nose.''

''But too big at the moment. I'm sorry, Tony, I really am. I just thought—well, never mind. You've managed thus far to get by without anyone's advice. I suppose we should catch up with—''

Regina didn't finish. Her eyes were caught by a magnificent black stallion prancing along at a slow canter to accommodate the pony beside it, but to see who was controlling the powerful beast made her groan inwardly. What horrid luck. Of all the people to encounter at this moment.

She glanced to see if Anthony had noticed Lady Roslynn yet. Of course he had. If the prime horseflesh hadn't caught his eye, the Irish green riding habit and sun-bright hair would have. But his unguarded expression was almost embarrassing to observe.

Good Lord, she had never seen him look at a woman like that before, and she had seen him with dozens of his ladyloves. Last night he had stared, yes, deliberately, a game of seduction played solely with the eyes. This was different. This was a look Nicholas might give Regina, of passion mixed with more tender feelings.

Well, that did it. She felt even more of an idiot now for having tried to warn Anthony off. It was obvious, at least to her, that something special was happening here. And wouldn't it be wonderful if something actually came of it?

Regina's thinking had undergone a complete about-face. She was now wondering how she might help get these two together. Anthony had his own ideas.

"Would you consider staying put, Reggie, while I pay my respects?" Her look said, *Not on your life.* His sigh was long and drawn out. "I didn't think so. Well, come along, then. You owe me one chaperonage, I believe."

Anthony didn't wait for her concurrence but rode straightaway to intercept Roslynn, hoping against hope that Reggie would give him at least a few minutes alone with her first. It wasn't to matter. James, blast him all to hell, chose that moment to return to see what was keeping them and managed to intercept the lady first.

Anthony arrived to hear James saying, "Delighted to see you again, Lady Chadwick."

Roslynn was nervous enough to have trouble controlling Brutus, a circumstance that caused acute embarrassment, since it had never happened before. She had seen Sir Anthony approaching, which was probably why the blond stranger startled her so, seeming to have appeared out of nowhere. It was even worse, and quite irritating, that he should lean forward to steady her horse. The move was so clearly indicative that she couldn't manage Brutus on her own.

Her tone was quite understandably sharp. "Do I know you, sir?"

"No, but I had the opportunity to admire you last evening in the Crandal garden. Unfortunately, you ran away before I could make your acquaintance."

Anthony watched the hot color seep into her cheeks and saw red. "For *that*, dear brother, I think I'll invite you back to Knighton's Hall."

James couldn't have cared less. Roslynn Chadwick by daylight was about the prettiest little lady he had ever encountered. That Anthony had found her first mattered not at all. It made it devilish awkward, but no more than that. Until the lady stated her preference, she was fair game as far as James was concerned.

Roslynn was staring at James, now that she knew who he was. She would never have guessed by his looks that he was Anthony's brother. And after what she had heard about him, she could understand why Anthony was considered the runner-up to being the worst rakehell of the two. They were both breathtakingly handsome, but where Anthony was a charming rogue, she sensed the blond Malory would be much more ruthless in his amorous pursuits—or in any pursuits, for that matter. He fairly reeked of danger. And yet she wasn't frightened. It was Anthony who threatened her peace of mind and rattled her composure.

"So you are the black sheep of the Malory clan?" Roslynn said. "Tell me, what terrible deeds have you done to earn that misnomer?"

"Nothing anyone can prove, I assure you, sweet lady." And then to Anthony he turned a challenging grin. "Where are your manners, dear boy? Introduce us."

Anthony gritted his teeth. "My brother, James Malory." Without the slightest change in tone, he added, "And that youngun about to run us down is his son, Jeremy."

Jeremy drew up at the last second, exhilarated from the ride and the near disaster. He was just in time to hear Roslynn's comment to James. "Your son? Now why didn't I guess that?" There was such irony in her voice that no one doubted for a moment that she didn't believe a word of it.

Jeremy began laughing hilariously. James was rather amused himself. But Anthony was getting angrier by the second. He had known this would happen, but why did it have to happen for the first time with her? And with the young scamp laughing his head off over the misassumption, there was no point in trying to correct it at present.

Roslynn was surrounded by Malorys now and quite wishing she had not been so cavalier in dismissing Timmy's groom this morning. For a simple ride in the park, she had thought it unnecessary to have a man along for protection. It was something she never did at home. But London was not home.

Anthony seemed to connect with her thoughts. "Have you lost your groom?"

Six-year-old Timmy piped up here. "Ros is my groom and I'm hers. She said all we needed was each other."

"And who might you be?"

"Lord Grenfell," Timmy said importantly.

With George Amherst's blond hair and gray eyes staring up at him, Anthony blundered with a "Know—that is to say, knew your father very well. But the next time Lady Ros thinks to be your groom, you must tell her—"

"I've already concluded that the park is not as safe as I had supposed, Sir Anthony," Roslynn cut in meaningfully. "I assure you I'll not assume the role again."

"Glad to hear it, but in the meantime, I'll escort you home."

James delighted in pointing out, "I hate to remind you, brother, but you already have one charge to look after. I, on the other hand, am available to see the lady home."

"The hell you will!" Anthony shot back.

Regina had held back, enjoying this little encounter without being noticed. But since it was about to get out of hand, she finally nudged her horse forward.

"Before you two come to blows, I think it prudent to point out that Jeremy is also available and will do nicely as an escort for such a short distance. And since I was meaning to call on Lady Frances, I think I'll join them, Tony, so I'll thank you now for indulging me this morning." And to Roslynn, belatedly, "Does that meet with your approval?"

Roslynn sighed in relief, for she hadn't been able to think how to politely refuse either Malory brother after she had already admitted her mistake in riding without an escort. "It does indeed, Lady Eden."

"Please, m'dear, none of that. You'll call me Reggie." She grinned at James before adding, "As most everyone does."

The remark seemed to improve Anthony's humor. He was smiling now as he gazed at Roslynn, and what a smile. She had to force herself not to look at him again even as they exchanged words in departure. She had been wise last night to conclude that it would do her no good to see the man again. This encounter, so innocent yet disconcerting, simply reinforced that conclusion.

Anthony, watching the foursome ride away, was quietly contemplating turning Reggie over his knee next time he saw her. "She's become unbearably bossy since she married Eden."

"Do you think so?" James chuckled. "Perhaps you just never paid any mind to it before, since it was never you she was bossing around."

Rubbed raw by James' humor, Anthony glared at him. "And you—"

James didn't give him a chance to work up a righteous anger. "Now don't be tedious, dear boy. After seeing the way she reacted to you, I can see I haven't much chance of stealing her away." He turned his horse around, then added with a devilish grin just before he put spurs to him, "But bad odds have never stopped me before."

Chapter Nine

"*Y*ou're being no help a-tall, Frances," Roslynn complained, mimicking, " 'Go if you like.' What kind of answer is that, I'd like to be knowing?"

Frances stopped short on the busy walkway fronting the shops on Oxford Street, bringing Nettie plowing into her back for not paying attention. Two packages dropped out of Nettie's hands, one round hatbox rolling toward the curb. Anne, Frances' abigail, made a frantic dash for it before it continued into the street. Frances didn't even notice.

"What's got into you, Ros? If you're having such trouble over a simple decision like this, I shudder to think what agonies you'll go through when it's time to choose your husband. Either you want to go to the Eden party or you don't. Yes or no, either or; how much simpler can it be?"

Roslynn grimaced. Frances was right, of course, at least as far as she knew. But then Roslynn hadn't told her about meeting Anthony Malory at the Crandals' ball. She had intended to, only their conversation on the way home that night had started by her asking if Lady Eden's husband had been a rake before they were married.

"He was indeed."

That answer had been said with such disgust, Roslynn had asked only one more question. "Are they happy together?"

"Actually, I've never seen two people happier or more in love."

This reply had been soft and incredulous, as if Frances couldn't quite believe it was possible. But after that, Roslynn knew her friend would become too upset if she learned that Roslynn had found Anthony Malory attractive, so she hadn't mentioned him at all. It was too obvious that Frances still abhorred men like him in the extreme.

But regardless of knowing how her friend felt, even being of the same mind, Roslynn had still been full of Anthony that night, so full of him that Nettie had noticed the minute Roslynn walked into her bedroom.

Her very first words had been, "Well, I see ye've met yer mon. What's his name, then?"

Brought out of her cloud, Roslynn had quickly prevaricated that there wasn't one him, but four, and she immediately launched into everything she knew about them so far, which wasn't much but managed to quell Nettie's first assumption quite nicely. Now she was putting too much importance on Lady Eden's invitation, when every other invitation she had received since her introduction to society had been decided on with barely a thought. Definitely out of character.

It was no wonder Frances thought something was wrong with her. But at least she couldn't guess what it was. Nettie, on the other hand, had been watching her like a hawk ever since she had returned from her ride with Timmy yesterday. How she had given herself away she didn't know.

"The decision might be simple for you," she said to Frances rather defensively, "but I have other things to consider."

"Such as?"

"The time involved, for one. Being out of the city for three or four days is just going to delay—"

"Didn't you tell me Regina promised to invite your gentlemen as well?"

"That doesn't mean they'll go, Frances. The season's only just started. She's picked an off time to have a weekend party in the country."

"Silverley's in Hampshire, not days away. And besides, you also mentioned that she promised to speak to her husband and give you all the information he has on your gentlemen as soon as you get there. For that reason alone, I would think you would want to go."

Logic, logic, how to refute it? "Who's to say he knows anything pertinent? It could turn out to be a complete waste of time."

"Then you can turn right around and be back in London the same evening."

"And leave you there?" Roslynn protested. "How would you get back?"

Frances shook her head. "I give up. You obviously don't want to go, so I won't either. We have a half-dozen other invitations for this weekend, so we'll—"

"Now don't be putting words in my mouth. I haven't said no yet."

"Well?"

Roslynn walked on, tossing her next words over her shoulder. "I still need to think on it."

She never should have brought up the party again to begin with, revealing her anxiety about it. She could almost hear the wheels spinning in Nettie's mind. Frances at least didn't have any idea what the trouble was. But Nettie knew her too well. And what could she tell Nettie when she got around to asking, and she would? More of the same excuses, even though Frances had just pointed out she really had none?

Hell's teeth! She was ready to wring her hands over this one. Everything logical said there was nothing to decide. She needed to go to Silverley if for no other reason than to get the information Regina would have for her. Also, she had only to ask herself, what if she didn't go, but all four of her "possibles" did? Then she would be stuck in London accomplishing nothing, and *that* would be a pure waste of time.

On the other hand, and it was a great big other hand, there was a chance Anthony Malory might show up at Silverley for this party, and seeing him again was something Roslynn didn't want to risk, didn't dare risk. He was just too tempting by half. That silly, girlish reaction she had had to him yesterday in the park, in broad daylight, even surrounded by others, proved it without a doubt.

She should have been more specific by asking Lady Eden if the one Malory she didn't want to see again would be there. But she hadn't wanted to give herself away. She had to be oh, so insouciant instead by asking if any Malorys would be there. So she deserved Regina's evasive "I never know when one or more of them will drop by. They know they're always welcome in my home, you see."

That was what she got for being so reticent, for pretending an indifference she was far from feeling. Now it was a matter of delaying her goal by several days or running into that rake again by chance.

There was really only one decision to make, so she might as well stop prevaricating over it. Another encounter with Anthony Malory was to be avoided at all costs. She had to accept the delay.

"Here we are, Ros. Dickens and Smith, my last stop for today," Frances said, then remonstrated, "You know, you're no fun at all to shop with. You could at least come in the shop, even if you don't want to buy anything.''

Roslynn couldn't quite manage a smile in her present depression to tease Frances out of her disgruntlement. ''I would if you hadn't picked such a hot day to drag me about. Going into the perfumers and the stocking warehouse was enough for me, thank you. I don't know how you could stand the bonnet warehouse and the silk mercers, but then I suppose you're used to it. But you forget we have a colder clime in Scotland. It's just too stuffy in these shops. At least there's a wee breeze out here, even if you can hardly notice it. Go on. I'll wait out here again with Nettie.''

It didn't take Nettie but two seconds to start in on her once the door of the drapery shop had closed on Frances and Anne. ''Now, lass, ye'll be telling me—''

''Och, Nettie, dinna be onto me now.'' Roslynn was quick to forestall her. ''I'm in no mood to be picked apart, none a-tall.''

Nettie was not one to let go easily. ''Ye'll no' be denying ye've been acting mighty strange.''

''I'm allowed, considering where we are and why and all I've got to be thinking about,'' Roslynn replied, her tone sharply defensive. ''Did you think this business of selecting a husband would be easy work? Hell's teeth! Sometimes I canna think for the worry of it!''

That managed to stir Nettie's sympathy. ''Now, hinny, it'll be over afore ye—''

''Shh,'' Roslynn interrupted with a frown. ''There it is again, Nettie. Do you feel it?''

''What?''

''That someone's watching us.''

Nettie gave her a doubtful glance, not at all sure whether Roslynn was simply trying to get the subject off herself or if she was serious. But the girl was certainly intent on slowly perusing the street this way and that.

"If someone *is* watching us, it's no' us they be watching, but ye. An admirer, nae doubt."

Roslynn looked back at Nettie impatiently. "I know what it feels like to be looked at like that, and this is not at all the same. I've felt it ever since we stood outside the bonnet warehouse waiting for Frances. I tried to ignore it, but the feeling persists."

"Well, then, it's nae doubt some pickpocket who's marked us, and no' surprising wi' all them jewels ye're wearing. Hold yer purse tightly, lass."

Roslynn sighed. "You're probably right. It'd be too soon for Geordie to have found me, wouldn't it? Still, I'd as soon wait in the carriage than out here in the open. Do you see our driver yet?"

Nettie stretched up on her toes. "Aye, about five shops down, but it appears he's stuck behind a wagon. See him? We can walk, though, and get ye settled inside. Then I'll come back tae tell Lady Frances."

It wasn't that Roslynn was paranoid, but she had never felt such a strange feeling before. It was no doubt her imagination run wild, but just the same, there was no point in her standing outside the drapery shop when the carriage was now in sight. Still, she gave one more glance around her, but there were so many pedestrians on the walkway and vehicles in the street, it was impossible to notice any one person staring at her.

They started down the street but got no farther than twenty feet when an arm snaked around Roslynn's waist from behind, lifting her right off her feet. She didn't think to scream, yet it was almost a relief that her suspicions hadn't been wrong, and she was prepared. No panic, no fear—yet. She simply let the upper half of her body drop over the steely arm that held her, grabbed the edge of her skirt, and plucked the dirk out of her walking boot.

Nettie, meantime, let out a screech to warn the whole of London. She immediately charged the fellow before he moved one foot, swinging her reticule left and right, catching his ear, whipping around his face to flatten his nose. It also caught Roslynn's bonnet as she raised herself, knocking it forward over her eyes so she couldn't see. But her target was felt, cutting off her air as it was. She didn't need to see the beefy arm to take a chunk out of it.

The fellow howled and let go, and Roslynn found herself sitting flat on her backside in the middle of the walkway. She tipped her bonnet back in time to see Nettie still after the man, getting a few more swings at his head and shoulders before he leaped into a dilapidated old carriage and the driver took off, tearing into the horses with a vengeance.

It gave Roslynn the shivers to know that the carriage had been so close, that only a few more steps and she'd have been thrown into it. And everything had happened so fast. There were people standing around her, but all obviously too slow in their reactions to have helped. Only now did one of the grooms from their carriage come running up to offer his assistance—too late.

Nettie turned around, tugging down her spencer, which had come all askew in her attack against the footpad, unable to stop the triumphant smile that was now turning her lips up at the corners. Not even seeing Roslynn sprawled on the ground could lessen her moment of victory—until she saw the dirk still grasped in Roslynn's fist. But still, *she* had made the blackguard run for his life, even if Roslynn had made sure she wasn't carried along with him. They had prevailed, and she was inordinately pleased.

So was Roslynn, come to that, even with her backside smarting. Gramp would have been proud of her for remaining calm and doing what she had to do without hesitation. She had drawn blood for the first time, but even now she didn't feel squeamish about it. What she felt was a good deal safer, knowing she really could take care of herself. Of course, she had been prepared. She might not always have that intuitive warning to put her on guard. And if more than just the one man had tried to grab her, that would be a different story too. She didn't dare get cocky about this success.

Roslynn accepted the groom's help in rising and calmly returned her dirk to her boot before dusting off her skirts. Nettie waved the anxious fellow back and the crowd too, with a few choice words about concern being unwelcome when coming so tardily. Huffily she gathered up the dropped packages, thrust them into the groom's hands, and grabbed Roslynn's arm, fairly dragging her on toward the carriage.

"I should've listened tae yer warning, lass. I will next time."

"Then you think it was Geordie's hirelings?"

Nettie took a moment to consider. "Truth is, it could've been, but I doubt it."

"What else, then?"

"Just look at ye, wearing those sapphires round yer neck like a beacon. They could've thought ye were the wife of some rich lord that'd pay a pretty piece tae be getting ye back."

"I suppose." They were both silent for a moment more, then Roslynn added unexpectedly, "I think I'll go to the Eden party after all. It won't hurt to leave London for a few days, just to be safe. If Geordie is here and watching, he'll think I'm onto him and fleeing again. And until then, I'll keep Frances' servants close to me when I go out."

"Aye, on that I'm in agreement. Ye need tae be more cautious than ye ha' been."

Chapter Ten

*I*t had been a simple matter, escaping London on Brutus' back, two stalwart grooms flanking her. Roslynn didn't bother with a disguise this time. If the town house was being watched, she wanted Geordie to be aware of her leave-taking, to see the hefty satchel of clothes she carried, to think she was fleeing London.

The subterfuge seemed unnecessary, however, when they were several miles away and it appeared no one followed behind them. The brilliant sunrise offered ample light by which to keep watch, but the roads were clogged mainly with farmers bringing their produce to market and with travelers coming to London for the weekend. Only one fancy coach was seen leaving town, and Roslynn left it so far behind it didn't matter whether it had been following her or not.

She had a pleasant breakfast while she waited in the inn where she had arranged to meet Frances, and when Frances showed up with nothing suspicious to report, Roslynn felt safe traveling the rest of the way to Hampshire in the Grenfell coach. Halfway there, she left one worry behind for another, but there was little she could do about this one except hope her concern was unfounded. In her favor was the likelihood that a man like Sir Anthony wouldn't care to leave the excitement of London for a small country gathering, and Lady Eden had confided that this party, planned for months in advance, would be attended mostly by her neighbors, country gentry like herself who generally avoided London during the season.

It was early afternoon when they arrived, quite the first to do so, but then few others were planning on staying over, living as near as they did. Frances opted to nap the rest of the afternoon. Roslynn gave the excuse she would do the same, yet once she was alone in the room allotted to her, she plopped herself down in front of a window facing the front of the house and anxiously watched the drive. Every arriving carriage was noted, every alighting male passenger thoroughly scrutinized. She even kept a close watch on the comings and goings of the servants, making sure no male missed her notice.

When Nettie entered much later to help her mistress prepare for the evening, her patience was tried to the limit by Roslynn's fidgetiness and her constant running toward the window at the least sound of a new arrival. It was taking a good half hour just to complete Roslynn's coiffure.

"And just who is it ye're looking fer, I'd like tae be knowing, that ye canna sit still fer even two minutes?" Nettie finally demanded when Roslynn once again sat down at the dressing table in front of her.

"And who would I be watching for but my gentlemen?" Roslynn replied defensively. "Only Sir Artemus Shadwell has shown up so far."

"If the others are coming, they're coming. Yer watching fer them won't change it."

"I suppose," Roslynn was forced to concede, since her answer had been a lie to begin with.

The truth was, since meeting Anthony Malory, she had given very little thought to her four "possibles." *That* would have to change.

Fortunately for her peace of mind, the last noise

she had leaped up to investigate appeared to be the last carriage to arrive. With no other sound from out front, Nettie was able to help her into the sky-blue gown of silk she had chosen for tonight, generously complemented by the Cameron sapphires around her neck and delicate wrists, and Roslynn was able to release some of her tension.

By the time Frances joined her so they could go downstairs together, Roslynn was quite relaxed. *He* wasn't coming, and if there was an annoying twinge of disappointment accompanying that knowledge, Roslynn determinedly ignored it.

Lady Eden met them at the bottom of the wide stairway that rose from the large main hall to divide in the center, one section going to the front of the house where the guest rooms were, the other to the back of the house where the master bedrooms were located. A railinged walkway surrounded this hall on the second floor to reach the many rooms upstairs, leaving the whole area below visible from above, with a mammoth chandelier hanging from the center of the domed ceiling, at the moment glittering down on the white marble floor.

Roslynn was looking forward to a tour of the rest of the house, and Regina didn't disappoint her, insisting her guests could wait. She further put Roslynn at ease with her bright chatter and charming manner as the three of them moved from room to room on the lower floors.

Silverley was an immense country house, almost castlelike with its central main block and corner turrets, but there was nothing medieval inside except perhaps the antique tapestries that graced many of the walls. It was tastefully furnished in different periods, Queen Anne and Chippendale dominating one room,

Sheraton another, still another in a combination, including a few quaint French Provincial pieces. Roslynn was left with the impression of a home, not a showpiece, though the latter term could certainly be applied.

The tour ended at the back of the house where the guests were gathered, and simply standing in the small antechamber with its floor-to-ceiling stained-glass windows, they were able to see into the drawing room on the left, which opened into a music room beyond. A large dining room was on the right, and off that was a lovely conservatory, which Roslynn promised herself a closer look at later. But at the moment, what with guests roaming through these connecting rooms, all of which fronted a vast parkland behind the house, Regina was cornered into making introductions before they had even entered the drawing room.

"There is one neighbor of mine I think you'll enjoy meeting," Regina commented to Roslynn when she was finally able to usher her and Frances into the drawing room. "Not everyone hies off to London for the season, you know. I wouldn't have gone myself if I hadn't promised, but I'm glad I did since I got to meet you. And don't worry, we'll have a chance later to discuss what Nicholas had to say about the gentlemen you're interested in."

"I see only Sir Artemus, Ros," Frances said uneasily, remembering how worried Roslynn had been about whether her "possibles" would be here or not.

"That's true," Regina said. "But there is still tomorrow, so I wouldn't discount the other gentlemen yet. I did have acceptances from all four of them. But in the meantime, you really must meet Lord Warton. Nicholas is so jealous of him, you know. In fact, I wonder sometimes what would have happened if I had met Justin Warton first.'' It was easy to see by her impish grin that she wasn't in the least serious about that last statement.

''Justin's not as old as your other gentlemen, Roslynn,'' Regina continued. ''Only about twenty-eight years old, I believe, but he's *so* nice, I just know you're going to like him. Devoted to his family and abhors London, so you wouldn't have been able to meet him otherwise. He goes to town only once a year to take his mother and sister shopping, and that off season. Now where is he?'' With her diminutive height, Regina had to stand on tiptoe to see over a few shoulders, but finally she smiled. ''There, by the fireplace. Come along, m'dears.''

Roslynn took two steps and stopped abruptly. She had immediately seen the large, handsome man sitting on a cream-and-gold sofa near the fireplace, flanked on one side by a young woman with the same blond looks as he and on the other side by an older woman, obviously Lord Warton's sister and mother, respectively. But she had in the next instant seen the two elegantly attired gentlemen several feet beyond, standing directly in front of the fireplace, the Malory brothers, and it was the dark one she locked eyes with, who made her pause, and groan, and feel the strangest rush of giddiness . . .

It took the greatest effort to tear her eyes away from Anthony Malory and continue to follow her hostess, who hadn't noticed her pause. She would have much preferred to turn around and retreat, rather than close the distance to a mere six feet from the fireplace where the sofa was situated, but there was no help for it. And since there wasn't, she decided it would behoove her to concentrate on the Wartons, Justin Warton in particular, and to keep her back to the Malorys.

It was easy to see why Regina might think Justin would interest her. He was terribly handsome with his blond hair, strong, chiseled features, and the loveliest pair of dark indigo eyes, eyes that were frankly admiring as they lit upon Roslynn. He was also quite the tallest man she had ever met, as she discovered when he rose from the sofa to take her hand and bring it up to his lips. He was large, with wide, wide shoulders, and he was solidly put together, firmly muscled. But with his immense size, if it weren't for his boyish smile and charming manner, he could have been quite intimidating.

As it was, he put Roslynn at ease immediately, and for several minutes she almost forgot who stood behind her—almost. The trouble was, she could actually feel those sensual eyes roaming over her body, could see them in her mind's eye as they had looked at her that night of the Crandal ball. Looked? No—*devoured* her across the space of a room, as they did now from only a few feet away. It was all she could do not to imagine what *he* was imagining as he gazed at her.

The interruption by a new arrival was a welcome distraction. "There you are, love," Nicholas Eden said as he slipped a possessive arm around his wife's tiny waist. "Why is it that whenever I leave the room, this big clod always manages to show up at your side?"

Whether he was jesting or serious was not evident either by his expression or tone, but Justin Warton didn't take offense. He laughed instead, as if he were used to such comments from his host.

"If I was of a mind to steal her away from you, Montieth, you'd know it," Justin replied with a wink for Regina, who was taking these remarks in stride.

"Now don't start, either of you," Regina admonished lightly. "Or you'll have these ladies believing you're serious. They're not, you know, not at all," she confided to her guests. "This, if you haven't guessed, is my husband." And she went on to complete the introductions, for although Frances knew of him, she had never actually met him.

Roslynn had expected someone as beautiful as Regina Eden to have an exceptionally handsome husband, and the Fourth Viscount Eden of Montieth was certainly that. He had gold-streaked brown hair and light brown eyes that glowed like amber each time they rested on his wife, and it was easy to see how he could have been called a rake as recently as a year ago and lived up to the reputation, and just as easy to see that he was now quite domesticated and thoroughly in love with his wife. What was surprising was that he was so young, no more than a few years older than she, Roslynn guessed, and yet his manner was that of an older man; in fact, he reminded her distinctly of Sir Anthony, which brought that rakehell promptly back into her thoughts.

"Come now, puss, how long do you intend to ignore us?" Anthony's deep voice suddenly broke into a lull in the conversation.

"All bloody night, if I have anything to say about it," Nicholas retorted none too pleasantly.

For a heart-stopping moment, Roslynn had thought Anthony was addressing her. But Nicholas' surprising reply, which earned him a sharp jab in the ribs from his wife, disabused her of that giddy notion.

"Oh, bother, must I always play referee?" Regina said to no one in particular, then promptly flounced over to the fireplace and gave each Malory brother a kiss. "As if anyone *could* ignore either of you for very long," she added with a laugh. "But I don't suppose for a minute that it's my attention you're so impatient for. Come along, then, and I'll introduce you." She hooked an arm through each of theirs and dragged them forward. "Lady Frances, I don't believe you've met my uncles, James and Anthony Malory, have you?"

Uncles? *Uncles!* Why was it that that wee bit of information hadn't surfaced sooner? Roslynn wondered angrily. She certainly wouldn't have come here if she had known the Malorys were *that* close to Regina Eden. Their niece. Hell's teeth!

The uneasiness was palatable with four in their group, the Wartons and Frances. Justin in fact made haste to leave with his womenfolk, protectively getting his sister out of the presence of two such notorious rakes. Roslynn could almost wish she had someone to look after her so diligently, someone to whisk her away from this present encounter. But she held her own. Not by look or word did she reveal that she was just as uneasy with the situation. Frances was not so inscrutable, however. Tight-lipped, curt during the introductions, her animosity for these two men couldn't have been more apparent, and she wasted little time in making her own excuses and moving on to the next group of people.

Which left Roslynn in a horrid predicament. To depart as well would have been grossly rude at this point. So she had to stand there, for a while at least, and suffer both Malorys' close scrutiny. And neither of them had any compunctions about openly staring at her.

Neither did James feel it necessary to ignore what had just happened. "I do believe the lass is embarrassed for us, Tony. You needn't be, Lady Roslynn.

My brother and I are quite immune to such reactions.''

''*You* might be, old man,'' Anthony remarked with a definite sparkle in his cobalt eyes. ''I for one could do with a little sympathy.''

Roslynn was left with no doubt as to what kind of sympathy he would like, since he was looking directly at her when he said it. She couldn't help smiling. He couldn't even wait until he found her alone to press his seduction. Now *that* was incorrigible.

Regina must have thought so too. ''Now, Tony, you promised you'd behave.''

''And so I am,'' he protested in all innocence. ''If I was inclined to do as is my wont, puss, you'd have a scandal on your hands.''

Roslynn had the feeling he was quite serious, even though Regina laughed as if he were teasing her. ''You're going to scare her off, Tony, if you're not careful.''

''Not at all,'' Roslynn demurred.

''There, you see, sweet?'' James put in. ''You can feel free to run along and attend to your hostessing. The lady will be quite safe in our hands.''

''Oh, I never doubted it for a minute,'' Regina said, only to add in parting, ''Nicholas, don't let either of them out of your sight.''

''Splendid.'' Nicholas scowled.

James chuckled. ''A decided lack of trust, that.''

''Unfortunately warranted,'' Nicholas grumbled beneath his breath.

''I do believe he still hasn't forgiven us, Tony,'' James said.

''Speak for yourself, brother. All I did was point out to him that it would be detrimental to his health if he didn't marry Reggie. You, on the other hand, were responsible for his being confined to bed for several weeks, not to mention your dragging him home from the West Indies when he proved such a reluctant spouse.''

''I was never—''

Roslynn interrupted Nicholas' snarl. ''Before this gets out of hand, I think I'll just—''

Anthony didn't let her finish. ''An excellent idea. While they squabble to their heart's content, you and I shall see what's blooming in the conservatory.''

Without giving her a chance to refuse, Anthony took her arm and began escorting her from the room. They moved no more than five feet before she tried to draw away from him. He wasn't letting go.

''Sir Anthony—''

''You're not going to turn coward on me, are you?'' His voice sounded near her ear.

Roslynn bristled that he should make it a challenge. ''I simply don't want to leave the room with you.''

''But you will.''

She stopped walking, forcing him to either drag her behind him or stop as well. He stopped, and the tiniest hint of a grin appeared as he bent his head to hers.

''Let me put it this way, sweetheart. Either I kiss you in the conservatory or I kiss you right here, right now. Whichever way, I *am* going to take you in my arms and—''

''The devil you are!'' Roslynn got out before she noticed how many people were suddenly watching them. ''Very well,'' she amended in a quiet hiss. ''I would like to see the conservatory, but there'll be no kissing, you scoundrel, and I'll have your promise first.''

His grin was wide and bold now. "Come along, then."

And he continued to escort her, stopping here and there to have a few words with people he knew, as if they were only strolling through the rooms. Roslynn caught Frances' eye along the way, and her friend's expression was quite disapproving and rightly so. But Roslynn didn't want to press her luck by trying again to extricate herself from this situation. Whether Anthony really would have kissed her in front of everyone was a moot point. She simply couldn't take the chance.

But she should have sealed the bargain. His "Come along, then" was not a promise by any means, which she found out not long after they entered the large conservatory.

"This is really lovely," Roslynn said uneasily as his arm slipped around her waist and he began to guide her along the plant-strewn walkway that circled the room.

"I couldn't agree more," he replied, only he was looking at her.

She kept her eyes averted, gazing intently at the statues along the walk, at the myriad flowers in full bloom, at the fountain that was on a lower level in the center of the room. Foremost in her mind was that hand resting on her hip, burning through the thin material of her high-waisted gown.

"I—I really should take you to task, Sir Anthony." Her voice was thin, shaky, and she had to clear her throat before continuing with more force. "That was devilish unfair of you to leave me no choice back there."

"I know."

"Was it necessary to be so high-handed?"

He stopped, turning her toward him, his eyes moving slowly over her face as he considered her question. In alarm, Roslynn realized that he had maneuvered them to the far side of the room, that thick branches from one of the trees growing below spread out at their level and effectively concealed them from the doorway. In actuality, they were quite alone for the moment, the sound of the party drowned out by the flow of the fountain.

"Yes, it was necessary," he finally answered huskily. "When all I've been able to think about since I first laid eyes on you is this."

To save her soul, Roslynn couldn't find the will to protest as his arm drew her closer. His other hand slid along her neck, the thumb tilting her chin up, and for the breath of a moment her eyes locked with his. Then she felt his lips, warm, beguiling, pressing ever so gently on her own, and her lids closed, accepting the inevitable. She had had to know, and now she did. And for the moment, nothing mattered but the taste of him, the feel of him pressed along her length.

Anthony didn't frighten her with his passion but kept it tightly leashed, even though he felt like an inferno about to explode. He couldn't remember when he had wanted something this much, and he took every care not to overwhelm her with what he was feeling, to fan her desire by slow degrees until she wanted him with equal intensity.

It was the hardest thing he had ever done, restraining himself when his body cried out to take her here and now. And in fact he was not as self-controlled as he supposed. Nearly mindless with wanting, he was unaware of the little things he was doing to her, that his fingers had slid into her hair, dislodging pins from her coiffure, that his knee had slipped between her own, far enough that she was practically straddling his thigh. But fortunately for him, she was as mindless as he was at this point. He just didn't know it.

Actually, that thigh rubbing against her groin was Roslynn's undoing, coupled as it was with his deepening kisses. He had gradually brought his tongue into play, teaching her the exquisite sensations it could invoke, using it to open her mouth, to taste the sweetness within. He eventually enticed her tongue to explore as well, and once it hesitantly passed between his lips, he wouldn't let it go, gently sucking it deeper and deeper into his mouth.

Helpless under his expertise, Roslynn was quite thoroughly seduced, ready and willing to let him do anything he wanted. When Anthony finally became aware of that fact, he groaned in frustration, for he had unwisely chosen his setting, never dreaming that he would be this successful this quickly.

Trailing his lips to her ear, he beseeched her, "Go to your room, sweetheart. I'll follow you there."

She was dazed, hypnotically so, unable to connect one thought with another. "My room?"

He had the urge to shake her. Now was not the time for confusion, for God's sake! He gripped her shoulders instead.

"Look at me, Roslynn," he said urgently. "We can't stay here. Do you understand? There's no privacy here."

She frowned up at him. "What would we be needing privacy for?"

Hell and fire! Was Regina right? Could Roslynn really be that innocent at her age? He found himself torn between chagrin and pleasure at the thought. If it were true, he risked losing what ground he had gained by bringing her back to her senses. And yet a tender cord was struck, heretofore dormant, wishing it were true.

Anthony sighed, dredging up a degree of patience to reach her. "We're going to make love, you and I. That is the natural conclusion to what we've been doing. And since we both want to, the thing to do is find someplace we won't be disturbed. You'll agree your room is the logical place."

Roslynn was shaking her head before he had finished. "Och, mon, what have you done? There was to be no kissing—I told you so."

Her lilting brogue served to stir him even more, and he pulled her tightly back against his chest. "It's too late to prevaricate, sweetheart, after you've surrendered in every way but one. Now be a good girl and do as I say, or I'll take you right here, I swear I will, and the devil take anyone who happens upon us."

If he meant to frighten her into complying, it didn't work. She almost laughed at his effort but didn't think he would appreciate that in this present mood that could make him say such a thing. Common sense told her he wouldn't do anything to cause his niece embarrassment. She should have realized that sooner, before she came in here with him.

"You canna use that bluff on me twice, laddie."

At this moment, Anthony wasn't sure it had been a bluff. But that she was boldly calling it restored his reason, even if it didn't completely cool his ardor. He had made a mess of the situation, and if she wasn't angry, she had every right to be.

His smile came with devastating effect. It was his melting smile. "If now just won't do, then I'll come to your room later tonight."

She pushed away from him, shaking her head. "You'll no' get past the door, I promise you that."

"Leave it unlocked."

"I'll no' do that either."

"Your window, then."

Her hazel eyes flared. "So you'll make me suffocate in my room, locking every window? Why canna you just take no for an answer? Have I no' made it plain enough for you?"

"It's the wrong answer, sweetheart, and until it's the right one, you don't really expect me to give up, do you? I must think of my reputation, you know."

She laughed at this, relieving some of her tension. God, but he was incorrigible, utterly lacking in morals, and oh, so tempting. She had never known a man could have such a powerful sexual allure, so strong that even in her saner moments, knowing full well that he was not the man for her, she could still be drawn to him. But whether he was serious or not in this bold pursuit of her, the only way she was going to survive this present encounter was not to take him seriously at all.

In control again, her eyes chiding him, Roslynn said, "Your reputation is precisely what *I* am thinking of, Sir Anthony."

"Then I must see if I can't chase such thoughts away—again."

"No!"

She gasped as he reached for her, and before she knew it, she was sitting on the railing, her balance precarious at best, and he was grinning at her. She had thought he meant to kiss her again. *This* she didn't find amusing at all. The drop behind her was at least eight or nine feet from the top of the railing where she sat to the ground, her feet were dangling off the floor, and she had nothing to grasp hold of if she should lose her balance—except him.

Scowling, she started to jump down, but Anthony stepped closer, and to Roslynn's horror, he flicked her skirt up to her thighs. Now he moved even closer, forcing her legs to part to accommodate his hips, and he leaned his chest into her, pushing her back, back . . .

"Hold onto me, or you're going to fall over." His voice broke through her panic.

She did, because there was nothing else she could do at the moment. Only he didn't straighten up so she could regain her balance. He kept her dangling half over the railing, his body her only anchor.

"You'll have to do better that that, sweetheart. Wrap your arms around my neck." With one arm he pressed her belly and chest to his. "Now hold tight, because I'm letting go."

"No, dinna—"

"Shh, sweetheart." His breath blew into her ear, sending delicious tremors down her back. "If you won't give in, at least give me this. I need to touch you."

She caught her breath as she felt a hand on each knee, slowly moving up the outside of her thighs, dragging her dress with them. "Stop! You're a bloody . . . let me down!" And then, in a husky whisper, "Anthony."

He shivered at the way she said his name. But before she could say any more, his hands reached her hips, and with a sharp pull he had their loins pressed tightly together.

Roslynn moaned softly, her head falling back, her limbs gone all buttery. He might as well have entered her, the feeling was that evocative. And now his lips burned a moist trail along the neck she had exposed to him, and Roslynn quite understandably forgot her precarious position.

"I don't suppose you'll thank me for intruding, Tony, but Lady Grenfell's searching for your little Scot, and she's bound to look in here at any moment."

With a curse, Anthony glanced at James several feet away, to see him tactfully looking down at the fountain, rather than at them. He lifted Roslynn off the railing, his hands still supporting her hips, and for just a moment more held her like that, savoring the feeling of her in this position, with her legs nearly wrapped around his waist. She was once again in the throes of passion, lips parted, eyes closed, face flushed. He doubted she had even heard James.

"Oh, Christ," he said as he let her slide slowly to her feet, frustrated now beyond measure. "We'll have to continue this another time, sweetheart."

She stepped back, her legs wobbly, and over several long moments he watched her eyes gradually focus, finally widen, and then promptly narrow. Fascinated, Anthony didn't even see her hand coming, but the palm cracked solidly against his cheek.

"There'll no' be another time, mon, for what you're wanting," she said quietly, but with enough force that he couldn't doubt her temper was boiling. "I dinna ken your rules, and you canna be trusted to play fair, so just stay away from me."

She flounced off in the direction they had been taking, continuing around the room. Anthony didn't try to follow her. He sat back on the railing, fingering his cheek, and watched her until she was gone from sight.

"I was wondering when that Scot's temper would surface." He grinned as James came up beside him.

"I'd say you were let off lightly."

Anthony's grin widened. "She didn't even know you were here."

"Bragging, brother?"

"Just feeling inordinately pleased, old man."

"Well, now that you've left her in this raging mood, I don't suppose you'll mind if I try my luck?"

Anthony's humor vanished instantly. "Stay away from her, James."

A blond brow shot up. "Possessive, aren't we? But I believe those words were hers—to you. And after all, dear boy, you haven't won her yet."

Chapter Eleven

*J*ustin Warton proved such delightful company that Roslynn's temper was able to subside completely in less time than she could have hoped for, considering what a foul temper she had when it was fully aroused. And she had been furious, the more so when Frances found her just coming out of the conservatory and promptly whisked her upstairs to repair her coiffure, which she hadn't even realized had fallen into such a telling state of disarray. Horrid man to leave her looking as if she had just been manhandled, which she had been, which forced her to suffer through a stern lecture from Frances, albeit deserved.

She *knew* she had been foolish, *knew* she had taken a terrible risk. She didn't need to be told so with such sterling clarity. But she couldn't take exception to Frances' anger in her behalf, since it was based on love and concern. She could only be more furious with herself, for upsetting Frances and for knowing better in the first place.

After a long harangue about Sir Anthony's sordid reputation, Frances had concluded with, "You simply must never find yourself alone with him again, Ros, especially since you are so obviously attracted to him."

"I never said that, Frances."

"You didn't have to. I saw it the moment Regina brought Sir Anthony forward to be introduced to us. And I saw the way he looked at you too. Kissing you in the conservatory was one thing, but you know it would't have stopped there if you had been in a less conspicuous place.''

Roslynn didn't volunteer that it had gone a step beyond kissing, even in that public place, or that she wasn't at all sure that it might not have gone much, much further if Anthony hadn't fortunately come to his senses and released her. *She* certainly hadn't been the one to break away, nor had she even tried, once she was held firmly in his embrace.

''You should have told me you had met him at the Crandal ball.'' Frances' tone suddenly turned hurtful. ''I could have warned you sooner, for it's obvious he's marked you for his next conquest.''

''Frances, Frances, you didn't have to warn me. I'd already heard the gossip about him at the ball. I knew what a disreputable rake he is.''

''And yet you still let him lead you off.''

''I told you, he tricked me!'' Roslynn cried in exasperation, then promptly regretted her tone. ''I'm sorry, but you must stop worrying. I've told him to stay away from me.''

Frances pursed her lips, her finely arched brows drawn tightly together. ''Do you think your wishes will make the least bit of difference to him? Men like him don't accept rejection, Ros. For some absurd reason, they only become more intrigued the harder the chase. And *that* one, Sir Anthony, is the worst of the lot, simply because he's the handsomest, the most sought after, and the most confirmed bachelor in the Realm. He'll never marry, Ros. He'll never settle for one woman. And why should he when hundreds scheme and plot to win his favor?''

''Frances, you're forgetting how unique my circumstances are. I'm not just another hopeful debutante on the marriage mart. I've got a goal to accomplish, and I'm not going to let anything upset it. The consequences are too abhorrent to me, not to mention dangerous, if I should fail to quickly secure a marriage.''

Frances sighed and gave a little apologetic smile. ''You're right, I was forgetting that. But you will be careful, Ros? A man like Malory, with his experience, could have you seduced before you even know it. I suppose we can just be grateful that that brother of his, just as unprincipled, hasn't set his eye on you too.''

Roslynn was to remember those words later, but when they returned downstairs and Justin Warton was quick to invite them to share the buffet with him, she was still simmering over her own naiveté with Anthony Malory to give his brother a single thought. And then Justin took her mind off her near catastrophe and she enjoyed herself for a while. He was so charming, his lovely indigo eyes so admiring, that she seriously found herself considering him as a likely candidate to add to her list, despite his young age. At least he was older than she, and he certainly made no attempt to conceal his interest in her, which was gratifying, especially after *she* had had to be so bold as to seek out her other candidates. And still had to, it seemed, since Sir Artemus had yet to approach her tonight, even though she knew he had seen her.

Unfortunately, Lady Warton broke up their threesome soon after they had eaten, complaining of a headache, and Justin was forced to see her home, though he extracted a promise from Roslynn that she would ride with him in the hunt planned for the next morning.

''Well, that was an easy conquest,'' Frances remarked after Justin had left with his mother.

"Do you think so?" Roslynn grinned. "He is rather nice, isn't he?"

"And so very upstanding. I've heard nothing but good things—"

"Frances, you needn't laud his sterling qualities. If you've noticed, Sir Anthony appears to have left. You can stop worrying."

Frances squeezed her hand. "Very well. I know you've got the sense to distinguish the good from the bad. And as long as Lord Warton has quit for the evening, shouldn't you be furthering your acquaintance with Sir Artemus while you have the opportunity?"

"Indeed." Roslynn sighed. "And I also need to find Lady Eden for the information she promised me. The sooner my list is narrowed down, the better."

But Regina Eden was having a lively conversation with several of her neighbors that Roslynn was loath to interrupt, and she found Sir Artemus embroiled in a game of whist, several such games having started up after dinner.

Roslynn moved near one of the open French doors to wait until she could catch Regina's attention, taking advantage of what little breeze wafted in off the vast parkland. As uncomfortably warm as the drawing room had become, she would have loved to step outside but didn't dare, not after the last time she had thought to escape to a garden had precipitated her first meeting with Sir Anthony. And just because she hadn't seen him since she left him in the conservatory didn't mean he wasn't still on the premises somewhere.

She almost thought to go and drag Frances outside with her just so she could cool off a bit when she was startled by a movement behind her.

"Enjoying yourself, Lady Roslynn?"

She turned around warily, recognizing James Malory's voice and afraid that Anthony would be with him, as before. She relaxed, however, to see he was alone, his golden hair slightly ruffled, obviously having just come in from outside. But her respite lasted only a few seconds, for the way he was pointedly staring at her, waiting for her answer, reminded her that this was the brother she had decided could be dangerous in his dealings, and nothing about him tonight changed that opinion, though she was now inclined to feel that Anthony was the more dangerous, at least to her.

She nodded slightly. "Yes, your niece has made me feel right at home, though I must say I was surprised to learn that she was your niece. She would be the daughter of one of your older brothers, I suppose?"

"Our only sister, Melissa," he corrected. "But she died when Regan was just a baby still, so my brothers and I had the pleasure of raising her."

Roslynn had the distinct impression that four young men really *had* found it a pleasure to raise their only sister's child, which made this particular Malory seem less threatening in her mind until he suggested, "Care for a stroll down to the lake?"

It was unexpected and instantly put her on guard. "No, thank you."

"Then just outside? You look like you could use a breath of fresh air."

"Actually, I'm rather chilled and was just thinking of fetching a shawl."

James chuckled at such a lame excuse. "My dear girl, that fine film of moisture on your brow says otherwise. Come along. You needn't be afraid of me, you know. I'm quite harmless in all respects."

When his hand gripped her elbow to escort her outside, Roslynn felt strangely as if this had happened before, earlier, that she was being rushed along the exact same course, leading to disaster. Only she had no chance to drag James to a halt as she had done with Anthony when he tried to escort her from the room. Just two steps and they were outside, and it was accomplished before she could even think to yank away, nor did he give her a chance to. Instead of walking on, he pulled her to the side of the door and pressed her back against the wall, and his mouth smothered her small cry of alarm.

It was done so swiftly, so cleverly, that Roslynn had had no opportunity to anticipate the trap or get out of it. Nor did she dare make any loud protests now, or she would draw the attention of the occupants inside, only several feet away on the other side of the wall, and she couldn't afford the gossip that that would entail. The most she could do was try to push him away from her, but it was as if she were squeezed in between two walls, his big, solid chest was so unmovable. And then she no longer tried. She could feel the blood pounding in her ears, because of the danger of discovery, she told herself, but actually, she found James Malory's kiss so reminiscent of his brother's that it could have been Anthony kissing her instead. Only it wasn't, and she held onto that thought for dear life.

"You and your brother must take lessons from each other," she hissed the moment he lifted his head.

James laughed despite his disappointment. "Do you think so, little Scot? Now why would you say that?"

She blushed furiously to have as much as admitted that Anthony had also kissed her. Defensively, she snapped, "Was that your idea of being harmless?"

"I lied," he said with a blatant lack of contrition.

"Indeed! Now let me pass, Lord Malory."

He moved back only enough to separate their bodies, not enough to allow her to slip by him. "Don't be angry, sweet. You can't blame a man for trying, though I now concede that Tony has bested me this time. It's devilish unfair that you happened to meet him first."

"What the devil are you blathering about?" But she gasped, afraid she knew. "If you two have placed wagers on me—"

"Never think so, dear girl. It's no more than sibling rivalry, and the simple fact that we share the same tastes, he and I." A finger came up to brush back the damp curls at her temple, and for a moment, Roslynn was mesmerized by intense green eyes. "You are incredibly lovely, you know . . . incredibly. Which makes it bloody difficult to accept defeat." His voice lowered to a husky pitch suddenly. "I could have made your blood sing, sweet lass. Are you quite certain you prefer Tony?"

Roslynn shook herself mentally, fighting off the potent spell he was weaving with little effort, yet with such ruthless success. Good God, these Malorys were devastating at their craft of seduction.

Stiffly, praying he would take her words to heart, she insisted, "I never said I preferred your brother, but that doesn't mean I prefer you to him either. The fact is, Lord Malory, I don't want either of you. Now will you let me pass, or must I throw caution to the winds and call for help?"

He stepped back, bowing slightly, a thoroughly maddening grin turning up his sensual lips. "I can't let you do that, dear lady. Being found out here alone with me would quite ruin you."

"Which you should have considered *before* you dragged me out here!" she retorted and promptly deserted him with all speed.

And as Anthony had done earlier, James watched her flounce away, only he didn't have Anthony's sense of eventual success to buoy his spirits. Quite the contrary. As much as he would have liked to win this particular lady, and no doubt could if he really set his mind to it, her reaction to his kiss was only a muted echo of her reaction to Anthony's. He hadn't left her in a state of bemusement, as his brother so obviously had. Her choice was clear, even if she was not yet aware she had made it. But if it were anyone else but Tony . . .

Damn, but she was a fine piece. His sense of humor returned, laced with irony. She had managed to stir him, and now he was sorely in need of a wench, which meant he would have to take himself off to the nearest village or else annoy Regan by seducing one of her neighbors. So there was nothing for it but to take himself off when he would rather not. Hell and fire, and a bloody pox on love at first sight!

Chapter Twelve

Roslynn rolled over, rubbed the sleep from her eyes, and squinted at the clock on the mantel. Damn. She had really meant to join the hunt this morning. She had even promised Justin she would ride with him and had been looking forward to showing off a bit to impress him with her equestrian talents. But the hunting party would probably be returning soon, if it hadn't already. There had been mention of a picnic planned for midday down by the lake, and it was nearly noon. Double damn.

She sat up, but not before she scowled down at the bed that had offered her no peace last night. Nettie had tried to wake her. She remembered that. But she doubted anything short of fire could have prodded her out of bed early this morning, because it had been dawn before she finally succumbed to sleep. Just one more thing she could lay at Anthony Malory's feet, drat the wretched man.

And there was no excuse for it. She had retired not long after midnight. Having arisen well before dawn yesterday to make the trip to Silverley, and not having napped in the afternoon as Frances had, she had really been exhausted last night. And she had had several hours to get over her chagrin at Anthony's brother for his outlandish conclusions concerning her preferences in men. She had even had her talk with Regina and now knew a good deal more about her ''possibles'' than she had before, though unfortunately, nothing had been revealed that would really assist her in whittling down her list as she had hoped.

Sir Artemus Shadwell was an avid gambler, but Roslynn had already concluded that observation for herself, and he was rich enough to afford this pastime. Lord Grahame, the distinguished Earl of Dunstanton, was a three-time widower. At least the poor fellow kept trying. Lord David Fleming, the viscount who was also heir to a dukedom, was a confirmed bachelor, his affairs so discreet his name had never been linked with any woman. Commendable. But the Honorable Christopher Savage was still an enigma to her. The Montieths simply weren't acquainted with the fellow.

But her gentlemen, much as they should have, hadn't occupied her thoughts last night as she lay tossing about in her bed. James Malory's effrontery had also been forgotten. It was that black-haired scoundrel with the smoldering blue eyes who had caused her hour after hour of insomnia in reliving those fateful minutes spent with him in the conservatory.

Well, there would be no more of *that*, by God, no more wasted thoughts on blackhearted rascals, and no more procrastinating. She *would* get down to business, and hoped, no, prayed, that the rest of her respected and highly suitable gentlemen would show up today.

Impatient now to quit the room, she rang for Nettie but didn't wait to start her toilette, and was dressed in a lovely peach percale day dress with short, puffed sleeves and heavily flounced at the hem before Nettie even arrived. Rushing Nettie with her coiffure earned her a snort and a brief lecture on the missed opportunities of slugabeds, but even so, the tightly woven chignon and numerous short ringlets that framed her face turned out most becomingly.

But Roslynn spared not a moment to admire the finished package. Snatching up a white satin bonnet adorned with ostrich feathers that matched her shoes, and a lacy parasol, she sped from the room, leaving Nettie to clean up the mess she had made of her wardrobe before Nettie's tardy arrival. And then she was brought up short, for standing at the end of the narrow corridor that led to the guest rooms, leaning casually against the railing that overlooked the central hall, was Anthony Malory.

It was not to be borne, it really wasn't, for he was obviously waiting for her. Hips against the rail, arms crossed over his chest, ankles crossed as well, he had an unimpeded view of her bedroom door, and since he was waiting where he was, there was no way she could have avoided him.

He was casually dressed, almost too casually, minus a cravat and with several buttons open on his embroidered cambric shirt, revealing a darkly tanned V of chest, a few hairs hinting at a thicker patch just below. His coat was dark navy, the shoulders and upper arms filled out tightly. Long, muscular legs were sheathed in soft buckskin, with shiny Hessians molded to his calves. Everything about him proclaimed him an avid outdoorsman, athletic, a bloody Corinthian, which was so contrary to the reputation that would have him a debauched creature of the night, devoted to sensual pleasures and late hours of dissipation. Well, whatever he was, he was dangerously appealing to her senses.

When it appeared that the lady wasn't going to budge another step that would bring her nearer to him, Anthony said, ''It's as well you came out now, sweetheart. I was just beginning to fantasize about slipping into your room and finding you still abed—"

"Sir Anthony!"

"Was the door unlocked?" he teased, but at her fulsome glare, finally chuckled. "You needn't bludgeon me with those pretty eyes, my dear. I don't mean a word of it. In fact, you can come ahead without the slightest qualm. Today I fully intend to offer my best behavior, to observe every propriety, and to bury all those wicked instincts that might cause you alarm."

"You promise?"

He grinned. "Must I?"

"Yes."

"Very well. My promise, solemn and most sincere, is yours until you take pity on me and give it back."

The sound of her husky laugh was like music to his ears. "You can have it back, Sir Anthony, when you're too old to want it, and not a day sooner."

She came forward then, stopping just in front of him, her parasol tucked under her arm, her bonnet swinging from the cord held in her hand. She was a vision, by God, with her full lips turned up in a generous smile, her firm little chin that had proved so stubborn, and those lovely gold-flecked eyes sparkling with humor now.

He had been wise to leave Silverley last night, he reflected now, wise indeed. If he had stayed, he would have been drawn to Roslynn again when she needed time to cool her temper. So he had taken himself off to the village to celebrate, for which there was ample cause. She might have slapped him, but by God, he had aroused her, and that was reason enough for his high spirits, and cause for wenching, since she had definitely aroused him as well.

Anthony could have laughed, remembering how his plans had gone awry. The problem was, by the time he had found a willing lass, a comely one too, in the little tavern where he ended up, he no longer needed one or wanted one, other than the one he had left behind at Silverley. So when James unexpectedly showed up at the same tavern not long behind him, he very happily turned the little doxy over to his brother and settled for getting pleasantly drunk while he plotted his next move.

He had decided, quite shrewdly if her present smile was any indication, to change his approach for the time being. And after a lengthy talk with his favorite niece this morning, he had come upon the perfect contrivance. He would offer the lady what she couldn't refuse—help to achieve her goals. Of course, if the advice he gave hindered more than helped, he wouldn't lose any sleep over it. Her goals simply weren't his.

She was waiting, patiently, to hear why he had put himself in her path. Ah, the power of a few words. She was at ease, her guard down, putting full trust in his promise. She had no way of knowing his passions far outweighed his whimsical honor, at least in dealing with those of the female gender.

He came away from the rail, his manner smooth, his voice impersonal. "It would be to your advantage, Lady Roslynn, to come along with me where we might talk privately."

Wariness returned. "I fail to see—"

His smile disarmed her. "My dear, I said talk, nothing more. If you can't bring yourself to trust me, how am I going to help you?"

Nonplussed. "Help me?"

"Of course," he replied. "That is what I had in mind. Now come along."

It was sheer curiosity that prompted Roslynn to hold her tongue and let him lead her downstairs and into the library. She simply couldn't fathom what he thought he was going to help her with. The only difficulties she was having at the moment were her attraction to him and her inability to scratch below the facade that her gentlemen presented to the public. Her gentlemen? No, he couldn't know about them, could he?

Whether he did or didn't, Roslynn found herself aghast to be blushing at the mere possibility. Fortunately, Anthony didn't notice, leading her directly to a sofa, then walking to the end of the long room and stopping before a liquor cart.

"Brandy?" he asked over his shoulder.

"At this hour?"

Her incredulous tone made him smile to himself. "No, of course not. How silly of me."

But he definitely needed one, for the thought flashed through his mind that he had her alone at last and only need lock the doors. But that wasn't what he had brought her here for, and he would have to keep *that* thought uppermost in his mind.

He tossed down the brandy and strolled back to stand before the sofa on which she sat so decorously, legs pressed together, parasol and bonnet in her lap. She was huddled in one corner, leaving him a good five feet of space to occupy himself. He would be a bore to sit next to her when it was perfectly clear she didn't want him to. He did anyway, though he conceded enough to allow a six-inch space to keep her from panicking.

She panicked just the same. "Sir Anthony—"

"D'you think you could start calling me Anthony, or better yet, Tony? After all, if I'm to be your confidant—"

"My *what?*"

He cocked a brow at her. "Too strong a word? Will friend and adviser do? After a long talk with my niece this morning, I realized you're sorely in need of both."

"She told you!" Roslynn's voice gasped accusingly. "Hell's teeth, she had no right!"

"Oh, it was done with the best of intentions, my dear. She wanted to impress on me how serious you are about getting married. Seems to think I have dishonorable intentions toward you. Can't imagine where she got that idea."

She glared at him, but it was impossible to keep her outrage alive after that bit of nonsense. Her laughter broke through, rich and delightful.

"You're a rogue, laddie. Do *you* never take anything seriously?"

"Not if I can help it." He grinned.

"Well, try long enough to tell me why you of all people would want to aid me on my way to matrimony."

"It simply occurred to me that the sooner you're married and bored with it, the sooner I'll have you in my bed," he answered caddishly.

Anything else Roslynn wouldn't have believed. *That* she believed completely.

"A rather long shot you're taking, wouldn't you say?" she bantered. "I could fall passionately in love with my husband, you know."

"Bite your tongue," he said with mock horror. "No one falls passionately in love these days, my dear, except young romantics and doddering old fools.

And you're going about this thing much too sensibly for that possibility to occur.''

"I'll concede that point for now. So what exactly are you offering to do for me?''

The loaded question brought a twinkle of amusement to his eyes. "Your situation is not unlike Reggie's was when she was looking for a husband. Her pressure came from having got through one season, as well as a tour of the Continent, with no luck whatsoever. Through no fault of her own, of course. She had to attend to finding a man my brothers and I could all agree was suitable for her.''

"Yes, I recall her mentioning something like that.''

"Did she tell you how she solved her problem?''

"She was compromised.''

Roslynn was surprised to see him scowl at that answer. "She had nothing to do with *that*. It was Montieth's cheeky idea of a jest on his current mistress that went awry. And we won't mention that again, if you please. But before then, Reggie had hired an old lord who knew absolutely everyone, and dragged him along with her to every function, as well as on her tour, so with a signal they had worked out together, he could tell her which men she met were worth considering or not.''

Roslynn's eyes flared. "I hope you're not suggesting I take you along with *me* everywhere I go, Sir Anthony, because—''

He was quick to forestall her. "Not at all, and unnecessary besides. According to Reggie, you already have several chaps under consideration. As it happens, I know them a damn sight better than Montieth does, since they're all closer to my age than his. Three of them belong to my club; the fourth frequents the same sporting hall I do. I just have one question for you, my dear. Why have you discounted someone closer to your own age?''

Roslynn averted her eyes before murmuring, ''An older man is likely to have more patience with my faults than a younger man.''

''You have faults? Never say so.''

''Everyone has faults!'' she snapped.

''A quick temper wouldn't be one of yours, would it?''

Her narrowed gaze brought a laugh, but she went on testily. ''An older man will be more settled, having sowed his wild oats already. If I am going to be faithful in this marriage, I must insist upon the same from my husband.''

''But you're not going to be faithful, sweetheart,'' he reminded her.

''If I'm not, then I won't expect him to be. But if I am, I will. Let's leave it at that. The fact is, it was my grandfather who suggested I find a man with a good deal of experience behind him, and truth to tell, the younger men I've met so far haven't impressed me—well, except one, and him I decided to add to my list.''

''Who?''

''Justin Warton.''

''Warton!'' Anthony sat up abruptly, exclaiming, ''He's a mama's boy!''

''You needn't be disparaging,'' she replied curtly.

''My dear girl, if all you want are pristine reports from me on your lucky chaps, then I don't see what help I can be to you. They all present an outward showing that is beyond reproach, which is to be expected of gentlemen of their stature. I had assumed it was the dirt swept under the carpet that you would be interested in.''

She felt warm under his censure. "You're right, of course. I'm sorry. Very well, in your opinion, which fellow would make the best husband?"

"You have no particular preference?"

"Not really. I find them all attractive, personable, and quite suitable from what I have been able to learn so far. That has been my difficulty. I don't know which one I should concentrate on to get this matter settled."

Anthony relaxed again, sitting back and casually placing his arm along the back of the sofa, just behind her head. She didn't seem to notice. She was impatiently waiting for him to answer her question, while he was going to carefully avoid doing so.

"It might help if you tell me what attributes you favor," he suggested.

"An easy temperament, a gentle hand, sensitivity, intelligence, patience, as I've said—"

"Delightful." His grin was wickedly maddening. "You'll be bored to tears, my dear, which will have us more intimately acquainted much sooner than I expected." Her pursed lips and scathing gaze elicited a chuckle, not in the least contrite. "You were saying?"

"There is also a marriage contract that must be signed," she said tightly. "It will prohibit my husband from having complete control over me or my holdings."

"Your idea?"

"My grandfather's. He was a stubborn old man with set ways. Since he was leaving his fortune to me, he wanted to make certain it stayed with me and wasn't put in the hands of some stranger he might or might not have approved of. He had the contract drawn up before he died."

"If he was so particular, why didn't he arrange you a marriage?"

Her look was wistful. "We had a special bond, Anthony. I didn't want to leave him while he still lived, and he would never have forced me to."

He smiled at her use of his name, slipping out without thought. It proved she was more comfortable with his company. She had even bent one knee to turn toward him while she spoke, more or less facing him now. It would be so easy to let his arm drop to her shoulders and draw her near . . .

Anthony shook himself mentally. "It's a moot point really. The only one I can think might object to this contract is Savage. Not that he'll be coveting your fortune. He's well enough off, I believe, for wealth not to be a criterion when he weds. But he's not a man who likes to have limitations placed on him. Still, if he wants you, it shouldn't matter."

"Then you recommend him?"

"My dear, I can safely say intelligence is the only criterion of yours that he meets. In fact, none of these chaps will meet every one of the qualities you're looking for. Warton, I suppose, comes closest to the mark, but if you marry him, you'll also be marrying his mother—that is, if she'll even allow him to marry. I've never seen a woman hold the strings so tightly as that formidable lady."

Roslynn was frowning long before he had finished speaking. "Very well, don't recommend one. Just tell me what you know of the others."

"Easy enough. Let's see, shall we start with Fleming? Affectionately known as the bungling viscount, since he must be doing something wrong that no woman will ever be seen with him twice, but perhaps you'll be the exception. He's soft. Some have even

called him a coward. Seems he was challenged once
by a young man to a duel but wouldn't accept. Never
did learn the reason for it. Has he shown a definite
interest?''

Actually, he hadn't, but that was not the issue here.
''Next?''

Anthony chuckled at her avoidance in answering
his query. No need to tell her yet that young Fleming's fancy leaned toward those who wore boots,
rather than satin slippers. If she could get the fellow
to marry her, which he doubted, she would very
quickly be looking outside the marriage bed for a
lover.

''The Earl of Dunstanton is a likable enough chap;
he just has a way with words that can cut a man to
shreds. He seems to be beset with tragedy, however,
what with three dead wives in the space of the past
five years. It's not common knowledge, but with the
death of each wife his estate has doubled.''

''You're not suggesting—''

''Not at all,'' he assured her, taking advantage of
her distracted alarm to bring his knee up to where it
just touched hers. ''It's no more than mere specula-
tion bandied about by envious chaps not so well off.''

The seed had been planted, even if it wasn't accu-
rate. Two of the wives had died in childbirth, which
truly was a tragedy, occurring one after the other.
The third had fallen off a cliff, messy business, but
the earl certainly wasn't culpable unless he had it
within his power to produce the freak storm that had
spooked the lady's horse and led to her fall.

''What about Sir Artemus?''

''Loves to gamble, but don't we all.'' This said
with a wink. ''And you'd have a ready-made family
if you go with him. He has dozens of little tykes—''

"I was told there were only five children!"

"Five who claim legitimacy. Yes, you'd have your hands full, and very little help from Shadwell, since he tends to forget the fact that he even has children. Are you planning to have some of your own?"

The blush did it, so utterly becoming that Anthony's good intentions flew straight away. His hand slipped to her neck, and without moving, he drew her full against his chest, fingers sliding up into her hair so he could position her mouth to receive his kiss.

It never happened. She pushed him back so quickly and forcefully that he lost his hold due to surprise.

"You promised!"

He sat up, raking a hand through his hair in a manner fraught with impatience and chagrin, yet his voice was a study in tranquillity. "Kindly remember, my dear, that this role of confidant is new to me and will take some getting used to." And then, with a sideways glance that caught the fury of her eyes, "Oh, for God's sake, don't fry me for conditioned instincts. It won't happen again, you may depend on it."

She stood up, faced him, gripping her parasol as if it were a weapon that could hold him off. "If you have nothing more to tell me—"

Oh, sweetheart, if only you knew that it is my will alone that keeps you safe for the time being. "Fact will have to be sifted from rumor. Give me a week or two—"

"One week."

He leaned back again, propping both arms behind him on the sofa, eyeing her languorously. That she was still speaking to him, still willing to depend on his advice, told him enough. She wasn't *that* angry with him.

"Fix your hair, my dear, and I'll escort you down to the lake."

He choked back a laugh at her murmur of exasperation on finding her coiffure once more disturbed by him. With impatient fingers she tightened the effect, then smashed her bonnet down over it. He did laugh then, gaining a murderous stare from her that only amused him the more.

But a few minutes later, as they strolled across the back lawn, she was treated to the full brunt of his charm, which had her smiling helplessly again, quite willing to forgive him his lapse. Only it didn't last, her improved humor. She hadn't realized how it might look, her having stayed behind, his having stayed behind, while everyone else rode to the hunt. But one look at Justin's bemused frown as they approached the gathering at the lake, and she was brought up short.

"I really don't think it's a good idea for us to be seen together," she said in an aside to Anthony as she caught sight of several more of her gentlemen in the party.

"I would agree if we were anywhere but here, my dear," he replied. "Here I am a relative of the hostess and quite naturally am expected to socialize."

His total lack of concern suddenly annoyed her, for Lord Grahame and Lord Fleming, having arrived for today's entertainments, had both noticed her as well. Whether they thought there was anything untoward in her tardy arrival on Sir Anthony's arm, she couldn't guess. But neither could she help remembering Regina's friendly warning to the gist that *any* lady seen to have gained this particular rake's interest was raw meat for the gossip mills.

At any rate, his escort down to the lake after they

both had missed the hunt couldn't help her cause, not when the men she was in actuality "courting" would surely wonder about it. Anthony should have known that. He was much more experienced in these things than she was. And so her annoyance was directed solely at him, enough to want to burst his bubble of nonchalance.

"You know, Anthony, even if I do find myself bored with my husband, that doesn't mean you're going to benefit from it."

He seemed to see through her deliberate taunt, at least his grin so indicated, and his answer sent a tingling thrill of apprehension down her spine. "On the contrary. You *will* eventually be my mistress, sweetheart. If I weren't absolutely certain of that, I never would have agreed to help you."

Chapter Thirteen

"No! Dear Lord, let me be dreaming!"

It was in fact a nightmare, to wake up in a room she had not gone to sleep in, to be unable to recall how she came to be there. Roslynn looked around wide-eyed, praying she wasn't really awake, yet knowing she was. Stained and peeling wallpaper. A chipped basin of water with a cockroach scurrying up the pitcher sitting beside it, resting precariously on a three-legged table propped in one corner because the fourth leg was missing. A single narrow bed, coarse woolen blanket covering her to her waist. Bare floor, bare walls, bare window.

How was this possible? She pressed her palms to her temples, trying desperately to remember. Had she been ill? Or had an accident? But all she could recall was last night, if it was last night and not days ago, with the time in between unaccounted for.

She had been unable to sleep, an annoying happenstance, recurring ever since she had met Anthony Malory. She and Frances had returned from the country three days earlier, but she had been unable to forget the time she spent with Anthony there, nor his unexpected about-face in offering to assist her, rather than seduce her.

And yet, despite his promise to end his pursuit of her, at least until after she married, he still hadn't left her alone that day. Oh, he had relinquished her so she could circulate with the other picnickers and work her wiles on her gentlemen, but whenever she noticed him in the crowd, her eyes met his, as if he were constantly watching her. That night, to her chagrin, he danced not once but three times with her, all in the guise of socializing. And he danced with no one else, not even his niece.

She had been furious when she realized what he was doing, but by then the damage had been done. Lord Grahame, the Earl of Dunstanton, had begged off from taking her to the theater after they returned to London, an engagement he had only made that afternoon. He claimed he had suddenly recalled a previous commitment, when it was so obvious he was simply intimidated by Anthony's blatant interest in her.

Yes, she had been unable to sleep last night, full of furious energy, because not one of her gentlemen had called since her return to London, and she didn't deceive herself that they were merely too busy. Anthony's innocent "socializing" had seriously set her back.

So if she remembered all that, how was it possible that she couldn't remember how she came to be here in this horrid little room? Anthony wouldn't . . . no, he wouldn't. And she doubted Frances had gone mad and somehow arranged this. That left only one alternative, unless she was so ill that this was all part of a delirium, and it was too real for that. Geordie had her. Somehow, some way, he had managed to abduct her right out of the house on South Audley Street in Mayfair, and where she was now was anyone's guess. Inconceivable, yet what else was she to believe?

Only there was a part of her that was unwilling to accept that Geordie had won, a part that was too optimistic, hoping there might be some other explanation. So her surprise was genuine when she saw the truth with her own eyes. Her fear was real too, nearly choking her with the tightening of her throat, her palms breaking out in a sweat. Geordie Cameron, in the flesh, walked as nonchalantly as you please into the room, a look on his face that was unmistakable triumph. And after all the things she had imagined would happen if he ever got hold of her, it was no wonder she was so overcome with anxiety that she could do no more than stare at him.

"Och now, it's glad I am tae see Mrs. Pym was right, that ye're awake at last. She's been sae obliging, sitting outside yer door, waiting tae hear ye stir sae she could come and tell me. She knows how impatient I've been, though the coppers in her pocket improved her diligence too. But dinna be thinking she'll be receptive tae yer blathering, lass, fer I've spun her a fine tale, I have, of rescue and returning ye tae the bosom of yer family. She'll no' believe a word ye try tae tell her if it differs from my tale."

After saying all this, he smiled, reminding Roslynn why she had never been able to abide this particular Cameron. His smiles were never genuine, always jeering or mocking, or more often sly, and they brought out the malicious evil in his icy blue eyes, eyes that could have been lovely otherwise.

Roslynn had always thought him tall until she met the Malorys, who were much taller. His carrot-red hair had grown shaggy since last she'd seen him, but then she doubted he'd had much time to attend to his grooming with the merry chase she had led him. He wasn't fat, no, not at all, but there was a beefiness about his body that she knew could overpower her if it came down to her fighting her way out of here. And yet he bore the Cameron good looks, at least when his true self didn't emerge from behind his expression; looks, sadly, that closely resembled Duncan Cameron when he was Geordie's age, so testified the only portrait of her grandfather at Cameron Hall.

"Ye're awful quiet, ye are," Geordie prodded her when she continued to just stare at him. "Have ye nae warm welcome fer yer only cousin?"

The incongruity of that question brought Roslynn back to her senses and dredged forth her anger. That he dared, *dared* do what she had feared he would! Of course, it was why she was here in London, why she was planning to marry when she didn't have to, why she had entered into a bizarre relationship with Anthony, accepting him as her confidant when she knew very well she should avoid him instead. But to be proved right! Her fear was forgotten in light of all the trouble and anxiety this greedy blackguard had put her through.

"Warm welcome?" she snorted. "The only thing I'm wanting to know, *cousin,* is how you managed it!"

He laughed, only too happy to expound on his cleverness and pleased that she hadn't asked why instead. That she knew why she was here saved him the explaining of that, and would save time in convincing her to go along with him. He didn't like being in England or dealing with English hirelings, and the sooner they were set for home, the better.

"It was sae easy, lass, sae very easy," he boasted. "I knew ye'd be trying something once the auld mon was laid tae his grave, only I didna think ye'd be coming here. But I had most of the roads watched, ye see, sae tae England was the only way ye could've traveled wi'out my knowing it."

"Clever you are, to make such a deduction."

His eyes narrowed at her sneer. "Aye, clever, clever enough tae ha' ye where I want ye."

Roslynn flinched, for he was right there. "But how did you find me so quickly, Geordie? London's no' such a small town, is it now?"

"I remembered ye had a friend here. It wasna hard tae find her, and sae tae find ye. But I would've had ye sooner if those bloody idiots I hired hadna been such cowards tae turn tail just because the street crowd was bestirred tae help ye that day on Oxford Street."

So it *had* been Geordie's doing that day she was nearly abducted off the street. But as for the crowd helping, that bit of news elicited a chuckle that Roslynn quickly turned into a cough. She could just imagine the tall tale those two footpads had told Geordie to account for their failure and to avoid his wrath.

"And then ye left town and I thought I'd lost ye," Geordie continued with a frown. "Ye put me tae a good deal of trouble and expense over that, lass, that ye did. I had tae send men oout in every direction tae find yer trail, but ye didna leave one, did ye, no' one that went very far? Only ye came back on yer own." Here he was smiling again, as if to say it was so typically female to make such a blunder. "And then it was only a matter of waiting—and here ye are."

Yes, here she was, and still ignorant of how Geordie had managed it. But his look said he was willing to enlighten her, wanting to in fact, because he was so very pleased with himself in having his plans work out so well, and wanted her to appreciate his cleverness. Oh, she appreciated it all right, like the plague. That had always been Geordie's problem. He was too clever and sly, like a bloody fox. All his life he had thrived on scheming and plotting the little pranks and accidents he was so fond of. Why should this be any different?

Perversely, Roslynn decided to take him down a peg instead of boosting his ego further with her avid curiosity. She yawned in the face of his explanations and said wearily, "So now what, cousin?"

His mouth dropped open. "Are ye no' the least bit interested in how ye came tae wake up here?"

"Does it matter?" she asked in a weary tone. "As you said, I'm here."

She thought he would burst a seam, he puffed up with such chagrin. "Well, I'll be telling ye, seeing as how it was the easiest but most ingenious part of my plans."

"By all means," she replied.

But she gave him another yawn for good measure and delighted in the way his light blue eyes spat daggers at her. He was so easily readable, so petty, and selfish, and hot-tempered. She supposed she ought not to push him anymore. She might have calmed down after her initial shock, but he was still a threat to her. And until she could figure a way out of this, if there was a way, she had best placate him.

"It was the maid, ye see, a clever lass I hired tae get inside the house. It was a simple matter of making certain one of the regular maids didna show up fer work and substituting my lass, claiming she was there tae take the other's place, being as she was sick."

Roslynn's temper sparked at this. "And just what have you done wi' the puir lass that didna show up for work?"

"Dinna fash yerself, cousin." His humor improved again now that he had her full attention. "She wasna harmed, save fer a wee bump on the head, and I've already sent a man tae release her, seeing as how yer absence will be known by now anyway. But as I was saying, wi' my hireling inside the house and in a position tae serve ye, she only needed tae wait until ye ordered something tae eat or drink afore ye retired, sae she could slip a sleeping draught in it."

The milk! The bloody warm milk she had asked for last night, hoping that it might help her sleep, never dreaming she would sleep so soundly she wouldn't even wake up for her own kidnapping!

"Aye, ye can see how it was done now, canna ye?" Geordie chuckled. "As soon as the lass was able, she slipped my men inside the house and hid them and went on home herself, her part over. Then when all the live-in servants had retired and the house was quiet, my men simply carried ye oout and brought ye tae me, and ye didna wake even once."

"So what are yer plans now?" she asked tightly, taunting. "Surely ye've something despicable in mind?"

"I've found me a mon of the cloth who's been persuaded he doesna need tae be hearing yer 'I do's' tae perform a wedding fer us. The gin-soaked sod'll be here as soon as my men can discover what alley he crawled into last night. But it willna be long now, cousin. And dinna think tae be causing a stir while we wait. Mrs. Pym will be keeping an ear open, and she's just outside the door."

As she watched him leave and heard the lock click on the door, she thought about calling him back. If he knew that both Nettie and Frances were aware of

her abhorrence for him and that she would never
willingly marry him, might he reconsider? But it was
his rampant greed that held her tongue. Marrying
her would bring him a fortune, and since he had
gone this far, it was likely he could go the next step
in eliminating anyone who opposed him. As it stood
now, his plan could be to simply lock her away
somewhere, and none would be the wiser. He could
as likely have a "regrettable accident" planned. But
it was a certainty that he wouldn't keep her alive if
he knew she had friends who would disclaim a marriage between them, and they would be in danger
too if she named them.

So where did that leave her? *Married to the blackguard,* was the loathsome answer. Hell's teeth, not
while she still had her wits about her. But panic was
beginning to take hold. Not long, he had said. How
much time did that give her? Even now the drunken
reverend could be arriving. And where the bloody
hell was she anyway?

Her eyes flew back to the window and she threw
off the covers, rushing to the opening. Her heart sank
as she saw the two-story drop, with nothing below
to break a fall. No wonder Geordie had taken no
precautions in boarding up the window. And if she
tried to call out it for help, the deceived Mrs. Pym
would have the door open in a flash, and Roslynn
would no doubt find herself bound and gagged for
her efforts.

Briefly, she thought of reasoning with Mrs. Pym,
but only briefly. The woman probably thought she
was insane or something. Geordie was clever *'* .t
way, his schemes well thought out, to cover al, pos-
sibilities. He would leave nothing to chance, not with
the fortune he had so long coveted at risk.

Hastily, she surveyed the room again, but only the water pitcher would make a likely weapon, and that only against the first person to come through the door. She had no guarantee that person would be Geordie, no guarantee either that the pitcher would hurt him enough to render him unconscious, or that he would be alone.

The window, then, was her only chance. It faced a lane of some sort, an alley really, though wide enough for traffic to get through. But there was no traffic. It was utterly deserted, dark and shadowed, as the buildings on each side rose far enough to hold back the daylight. Sticking her head out the window, at each end of the lane she could see streets brightly lit, wagons passing, a child running by, a sailor strolling arm in arm with a garishly dressed woman. A good shout could probably draw someone's attention. Neither end of the lane was *that* far away. But a good shout would draw Mrs. Pym's attention too.

Roslynn ran back to the bed, yanked off the scratchy blanket, and, rushing back, stuck it out the window. She waved it furiously, leaning out the window as well, until finally her arms became exhausted, her breath labored. Nothing. If anyone noticed, it no doubt appeared she was simply airing the blanket, nothing to elicit curiosity.

And then she heard the wagon. Her head swung around to see it slowly entering the lane, and her heart began to race with excitement. It was filled with barrels, possibly using the lane as a shortcut to reach the other street. The lone driver was whistling as he prodded his mule, pausing only to sweet-talk the animal.

Roslynn dropped the blanket, giving up waving it, waving her arms instead. But without her making a sound, the driver simply didn't notice. His hat was wide-brimmed, and since she was above him, she was blocked from his view. The nearer he came, the less chance there was that he would see her at all, and the more she panicked. She hissed, and said *psst*, and waved even more frantically to draw his attention, but to no avail. By the time she thought to throw the water pitcher down at him, he was already too far past her window. Besides, with the noise the wagon was making over the cobbled lane, she doubted he would have heard the crash unless she landed a direct hit, which was unlikely as sore as her arms were already.

Disappointment washed over her and she slumped back against the wall beside the window. This just wouldn't do. Even if the fellow had noticed her, how could she have explained her predicament in a whisper? He wouldn't have been able to understand her. And if she spoke any louder than a whisper, she would give herself away to Mrs. Pym.

Hell's teeth, was there nothing else she could do? She eyed the water pitcher again, but she had little hope she could succeed with it. When Geordie came again, he was likely to have the reverend with him, as well as the men who had fetched him, for witnesses to this unholy ceremony would be needed.

Roslynn was so distraught by picturing herself actually married to Geordie Cameron that she didn't hear the second vehicle passing through the lane until it was almost too late. When she turned at the sound, the hay wagon was nearly beneath her window. This driver, also alone, was cursing the two nags pulling the load of hay, emphasizing his apparent ire by shaking the gin bottle in his hand at them, swilling a long draft, then shaking

it with another curse. *He* wouldn't hear her for the noise
he himself was making, and he was so close already.

There was nothing for it. She might not have another chance. So without thinking about it, for that
would have terrified her and kept her inside, Roslynn
climbed up on the window ledge, waited the few seconds until the wagon was directly below, and jumped.

Chapter Fourteen

It was an insane thing to do. That thought passed through Roslynn's mind as she was falling, falling, her feet flying up in front of her eyes, her hands instinctively clutching at air, knowing she was going to die. She cursed Geordie with her last breath, but at least there was some satisfaction that he would think she preferred death to marrying him, though not enough satisfaction to make it worthwhile, for she was the one dying, while that greedy cur would probably produce a marriage certificate and claim her fortune anyway.

She landed with a bone-jarring impact, flat on her back. Breath and wits deserted her, and for a moment she actually passed out. A missing cobblestone was responsible for the wagon's jolt that brought her back to her senses. She groaned, thinking she must surely have a dozen broken bones. But the next jarring of the wagon caused her no discomfort. Incredible. To have done something so stupid, yet come through unscathed. She was surely blessed, but then fools usually were, and she was the greatest of that number today. She could have broken her neck, and well she knew it! But thank God for the cushion of hay. If it had been any other load this wagon was carrying . . .

Miraculously, the drunken driver was unaware he had gained a passenger, but Roslynn supposed her impact with the wagon seemed no different to him in

his sottish condition from the wagon hitting a particularly deep rut. Either that, or the man was deaf.

Scattered hay nearly covered her from head to foot,
but one glance at the window she had just leaped
from, and she swiftly yanked handfuls to complete
the camouflage. And not a moment too soon. The
wagon rolled out of the shadowed lane into the con-
gested, brightly lit street, and Roslynn finally realized, horribly, that she was wearing nothing more than
the thin white cotton nightgown she had gone to sleep
in last night, and was barefoot as well.

But she could be thankful for small favors. At least
the gown wasn't one of the skimpy negligees that had
been made for her trousseau. It covered her from neck
to ankle, with flowing long sleeves cuffed at the wrist,
and she supposed if she could find something that
would make do for a belt, it might pass for a dress at
first glance.

Unfortunately, Roslynn had little time to think of
that or how she was going to get home without money.
The wagon rolled into a stable and stopped, and she
just managed to scurry out of it and hide behind an
empty stall before the driver came around back to
begin unloading the hay. Another man, big and burly,
joined him, cursing him in a good-humored way for
being late. While they both tackled the hay, Roslynn
reconnoitered.

A stable wasn't such a bad place to end her journey
thus far. Actually, it was ideal. If she could just rent
a horse and get directions to Mayfair, for she still had
no idea what part of the city she was in now, she
could be home before long and without further incident. The trouble was, the only thing of value on her
person was her mother's crucifix, which she wore
whenever she wasn't decked out in her more costly

jewels, and it was unthinkable to part with it. Still, it
didn't look as if she would have much choice in the
matter, unless she was closer to Mayfair than she realized. Then she could chance walking, even barefoot.

Roslynn frowned at that idea. It wasn't one of her
better ones, and she was forgetting the sort of street
traffic she had seen passing by the lane—delivery
wagons, drunkards, sailors walking with their doxies,
but not one carriage. And this stable wasn't so very
far from where she had escaped. Whatever part of
town this was, it certainly wasn't elite, and trying to
walk through it would likely give her more trouble
than she had started with. Which left her again with
the desperate need to rent a horse.

Not knowing if Geordie had discovered her absence
yet and might already be searching for her in the
nearby vicinity made Roslynn a bundle of nerves as
she waited for the gin-guzzler to depart with his hay
wagon. But she had decided to risk being alone with
the other fellow to state her case, for the less people
who saw her in her present condition, the better. She
could just imagine the scandal should any of this get
out. *Lady Chadwick cavorting through the slums in
her nightgown.* How the *ton* would eat that up, and
down the wayside would go her last chance for a
quick, decent marriage.

Still, she had to mentally push herself out of her
hiding place once it appeared she was finally alone
with the stableman, mortified that anyone, stranger or
not, should see her in her bedclothes. And her embarrassment increased a hundredfold when the big
fellow actually noticed her and his eyes fairly popped
out of his head. Standing with one bare foot unsuccessfully trying to hide the other, her arms crossed

over her chest because even though she was completely covered, she still *felt* naked, and her hair streaming about her upper torso, ribboned with straw, she was a sight to behold—a very fetching sight, actually, though she would be the last to think so.

The man must have thought so, however, because he continued to stare, unmoving, unspeaking, his mouth hanging open. He was middle-aged, brown hair feathered with gray, gray stubble on a too-wide jaw. Whether he was proprietor or employee she couldn't tell. It didn't matter, though. He was all she had to help her, and knowing that filled her with a nervousness she wouldn't otherwise have felt.

Roslynn blurted out her predicament with the briefest explanation, but so swiftly, it was doubtful the fellow understood even two words of it. And in fact, it was several long moments before he gave any indication that he had heard her at all. Then he chuckled, hitching up his pants and walking toward her.

"A 'orse, eh? Ye should 'ave said right off, miss. 'Ere I was thinking me good friend Zeke 'ad sent o'er a right fine birthday present. A 'orse?" He chuckled again, shaking his head. "Can't blame a man fer wishful thinking."

Roslynn was blushing furiously before he had finished laughing. "Do you have one to rent?"

"Two I 'ave, both nags, but the good stock goes out early, it does."

"Will you take this, then?" She lifted the cross off her neck and handed it to him. "It'll buy both nags plus several more, but I'll be wanting it back. I'll send someone back with the horse and the proper payment."

He turned the cross over in his hand, then had the

audacity to bite on it before nodding his head. "It'll do."

"I don't suppose you'd have a pair of shoes I could borrow too?"

He took one look at her dainty feet and snorted at the request. "Not likely, miss. Me children's all growed an' gone, they are."

Desperately she asked, "A cloak, then, or something to cover myself with?"

"Now, that I can manage. Aye, an' best I do, or ye'd be causing a bleeding riot in the streets, ye would."

Roslynn was too relieved to be annoyed at the sound of his laughter as he went off to fetch her the nag.

Chapter Fifteen

*T*he shadows of twilight grew darker with each passing second. What should have amounted to a thirty-minute ride had turned into a three-hour excursion of wrong turns, delays, and increasing aggravations. But at least Roslynn knew where she was now, and in fact she was grateful for the dark, for in her eagerness to be home she hadn't taken into consideration the ride down South Audley Street, where any number of people might have recognized her. The dark came in handy for concealment, and handier still was the hood of the old moth-eaten cloak the stableman had tossed her.

Hell's teeth, this day couldn't end soon enough for her, but it was far from finished yet. She could no longer stay with Frances, not even for tonight. And she could no longer delay getting married. Geordie's locating her had changed everything. She even expected to find him waiting on the doorstep for her, or secreted in a carriage ready to pounce on her the moment she reached the house.

Luck stayed with her, however, at least in letting her reach home without further mishap. And she even considered it fortunate that Frances wasn't there, for she would have disapproved of what Roslynn meant to do, would have tried to stop her, and Roslynn didn't have the time it would take to convince her she knew what she was doing.

Nettie was another matter. After sending one of the footmen back to the stable with the old horse and the money to retrieve her cross, and briefly assuring the butler and other servants she passed along the way that she was fine, but giving them no explanation, Roslynn rushed upstairs to find Nettie in her room, anxiously pacing the floor and looking more haggard than she had ever seen her. But at first sight of Roslynn, her face filled with surprise and relief.

"Och, hinny, if ye didna give me the worst scare of my life!" And then almost in the same breath, her tune changed. "Where the devil have ye been, I'd like tae be knowing? I thought yer cousin had ye fer sure."

Roslynn nearly smiled at Nettie's ability to jump from one emotion to another with such startling swiftness, but as harried as she was herself, she couldn't even spare a moment for the amusement her abigail stirred, so welcome after such a ghastly day. She hurried straight to her wardrobe, tossing over her shoulder, "He did, Nettie. Now help me dress, quickly, while I tell you about it."

She did, and Nettie interrupted only once with "Ye did what?" when she came to the part about jumping out of the window. After she had finished, the anxiety was back in Nettie's expression.

"Then ye canna stay here nae longer."

"I know," Roslynn replied. "And I'm leaving tonight, we both are, but not together."

"But—"

"Listen now," Roslynn interrupted impatiently. "I've had all afternoon to think what's best to do. Geordie's made his move. Now that his scheme is out in the open, what's to stop him from forcing his way in wherever I am and taking me again, and next time maybe hurting someone in the process? It took me so long to get home, I thought for certain he'd be here waiting. But perhaps he didn't think I could make it this far without money or clothes.''

"Then ye think he's still searching fer ye near where ye escaped him?''

"Either that, or he's working on a new plan already. But there's also the likelihood he sent someone here to watch the house. Although I didn't see anyone, that doesn't mean no one's out there, so we've got to confuse them, and pray it's only one man. If we leave together at the same time but in different directions, he'll not know who to follow."

"But where are we going?''

Roslynn finally smiled. "Back to Silverley. He'll have no way to trace us there."

"Ye dinna know that."

"It was Geordie who tried to have me snatched off the street that day. He knew where I was, but apparently no one was watching the house the morning I left so early for the country. When he realized I had gone, he sent men out in all directions, but the trail was lost after we left that inn where we joined up. As long as we avoid public places and aren't followed, we'll be safe."

"But, lass, that accomplishes nothing but tae hide ye fer a time. It doesna get ye married, and ye'll no' really be safe from that blackguard until ye wed."

"I know, which is why I'll be sending for the gentleman of my choice to meet me there and put my proposition to him. If all goes well, I can be married at Silverley too, if Regina doesn't mind."

Nettie's brows shot up. "Then ye've decided which one tae marry?''

"By the time I get there, I'll know which one I want," Roslynn hedged, for that was the only thing still in doubt. "The important thing at the moment is to get there without leaving a trail Geordie can follow. Now, I've already sent one of the servants to fetch us each a rented hack."

"What of Brutus?" Nettie asked, then glanced with wide eyes at Roslynn's full wardrobe. "And all yer clothes? There's nae time tae pack—"

"They must be left here until after I'm wed, Nettie. We can both take a few things now, and I'm sure Regina has a competent seamstress who can supply whatever else we need to see us to the wedding. All I need to do is leave a note for Frances; then we can be off. Where is she, by the way?"

Nettie grunted. "After she fair wore the carpet down tae a frazzle all morning long, one of the maids mentioned she had a brother who knew a certain fellow, who knew how tae go about hiring the kind of men who could find ye quicker than the authorities—"

"Authorities!" Roslynn gasped, horrified that the scandal she had worried about all day was going to break around her head anyway. "Hell's teeth! She didna report me missing, did she?"

Nettie quickly shook her head. "She was near tae doing it, though, that worried she was, but knew once she did, it'd never be kept secret. And if ye'd no' be completely ruined, the talk would still hurt yer efforts tae get a decent husband. That's why she jumped on the maid's suggestion, and even insisted on going herself tae arrange the hiring."

Roslynn frowned. "Still, with so many servants knowing—"

"Och now, ye're no' tae worry as tae that, lass. They're good people Lady Frances has, but tae be safe, I had a wee talk wi' each of them. They're no' likely tae breathe a word outside this house about yer absence.''

Roslynn chuckled. ''You'll have to tell me some-time what threats you used, but right now we've no more time. Go and pack up several changes of clothes, and I'll do the same, then meet me down-stairs. We should leave at exactly the same moment. And, Nettie, head north until you're certain you're not followed; then you can turn toward Hampshire. I'll go south and then backtrack too. But if I don't arrive close behind you, you're not to worry. I'll be going far out of my way first, just to be safe. I don't intend to fall into Geordie's hands again no matter what. He won't be so careless the next time.''

Chapter Sixteen

It seemed like an eternity before the front door finally opened to Roslynn's repeated pounding, and pounding she was doing before she finished. She was in such a state of nerves, in fact, expecting to be seized at any moment, that even her own shadow gave her a start when she glanced behind her to make sure the old carriage was still waiting, the driver still keeping an eye on her. Not that he would be much help if Geordie and his hirelings found her.

It was the risk that had her in a such a state. She shouldn't be stopping here. She had promised Nettie she would make all haste out of London, yet she had come directly here instead, not allowing herself time to lose anyone who might have followed her. That was what had her heart hammering to the tune of her fist against the door. Geordie could be sneaking up on her at this very moment, getting closer and closer, while she stood here waiting for the bloody door to open.

When it did open, she shoved her way inside so forcefully, she nearly knocked the butler down. She closed the door herself, leaning back against it, then looked aghast at the fellow, who was looking even more aghast at her.

He collected himself first, straightening his coat with a sharp tug, gathering his dignity about him like a cloak. "Really, miss—"

She jumped in to forestall him, unthinkingly giving him an even worse impression of her. "Och, mon, dinna scold me. I'm sorry to be barging in, but this is an emergency. I must speak wi' Sir Anthony.''

"Out of the question," he stated with haughty disdain. "Sir Anthony is not receiving tonight."

"He isna here, then?"

"He is unavailable to callers," the butler stated more bluntly. "I do have my orders, miss. Now if you would be so good—"

"No!" she gasped as he reached for the door handle to show her out. "Did you no' hear me, mon? I *mun* see him!"

Without a pause, he opened the door, forcing her to move away from it. "There are to be no exceptions." But when he reached for her arm to literally shove her outside, Roslynn clobbered him with her reticule. "Now see here!" the man gasped, outraged.

"Och, but you're a dafty, you are," she said calmly enough, but her eyes glared at him furiously. "I'm no' leaving here until I've seen Anthony. I didna take the risk of coming here just to be turned away, you ken? Now tell him—just tell him there's a lady to see him. Do it, mon, or I swear I'll—"

Dobson turned away before she could complete the threat. Stiff-backed, he mounted the stairs, deliberated taking his time. Lady indeed. Never in all his considerable years in Sir Anthony's employ had he seen the like. Ladies didn't accost a man just for doing his duty. The very idea. What *had* Sir Anthony stooped to, to become involved with such a brazen creature?

Out of sight of the foyer where he had left her, Dobson considered waiting a few moments and then simply returning to try again to oust the woman. After all, Sir Anthony had come home in a foul disposition because he was late for a family gathering at his brother Edward's house. Lord James and Master Jeremy had already left for it. Even if Sir Anthony were inclined to see this particular woman, he had no time. He was changing now, and in fact would be down shortly. He would *not* care to be confronted with any further delay in the form of a pushy female of questionable quality. If it were any other appointment, it wouldn't matter so much. But family came first with Sir Anthony. It always had and always would.

And yet . . . Dobson couldn't shake the implied threat from his mind. He had never encountered a caller so insistent on having her way, discounting Sir Anthony's own family, of course. Would she scream, or worse, become violent again? Unthinkable. But perhaps he ought to at least inform Sir Anthony of the problem.

The answer to his knock was curt. Dobson stepped warily into the room. He had only to look at Willis, Sir Anthony's valet, to see there had been no improvement in disposition. The man's expression was harried, as if he had already had a full measure of Sir Anthony's acerbic tongue.

And then Sir Anthony swung around, giving Dobson pause. He rarely saw him in this state of undress. He wore only his trousers and was in the process of towel-drying his thick black hair.

Again the impatient curtness. "What is it, Dobson?"

"A woman, sir. She pushed her way in, demanding to speak with you."

Anthony turned away. "Get rid of her."

"I tried, sir. She refuses to leave."

"Who is she?"

Here Dobson couldn't conceal his disgust. "She wouldn't give her name, but claims to be a lady."

"Is she?"

"I have my doubts, sir."

Anthony tossed the towel aside with obvious annoyance. "Bloody hell, she's probably here for James. I should have known his tavern doxies would start showing up on my doorstep if he stayed for any length of time."

Dobson was reluctant to clarify. "Begging your pardon, sir, but she mentioned your name, not Lord Malory's."

Anthony scowled. "Then use your wits, man. The only women who come here come by invitation. Am I correct?"

"Yes, sir."

"And would I have extended an invitation tonight, with a previous engagement?"

"No, sir."

"Then why are you bothering me with this?"

Dobson could feel the heat rising under his collar. "For permission to force her out the door, sir. She won't leave of her own accord."

"By all means," Anthony replied dryly. "Use one of the footmen if you don't think you can manage on your own, but get rid of her before I come down."

The heat crept up Dobson's cheeks. "Thank you, sir. I will get help, I think. I don't care to confront that Scot's temper again on my own."

"What was that?" Anthony asked so forcefully, Dobson's color washed clean away.

"I—I—"

"Did you say she's Scottish?"

"No, no, she only sounded—"

"Blister it, man, why didn't you say so? Show her up here and hurry, before she decides to leave."

"Before she—" Dodson's mouth dropped open, but a glance about the room prompted a *"Here,* sir?"

"Now, Dobson."

Chapter Seventeen

Anthony couldn't believe it. Even when she walked through the door, tossed Dobson a withering look, then turned the same lethal glare on Anthony, he still couldn't believe it.

"That's a very rude mon you have for a butler, Sir Anthony."

He simply grinned at her, standing there with her foot tapping and her arms crossed over her chest. "When I gave you my address, sweetheart, it was so you could send me a message if the need arose, not for you to show up on my doorstep. You do realize the impropriety? This is strictly a bachelor's residence. I even have my brother and nephew staying with me—"

"Well, if they're here, then I'm no' alone wi' you, am I now?"

"I hate to disappoint you, my dear, but they are out for the evening and you are in fact very much alone with me. As you can see, I was preparing to go out myself, which is why Dobson was so reluctant to admit you."

What she saw, when she got a good look at him through the fumes of her anger, was that he looked more as if he were prepared for bed. He wore a short quilted robe of silver-blue satin over trousers, and nothing else. The robe he was just now belting, but not before she had had a glimpse of his bare chest and the sparse mat of black curls there. His hair was damp, hand-combed back from his forehead, with drying tendrils beginning to curl over each temple. He looked more sensual than she had ever seen him, and it was all she could do to tear her eyes away and even remember why she was here.

The trouble was, her eyes lit next on a bed, and it struck her with the force of a blow where he had received her. His *bedroom*. Hell's teeth!

"Did you know it was me—no, you couldna," she answered herself, her eyes flying back to his. "Do you receive all your callers up here?"

Anthony chuckled at this. "Only when I'm in a hurry, my dear."

She frowned, not at all amused, but made a concerted effort to pull herself together. To do that, she had to look away from him again.

"I won't keep you long, Sir Anthony. I haven't the time to waste myself. Something happened—well, that needn't concern you. Suffice it to say, I've run out of time. I need a name from you, and I need it now."

His humor fled. He was afraid he knew exactly what she was talking about, and that certainty produced a tightening in his belly that was most uncomfortable. His being her confidant had been no more than an excuse to get close to her. Not bloody likely would he defeat his own purpose by helping to get her married. He had meant to delay that eventuality indefinitely and seduce her before it ever became a fact. Now here she was demanding a name from him, which he should have if he had actually done what he had told her he would do, which he hadn't. Obviously, her need for a confidant was at an end. If he didn't give her a name, she would make her own choice, good or bad. He had no doubt a-tall.

"What the bloody hell happened?"

She blinked at his harsh tone, coming so unexpectedly. "I told you, that doesn't concern you."

"Then humor me, and while you're at it, you can tell me why you're going about this marriage business in an either-or fashion, and why the rush."

"It's none of your business," she insisted.

"If you want a name, my dear, you'd best make it my business."

"That's—that's—"

"Not very sporting of me, I know."

"Beast!"

His humor returned in the face of her rage. God, she was beautiful when her eyes flashed like that. The golden flecks seemed to blaze, to match the fire of her hair. It dawned on him suddenly that she was really in his house, in his bedroom, where he had imagined her countless times but had been unable to figure a way to get her there himself.

The grin that curled his lips infuriated her even more. *You've come to my lair, sweetheart,* he couldn't help thinking. *I have you now.*

To her, he suggested, "A drink?"

"You'd drive a saint to it," she retorted, but nodded just the same and took a hefty swallow of the brandy he handed her a moment later.

"Well?" he prompted when she did no more than continue to glower resentfully at him.

"It has to do with my grandfather, and his making me promise I'd marry as soon as he passed away."

"I know that," Anthony said calmly. "Now tell me why he wanted such a promise."

"Very well!" she snapped. "I have a distant cousin who means to marry me at any cost."

"So?"

"I didn't say he wants to, but means to, whether *I*

want to or not. Do you ken now? If Geordie Cameron gets his hands on me, he'll force me to it.''

''I take it you'd rather not have him?''

''Dinna be daft, mon,'' she said impatiently, beginning to pace a circle around him. ''Would I be willing to wed a near stranger for any other reason?''

''No, I don't suppose so.''

Roslynn gasped, catching his smile. ''You think it's amusing?''

''What I think, sweetheart, is that you've made too much of it. All you need is to have someone persuade this cousin of yours that he'd be healthier if he looked somewhere else for a wife.''

''You?''

He shrugged. ''Why not? I wouldn't mind doing you such a service.''

She nearly hit him. She finished off her brandy instead, grateful for its calming effect.

''Let me tell you something, Anthony Malory. This is my life you're suggesting you gamble with, not yours. You don't know Geordie. You don't know how obsessed he is with getting his hands on my grandfather's fortune through me. He'll do anything to get it, and once he does, what's to stop him from arranging a convenient accident for me, or locking me up somewhere and claiming I've gone daft or something? A little warning from you wouldn't scare him off, even if you could manage to find him to do so. Nothing will. The only way I can protect myself is to marry someone else.''

Anthony had taken her glass, refilled it, and handed it back while she laid into him with these facts. She didn't even seem to notice.

''Very well, now I know why you think you must marry quickly. So tell me, what's made it immediate?

What brought you to risk your reputation by coming here tonight?''

She flinched at the unnecessary reminder of *that* danger, which had seemed the lesser evil at the time. ''Geordie's found me. Last night he managed to have me drugged and taken right out of Frances' house.''

''The hell you say!''

She went on as if she hadn't heard his outburst. ''I woke up today locked in a strange room down by the waterfront, just waiting for the deceitful parson Geordie had found to arrive. If I hadn't jumped out the window—''

''Good God, woman, you can't be serious!''

She stopped her pacing for a moment to fix him with a look that was frankly contemptuous. ''I've no doubt still got some straw in my hair from the hay wagon I landed in. It took me so long to find my way home that there was no time to brush it all out. I would show you, but Nettie's not here to redo my hair if I take it down, and I doubt your Dobson could manage it. And I will *not* leave your house looking as if—as if—''

Anthony threw back his head in laughter when she failed to complete the provocative thought. Roslynn gave him her back and headed straight for the door. He got there at the same moment, his hand sliding past her shoulder to press firmly against the only exit.

''Was it something I said?'' he asked in all innocence next to her ear.

Roslynn didn't hesitate to give him the full impact of her elbow, which landed unerringly at such close range. Satisfied with his grunt of discomfort, she slipped around him, putting a more breathable distance between them.

"I believe you've had enough amusement at my expense, Sir Anthony. I only intended to be here a few minutes, and I've wasted all this time on unnecessary explanations. I have a driver waiting and a long trip ahead of me. You said you were in a hurry as well. The name, if you please."

He leaned back against the door, that "long trip" sending off tremors of panic through his body. "You're not leaving London?"

"Of course I am. You don't think I can stay here now that Geordie's found me, do you?"

"Then how do you intend to entice one of your admirers into a marriage proposal if you're not here to help the courtship along?"

"Hell's teeth! As if I have time for a courtship now," she said, exasperated by his never-ending questions. "I'll be doing my own proposing, if you'll—just—give—me—a—name!"

Her furious emphasis on each word warned him to change tactics, and yet he was at a momentary loss. He wouldn't give her a name even if he had one to recommend, but if he told her that, she'd be out of the room in a flash and gone who-knew-where. He wondered if he dared ask her destination. No, she was fed up with his deliberate evasions.

He walked toward her, indicating the thick lounge chair in front of the fireplace. "Sit down, Roslynn."

"Anthony . . ." she began warningly.

"It's not that simple."

Her eyes narrowed suspiciously. "You've had ample time to sift fact from rumor, as you promised to do."

"I asked for a week, if you'll recall."

Her eyes flared in alarm. "Then you haven't—"

"On the contrary," he cut in quickly. "But you're not going to like what I've found out."

She groaned, ignoring the offered chair, and began pacing again. "Tell me."

Anthony's mind raced ahead, scavenging frantically for possible dirt he could pile on her contenders. He began with the only piece that was actually true, hoping inspiration would follow for the rest.

"That duel I told you David Fleming refused to participate in. It not only branded the poor fellow a coward but also—well, actually—"

"Out with it! I suppose it involved some woman? That's hardly surprising."

"The argument wasn't over a woman, my dear, but another man, only it was still a lover's quarrel." He took advantage of her moment of shock to refill her brandy glass once more.

"You mean—"

"I'm afraid so."

"But he seemed so—so, och, never mind. *He* certainly won't do."

"You'll have to scratch Dunstanton too," Anthony said. Since she was leaving London, she couldn't confirm his next words: "He's just announced his betrothal."

"I don't believe it!" she gasped. "Why, just last weekend he asked me to the theater. Of course, he canceled but . . . oh, very well. I wanted the list narrowed down, and so it is. What about Savage?"

Anthony was inspired by the name. "He won't do at all, my dear. Somewhere along his misspent youth he must have taken his name to heart. The man's a sadist."

"Oh, come now—"

"It's true. He enjoys hurting anything weaker than he is—animals, women. His servants are terrified . . ."

"All right! You needn't go into detail. That still leaves Lord Warton, whom even your niece recommended to me, and Sir Artemus."

It was Anthony's turn to pace, for he drew a blank where Warton was concerned. Shadwell's love of gambling could be played up, but there was absolutely nothing to discredit Warton with. In fact, the chap would no doubt make an ideal husband for Roslynn. Fortunately for Anthony, that knowledge so annoyed him, he managed to dredge up the perfect muck to swill on the fellow.

He turned toward Roslynn, imitating a suitably reluctant look. "You might as well forget Warton too. His interest in you was only to throw his mother off the scent."

"What the devil does that mean?"

"He's in love with his sister."

"*What?*"

"Oh, it's a well-enough-kept secret," Anthony assured her. "Reggie certainly doesn't know, for it's not something Montieth would want to disillusion her with. After all, she's quite friendly with all three Wartons. And he wouldn't have told me if I hadn't mentioned to him your sudden interest in the fellow. But he came upon them in the woods once, quite an embarrassing moment, I would imagine—"

"Enough!" Roslynn finished off her third brandy and handed him the glass. "You've done exactly as I asked, and I thank you. Sir Artemus was the first to appear on my list, so it seems fitting that he should end up being my choice."

"He's destitute, my dear."

"No problem." She smiled. "I have enough money to plump up his purse again."

"I don't think you understand, Roslynn. In the last few years his gambling has become a disease. He's gone from being one of the most wealthy men in England to having nothing. He's had to sell off every estate he owned except the one in Kent, and that's heavily mortgaged."

"How can you know that?"

"My brother Edward has handled the sales."

She was frowning, but insisted stubbornly, "It doesn't matter. In fact, it assures me that he can't possibly refuse the proposal I'll put to him."

"Oh, he'd jump on it, all right. And within a year you'd be just as destitute as he is."

"You're forgetting I will have control of my fortune, Anthony."

"True, but you're overlooking the simple fact that a man can and does gamble on credit, which is utterly impossible to monitor. And his creditors won't hesitate to come to you as his legal wife for payment, nor even to take you to court. And the courts, my dear, will hardly favor your contract when it can be proved you married Shadwell with full knowledge of his penchant for excessive gambling. You would be forced to honor his debts whether you want to or not."

Roslynn paled, eyes wide and incredulous. With so little knowledge of the law herself, she had no reason to doubt Anthony's predictions. She was forced to believe him. And to think she had once assumed a down-and-out gambler would be a perfect choice for her, never dreaming he could actually be the one man to lead her into penury. She might as well give her inheritance to Geordie as settle for a gambler.

"They were all so suitable," she said absently, miserably, before she turned large hazel eyes on Anthony. "Do you ken you've left me no one?"

Her woebegone expression struck right to his heart. He was responsible, with his half-truths and fabrications. He had interfered with her life with the most selfish of motives. Yet he couldn't bring himself to push her toward another man. He just couldn't do that. And it wasn't only that he wanted her himself. The thought of another man touching her had the strangest, gut-wrenching effect on him.

No, he couldn't regret that he had left her with no one, for his relief was too great on that score. But he couldn't bear her misery either.

In an effort to cheer her, he offered lightly, "Fleming would have you, you know, if only for appearance' sake." If he thought *she* would have *him,* however, he'd simply have to kill the fellow. "For your purposes, he'd be ideal, and then I could be assured of having you all to myself."

If nothing else, he succeeded in sparking her anger again with that observation. "I'd no' take a mon who'd be loath to touch me. If I have to marry, I'm wanting children out of it."

"That can be arranged, my dear, most willingly on my part," he replied softly.

But she was no longer listening to him. "I suppose I could return home and marry a crofter. What difference who I marry now? The thing is to get it done."

He saw his every effort tumbling down the wayside. "Bloody hell! You can't—"

She was still lost in the world of her few remaining

options. "It's what I should've done from the start. At least I'll know what I'm getting."

He caught her shoulders, forcing her to hear him. "Confound you, woman, I'm not about to let you throw yourself away on some dirt farmer!" And before Anthony even realized what he was going to say, the words tumbled out. "You'll marry me!"

Chapter Eighteen

*W*hen Roslynn's laugher died down to a trickle of chuckles, she realized belatedly that her amusement could be nothing short of a gross insult to Anthony. While she had been blinded by tears of humor, he had moved away from her. She located him now, sitting on the bed, casually leaning back on one elbow.

He didn't *look* insulted. He looked rather bemused, actually. Well, at least her faux pas hadn't aroused his anger, which she wouldn't have blamed him for in the least. But it was so ridiculous. Marry him, indeed. London's most notorious rake? He couldn't possibly have meant it anyway.

But she felt better for having had a good laugh, considering what she was yet facing. With a lingering smile, she took a few steps closer to him, bending her head at an angle to try to gain his attention.

"That's a rare talent you have, Anthony, for lifting the spirits, but then no one could ever accuse you of lacking charm. But it's plain to see you're out of your element when it comes to proposing marriage. I believe the words should come in the form of a request, not a demand. You really must remember that the next time your sense of humor leans toward the absurd."

He said nothing at first, but his eyes rose to meet hers. She grew suddenly uncomfortable under his level stare.

"Quite right, my dear. I'm afraid I lost my head.

But then I rarely do things in a conventional manner.''

"Well . . ." She drew her ermine-trimmed pelisse closer together. It was a nervous gesture on her part. "I've taken up enough of your time."

He sat up straight, hands pressed to knees. "You're not leaving yet, not without giving me your answer."

"Answer to what?"

"Will you marry me?"

Put to her conventionally, the question sounded no less absurd. "But you were joking!" she said incredulously.

"Afraid not, sweetheart. Though it's as much a surprise to me as it is to you, I'm quite serious."

Roslynn's lips compressed tightly. *This* was not funny at all. "It's out of the question. I wouldn't marry you any more than I would Geordie."

Her previous laughter was understandable. And her reaction to his demand that she marry him was mild compared with his own surprise. But although the words had come of their own volition, once said, Anthony realized the idea of marriage, always so appalling before, suddenly had merit.

Not that he couldn't be talked out of it if she weren't standing there looking so fetching. He had gone thirty-five years without needing a wife and he certainly didn't need one now. So what the bloody hell was he doing insisting he was serious when she had given him an out by doubting him?

The trouble was, he didn't like being backed into a corner, and her threat to marry merely anybody did just that. And he liked even less the idea of her walking out of his life, which she was also threatening to do. For that matter, her leaving this room was the last thing he wanted. She was here. He was bloody well going to take advantage of it.

Her flat refusal to accept him, however, was the seed that tipped the scale. She *would* have him, by God, if he had to compromise her to get her agreement.

"Correct me if I'm wrong, my dear, but you haven't another offer forthcoming, have you? And I recall your saying that it made no difference who you marry as long as you get it done."

She frowned at him. "That's true, but you happen to be the one exception."

"Why?"

"Let's just say you'd make a terrible husband."

"I always thought so," he surprised her by agreeing. "Why else would I have avoided matrimony so long?"

"Well, then, you've made *my* point, haven't you?"

He grinned now. "Just conceding the possibility, sweetheart. But let's also look at the other side of the coin. I could as likely take to marriage right handily. Montieth did, and I'd have been the first to say he was doomed to failure."

"*He* happens to love his wife," she pointed out with annoying emphasis.

"Good God, you're not waiting to hear me say I love you, are you? It's rather soon—"

"Certainly not!" Roslynn cut in stiffly, cheeks flaming.

"But we both know I want you, don't we? And we both know you—"

"Sir Anthony, please!" If it was possible for her face to get any hotter, it did. "There's nothing you could say to me to make me change my mind. You just willna do for me. I swore I'd never marry myself a rake, and you've admitted to me that's what you are. And you canna change what you are, mon.''

"I suppose I have Lady Grenfell to thank for your inflexibility?''

Taken aback, she didn't even wonder how he came to that conclusion. "Aye, Frances knows firsthand what happens when you lose your heart to a rake. Hers took to his heels when she needed marrying, forcing her to take what she could, which was an old man she loathed.''

The exotic slant to his eyes was much more prominent when he scowled. "I think it's time you heard the full story, Roslynn. Old George simply panicked when faced so unexpectedly with fatherhood. He went off on a two-week spree to resign himself to the loss of his bachelorhood, and by the time he came to his senses, Frances was already married to Grenfell. She never once allowed him to see his son. She refused to see him when Grenfell died. If your friend has been miserable over the whole affair, so has mine been. The truth of the matter is, George would marry her now if she'd have him.''

Roslynn moved over to the lounge chair and sat down, dazedly staring at the cold hearth. Why did he have to know George Amherst? Why had he told her that? Frances would probably marry Amherst in a minute if she could bring herself to forgive him for what had doubtless been a most natural reaction on his part, considering what a rakehell he had been at the time. And what about Roslynn herself?

Hell's teeth, there would be nothing she would like better than to marry Anthony Malory . . . *if* he loved her, *if* he would be faithful, *if* she could trust him. None of that was true, however. Nicholas Eden might love Regina, her grandfather might have loved her grandmother, George Amherst possibly had loved Frances and still did, but Anthony had admitted he didn't love her. And unfortunately, it would be too easy for her to love him. If that weren't the case, she would accept his offer. But she wasn't fool enough to leave herself open to the kind of hurt Anthony could and would bring her.

She glanced around to face him, only to see the bed empty now. Startled, she felt her bonnet being tugged on and shot forward to the edge of the chair. She turned to find Anthony casually leaning against the chair, his arms braced on the back.

It took a second for Roslynn to adjust to his nearness and, clearing her throat, she managed to get out, "I'm sorry, but what you've said about Frances and George doesn't change my mind about you."

"Somehow I didn't think it would," he said, shaking his head, and the slow smile appearing added to Roslynn's unease. "You're a stubborn Scot, Lady Chadwick, but that's one of the things I find endearing about you. I give you what you desperately need, and you spite yourself by refusing, and for some ridiculous reason that is pure supposition. I could turn out to be the most exemplary of husbands, you know, but you won't give me the chance to find out one way or the other."

"I told you, I'm not a gambler, Anthony. I'd rather not risk the rest of my life on a 'maybe' when the odds are so stacked against it."

He bent forward to rest his chin on his crossed arms. "You do realize that if I keep you here overnight, you will be quite compromised. I wouldn't even have to touch you, my dear. Circumstances speak for themselves. It's what got Reggie married, when her first meeting with Montieth had been quite innocent.''

''You wouldn't!''

''I believe I would.''

Roslynn shot to her feet, glaring at him with the chair safely between them. ''That's—that's . . . it'd no' work anyway! I'm going home to Scotland. What do I care if my reputation's ruined here? I'd still have my—'' She couldn't get the intimate word out, so skirted the thought. ''My husband would know the difference, and that's all I care about.''

''Is it?'' he asked, a devilish gleam appearing in his cobalt eyes. ''Then you don't leave me much choice, sweetheart, if I'm to help you despite yourself. So it's to be compromised in truth rather than by pretense?''

''Anthony!''

Her wail brought a grin to his lips. ''I rather doubt I could have settled for the pretense anyway. It was good of me to consider it, but I'm too much the rake, as you keep pointing out, not to take advantage of your presence in my bedroom.''

She began backing toward the door, more quickly when he came around the chair to follow her. ''I'll— I'll settle for the pretense.''

He shook his head at her. ''My dear girl, if everyone is going to assume you've shared my bed, why deny yourself the pleasure?''

Roslynn had to fight down the thrill of anticipation those words gave her, even though she was sure he was just toying with her. And his teasing manner kept her from being truly alarmed, yet the closer he got, the more she became alarmed in another way.

She knew what could happen if he kissed her. It had happened before. Whether he was serious or not about this supposed seduction, if he touched her it was likely to happen, regardless, and with very little effort on his part.

"I don't want—"

"I know," he said softly as he caught her shoulders and pulled her up against his chest. "But you will, sweetheart. I can promise you that."

He was right, of course. He knew what she wanted, deep down, what she couldn't admit to him or herself. She could fight against it till the sun ceased to shine, but it wouldn't go away. He was the most exciting, compelling man she had ever known, and she had wanted him from the moment she met him. Such intensity of feelings had nothing to do with logic and reasoning. It was the yearning of heart and body, common sense be damned.

Roslynn let go, giving herself up to the senses as he gently enclosed her in his embrace. It felt like coming home, so often had she imagined being held by him again. The warmth of his body, the strength of his arms, the headiness of his passion, she remembered, yet it was all new again, wonderful, and so very welcome.

But his kiss, when it came, was actually so hesitant she barely felt it. And she realized he was giving her this last chance to stop him before he took complete control. He knew very well that he was experienced enough, skillful enough, to overcome any reluctance she might still harbor. He had done it before. That he was holding back warmed her heart more than anything, making her want him even more.

Roslynn said yes simply by slipping her arms around his neck. She was crushed then by the might of his relief, until he recalled himself. But she didn't mind. Breathing was incidental in light of the magic Anthony was now wielding with his mouth. His lips were warm, dry, moving carefully across her own, slowly fanning the heat between them.

He held her like that for a long while, kissing her, letting her feast on the delicious sensations he was evoking. When he leaned back, it was to begin working the buttons on her dress. Her bonnet and cloak had already been discarded without her even realizing he had removed them. Now she watched him begin to slowly undress her, and she couldn't move, didn't want to anyway. His eyes were mesmerizing her, grown dark and heavy-lidded, seeing into her soul. She couldn't look away, even when she felt her dress slithering over her hips to puddle at her feet, or her undergarments following the same path.

He didn't touch her then, except with his eyes as they took a slow journey down her length and back up again. On his lips appeared that sensual smile that had the power to liquefy her limbs, dangerous when her senses were already melted. She swayed, and his hands came out to steady her, grasping her hips, but they didn't stay there. With exquisite slowness, he savored the feel of her bare skin, around her hips, over her narrow waist, stopping finally at her breasts, his thumbs hooked beneath. He didn't touch her in any other way, yet her nipples tightened, her heartbeat accelerated, and a new warmth uncoiled inside her.

And his smile widened. It was positively triumphant, as if he could see inside her and knew exactly what she was feeling. He was a man victorious, rejoicing. And she didn't care. She was smiling herself, but inwardly, because if he had won, so had she, defeating her own common sense to have what she had wanted all along, to make love with this man, to have him initiate her and be her first lover, because with him she knew it would be beautiful.

But as long as she was going to give in to her desires, she wanted to take an active part. She had thought before of undressing him, wondering what he would look like. Her imagination had produced an Adonis. Before her was the man, much more intimidating than a fantasy, yet desire made her bold.

She tugged loose his belt so that his robe fell open, and placing her palms against his skin as he had done against hers, she moved her hands up, touching him as she had longed to do, skin to skin, spreading the robe wide, pushing it back at his shoulders. He let it drop from his arms and reached for her, but she held him at arm's length, wanting to look her fill. Revealed to her was warm skin and muscle, dark, curling hair, a chest that made her fingers tingle. Solid, powerful, he was so much more than she had imagined. She had a strong, compulsive urge to wrap her limbs around him, to get as close as was humanly possible, and there was so much of him to get close to.

"Och, but you're a bonny mon, Anthony."

He had been spellbound, watching Roslynn's fascinated scrutiny of him, but her husky words were the stimulus that nearly sent him over the edge. He yanked her to him, his mouth coming down hard to slash across hers. At the same time he lifted her in his arms and bore her to the bed.

He let her down gently, then leaned back, his eyes smoldering on her face, down her body once more, all of her lying in his bed. How often he had pictured her here, her skin flushed with desire, her eyes heated, beckoning. She was exquisite, more so than he had envisioned, curves perfectly rounded, womanly, and she was here, his, and she wanted him.

He wanted to shout with joy. Instead he cupped her cheeks with exquisite tenderness, fingers moving over her face, into her hair, down her neck. He would never get enough of touching her.

"You can't imagine what you do to me."

"I know what you do to me," she said softly, watching him. "Is it the same?"

The sound he made was half groan, half laugh. "God, I hope so."

And he kissed her, his tongue parting her lips to plunge inside, his chest settling over hers. When she lifted her arms to wrap around him, he caught them, spreading them out wide, twining his fingers with hers to hold them there. She couldn't move, but she could feel, and what she felt was his chest moving across her nipples, back and forth, electrifying the hard little nubs with just the barest sensual touch.

Next he lowered himself to take one sensitive breast into his mouth, gently suckling, or slowly circling his tongue around it. But he wouldn't release her hands, and she felt she would go mad with the need to hold him, caress him.

The moan came from deep in her throat. He paused, grinning up at her.

"You're a devil," she told him, seeing his wicked delight.

"I know." And he licked at her other nipple. "Don't you like it?"

"Don't I like it?" she repeated, as if she had never heard such a ridiculous question. "What I'd like is to be touching you as well. Will you let go?"

"No."

"No?"

''Later you can touch me to your heart's content. Right now I don't think I could bear it.''

''Oh.'' She sighed. ''Well, as to that, I canna bear much more either.''

He buried his head between her breasts, groaning. ''Sweetheart, if you don't hush, you'll have me behaving like an inexperienced boy.''

Roslynn chuckled, and the throaty sound was Anthony's undoing. He whipped off his trousers but fortunately recalled himself before literally pouncing on her. There were still her stockings and shoes to remove, and he saw to them in quick order. Desire was riding him hard now, his previous unhurried pace at an end.

It was the dirk falling out of her shoe that returned a measure of control to him. He grinned inwardly, amazed. She was full of surprises, his little Scot. Marriage to her would be not only extremely pleasurable but interesting as well, and he was suddenly looking forward to it, all previous doubts forgotten.

He hefted the dagger in his hand. ''Do you actually know how to use this?''

''Aye, and I did when one of Geordie's hirelings tried to snatch me off the street.''

Anthony tossed the dirk aside, his smile meant to reassure her. ''That's one worry you won't have after tonight, sweetheart.''

Roslynn had her doubts about that but kept them to herself. Nothing was settled. He still wasn't the type of man she could enter into a marriage with, no matter how much she wished it were otherwise. He was a lover, and as such she could readily accept him. What did she need with her virginity anyway, since recent events assured her that her marriage, when it came about, would now be no more than a business arrangement?

But tomorrow's decisions were a long way off, and Anthony's hands were gliding up her legs, parting them, and making it impossible for her to think of anything else. He bent to kiss the inside of her thigh as he moved up as well, her hip, dipped his tongue into her belly button. Hot flames curled her toes, made her squirm. She clasped his head, pulling on him, but he still stopped to pay homage to her breasts again, lathing each sensitized peak until she was mindless with wanting. Her back arched, molding her belly to his chest, demanding the contact. It wasn't enough. She didn't know exactly what was needed but understood instinctively there had to be some purpose to the fires ravaging her senses.

She pulled on him frantically now, but he was un-movable, fully in control. Not until he was ready did he slide up a little more, assaulting her neck with lips that were now scorching, moving toward her ear. When his tongue slipped inside, the jolt was so powerful her body bucked, nearly dislodging him, and then settled into a delicious trembling that made her want to curl into him.

Her loins were aching, an inferno of moist heat, and when she felt something touching there for the first time, her body instinctively closed around it, hungering for the pressure in that burning region. And it managed to fill her, a glorious, welcoming fullness that she pushed against, locking her legs around him so she wouldn't lose it, finally feeling she had gained a measure of control. She wouldn't let go, and the pressure built in her, grew, until it seemed to pop, opening a new channel of feeling deep inside her that brought a certain relief of the tension, but not enough relief to last.

He was kissing her again, deeply, with a fierce hunger that matched her own, his arms locked on both sides of her like iron bars, his fingers threaded in her hair, holding her, controlling her. And his body was moving against her with a kind of urgency that she responded to, felt also, as the tension grew again, pulsed, and then finally exploded into blissful oblivion.

Moments later Anthony collapsed on her, his own climax draining him so completely that for a while he was too weak to even lift his head. Never had he experienced anything like it, and he was about to tell her so when he realized she was out cold. Whether she had fallen into exhausted slumber or had fainted, he didn't know. He smiled, though, smoothing back the hair from her cheeks, inordinately pleased with himself and her.

He had the consuming urge to wake her, to start all over again, but he tamped it down, recalling the barrier he had felt that marked her a virgin. Reggie had said she was. Roslynn's passionate responses disclaimed it. The truth filled him with an inexplicable pleasure. And although she hadn't even seemed to notice the breach of her maidenhead, the loss demanded recovery. There was the morning. There was the rest of his life.

He shook his head, bemused. When had he become so bloody chivalrous?

Carefully he left the bed, drawing the covers up over her. Her languorous stretch and sigh made him smile. God, she was beautiful, and so alluring she made a man ache with wanting to know every inch of her. He promised himself he would. But for the moment, he donned his robe, gathered up her clothes, and quietly left the room. There was her driver to dismiss, arrangements to be made—the lady wasn't going anywhere.

Chapter Nineteen

$Roslynn$ came awake to the tickling of rose petals against her cheek. She opened her eyes, focused on the pink rose first with confusion knitting her brow, then saw the man behind it, smiling at her.

"Good morning, my dear. And it is, you know. The sun has decided to shine for our wedding."

Roslynn groaned and turned over to bury her head in the pillow, unwilling to face the day and the consequences of her own actions. Hell's teeth, what had she done? Nettie would have gone on to Silverley and would be out of her mind with worry, thinking their ruse had failed, that Geordie had grabbed her again. And her driver! How could she have forgotten leaving the fellow to wait for her? Granted, she had tipped him well, but not well enough to wait all night. He had probably gone off with her bag of clothes, which also contained most of her jewels and important papers, including her marriage contract. Drat those three brandies!

Amidst the mounting consequences running through her mind, Roslynn felt Anthony's hand roving over her backside to the accompaniment of his chuckle. "If you really want to stay in bed—"

"Go away!" she mumbled into the pillow, furious with herself for feeling a thrill at his touch even in the face of her misery, and furious with him for sounding so cheerful.

"I don't see what the problem is," he said reasonably. "I have taken the tedious chore of decision making out of your hands. You are well and truly compromised, sweetheart.''

She swung around. "The devil you say. I felt no pain, only—"

He laughed as the blush spread across her cheeks and her mouth snapped shut. "I admit to a certain finesse, but I didn't realize I was *that* skillful. I felt your maidenhead give way, dear girl.'' He quirked a brow at her, his grin maddening. "Are you saying you didn't?"

"Oh, be quiet and let me think!"

"What's to think about? While you whiled the night away in sated slumber, I obtained a special license that will allow us to marry immediately without hying off to Gretna Green. I never realized until now how beneficial it is to hold the markers on men with influence."

He seemed so bloody proud of himself she wanted to hit him. "I haven't said I'll marry you."

"No, you haven't. But you will." He walked to the door, opened it, allowing the well-remembered butler to step into the room. "Lady Chadwick would like her clothes and some breakfast, Dobson. You are hungry, aren't you, sweetheart? I always find I'm ravenous after a night of—"

The pillow hit him squarely in the face, and he had to choke back his laughter as he caught sight of his butler's incredulous expression. "That will be all, Dobson."

"Yes, yes, of course, sir. Very good, sir."

The poor, embarrassed man couldn't leave the chamber fast enough, but the moment the door had closed, Roslynn lit into Anthony with a fury. "You're a bloody beast, a damnable swine! Why did you have to tell him my name?"

He shrugged, not in the least contrite over his deliberate ploy. "Just a little insurance, sweetheart. Dobson wouldn't dream of spreading tales about the future Lady Malory. On the other hand . . ." He left the thought unfinished, but it wasn't necessary to spell out these new consequences.

"You're forgetting I dinna care if my reputation's ruined here."

"Now that's not exactly true," he replied smoothly, confidently. "You would care. You just don't have your priorities in the right order at the moment."

True, but irrelevant. She tried turning the tables on him. "I'm wondering why a mon like yourself would be wanting to marry so suddenly. Is it my fortune you're interested in?"

"Good God, where did you get that idea?"

He seemed so surprised, she felt rather ashamed for having mentioned it but pointed out, "You're a fourth son."

"So I am. But you're forgetting that I'm already aware of your unusual marriage contract, which, by the by, I'm quite willing to sign. You're also forgetting the fact that we made love last night, Roslynn. You could at this moment be carrying my child."

She glanced away, chewing on her lower lip. They had, and she could be. She had to tamp down the pleasure that thought gave her.

"What do you get out of this marriage, then?" she asked reasonably.

He came back to the bed on the side she was closest to. He pulled a piece of straw out of her hair and examined it, smiling. "You," he said simply.

Her heart seemed to flip over. It was sounding too bloody good, so much so that she couldn't seem to remember what her objections were. This simply wouldn't do.

She let out an exasperated sigh. "I canna think when I just wake up. You didna give me time to think last night either." This in an accusing tone.

"You're the one in the all-fired hurry, sweetheart. I'm only trying to accommodate you."

Must he point out things like that? "I need time to consider."

"How much time?"

"I was going to Silverley. My abigail's already gone there, so I still have to. If you'll give me until this afternoon, I'll have an answer for you. But I must tell you, Anthony, I can't see myself marrying you."

Abruptly, Roslynn found herself lifted up and kissed with a thoroughness that curled her toes. "Can't you?"

She pushed away from him until he let her fall back on the bed. "You only prove that I canna think at all when I'm around you. I'll be leaving now, if you'll just get me my clothes. And what the devil were you doing by taking them away?"

"Just making sure you would still be here when I got back from obtaining the license."

"Did you . . . sleep with me?"

He grinned at her hesitation. "My dear, I made love to you. Sleeping with you is rather beside the point after that, wouldn't you say?"

She decided to say nothing more to that, regretting having brought up the subject at all. He could talk circles around her anyway.

"My clothes, Anthony?"

"Dobson is bringing them. And the portmanteau you left in your carriage is in my dressing room, if you need anything from it."

Roslynn's brows shot up. "You retrieved it? Thank heavens!"

"Good Lord, don't tell me you were careless enough to leave something of value in a hired hack?"

She resented his censure. "I was upset when I came here," she said tartly in her defense. "And more upset after I got here, if you'll recall."

"Quite so," he conceded. "But you had better check to see that nothing is missing."

"It was only the marriage contract I was worried about. It would take too long to have another drawn up."

"Ah." Anthony smiled, humor dancing in his cobalt eyes. "The infamous contract. You may as well leave it with me so I can get the reading of it out of the way."

"And have you conveniently lose it? Not likely."

"My dear girl, you really must try trusting me just a little. It really would make for a more agreeable relationship, don't you think?" When she stubbornly refused to answer, he sighed. "Very well, have it your way." But to give her a taste of her own distrust, he added, "You *will* be at Silverley when I show up, won't you?"

Roslynn had the grace to blush. "Yes. You were kind enough to make the offer. I owe you an answer. But I'll have no arguing over it. You must accept my decision, whatever it is."

With a grin that lacked concurrence, Anthony left the room. The fact was, he trusted her at this point no more than she did him. He would have to have someone follow her to make sure she didn't take off straight for Scotland. He needed someone to keep Warton away from Silverley while she was there too.

Couldn't have them meeting again after he had blackened the fellow with such a walloping lie.

As for her coming up with the right answer, that didn't worry him. Her cousin wasn't the only one who could see them married one way or another.

Chapter Twenty

"*I* don't believe it! Tony asked you to marry him? *My* uncle Tony?"

"I know what you mean," Roslynn said, considering Regina's wide-eyed wonder rather amusing. "I find it difficult to believe myself."

"But it's so sudden . . . well, of course he knows your circumstances. It would have to be sudden, wouldn't it, if he was going to get you? Oh, this is famous! Uncle Jason is going to just die! The whole family is. We never thought he'd do it, you know. Oh, it's just wonderful!"

Whether it was wonderful or not was debatable, but Roslynn smiled, not wanting to put a damper on Regina's obvious delight. She had made her decision on the long ride to Silverley, which was fortunate, because she hadn't had a moment's respite since she arrived. First Nettie had laid into her, deservedly, blistering her ears with a thorough scolding for her thoughtlessness. Then Regina had had to hear all about the abduction and the harrowing escape from Geordie firsthand, which Nettie had mentioned as their reason for the unexpected visit.

Now Roslynn had had to admit that Anthony would be here soon for her answer. That Regina hadn't thought to ask what that answer would be was telling. Of course she would be prejudiced. She wouldn't be able to understand how a woman might have doubts about marrying someone of Anthony's good looks and wicked charm, even if he did have a rakehell past.

"Everyone will have to be notified," Regina continued enthusiastically. "I'll do that, if you like. And I'm sure you'll want the wedding just as soon as the banns—"

"No banns, puss." Anthony sauntered into the drawing room without warning. "You can let the family know that congratulations are in order, but I've already sent for the parson, inviting him to dinner, and afterward we'll have a little ceremony. Is that quick enough to suit you, Roslynn?"

Forcing her to reveal her decision in this casual way, the moment he walked in, was not how Roslynn had imagined it. But he was looking directly at her, waiting for her confirmation or denial, and if she didn't know better, she would have sworn he seemed different. Nervous, perhaps? Could her answer really be that important to him?

"Yes, those arrangements will do . . . but we have some things to discuss first."

Anthony let out his breath slowly, a wide grin curling his lips. "By all means. Will you excuse us, puss?"

Regina jumped up and threw her arms around his neck. "Excuse you? I could clobber you! You never even let on."

"And spoil the surprise?"

"Oh, it *is* wonderful, Tony," she agreed happily. "And I can't wait to tell Nicholas, so I'll just run along." She laughed here. "Before you throw me out."

Anthony smiled fondly after her, delaying the moment he must face the music. He supposed he shouldn't have put Roslynn on the spot like that. And her "things to discuss" had sounded too serious by far.

"I hope you're not always going to be so high-handed?"

Roslynn's voice could have cut through lead. Anthony spun about, offering a crooked grin.

"Never think so. I can be putty in the hands of the right woman."

She wasn't amused. If anything, her expression turned more frigid. "Sit down, Anthony. There are some things you'll have to agree to before I'll marry you."

"Is this going to hurt?" When her eyes began to narrow, he sighed. "Very well, give me the worst of it."

"I want a child."

"Only one?"

Hell's teeth, she wanted to throw something at him! Could he ever treat anything seriously?

"Actually, I would like at least three, but one will do for now," she bit out.

"Well, this is cause for sitting down, isn't it?" he said and joined her on the sofa. "Have you a preference for gender too? I mean, if it's girls you want but we only have boys, I'm willing to keep on trying if you are."

His tone might be jesting, but she had the feeling he actually meant it. "You don't mind having children?"

"My dear girl, whatever made you think I would mind? After all, the mode of getting them has always been a favorite practice of mine."

The blush spread clear to her roots. She glanced down at her hands, held tightly in her lap. She could feel his eyes smiling at her, amused by her embarrassment. Well, he hadn't heard all of it yet.

Still avoiding his eyes, she said, "I'm glad you're

being so reasonable about it, but I have another condition you must agree to that is rather unorthodox, though related in a way. Your mistress, or mistresses, as the case may be—''

His hand on her chin stopped her, turning her face to his. "This isn't necessary, you know," he said gently. "A gentleman always gives up his mistresses when he marries."

"Not always."

"Be that as it may, in my case—"

"You should have let me finish, Anthony." Her voice was sharp again, her little chin at a stubborn tilt. "I'm not asking you to give up anything. On the contrary. I insist you keep your mistresses."

He sat back, shaking his head. "I've heard of accommodating wives, but don't you think you're overdoing it a touch?"

"I'm serious."

"The devil you are." He scowled, infuriated not only that she really seemed to be serious, but also with the suggestion itself. "If you think for one bloody minute I'll agree to a marriage in name only—"

"No, no, you misunderstand." She was frankly surprised at this show of anger on his part. She had thought he would be delighted with this arrangement. "How can I get a child if our marriage is in name only?"

"How indeed!" he snapped.

"Anthony." She sighed, realizing he must be exhibiting wounded pride. He obviously expected a jealous wife, and that he wasn't getting one was deflating. "I intend to be a wife to you in every way. It's the least I can do, after you've come to my rescue, so to speak. If you'll just listen to me for a moment."

"My breath is bated."

She sighed again. Why was he fighting her on this of all things? It had seemed the ideal solution. In fact, she couldn't marry him otherwise.

She tried again. "I don't see what you're so up in the air about. You don't love me. You said as much. And my feelings aren't involved yet either. But I do like you, and we are—at least I am attracted to you."

"You know bloody well the attraction is mutual!"

She ignored his snarled interruption. "That was one of my prerequisites, that the husband I finally choose at least be pleasing in appearance so that I wouldn't mind too much—"

She broke off at his snort, knowing full well he was thinking of last night and how well she had enjoyed it. No, it wasn't necessary to mention that with him she would find certain marital duties quite pleasurable.

"You are personable," she continued. "And charming. There's no denying that. And I'm sure we can deal well with each other. But because there's no love involved, you're not committed. Neither am I, for that matter, though I'm the one in desperate need of a husband. In your case, however, it would be unrealistic of me to expect you to be completely faithful to your vows, don't you see? And so I'm not asking you to be. What we will have is a business arrangement, a marriage of convenience, if you like. Trust isn't required."

He was staring at her as if she had lost her mind. She supposed that *was* doing it up a bit much, but how else could she put a nice dressing on the simple fact that she didn't trust him and probably never would? Hell's teeth, he was the first to admit he was a rake. And a rake doesn't reform unless his heart is caught—her grandfather's own words, and words she could well believe because they made sense. Anthony had no business getting annoyed with her. *She* should be angry that it was necessary to even make this stipulation.

"Perhaps we should just forget it," she said stiffly.

"A splendid notion finally," he drawled.

Her lips thinned out at his quick agreement to *that.* "I didn't want to marry you to begin with. I told you so."

"What?" He sat bolt upright. "Now wait a minute, Roslynn. I didn't mean not getting married was a splendid notion. I thought you meant—"

"Well, I didna!" she snapped, quite losing her temper at last. "And if you willna agree to keep your mistresses, then we've nothing further to discuss, have we? It isna as if I'm no' asking for an equal share of your body. But I ken what you are, mon, and that your eyes will be wandering again once the novelty wears thin. You canna help it. It's your nature."

"Bloody hell."

She went on as if she hadn't heard his curse. "But I was willing to have you anyway, fool that I am. You would have given me bonny bairns. You would have saved me from Geordie. That was enough. I wasna asking for more."

"Perhaps I am willing to give you more. Or hadn't that thought crossed your mind when you came up with this magnanimous gesture?"

Roslynn stiffened under his derision, but she was in control again. "It comes down to one simple thing, Anthony. I could never trust you where other women are concerned. If I should . . . should come to care for you eventually, a betrayal would be too painful. I would rather know from the start that you won't be faithful to me; then our relationship will progress no

further than it is now. We would be friends as well
as—''

"Lovers?"

"Yes, well, there you have it. But since you won't
agree, that's an end to it, then, isn't it?"

"Did I say I wouldn't agree?" His voice was calm
again, but it was a forced calm. His set expression,
his rigid posture, said he was still simmering. "Let
me see if I have this right, my dear. You want to get
a child by me, but at the same time you don't want
my full devotion. You will act the wife in every way,
but I'm to go on as I have been, seeing as many
women as I like."

"Discreetly, Anthony."

"Ah, yes, discreetly. I can see where you might
not want it bandied about, especially since you're
pushing me out the door before I've even gotten inside it. So if I don't come home two or three nights
a week, you'll be happy, I take it?"

She wouldn't deign to answer that. "You agree?"

"Of course." His smile was brittle, lacking
warmth, but Roslynn didn't notice. "What man could
resist having his piece of cake so thickly frosted?"

Roslynn didn't know if she liked that analogy. She
didn't know if she liked his surrender either, now that
she had it. He certainly hadn't argued very long. A
token resistance, then grudging acceptance. Hah!
Wretched man. He was undoubtedly delighted with
her terms, and now she had to live with them.

Chapter Twenty-one

The Eden coach was well sprung, comfortable, with conveniences in the way of pillows and blankets, glasses and champagne. Roslynn had no need of the former, her husband's shoulder doing quite nicely in that capacity. She declined the champagne as well, having tipped enough glasses in toasts after the ceremony.

They had really done it, gotten married. Made love one night, married the next. It was so incredible that Roslynn had to wonder if unconsciously she hadn't wanted this to happen all along, if this wasn't why she had gone to Anthony's last night instead of going straight to Silverley as she had intended. But no, it wasn't going to be an ideal marriage. She had seen to that with her own perversity and mustn't forget it. And yet she still had him, didn't she? He was her husband, part-time or not.

She smiled, snuggling up close to him, glad that she was feeling just intoxicated enough not to feel self-conscious about it. Anthony was sipping champagne himself, staring thoughtfully out the window. The silence was companionable, the champagne she had already consumed making her drowsy.

She wasn't sure why they weren't staying the night at Silverley, as she had assumed they would. Anthony had said something about not wanting to worry about the noise, and his own bed, and starting things out right. It had sounded rather ominous at the time, the part about the noise, but she couldn't remember why now. Probably only bride's jitters. After all, she had just signed away her independence, giving herself into the hands of a man she barely knew, and one who was full of surprises, least of which was that he' wanted to marry her.

She had every right to be nervous before and after the fact. Hadn't he surprised her twice today, first by arguing about her conditions, and second by signing the marriage contract without having read it first? Nicholas, who was witnessing the signing, had protested. She had herself, for that matter. But even after signing the damn thing, Anthony had still refused to read it. And now he was taking her back to London, the last thing she'd expected for tonight.

Frankly, she would have felt a lot more secure staying with the Edens this first night of her marriage. But she had made enough demands for one day and so hadn't protested when Anthony cut the celebrating short to leave. Granted, they'd had an early dinner, and the wedding ceremony had taken no time at all. It wasn't that late in the evening, though it would probably be midnight before they arrived at Anthony's town house.

She supposed she ought to take advantage of the ride and get some sleep while she could. She smiled again, for her first thoughts on seeing the blankets and pillows piled on the seats hadn't been about sleep. She had been appalled to think they would be having their wedding night in the coach. After all, Nettie had been relegated to a smaller carriage to follow at a slower pace. They were alone, just the two of them, in a coach that was certainly roomy enough to accommodate them for anything they might have in mind. The yellow glow of the coach lamp gave off a soft, romantic light. But no, Anthony had only suggested she nap for the return ride to London. He hadn't even taken advantage of their solitude to kiss her, just pulled her close and settled her against him.

She could blame the champagne for making her think her wedding night was going to start early. She wasn't even sure she was going to have a wedding night. After the fuss Anthony had made over her conditions, even if he did agree to them, she wouldn't be surprised if he just dropped her off and went on to visit one of his many women. And what could she say about it? In his own words, she had pushed him out the door.

Anthony heard his wife's sigh and wondered what she was thinking. Probably devising more ways to keep herself detached from this marriage. It was laughable, it really was, but of course he hadn't thought so earlier. Here he was taking a wife for the first time in his life, and she wanted to be no more than a mistress, and not even a possessive one. Did she feel nothing for him that she could blithely let him go from her arms to those of another woman? If he had wanted to continue to tomcat about town, he could have remained a bachelor.

It was perhaps a half hour later that the pistol shot shattered the quiet of the late hour and the coach came to a jostling halt. Roslynn jerked upright, blinking her eyes awake, in time to hear Anthony's soft curse.

"Have we arrived?" she asked, confused, as she glanced out the window to see nothing but pitch black.

"Not quite, my dear."

"Then—"

"I believe we're about to be robbed."

Her eyes swung to his. "Highwaymen? Then why are you just sitting there, mon? Are you no' going to do something?"

"My dear girl, this is England, and robbery is such a common occurrence that you come to think of it as donations to the needy. No one in his right mind travels these roads at night with anything of real value. We empty our pockets and go on our way, with no real harm done. It will be over in a matter of moments."

She stared at him, aghast. "Just like that? And what if I dinna want to be robbed?"

He sighed. "I assume this is your first time?"

"Of course it is! And I'm amazed that you can sit there calmly doing nothing."

"And what would you suggest I do when I haven't a weapon at my disposal?"

"*I* have one."

He caught her wrist as she reached for her boot and the concealed dirk. "Don't even think about it," he warned.

"But—"

"No!"

She sat back in a huff, glaring at him. "A fine thing when a husband willna protect his wife from brigands."

"Give over. Roslynn," he replied impatiently. "It's only a few pounds and trinkets."

"And a fortune in jewels in my portmanteau."

He gave her a level look, glanced at the bag on the seat opposite them, the same damn bag she had carelessly left in the hired hack last night, and snarled, "Bloody hell! You *would* cart about a fortune, wouldn't you? Very well." A quick examination of the interior inspired no strategy. His eyes came back to settle on Roslynn speculatively. "Toss your cloak back over your shoulders . . . yes." The deep scoop of her décolletage revealed the upper swell of her breasts, but the neckline was rather demure actually, in comparison to some others in this day and age. "Now, lower your dress a little—"

"Anthony!"

"This is no time for offended modesty," he explained wearily as he moved to the seat across from her. "You're to be a distraction."

"Och, well, in that case."

"That's quite low enough, my dear." He frowned at her. "*You* might not care if any number of women view my body in the nude, but I'm not quite so generous when it comes to other men and your charms."

"I was only trying to help," Roslynn retorted, annoyed with the reminder of the bargain she had insisted on.

"Commendable, but we want the chap to ogle you, not bust his breeches."

"Bust his breeches? Whatever are you talking about?"

He finally smiled. "I will be delighted to demonstrate at another time."

Anthony might have said more, but the highwayman made his appearance just then, yanking the door open and thrusting his head inside. Roslynn gave a little start. It was one thing to talk about being robbed even when you were about to be robbed, but quite another thing to meet the robber face-to-face.

The coach was high enough off the ground that only the man's upper torso was framed in the doorway, but it was a huge torso, great-brawny shoulders in a too-tight jacket, dark, scraggly hair on a large head wrapped in a dirty scarf. Fat fingers gripped an old, rusty pistol, also thrust into the coach and pointed directly at Anthony.

Roslynn could do nothing but stare at the pistol,

her heart beginning a drumroll. This was not how she had imagined it . . . well, she hadn't really imagined anything. Not knowing any highwaymen personally, how was she to know how very dangerous they could be? But she had goaded Anthony into doing something, so it would be her fault if he got shot. And for what? Some stupid jewels that were replaceable?

She glanced at Anthony, wondering how she could tell him to forget it, when the highwayman spoke up. "Evenin', m'lord," he said congenially enough, his voice muffled behind the scarf. "Good o' ye t' sit tight and await me, it was. 'Ad a bit o' trouble wi' me 'orse after lettin' yer driver know what's what. But I'll be relievin' ye o' yer—cor!"

It was at this point that the chap caught sight of Roslynn in the dim light. It took only a moment more for Anthony to grab hold of his wrist and jerk it forward, which brought the fellow's face slamming into Anthony's fist.

It happened so fast it was over with before Roslynn had time to be alarmed that it was the hand holding the pistol that Anthony had grabbed. The highwayman, unsuspecting lout, was out cold, facedown on the floor. And as calmly as you please, Anthony placed a foot on his back to keep him from sliding out the door while he pried the pistol loose.

"Be a good girl and stay put while I see if he rode alone or has chums lurking about."

Before Roslynn could say a word, Anthony was out the door, the highwayman slid out the other one, and she was left in the empty coach, the words dying on her lips. She had never been so frightened in her life, not even for herself. Anthony in danger was a revelation. She found she couldn't stand the suspense, waiting to hear more shots fired.

Fortunately, it was only a matter of moments before he was back, smiling now. "According to our very shaken driver—it seems this was his first robbery too—the chap was alone."

Roslynn's relief came out in an explosive "What the devil do you mean, scaring me to death like that? You could've been killed!"

Both brows shot up in amazement at her vehemence. "My dear girl, what did you expect me to do when you demanded I *do* something?"

"I didna mean for you to get yourself killed!"

"Glad to hear it," was his dry reply. "But it's done now, so enough."

"Dinna be telling me—"

He yanked her across his lap and smothered her words with a very forceful kiss. A moment later it became soft nibbles, and finally he grinned at her.

"That's better. Now you have something else to think about, and you can be sure we'll continue this later." He set her gently back on the seat beside him and reached for the bottle of champagne. "But right now I could use another drink, and you can go back to sleep."

"As if I could," Roslynn retorted, but the steam had gone out of her anger.

"You'd best try, sweetheart, because I promise you, you won't have much opportunity to sleep later."

She said nothing to that but waited until he sat back with glass in hand and settled herself against him again. Her heart rate had returned to normal, although she could have done without the experience. This was her wedding night, for God's sake. Things like this just didn't happen on one's wedding night.

Peevish now that she had gotten so frightened for nothing, she said, "Next time pay me no mind and don't be so heroic. The jewels weren't *that* important.''

"Perhaps, but it would have fallen to me as your husband to replace them, and I would rather not so dent my pocket.''

"So you *did* marry me for my money?''

"Why else?''

With such irony in his tone, she glanced at him to see his eyes fixed on the bodice of her gown, which she had yet to raise. She nearly laughed. Why else indeed! The man was a rake through and through, but she had known that, knew too that there was no hope of changing him.

She sighed, briefly wondering if she ought to tell him that if he had married her for her money, he would be pleasantly surprised. Her marriage contract dealt very generously with him. And even though Anthony was obviously well-to-do enough not to have to work for a living, he was still a fourth son and couldn't possibly be rich enough to scorn what she had brought him through the marriage.

She would have to tell him, but not now. The excitement of the attempted robbery had drained her. Within moments, she was fast asleep again.

Chapter Twenty-two

Anthony shook Roslynn awake as they turned off the King's Road onto Grosvenor Place. They were nearing Piccadilly now, where his town house was located across from Green Park. He hoped that James would still be out for the evening and Jeremy would be in bed, because, as late as it was, the last thing he wanted to do was tender explanations. Besides, he had spent the whole of the ride home, less the short interruption by the highwayman, contemplating the delights of his bed. He didn't think he could wait much longer.

Roslynn couldn't have cared less at the moment. She had slept soundly this second time and couldn't seem to rouse herself sufficiently to appreciate that they had finally arrived. She just wanted to continue sleeping. Thoughts of her wedding night, of her new husband, of anything, were far removed. And yet someone continued to shake her.

Anthony was nonplussed when all Roslynn did was sigh an irritated moan and slap his hand away, refusing to open her eyes. Women didn't usually sleep in his presence, so he was unaccustomed to dealing with one who wouldn't wake up. He had suggested a nap to refresh her, not to put her out for the night, for God's sake.

He tried once more. "Come on, my girl, or have you forgotten what day this is?"

"Mmm?"

"Do wedding bells bring anything to mind? Or a

husband thinking about you slipping into something sheer and sexy for his delectation?''

She yawned, but did manage to sit up, blinking her eyes several times before rubbing the sleep from them in a very childlike way. "I don't travel with anything like *that*.''

He grinned to himself. At least her mind was finally working, even if it was a bit slow in realizing he was only teasing her.

"Not to worry, my dear. I sent for your things this morning.''

That certainly woke her up. "You didn't! That was a fool thing to do when you didn't even know yet if I'd marry you or not. Geordie could have been watching and waiting for just that so he could follow and find out where I've gone.''

Anthony certainly hoped so. That was just why he'd done it. And with any luck, the man he'd set to follow the "followees" would have an address for him tomorrow. But as to her concern, he chuckled.

"I know it's not every day that you become a bride, sweetheart, but it's a bit disconcerting, not to mention a blow to the ego, that you keep forgetting your changed status. You're married now. The sooner your cousin knows it, the sooner he'll trouble you no more.''

The smile began hesitantly but blossomed into a dazzling display of delight. "That's true, isn't it? I'm so used to hiding from Geordie, I suppose it'll take me a while to relax now that I don't have to anymore. It's done. I'm free.''

"Not quite free, my dear.''

"No, I didn't mean—''

"I know.'' He chucked her under the chin. "But

you are in fact mine now, and I am discovering, very quickly, what a possessive bore I can be.''

How utterly absurd was that statement, but Roslynn was certain he was joshing her, as was his habit. If and when he ever treated a subject seriously, she would probably perish from the shock.

On a new thought, she asked, ''Anthony, why did you insist on returning to London tonight?''

His eyes twinkled with amusement. ''Brides are nervous enough on their wedding night. I thought you might be more at ease in a bed you're already familiar with.''

Blushing, she got out in a whisper, ''I asked for that, I suppose.''

''You did.''

''But you mentioned noise?''

''Did I? Think nothing of it. Like as not, we'll be as quiet as church mice.''

He was teasing her again. She wasn't sure she liked it tonight. She wasn't sure she would ever get used to it, his allusions to lovemaking. But tonight . . .

She yawned, Anthony grinned, and the coach stopped.

''At last,'' he said and leaped down without awaiting the coach step. 'Come, my dear, and I will endeavor to carry you over the threshold.''

She took his hand and was lifted to the ground. ''It isn't necessary—''

''Allow me to play my part,'' he cut in, at the same moment sweeping her off her feet. ''After all, they must have invented this quaint custom for a reason. Perhaps so the bride can't possibly escape?''

''What nonsense.'' She chuckled, wrapping an arm about his neck. ''More likely it was a few brides fainting on the threshold so they had to be carried inside that started it."

"Only a few?" he teased. "I assure you that ignorance of the marriage bed is more widespread than that. Mothers just can't bring themselves to discuss such things these days, you know. A shame, because it makes it devilish hard on the poor grooms, easing fears and nervousness when they'd rather get right to the deflowering."

"Anthony!" she cried, though it was difficult not to smile at his wicked grin. "*Must* you say such things?" But she added, to have the last word, "Besides, some brides don't have mothers to enlighten them."

"Ah, now we're getting personal." He reached the door and pounded on it before giving her a tender look. "But you weren't frightened, were you, sweetheart?"

"You didn't exactly give me time to be frightened," she admitted, warming with another blush.

"And now that you know what it's all about?"

"I believe I feel a faint coming on."

He burst into laughter, but coughed it down as the door opened and a stoic-faced Dobson stared out at them. Roslynn was a trifle disappointed that the fellow could look so blasé, as if he were quite accustomed to finding his employer at the door with a woman in his arms. But she was mollified a moment later as they passed him and she caught Dobson's unguarded expression. That was more like it, astonishment in the extreme. She hid her smile against Anthony's shoulder.

But watching the butler, she missed seeing James Malory just stepping into the hall, a drink in hand. If he was surprised, he didn't show it. The voice that drew Roslynn's attention to him was bland as well.

"I don't suppose I should be witnessing this."

"I was hoping you wouldn't," Anthony retorted without breaking his stride toward the stairs. "But since you have, you may as well know I married the girl."

"The devil you say!"

"He really did." Roslynn chuckled, delighted with this reaction even more than with Dobson's. "You don't think I'd allow just anyone to carry me over the threshold, do you?"

Anthony stopped short, rather amazed himself that he had managed to discompose this particular brother. "Good God, James, I've waited a lifetime to see you at a loss for words. But you'll understand if I don't wait around for you to recover, won't you?" And he didn't, continuing on his way.

At the top of the stairs, Roslynn whispered, laughter in her voice, "That was naughty of us, don't you think?"

"Not a-tall, dear girl," he promptly disagreed. "If I'm to have you to myself for a while, rendering my brother speechless was not only necessary but priceless. We will be bombarded with the family's good wishes and endless questions soon enough." Inside his room, he leaned back against the door with a sigh. "Alone at last."

Before Roslynn could say anything, he let her legs drop, turning her toward him at the same time. She ended up practically lying on him, a position they both savored for several long moments while he teased her lips with soft nibbles.

The backs of his fingers caressed her cheek, bringing her eyes slowly open. His own were grown dark and heavy-lidded with passion. And his voice was a caress too, his breath warm against her lips.

"Did you ever stop to think that this is the one night of your life when everyone knows you intend to make love? Ah, sweetheart, I love it when you blush for me."

"It's something I've been doing only recently— since I met you."

For some reason, her husky reply savaged Anthony's senses. He set her away from him, his hands trembling, a soft groan in his throat.

"I was a bloody fool to wait this long. I'll give you five minutes to do whatever you have to, but for God's sake, take pity on me, Roslynn, and be in bed when I return."

"Wearing something sheer and sexy?"

"Good God, no!" he exclaimed. "I don't think I could bear it now."

With that he disappeared into his dressing room, leaving Roslynn with a silly smile on her lips and a warmth of anticipation churning in her belly. Had she done that to him, made him lose control like that? Extraordinary. But she wasn't too composed herself. Knowing what was going to happen was a lot different from not knowing. It made it easier. There was an eagerness. But she was still too inexperienced not to be a trifle nervous too.

Her fingers were rather clumsy in stripping off her clothes, though she made quick work of it. Her heart was pumping at an abnormal rate. Her ears were attuned to the door as she waited to hear it open. Climbing into the bed, she was undecided whether to pull the sheet over her completely or to leave it only partially draped. Modesty won out, for now. She wondered if frequency would help, if she might eventually manage a certain detachment. With Anthony, she doubted it. This was more likely to become habit-forming.

He was wearing a long robe of crimson velvet when he finally returned. With acute embarrassment, Roslynn realized that she hadn't even thought to put on a nightgown. Not that it would have stayed on for long, but wasn't it unseemly for a wife to wait naked in bed for her husband? Perhaps not—at least not tonight. And Anthony's appreciative smile as he approached the bed said he certainly approved.

"May I?" He sat down next to her and began removing the pins from her hair.

She touched a red-gold lock that fell onto her shoulder. "I forgot."

"I'm glad."

He was. He loved her hair, loved touching it and running his fingers through it. Setting the pins aside, he massaged her scalp until her eyes closed and a dreamy smile appeared on her lips.

"That's nice," she breathed softly.

"Is it? And what about this?"

His lips pressed to her temple, moving down, stopping at her mouth for a long, deep kiss before continuing down her neck in a path that led to her breasts. Ripples of warmth shot along her nerves, making her toes curl.

"That's *too* nice," she murmured.

Anthony's chuckle was rich with pleasure. "Ah, sweetheart, was it only last night? It seems an eternity has passed between now and then."

She reached out to cup her palm to his cheek and ended by running a finger over his lips. "Only an eternity?"

He said her name impassionedly before he caught

her wrist and kissed her palm, his dark eyes never leaving hers. An electricity passed between them, hot and tingling. And his intense stare continued to hold her transfixed as he shrugged out of his robe, yanked the sheet down, and covered her body with his. He commenced then to kiss her so long and passionately that she was in a state of mindless need when he finally entered her, so much so that her climax was immediate and earth-shattering, her cry of fulfillment sending Anthony over the edge as well.

In a cocoon of contentment, Roslynn held his sweat-moistened body, waiting for their breathing to return to normal. She was in no hurry to have him move, and so her hold was rather tight. Not that it could have kept him there, but he was in no hurry to move either. His head rested on her shoulder, his breath fanning her neck, stirring the hair there, tickling her. Gooseflesh rushed down her arms and she gave a little shiver, enough for him to notice.

"I have managed to act the typical groom," he said with a sigh. "Impatient, speedy, and now contrite." He lifted his weight onto his elbows, which gave her a little thrill as his groin pressed more tightly to hers. "I give you leave to castigate me, my dear."

"For what?"

"Well, if you don't know—"

"For what, Anthony?"

"For my lack of control, of course. A man of my age and experience has no excuse, so I must put the blame on you. You quite make me lose my head."

"Is that bad?"

"I'll let you be the judge in a little while, when I make love to you at a more leisurely pace."

Her laugh was deep in her throat. "If I didn't know better, I'd say you were fishing for compliments. You must know your performance wasn't lacking. Quite the contrary. You were wonderful.''

He gave her his melting smile, which sent a weakness racing through her limbs. She gasped, her lips parting, tempting him to bend down and brush them lightly with a kiss.

But then he got up, surprising her by tossing the sheet up over her and retrieving his robe where he'd carelessly dropped it on the floor. He sat down again on the edge of the bed, but at a distance, which should have given her warning.

With a mock sigh, he said, ''And now for the noise.''

Hazel eyes blinked. ''The noise?''

''The unleashing of your Scot's temper.''

Roslynn grinned at him, thinking he was once again teasing her. ''I'm going to lose it, am I?''

''More than likely, since I'm honor-bound to tell you that I lied to you today.''

Her amusement fled. ''About what?''

''Can't you guess, my dear? I have no intention of keeping a mistress on the side now that I've married. It utterly defeats the purpose, doesn't it?''

''But you agreed!''

His smile was one of sheer male satisfaction. ''I can safely say I would have agreed to anything today to make you legally mine, even to putting it in writing, which fortunately you didn't think to request.''

Roslynn stared at him incredulously, hot anger banishing the languor of her limbs. She felt tricked, cheated. She was furious.

''You married me falsely!''

''I married you in good faith.''

''I offered you an ideal situation, mon!''

''One I didn't ask for or want. And, my dear, if

you'll just think about it, you'll see how utterly absurd your request was. You didn't ask me to marry you, I asked you, and I'll have you know I've never done that before. Nor is it something I would have done lightly. I've had mistresses enough to last me a lifetime. What I want now is a wife.''

It was ludicrous how calm he was next to her fury, shaming her into lowering her voice. ''You say so now, but what of next month, next year? Your eyes will be a-wandering again soon enough.''

Anthony grinned at her, knowing that would probably infuriate her all the more. ''My eyes have been a-wandering, as you put it, for the last nineteen years. Give them a rest, Roslynn. They settled on you and don't want to move on.''

Her own eyes narrowed to a seething glare, just as he had anticipated. ''So you think it's a matter to be joking about, do you? Well, let me tell you—''

She didn't get a chance to. He reached over and caught her around the waist, dragging her across the bed and up against his chest. The sheet was lost in the process, but Roslynn was too angry to notice. Anthony wasn't. And the new stirring below his belt demanded he end this bickering soon and get back to the pleasures of the wedding night. The silly girl. All this fuss because he wanted no one but her. She ought to be happy about it instead of raising hell. But he had expected this, and had an answer for her.

''What say we compromise, sweetheart? D'you still insist I keep a mistress?''

''Hell's teeth! Now isna that what I've been saying?'' she retorted.

''Very well.'' His eyes caressed her face, stopped on her lips, and his voice deepened. ''Are you prepared to fill the role?''

"Me?"

His grin was back, maddeningly. "Who else? You happen to be the only woman I'm interested in at the moment."

"That's no' what I meant, and you know it!"

"Perhaps, but it's the best I can do."

Roslynn didn't believe this for a moment. "You must have a woman you've been seeing."

"Assuredly. Several, in fact. But none could actually be called my mistress, sweetheart. And if you must know, I haven't seen any of them since I met you. But that's beside the point, isn't it? The point is, I have no desire to take any of them to my bed again, or anyone else for that matter. You are quite stuck with me."

"Anthony, be serious just for once!" she pleaded in exasperation.

"My dear, I've never been more serious in my life. How can I make love to another woman when you're the only woman I want? It can't be done, you know. Desire isn't just called forth at will. Or hadn't you thought of that?"

She was looking at him with confusion and a touch of wonder, only these expressions quickly turned to a frown and a tightening of her lips. "But that doesn't mean you'll no' see someone eventually that you'll be liking."

Anthony sighed wearily. "If that day comes, I swear to you, Roslynn, it won't matter in the least. I'll have only to imagine you, here like this, and be a contented man."

She made a sound that was very nearly a snort. "Very prettily said. I give you that. But you're forgetting you dinna love me."

He tossed her back onto the bed and quickly covered her body with his own. "Then let us examine what I do feel, shall we?" His voice purred, but it was obvious he had lost patience with her. "There's lust, in abundance. It's been bloody hell keeping my hands off you until now. There's possessiveness, which I've only recently discovered. There's jealousy, which I've known about for weeks." His brow rose sharply as her eyes rounded. "Don't tell me I've actually surprised you, my dear."

"You were jealous? Of who?"

"Bloody well everyone, even my blasted brother. And you may as well know, while we're at it, that the gentlemen you were considering for marriage were all immensely suitable, with the exception of Fleming, who really is a queer fellow. It was all lies, Roslynn, because I couldn't stand the thought of any of them having you."

He was holding her down now, because he fully expected her to become violent after this particular confession. But Roslynn was perfectly still, rage at what he'd done overshadowed by utter amazement.

"Then you must . . . care a little?" Her question was whisper-soft, hesitant.

"Bloody hell!" he finally exploded. "Would I have married you if I didn't?"

Not the least bit intimidated, she reminded him, "You married me to help me out of a horrid situation, which I'm grateful for."

Anthony closed his eyes for a moment, pleading for self-control. When he opened them, there was a hard gleam there. But his voice was moderate, if a touch arrogant.

"My dear, if I had only wanted to help you out, as you put it, I could have hurried your bothersome cousin to an early demise with little difficulty. But I

wanted you for myself, it's that simple." Here his
tone changed, became stern. "And if you tell me once
more to enjoy other women when I'll be bloody
damned if I will, I'll play the archaic husband for you
and thrash you soundly. Have I made myself clear?
There will be no other women, not now, not ever!"

He waited for her temper to snap again. He got a
smile instead, a very beautiful one that reached her
eyes, brightening the golden flecks there.

Anthony didn't know what to make of this sudden
change, until she said, "Dinna you mention earlier
doing something at a more leisurely pace? I was suppose to judge—"

His laughter cut her off, deep and exultant. "Never
change, sweetheart. I wouldn't have you any other
way."

And he proceeded to have her his way, with her
full and delighted cooperation.

Chapter Twenty-three

"Och, now, what is this? Sitting there grinning at yerself, are ye?"

Roslynn turned the hand-held mirror slightly and caught Nettie's image reflected behind her. Her grin widened, and her eyes, already sparkling, tried for a look of innocence as she swung around on the stool.

"Was I grinning? I can't imagine why."

Nettie snorted, but her lips were twitching at the corners too. "Pleased wi' yerself, ain't ye?"

Roslynn gave up the pretense. "Yes! Oh, Nettie, I never thought I could be this happy!"

"Aye, it's nae wonder. That's a bonny-looking mon ye caught. But did ye have tae be keeping him such a secret?"

"There was no secret. He wasn't really under consideration, Nettie. His asking to marry me was as much a surprise to me as to anyone."

"Well, now, as long as yer happy wi' him, that's all I could be asking, and sae much more than I was expecting, wi' all the haste. It doesna even matter that this house is sae Spartan and the servants boorish snobs."

Roslynn chuckled. "You've met Dobson, I take it?"

"Aye, that lout. What a cold one. But it's nae wonder he's sae snooty, him being in charge of all the servants here. There's nae housekeeper, nae other women servants a-tall, just two maids who come in several times a week tae clean. Even the cook's a mon, and there's another uppity one fer ye."

"I see you have a few complaints, Nettie. But don't take it so to heart. You're forgetting this was a bachelor residence until now. I'm sure Anthony won't object if we make some changes. There's new furnishings to buy." At this she glanced about her new bedroom, envisioning putting her touch to it. "New servants to hire. We'll be busy in the next few weeks, you can be sure."

"Now dinna be going off on a spending spree on my account. And remember ye've a husband now tae be asking afore ye go spending his money. The creatures are particular about such things as that."

"Don't be such a worrier, Nettie. I'm not going to use *his* money when I've so much of my own."

"Ye better talk that over wi' him first, lassie. A mon's funny about wanting tae pay his wife's bills, ye know? Yer trouble is, ye've been doing fer yerself too long, even afore Duncan, bless him, passed on. But yer married now. Ye've got tae make allowances and do things a might differently if ye want tae be keeping the peace atween ye." A knock sounded on the door just then, and Nettie explained. "That'll be yer bath water. Are ye in a hurry tae be joining yer mon fer lunch, or have ye time—"

"There's plenty of time, Nettie. Anthony went out, I believe." Roslynn blushed here. "I was still half asleep when he told me. But he mentioned something about his daily ride and attending to a few things. I don't expect him back before dinner, however, so I can spend the day acquainting myself with the house and servants. And I really must send a note off to Frances to let her know what's happened." After getting so little sleep last night, Roslynn thought those were enough priorities for one day.

An hour later, wearing a cool muslin dress of yellow-and-rose spring flowers on a beige background, Roslynn left Anthony's room, *their* room now, and started down the short hallway. She had seen next to nothing of his home the last time she was here, nor last night either, but that would soon be corrected. She would need Dobson's help, though. Since there were other Malorys in residence, she couldn't just open doors indiscriminately.

She spared a moment's thought for the other two occupants of the house, Anthony's brother and son. She wondered if her husband would now admit that Jeremy Malory was his son. There was no reason for him to still deny it, at least not to her. He was a handsome lad, a boy to be proud of, and the image of his father. Actually, it was ludicrous for Anthony to deny patrimony when anyone merely had to look at Jeremy to know who sired him.

She would need to make friends with the lad, but she could foresee no difficulty there. James Malory was another matter. There was no reason to get too friendly with him, and every reason not to. Should she tell Anthony about James having kissed her once? Or maybe he already knew. He *had* said he had been jealous of his brother.

She smiled, remembering their crazy conversation last night. She didn't know how he had done it, but she had let him convince her he was going to make a wonderful husband. All of her long-standing, preconceived notions about rakes were put to rest. He was going to be faithful. She felt it, believed it now wholeheartedly, and was ecstatic about it. What more could she have asked for than to have Anthony Malory all to herself? His love, she reminded herself. But that would come. It would. It had to.

"Hell's bells, what are *you* doing here?"

Roslynn paused at the top of the stairs. Jeremy Malory, on his way up, stopped dead in his tracks too, his mouth left open in an O of wonder after he had got his question out. The imp in Roslynn decided to be mischievous, since it was obvious he hadn't heard of the marriage yet.

"I spent the night, don't you know."

"Spent the night?" he repeated.

"Yes, and I'm thinking of moving in."

"But—but there's only bachelors here!"

"But there's lots of room, don't you think? And this house could use a woman's touch."

"It could?" he said in bemusement, only to shake his head. "But it wouldn't be proper, would it? I mean, you're a lady—I mean, well, you know what I mean. It just wouldn't be proper."

"No?" Roslynn grinned. "Then I'll have to speak with your father. He's the one insisting I stay."

"*He* did?" Jeremy nearly choked. "Hell's bells, he's gone and done it now! Uncle Tony's going to fly through the roof. He had his eye on you himself. Hell's bells, he'll probably throw us out now."

"Jeremy," she began gently, giving up the game. She hadn't thought he would be this upset. "There's no need to keep up the pretense. I know Anthony is your father. And I'm sorry I teased you like that. The reason I'm staying is because I married your father yesterday. He really should have told you."

His mouth dropped open again, but this time he was quicker to recover. "My father, meaning—Anthony? You married Anthony Malory?"

"You don't have to sound *that* surprised."

"But . . . I don't believe it. Tony getting married? He wouldn't."

"And why not, I'd like to be knowing?"

"He just wouldn't. He's a confirmed bachelor. He's got all the women he could want chasing after him. What would he need a wife—"

"Careful, laddie," Roslynn warned stiffly. "You're getting very close to insulting me."

Color flamed his cheeks. "I—I beg your pardon, Lady Chadwick. Truly, I meant no offense."

"It's Lady Malory now, Jeremy," she said, holding up her hand in front of him and tapping her wedding ring. "It happened last evening at Silverley, with your cousin Regina as witness. So you might as well believe it, laddie. I've no reason to lie about it, and you can ask your father as soon as he comes home."

"My father was there too?"

Roslynn sighed. "How could he not be at his own wedding?"

"No, I meant James. He *is* my father, you know. He really is."

It was Roslynn's turn to be surprised, because Jeremy was too earnest to be lying about it now. "But you look so much like Anthony!"

"I know." He grinned. "But so does Reggie, and so does Amy, Uncle Edward's daughter. And my aunt Melissa, Reggie's mother, did too, though I never met her. She died when Reggie was still a baby. All the rest of the Malorys are blonds. It's just us five who took after my great-grandmother Malory."

"I can see I've a lot to learn about this family, there's so many of you."

"Then he really married you? He really did?"

"Yes, Jeremy, he really did." She grinned, coming down a few steps to lock arms with him. "Come along and I'll tell you all about it. James—your father—was here last night when Anthony carried me over the threshold, you know. Now, if you think *you* were surprised, you should have seen him.''

"I'll bet." His chuckle was deep for someone so young, but infectious.

Chapter Twenty-four

*W*hen Anthony and James walked inside the tavern and paused to look over the crowded room, the same phenomenon occurred that had happened again and again throughout the afternoon. One by one, the occupants of the room noticed them, nudged their companions, and the room began to quiet, until the silence was as thick as the cloud of smoke floating above the scarred tables.

The riffraff of the wharves didn't take too kindly to the gentry invading their territory, and there was usually always some down-on-his-luck fellow filled with enough resentment of the upper classes to pick a fight with the unsuspecting slummers, as any well-dressed gents were assumed to be. It could be the highlight of an evening, a chance for the lower masses to get a little of their own back from the wealthy who think it their due to exploit them, by wiping the floor with the nabobs' beaten bodies and casting them out in the street half dead, and sometimes, actually dead.

But the sheer size of these two aristocrats gave even the meanest bruisers pause. They didn't have the look of the dandies who thought it a lark to frequent establishments they scorned in the sober light of day. No, these two were obviously of a different quality, the menacing aura about them penetrating even the most sodden brain. Anyone who briefly thought of causing trouble quickly changed his mind at a second look and went on with his drinking and revelry, determined to ignore these particular nabobs.

The silence had lasted perhaps twenty seconds. Anthony didn't even notice it this time. He was tired, frustrated, and just a little bit intoxicated, since they had ordered drinks in each of the nine taverns they had entered while questioning the barkeeps. James did notice, and was berating himself once again for not dressing properly for this excursion. Clothes fitted a man to his elements, and theirs were distinctly out of place in these elements. But how had either of them known this would turn into an all-day excursion?

Anthony was deciding he had had enough for one day when his eyes lit on a thatch of bright red hair. He looked at his brother and rolled his eyes toward the bar. James followed the indicated direction and saw the fellow too. Red hair did not make him Geordie Cameron, but it did raise the odds that he was likely a Scotsman. James sighed, hoping this was the end of their search. Wild-goose chases were not how he preferred to while away his time.

"Why don't we take that table near the bar and see what we can overhear?" James suggested.

"Why don't I just go ask him?" Anthony countered.

"Men of this ilk don't like to be questioned, dear boy. They've usually, every one of them, got something or other to hide. Haven't you surmised that yet?"

Anthony scowled but nodded. James was right. They had had deuced little cooperation from everyone they'd questioned today, but blister it all, he wanted this done with so he could go home. He had a wife waiting for him, and this was not how he had imagined spending the second day of his marriage.

What was supposed to have taken only a few hours' time at the most this morning had turned into a com-

edy of exasperation. Anthony had been in the process
of explaining to James about Geordie Cameron, the
reason that he had married in such haste, when his
man John had interrupted their breakfast with the fellow's address, having successfully followed Cameron's hirelings yesterday to his lair.

It must have been the look of predatory delight on
Anthony's face that prompted James to offer to come
along. Not that Anthony was going to really harm the
scoundrel. No, just impress him with a sound thrashing, give him the good news that Roslynn was out of
his reach, since he wasn't taking any chances that
Cameron might miss the notice of her marriage in the
papers, and send him off with a warning to trouble
her no more. Very simple. He didn't need James'
help, but he was glad of his company as the day wore
on.

The first in a long list of frustrations was to find
Cameron vacated from the flat he had rented. That he
hadn't left until last night, when Roslynn had escaped
him the day before, was interesting. He was either
confident that she wouldn't alert the authorities of her
kidnapping or just plain stupid. Whichever, he had
smartened up by last night and had changed loca-
tions. And since it was too soon for him to have found
out about Roslynn's marrying, Anthony doubted the
chap had given up to return to Scotland, which was
why he had spent the rest of the day making inquiries
at every lodging and tavern in the vicinity, albeit
fruitlessly.

All he had was Geordie Cameron's description from
his landlady, but this fitted the fellow at the bar. Tall,
carrot-red hair, light blue eyes, presentable, and oh,
yes, very good-looking, according to Mrs. Pym. Anthony couldn't see the eyes yet, and whether the chap

was good-looking or not was a matter of opinion, but
the rest agreed with him, even to the halfway decent
togs he was sporting. The man had a companion,
perhaps one of his hirelings, standing there with him,
a short chap with a woolen cap pulled so far down
over his head, his features were obscured even from
a side angle.

They were talking together, at any rate, and James'
suggestion to listen in on the conversation was reasonable, despite the fact that Anthony's patience was
worn thin. After all the trouble he had been through
today, he was no longer just looking forward to
thrashing the fellow, but pleasantly contemplating an
alternative of a more permanent nature. Missed his
lunch, missed his dinner, missed making love to his
wife all day. He bloody well hoped she would appreciate his efforts on her behalf.

He followed his brother across the room to a table
already occupied by two rough-looking men and felt
a small bit of his humor returning as he watched
James stop there and stare the fellows into hastily va-
cating their seats. "Amazing how you do that, old
man."

James grinned innocently. "Do what?"

"Put murder and mayhem in those two little green
orbs of yours."

"Can I help it if the chaps thought I meant them
bodily harm? I didn't, you know. I am the most
peaceable fellow this side of—"

"Hell?" Anthony suggested with a wry smile. "It's
a good thing Connie's not here, or he'd choke on that
fairy tale."

"Put a lid on it, puppy. We need a drink if we're
not to look any more inconspicuous than we already
do."

Anthony turned around to locate a barmaid and got more than he bargained for. The wench was curvaceous without being plump, amazingly pretty for such a rough establishment, and had set herself down on his lap, wrapping soft arms about his neck in blatant invitation. It was done too quickly for him to discourage her, and he was so surprised by her action that he drew a blank for a moment on how to get rid of her.

James took pity on him, however, vastly amused at Anthony's dilemma. "You've chosen the wrong lap, dear girl." His dry tone brought the barmaid's head around to him, and at her bemused look, James grinned. "You see before you one of the world's most pitiable creatures—a married man—also one very preoccupied this evening. Now, if you'd care to bounce your pretty little backside over to this side of the table, you might get a rise for your trouble."

The maid giggled at James' crudity, words she was used to but not expecting from such an elegant-looking nabob. Yet she gave a last wistful look at Anthony, the one who had first boggled her eyes when the men walked in. He was worth at least another try, though the other one was just as appealing, now she'd had a better look at him.

She ignored Anthony's frown of displeasure, caused by James' words, and wrapped her long blond hair around his neck to pull him closer to her, while below the table, her buttocks wiggled in his lap provocatively. "Sure ye don't want some, luv. I'd be 'appy—"

His wits returning *too* quickly, Anthony lifted her up and set her on her feet, giving her a little shove in James' direction. "Another time, luv," he said not unkindly, but his eyes were narrowed when he met James' amused gaze.

James wasn't in the least perturbed. He caught the girl around the waist, caressed her backside with promise, whispered a few words in her ear, and sent her off with their order for two ales.

"Caught your fancy?" Anthony sneered.

"Whether this is your man or not, dear boy, I'm done for the day. I might as well have some compensation for my trouble, and she'll do nicely."

Anthony finally smiled. "Yes, I suppose she will. But you'll recall whose lap she preferred."

"Your recent victory has apparently gone to your head, lad. I hate to bring you back to earth, but you obviously need to be reminded that all you can do is look from now on—while I on the other hand can still sample to my heart's content."

"You don't see me bemoaning my state, do you?"

"Remember those words when you do. Women are to be savored for the moment. Anything longer is a threat to a man's sanity."

Anthony smiled serenely, even though those used to be his own sentiments as well. James didn't notice. His eyes had drifted to the two at the bar in such intimate conversation, particularly to the shorter fellow, and he frowned, looking at the cutest little backside to ever grace a supposedly male anatomy.

Anthony was distracted as well a moment later when the redhead, no more than six feet away, raised his voice a little. The thick Scottish brogue was unmistakable, reminding him forcefully of why they were here.

"I've heard enough," Anthony said tersely, swiftly rising to his feet.

James grabbed his arm, hissing, "You've heard

nothing. Be sensible, Tony. There's no telling how many of these chaps in here might be in his pay. We can bloody well wait a little more to see if he might leave the premises.''

''*You* can wait a little more. I have a new wife at home I've kept waiting long enough.''

Before he took another step, however, James sensibly called out, ''Cameron?'' hoping for no response since Anthony was no longer in a reasonable state of mind. Unfortunately, he got ample response, both characters swinging around at once and searching the room, one fearful, the other assuming an aggressive stance. Both pairs of eyes lit on Anthony as he shook off James' hand and closed the distance in two steps, but he had eyes only for the tall Scot.

''Cameron?'' he asked in a deceptively quiet tone.

''The name's MacDonell, mon, Ian MacDonell.''

''You're lying,'' Anthony growled, catching the man's lapels in his fists and jerking him forward and up, until their eyes were at a level only inches apart.

Too late, Anthony saw his mistake. The narrowed eyes now blazing at him were light gray, not blue. But at the same moment Anthony realized it, the little man next to them slipped a knife out of his sleeve.

James intervened at this point, since Anthony was too involved with the redhead to take notice of his companion. He neatly knocked the knife aside, only to be attacked for his trouble, fists and feet both flying his way. Hardly any damage ensued. The little bugger had no more strength than a child. But James was not about to just stand there and take this barrage. With no effort at all, he flipped his opponent about and hefted him off his feet. Somehow he wasn't surprised to find a full, soft breast cupped in his hand.

Anthony had glanced their way at the start of the

commotion, but now his eyes widened as he took in the delicate chin, smooth lips, and pert little nose. The cap had come down further to completely cover the eyes, but the perfectly molded cheekbones were unmistakably feminine too.

His voice was a trifle loud in his surprise. "Good God, *he's* a woman!"

James grinned. "I know."

"Now you've done it, you miserable curs!" the girl snarled at them both as several men within hearing glanced their way. "Mac, do something!"

MacDonell did. He pulled back his arm and swung at Anthony. The decision was made quickly not to fight, much as Anthony needed that outlet to let off some of his frustration. He caught the fist and slammed it down on the bar.

"There's no need for that, MacDonell," Anthony said. "I made a mistake. I apologize."

MacDonell was disconcerted at how easily he had been outmaneuvered. He wasn't that much smaller than the Englishman, yet he couldn't raise his fist off the bar to save his soul. And he had the feeling that even if he could, it wouldn't do him much good.

Prudently, the Scotsman nodded his acceptance and got his release by doing so. But his companion was still held tight, and it was to James his aggression turned now.

"Ye'll be letting go, mon, if ye ken what's good fer ye. I canna let ye monhandle—"

"Be easy, MacDonell," Anthony interjected in a hushed tone. "He means the lass no harm. Perhaps you'll let us accompany you outside?"

"There's nae need—"

"Look around you, dear fellow," James interrupted the Scot. "There appears to be every need, thanks to my brother's loud blunder."

So saying, he hefted the wench under his arm and started for the door. Her protest died with a tight squeeze about the ribs, and since MacDonell heard no complaint from her, he followed behind. Anthony did as well, after tossing a few coins on the table for the ales that had never arrived. He spared a glance for the room to see that most eyes were still on James and the girl, or rather, just on the girl. He wondered how long she had been in the tavern before her disguise was uncovered. It didn't matter. Dressed as she was in skin-tight breeches, even if her sweater was baggy in the extreme, there probably wasn't a man there who wouldn't have made a try for her if James didn't have her firmly in hand.

Anthony supposed it was too much to hope that they could exit the place without some further incident occurring. He caught up with the others only because the barmaid had appeared out of nowhere, it seemed, and latched possessively onto James' arm, stopping him.

Anthony arrived to hear her demand, " 'Ere now, ye're not leavin', are ye?"

James, instead of brushing her off, gave her a smile to quite dazzle her. "I'll be back later, my dear."

She brightened, not even bothering to glance at the bundle under his arm. "I finish work at two."

"Then two it is."

"Two's one too many, I'm thinking." This from a brawny sailor who had stood up and was now blocking James' path to the door.

Anthony sighed, coming up to stand next to his brother. "I don't suppose you'd care to put her down and take care of this, James."

"Not particularly."

"I didn't think so."

"Stay out of this, mate," the sailor warned Anthony. "He's got no right coming in here and stealing not one but two of our women."

"Two? Is this little ragamuffin yours?" Anthony glanced at the bundle in dispute, who had pulled her wool cap up enough to see by and was peering at them with murder in her eyes. He was almost hesitant to put it to the test. "Are you his, sweetheart?"

She was wise enough to give a negative shake of her head. Fortunately, the sailor was an ugly-looking brute, or she might have given a different answer, she was so angry at the way she was being manhandled. Anthony couldn't blame her. James was holding on a bit tighter than necessary, and the position he had her in was far from dignified.

"I believe that settles it, doesn't it." It was not a question by any means. Anthony was tired of the whole affair, especially when he had no one to blame but himself for being there in the first place. "Now be a good chap and move out of the way."

Surprisingly, the sailor stood firm. "He's not taking her out of here."

"Oh, bloody hell," Anthony said wearily just before flattening his fist on the fellow's jaw.

The sailor landed several feet away from them, out cold. The man he had been sitting with rose from their table with a growl, but not soon enough. A short jab and he fell back in his chair, his hand flying up to stanch the blood now seeping from his nose.

Anthony turned around slowly, one black brow arched questioningly. "Any more comers?"

MacDonell was grinning behind him, realizing now how fortunate he had been not to take on the Englishman. Not another man in the room made a move to accept the challenge, drawing the same conclusion. It had happened too quickly. They recognized a skilled pugilist when they saw one.

"Very nicely done, dear boy," James congratulated him. "Now can we quit this place?"

Anthony bowed low, coming up with a grin. "After you, old man."

Outside, James set the girl on her feet in front of him. She got her first good look at him then in the glow of the tavern lamp above the door, enough to make her hesitate a hairbreadth before she kicked him in the shin and bolted down the street. He swore violently and started after her, but stopped after a few feet, seeing that it was useless. She was already out of sight on the darkened street.

He turned back, swearing again when he saw that MacDonell had disappeared as well. "Now where the bloody hell did the Scot go?"

Anthony was too busy laughing to have heard him. "What's that?"

James smiled tightly. "The Scot. He's gone."

Anthony sobered, turning around. "Well, that's gratitude for you. I wanted to ask him why they both turned when they heard the name Cameron."

"To hell with that," James snapped. "How am I going to find her again when I don't know who she is?"

"Find her?" Anthony was chuckling once more. "Gad, you're a glutton for punishment, brother. What do you want with a wench who insists on damaging your person when you have another one counting the minutes until you return?"

"She intrigued me," James replied simply, then

shrugged. ''But I suppose you're right. The little barmaid will do just as well.'' Yet he glanced down the
empty street again before they headed toward the
waiting carriage.

Chapter Twenty-five

Roslynn stood by the window in the parlor, her cheek pressed to the cool glass, her hands gripping the blue tasseled drapes next to her. She had stood like that for the past thirty minutes, ever since she had left the dining room and an uncomfortable dinner with Jeremy and his cousin Derek, who had come by to take the youngster out for the evening.

At least Derek Malory's arrival had proved a diversion for a while. The marquis' heir was a handsome young man about her own age, with an unruly thatch of blond hair and eyes more hazel than green. He cut quite a dashing figure in his evening togs, and it took Roslynn only half a minute to discover he was fast following in his uncles' footsteps—another rake for a family that had too many already. But there was still a certain boyish quality about Derek Malory that made him seem harmless and quite charming.

He reacted to the news of his uncle's marriage just as Jeremy had, at first with disbelief, then delight. He was also the first to call her Aunt Roslynn, and not in jest, giving her quite a start for a moment. She really was an aunt now, to a whole brood of nephews and nieces. An instant family, thanks to her marriage to Anthony, and a warm and loving one, if Jeremy was to be believed.

But Jeremy and Derek were gone now, and Roslynn had gone back to her brooding, hardly even aware that she had stood in the same spot for the past half hour, gazing out at the passing traffic on Piccadilly.

On the one hand, she was worried sick. Something had happened to Anthony. He was hurt, unable to get word to her. That was the only reason the whole day had gone by and she had heard nothing from him. On the other hand, what had started as a slight irritation upon being abandoned, so to speak, had grown to a simmering anger as the hours dragged by, especially when Derek arrived and she couldn't explain Anthony's absence. He had simply gone about his business for the day without a by-your-leave, never mind that he had a wife now who might worry about him.

These conflicting feelings hadn't sat well together and had spoiled her appetite for the special dinner that she had held up for more than an hour, hoping Anthony would arrive in time. He hadn't, of course, and her anxiety was growing now, taking precedence over the anger, tying her belly up in knots.

Hell's teeth, where was he? This was only the second day of their marriage. Had he completely forgotten that fact? They should have spent the day together, getting to know each other better.

A carriage finally stopped in front of the house. Roslynn raced out of the room, waving Dobson away when he started for the door. She yanked it open herself before Anthony even reached it, and scanned his tall frame for injuries. There were none. He was all right. She wanted to hug him and clobber him at the same time. She stood there gripping her hands instead, to keep from giving in to either urge.

When Anthony spotted her, looking like a confection in a pale green gown with delicate white lace trim, his face lit up with a dazzling smile. "God, you're a sight for sore eyes, sweetheart. I can't tell you what a bloody rotten day I've had."

Roslynn didn't move so he could enter, but stood

her ground in the center of the doorway. "Why dinna you tell me anyway?"

The brogue gave her away. He stepped back to get a better look at her and noted the mulish angle of jaw, the tightly compressed lips.

"Is something amiss, my dear?"

"Do you ken what time it is, mon?"

"Ah, so that's it." He chuckled. "Did you miss me, sweetheart?"

"Miss you?" she gasped. "Ye conceited toad! I dinna care if you go off for days at a time if that's your wont. But it's common courtesy, isna it, to be telling someone when they're no' to expect you home?"

"Yes, I suppose it is," he surprised her by agreeing. "And I'll be sure to remember that the next time I spend the day trying to track down your elusive cousin."

"Geordie? But—why?"

"Why else? To give him the good news. Or hadn't you realized that until he is made aware of your new status, he's still a danger to you?"

Roslynn could feel the blush starting, and it was a furious one. He was late on her behalf, and how did she meet him at the door? Like a shrew.

"I'm sorry, Anthony."

Her contrite, downcast look was irresistible. He pulled her close until her head rested on his shoulder. "Silly girl," he teased her gently. "You've nothing to be sorry about. I rather like having someone worry about me. You *were* worried, weren't you? That's why all the fuss?"

She nodded, having heard him, but she wasn't that attuned to what he was saying. Her nose was twitching, assaulted by an offensive, sweet smell coming from his coat, almost like . . . perfume, cheap perfume at that. She leaned back, frowning, and caught sight of a thin yellow string on his shoulder—no, not a string, a blond hair. She picked it off and pulled, but it kept coming, until at least a twelve-inch length dangled from her fingers. She might have thought it was her own, even though it was so light in color, but it was brittle, not fine.

"I knew it!" she hissed, looking up at him with outraged fury in her eyes.

"Knew what? What's got into you now?"

"This!" She shoved the hair in his face. "It's no' mine, mon, and it certainly isna yours, is it now?"

Anthony scowled, swiping the hair from her fingers. "It's not what you think, Roslynn."

She stood back, crossing her arms over her chest. "Oh? I suppose it was some brazen wench who just happened to plop down on your lap uninvited, rubbing her cheap smell all over you before you could be stopping her?"

Good God, he groaned inwardly, *did she have to hit it right on the nose?* "As a matter of fact—"

"Hell's teeth, you canna even make up your own tales!" she shrieked.

This was so ridiculous, it was laughable, but Anthony didn't dare laugh when her expression at the moment boded murder. Very calmly, he said, "Actually, it was a barmaid. And I wouldn't have been in a position to have found her tumbling into my lap if I wasn't in a tavern, one of many, mind you, looking for your cousin."

"Aye, put the blame on me for your unfaithfulness. That's typical of a mon's arrogance, isna it? But I'll be telling you what I'm to blame for, and that's believing you last night! I'll no' be making *that* mistake again!''

''Roslynn—''

She jumped back when he reached for her, and before he could stop her, she slammed the door in his face. Anthony swore foully, his temper finally unleashed, but with nothing to vent it on now.

He turned around, facing the empty street, gritting his teeth. At least James had gone on in the carriage to White's to kill a few hours before his rendezvous with self-same barmaid. He didn't think he could have borne having his brother be a witness to this absurdity and watching him laugh his head off as he reminded Anthony about marital bliss.

Bloody everlasting hell. Kicked out of his own house! A fine topping for a day that had gone from bad to worse. If the *ton* ever got wind . . .

Anthony's head came up with a jolt. It was *his* bloody house. What the devil did she think she was doing, kicking him out of his own house?

He swung around and started to kick the door, he was so angry. He thought better of that at the last moment and tried the latch first. But finding it unlocked, he threw it open forcefully. The resounding bang was satisfying; however, it did nothing to appease his temper. Nor did the fact that he caught his wife by surprise, halfway up the stairs.

''Get back down here, Lady Malory. We haven't finished this discussion.''

He was amazed that she obeyed him immediately, coming stiffly down the stairs. But when she reached him, it was to give him a look of contempt.

''If you'll no' go away, then I will,'' she said, and she actually walked toward the still-open door.

Anthony caught her wrist and spun her around.

"The devil you will! You aren't leaving this house, and neither am I. We're married, remember? Married people live together, last I heard."

"You canna make me stay here!"

"Can't I?"

He could, and it infuriated Roslynn more that she had given him that right.

She jerked her hand away from him, rubbing the wrist that would be bruised come morning. "Very well, but I'll be taking another room for myself, and if you've anything to say about that, you can save it for another time."

She turned back toward the stairs, only to be brought around again with a hand to her shoulder. "I prefer right now, my dear," he said darkly. "You're condemning me out of hand."

"You've brought the evidence home wi' you, mon. It speaks for itself."

His eyes closed in exasperation for a moment. "Even if that were true, which it isn't, you're not allowing me to speak in my own defense. Unfair, by any means."

"Unfair?" she retorted, eyes frying him. "I'm only saving you the trouble, because no matter what you say, I'd no' believe it now."

Again she tried to turn away. Again he jerked her back. "Confound you, woman, I was looking for Cameron!"

"Maybe you were, but you made a wee detour too. So be it. I gave you leave."

He was ready to pull hairs at this point. "Then why are you raising bloody hell about it?"

"You lied to me! You tried to make me believe it'd be otherwise, and for that I'll no' forgive you!"

She turned away in a huff. His voice stopped her

this time, deliberately taunting. "Go ahead, and I'll turn you over my knee."

"You wouldna dare!"

His eyes had narrowed to mere slits. "At the moment, sweetheart, I assure you it would be a pleasure. Now, I'm going to tell you this only once. Whether you believe it or not, I frankly no longer care. The little wench who crawled all over me was just doing her job. She made the offer, I refused it. There was no more to it than that."

With icy control, Roslynn demanded haughtily, "Are you finished?"

After her repeated attempts to do so, it was Anthony who turned and walked away.

Chapter Twenty-six

Roslynn cried herself to sleep that night, the first time she had done so since she was a little girl. That Anthony didn't even try to disturb her in the new room she had moved to was a relief, and yet for some reason she cried the harder. She hated him, never wanted to see him again, but she was stuck with him.

If only she wasn't such a naive little fool. But she had let him convince her that they could have a normal marriage, and now she was paying for her gullibility, with resentment she couldn't seem to help feeling and with a bitterness that was wholly unfamiliar to her. For a few hours that morning she had been in heavenly bliss, which made coming back down to earth so much harder to bear. She wouldn't forgive him for that, for her lost chance at happiness.

Why couldn't he just leave things as they were? Why did he have to give her hope, then turn right around and dash it to bits?

Nettie, not having to be told what happened, since the whole household couldn't help but hear the loud argument, had wisely kept her mouth shut while helping Roslynn change rooms. The next morning, she had cold compresses ready to apply to swollen eyes, again without comment, bless her. And Roslynn's eyes were rather puffy. Chalk up another point against the cur. He was ruining her appearance.

But Nettie's herbal solution erased all evidence of the miserable night her mistress had spent. Too bad she didn't have a magic tonic for what ailed Roslynn inside. Yet when she came downstairs in a sunny yellow dress to counteract her mood, it was virtually impossible to tell that she was still a boiling pot of emotions, none of them good, which was fortunate, since she walked unawares into a parlor full of Malorys, by the looks of them, minus her husband, thank God.

So it had started. Gad, at what a time, when she didn't know if she could bear the sight of Anthony today. And she had no idea what sort of mood he would be in when he came down. He could very well give their troubles away, but she wasn't going to.

She formed a welcoming smile. Just because she wasn't able to get on well with her husband didn't mean she had to be at odds with the rest of the family.

James was the first to notice her entrance and rose immediately to make the introductions. "Good morning, dear girl. As you can see, the elders have arrived to look you over. My brothers Jason and Edward—the blushing bride."

Jason was scowling already, but at James' choice of words. Both men were big, blond, and green-eyed, with Edward the stockier of the two. Jason appeared an older version of James, serious, even to having that aura of ruthlessness about him. Edward was the exact opposite, as she was to learn, good-humored, easygoing, certainly jolly, but staid where business was concerned.

Both men rose, Edward to give Roslynn a hearty hug; Jason, more reserved, bringing her hand to his lips. Jeremy, who didn't need another introduction, simply winked at her. Thank goodness he and James hadn't been home last night to overhear that embarrassing scene in the hall.

"You can't know what a pleasure this is, my dear," Jason was saying, giving her a warm smile as he led her to the sofa to sit next to him. "I had despaired of Tony ever marrying."

"Didn't think the lad had it in him to settle down," Edward added jovially. "Delighted to be proved wrong, though. Simply delighted."

Roslynn didn't know what to say to that, under the circumstances, because Anthony was anything but ready to settle down. But they wanted to believe he was, obviously, so she wouldn't set the record straight on that score. However, she couldn't let them think this was some sort of love match either. It certainly wasn't that by any means.

She began to speak hesitantly. "There were reasons why we married that you should be aware of—"

"Already know, my dear," Edward interrupted. "Reggie's filled us in about your cousin. Doesn't matter, you know. If Tony wasn't ready, he wouldn't have taken the plunge."

"He did it to help me," Roslynn said, only to get three doubting-Thomas smiles, making her insist, "Well, he did."

"Rubbish," Jason replied. "Tony's not the sort to play hero, saving damsels and all that."

"Just the opposite." Edward chuckled.

James added his opinion. "One has only to look at you, dear girl, to know what motivated the lad. Can't say as I blame him in the least."

Jason intercepted the wolfish grin bestowed on Roslynn that had her cheeks blooming. "None of that, now." He scowled at James.

"Oh, give over, Jason. She became safe from me the moment she married."

"Since when did that ever stop you?" Jason demanded brusquely.

"True." James shrugged. "But I draw the line at seducing sisters-in-laws."

Roslynn had no way of knowing this was only bantering. But then she had no way of knowing that these brothers were happiest when they were arguing, even in jest.

"My lords, please," she intervened. "I'm sure James meant no offense."

"There, you see, old man," James said smugly to his brother. "She knew not to take me seriously. What's a look, anyway?"

"Usually an extension of one's true feelings," Jason retorted, still scowling.

"Ah, but never mine. I find it much more amusing not to give myself away so obviously—as you do, brother."

Edward laughed. "He's got you there, Jason. You do look rather fierce at the moment."

"Yes," James agreed, rubbing it in. "You look fierce enough to make the newest member of the family think *you're* serious."

Jason's brow smoothed out as he glanced at Roslynn. "I'm sorry, my dear. What must you think of—"

"That you're a tyrant, and she wouldn't be far off the mark," James couldn't resist saying, even if it did bring Jason's narrowed gaze back to him.

"Not at all," Roslynn intervened again. "I'm an only child myself, so it's . . . interesting, seeing how a large family interacts together. But tell me, who in the family is the referee?"

The question brought hearty laughter, more than she had hoped for. It transformed James, making him even more handsome, if that were possible. It softened the lines on Jason's face too, showing her he was still a devilishly good-looking man at forty-six and not nearly as intimidating as he had seemed. Edward, it just made more lovable. Gad, these Malorys were dangerous to a girl's equilibrium. And, heaven help her, she had married one.

"I told you she was a gem," James said to his brothers. "Has Tony met his match or hasn't he?"

"It would seem so," Edward agreed, wiping the tears of laughter from his eyes. "But I thought you said she was Scottish. I detect no brogue."

A quiet voice from the doorway answered before James could. "It comes with a temper, in moments least expected."

James couldn't let that one pass. "You know from experience, no doubt?"

"No doubt at all," Anthony replied, looking directly at his wife.

Roslynn's fingers clenched into fists, her reaction to seeing him there, oh, so casually leaning a shoulder against the doorframe, arms crossed, one knee bent to cross his feet at his ankles. How dared he? So he wanted to play with words, did he?

She gave Anthony a syrupy sweet smile as she took up the challenge. "Dinna fash yourself, mon. I only hold grudges when they're truly deserved."

James twisted the knife. "Well, then, you've nothing to worry about, Tony, have you?"

"When *does* your ship sail, brother?" was Anthony's retort, gaining a hoot of laughter from James.

The two older brothers and Jeremy came forward

then, offering congratulations and good-natured rib-
bings. Roslynn watched this happy scene, fuming.
So he was going to pretend nothing was wrong, was
he? Well, she could too, she supposed, as long as
his family was here, and as long as he kept his distance from her. But he didn't. He joined her on the
sofa, taking Jason's place, and put his arm around
her shoulder in a too-husbandly fashion.

"Pleasant night, sweetheart?"

"Go to the devil," she hissed under her breath,
but she was smiling as she said it.

Anthony chuckled, managing to keep from wincing when the effort nearly split his head open. He
had a royal hangover, thanks to his little wife's stubbornness last night. He would have preferred to simply remain in bed, but couldn't after Willis informed
him the elders had arrived. Bloody inconvenient. He
couldn't very well have it out with Roslynn with an
audience present.

What he should have done was finish it last night.
But, fool that he was, he had thought a night's sleep
would make her more receptive to reason, and so he
had gotten smashed to keep him from breaking her
door down. He should have broken the door down.
She was nursing her grudge anyway, so it couldn't
have made her any angrier. Bloody hell. He'd like to
shoot the man who ever said women were malleable
creatures.

For the moment, Anthony chose to ignore his wife,
but perversely, he kept his arm around her. "So,
Eddie, where's the rest of your brood?"

"They'll be along as soon as Charlotte can round
them all up. By the by, she wants to give you and
Roslynn a party, since we missed the wedding.

Nothing too big, mind you. Just family and friends.''

"Why not?'' Anthony agreed. ''Might as well spread some of our happiness around.''

He smiled to himself as he heard Roslynn choke.

Chapter Twenty-seven

"*I* came by yesterday, you know, but you had so many guests—"

"So you just left?" Roslynn stopped buttering her muffin to stare pointedly at Frances. "I wish you hadn't."

"I didn't want to intrude."

"Fran, it was just his family, come by to meet me and wish him well. You would have been welcome, believe me, especially by me. Can you imagine how alone I felt, meeting the whole Malory clan?"

Frances said nothing for a moment. She took a sip of tea, fooled with the napkin on her lap, played with the pastry on her plate that she hadn't touched. Roslynn watched her, holding her breath. She knew what was coming, what hadn't been said yet. She was dreading it, especially now, when she was so regretting her hasty marriage to Anthony. And this was the first she had seen Frances since that marriage. When she had stopped by unexpectedly this morning, just as Roslynn was sitting down to breakfast, she knew she would be eating a dose of censure along with the cook's tempting array of food.

She tried delaying the subject. "I hope you weren't too worried the other night." Hell's teeth, was it only four days ago that she had woken up in Geordie's clutches?

"Too worried?" Frances laughed bitterly. "You were taken from my own house. I was responsible!"

"That you weren't. Geordie was just too tricky for

us. But I hope you understand why I had to leave before you got back.''

"Yes, that I understand. You couldn't stay with me after he had discovered your whereabouts. But that note you sent me two days ago. *That* I'll never understand. How could you do it, Ros? Anthony Malory, of all men?''

Well, there it was, the question she had dreaded, the same one she had been asking herself. The answers just didn't hold up, at least not for her, but she owed them to Frances.

"The night Nettie and I left, I stopped by here to see Anthony.''

"You didn't!''

Roslynn flinched. "I know I shouldn't have, but I did. You see, he had offered to help me when we were at Silverley. Regina's husband didn't know my gentlemen that well after all, but Anthony did. He was supposed to clarify certain rumors about them—well, anyway, after that run-in with Geordie, I had run out of time. I came here for a name, nothing else, just a name of the one man out of the five who was most suitable for me to propose to.''

"All right. That's reasonable, I suppose, even if highly improper,'' Frances conceded. "You were frightened, upset. You couldn't have been thinking very clearly that night. So how could it have gone wrong? How did you end up with Sir Anthony instead?''

"He lied to me,'' Roslynn said simply, her eyes fixed on the uneaten muffin still in her hand. "He convinced me that all five of my gentlemen were so unsuitable, I couldn't possibly marry one of them. Oh, you should have heard some of the horrid stories he invented, the regret he managed in the telling. I never once suspected that he might be lying.''

''Then how do you know—''

Roslynn laughed shortly. ''He admitted it later, after we were married. Arrogantly confessed the whole thing.''

''The cad!''

''Yes, he is that.'' Roslynn sighed. ''But that's not the point. That night I was already desperate when I came here, and then to be told that I was more or less back to the starting point, well, I truly didn't know what to do.''

''So you asked him to marry you.'' Frances drew her own conclusion. ''Well, at least I understand now—or think I do. I suppose you felt you had no other choice.''

''That's not exactly how it happened,'' Roslynn admitted, though she decided then and there not to mention her seduction. Frances didn't need to know *everything.* ''Even then I didn't consider Anthony as a solution to my problem. Hell's teeth, I was ready to go home to Scotland and marry a crofter. It was Anthony who suggested I marry him instead.''

Frances' mouth dropped open. ''*He* did?'' She collected herself quickly from her surprise. ''Well, I naturally thought you would have . . . I mean, you did say before that you wouldn't be afraid to make the proposal, that it would probably be necessary since you had so little time for courting. And here you had run out of time, so I naturally assumed . . . He really did?''

''Yes, and I was just as surprised. In fact, I thought he was joking.''

''But he wasn't?''

''No, not at all. I refused, of course.''

Frances' mouth dropped open again. "You did?"

"Yes, and went on to Silverley." Frances didn't need to know this had happened the next morning. "But as you can see, I changed my mind. He was offering me a solution, and I decided to treat it as a business arrangement. I still haven't figured out why he did it, but there you have it, the whole story." Less the parts Roslynn couldn't bring herself to mention.

Frances sat back, herself again. "Well, I just hope you don't come to regret it. For your sake, I'll pray for a miracle, that Sir Anthony might somehow turn out to be another Nicholas Eden."

"Good God, bite your tongue, madam," Anthony said as he casually sauntered into the room. "I can barely tolerate the fellow."

Poor Frances turned beet red. Roslynn glared furiously at her husband. "Taken to eavesdropping, my lord?"

"Not at all." He smiled at her, belying the denial. "So the reinforcements have arrived, eh?"

He had Roslynn blushing now as he looked pointedly at Frances with that question. She was remembering that all day yesterday, every time he had tried to talk to her, she had moved off to speak with a member of his family, all of whom had stayed for dinner and much later, giving her excuses to avoid him the whole day. Now they still weren't alone, only this time the visitor was firmly in her camp. His use of the word "reinforcements" was apt, though Frances didn't know what he was referring to.

"You're on your way out?" Roslynn asked hopefully.

"Actually, I'm off to continue the hunt for your dear cousin."

"Oh? And another detour?" She jabbed for blood. "Then I'll see you—when I see you, I suppose."

Anthony braced his hands on the table across from her, leaning forward, his eyes dark with meaning as they locked with hers. "You will *see* me this evening, my dear. You may depend upon it." And then he straightened, his smile tight. "Good day, ladies. You may continue raking me over the coals now."

He turned on his heel and sauntered out as nonchalantly as he had entered, leaving Roslynn bristling and Frances uncomfortably aware that much more had just transpired than was said. But as quietly as he had left the room, he slammed out of the house.

Roslynn grimaced, hearing the noise. Frances raised a questioning brow. "He's displeased about something?"

"You could say that."

"So are you?"

"Frances, I really don't want to talk about it."

"That bad, eh? Well, all I can say is you agreed to this marriage, knowing what he was like. I don't imagine he'll be an easy man to live with, but you must make the best of it. Just don't expect too much."

That was laughable. She hadn't expected a thing, until Anthony had deluded her into thinking he could change. And not twenty-four hours' married and he proved he couldn't. She could have understood a month later, or even a week, but the very next day after he swore he wanted no one but her? The trouble was, she couldn't seem to break through the anger to get back to her original reconcilement to take him as he was.

Anthony's thoughts were simmering along the same lines as he threw himself into the waiting carriage outside. He had every right to be furious and he was, immeasurably so. A business arrangement! He'd like to know what the bloody hell he was to get out of this "business arrangement" as it stood now.

Stubborn, unreasonable, vexing woman. And illogical, for God's sake. If she'd just use some common sense, she'd see how absurd her accusations were. But no, she wouldn't even talk to him about it. Every time he had tried yesterday, she had bestowed her false smile on him and flitted away, using his own family as a barrier against him. And they loved her. And why not? She was charming, intelligent—except in some matters—and beautiful, and they looked on her as his salvation. More likely she was the devil's advocate, sent to drive him mad.

Well, he'd be doubly damned if he'd lose another night's sleep over the contrariness of his wife. She belonged in his bed, not nursing her foolish grudges across the hall. Tonight they'd talk, by God, and without interruption.

Now, how to word a message to James, to suggest he take himself and Jeremy off for the evening, without telling him why?

Chapter Twenty-eight

A while after Frances left, Jeremy came in with a stack of newspapers and a jaunty smile, telling Roslynn the notice would run for two weeks. She found it in each paper, the announcement of her marriage, but she had to admit that Anthony was right in this matter. There was no guarantee that Geordie would see it. So she couldn't help feeling grateful that, even though Anthony was annoyed with her, he was still making an effort to find Geordie to warn him off.

She might be safely married, but if Geordie didn't know it, then how safe was she really? He could at this very moment be working on a new scheme to snatch her and drag her to the altar. He knew where she was—at least he knew that her clothes had come to this address. And if he succeeded in abducting her again, and she had to be the one to tell him he was too late, well, there was no telling what he might do to her in his anger at being thwarted.

Because of that, she elected to stay close to home for a while. Any remodeling she was planning could be done by having the tradesmen come to her, rather than her going to them. And she did plan extensive redecorating of Anthony's house. Nor was she going to bother to tell him about it. And when he saw the damage to his purse, because she had changed her mind about paying for it herself and intended to use only his money, well, he might think twice

before getting in her bad graces again with more
lies.

A wee voice whispered that she was being wickedly
spiteful. Roslynn didn't listen to it. She was going to
spend Anthony's money as if he were made of it. She
might even insist he build her a new house, a mansion
in the country perhaps, but after she had redecorated
this one, of course. After all, the town house wasn't
that large. It didn't even have a ballroom. How was
she expected to entertain?

She could even pauperize the wretched man if she
were of a mind to. Yes, there was an idea worth considering. A picture of Anthony humbled and having
to come to her for an allowance was delightful indeed, and no more than he deserved for disillusioning
her.

But Roslynn didn't devote too much time to vengeful thoughts today, not with Anthony's implied threat
hanging over her head that there would be a confrontation between them tonight. She couldn't deny that
worried her no small amount. And her nervousness
increased during the afternoon, so much so that when
James informed her during dinner that he and Jeremy
were off to Vauxhall Gardens for the evening, she
almost asked to join them. Why tonight of all nights
did they both have to go out, never mind that this was
the norm rather than the exception? Even though Anthony wasn't home yet, she didn't doubt for a minute
that he would show up eventually.

But she didn't ask to intrude on the two Malorys
who were still bachelors. She wasn't that much of a
coward. At least that was what she told herself before
James and Jeremy left. Nevertheless, as soon as the
door closed behind the dashing pair, leaving her alone

with the servants, Anthony's servants—Nettie didn't count—she found she was a coward after all.

It was a ridiculously early hour to be retiring for the night, but retreat to her bedroom she did, and with all haste. Dobson was told to inform Anthony when he finally came in that she wasn't feeling well and wasn't to be disturbed, for any reason. Whether that would put him off remained to be seen.

In case it didn't, however, she wasn't taking any chances. She donned her most unappealing nightgown, a heavy cotton garment more suitable for a cold Scottish winter in the Highlands, stuck her hair under an ugly nightcap that she borrowed from Nettie, never having liked the use of them herself, and finished her ensemble with a bulky robe that she usually wore only after her bath.

She also considered putting one of Nettie's thick night creams on her face, but that would be doing it up a bit too much. A glance in the mirror showed her that she looked appalling as it was. Anything more would just be obvious arsenal that Anthony might find funny instead of discouraging.

Of course, now that she was so bundled up, she was too warm for bedcovers. But that was just as well. Curled up with a book would be a more natural touch, rather than pretending sleep, which Anthony would likely doubt if he arrived while it was still so early.

No, she had to appear normally indisposed, as if she weren't trying to deliberately avoid him. He would then have to give her the benefit of the doubt and leave her alone. That was, if he didn't heed Dobson's message. That was, if he came home at all.

Hell's teeth, none of this would be necessary if Dobson had been able to find the cursed key to the door yesterday when she had asked for it. But then, might not locking Anthony out be taken as a challenge by someone like him? It would certainly be a clear statement that she didn't want to talk to him, not now, not any time soon. No, this way was better. Let him come, if he must, but she would make him feel guilty as hell for disturbing her when she was feeling, and looking, so poorly.

The book she had on hand was a boring collection of sonnets, gushy in sentimentality, left behind by the previous occupant of the room, whoever that had been. But she was stuck with it. It was too late to risk going down to Anthony's study, where a small library was kept. It would be just her luck that he would walk in and catch her out of bed, ruining the effect she was striving for.

She gave up reading the silly book, however. At any other time she might have been enthralled, for love sonnets, which she surmised most of them were as she flipped through the pages, usually sparked a tender chord in her. But she was in no frame of mind to be romantic tonight. Anything but. She let her mind wander instead, wondering if she ought to allow her malady to last through tomorrow. She could use the time alone to think, to get in control of her emotions again.

Fortunately, Roslynn was still holding the book in front of her and appeared to be reading, because she had no warning that Anthony had returned. The door to her room simply opened and he was there. Unfortunately, he wasn't so easily fooled.

"Very amusing, my dear." His tone was dry, his expression inscrutable. "Did it take all day to think this up, or were you inspired when the Hawke and his pup deserted you?"

Since she had no idea what he was talking about in reference to birds and dogs, she ignored the question altogether. "I asked not to be disturbed."

"I know you did, sweetheart." He shut the door, his smile unnerving. "But a husband is allowed to disturb his wife—anytime, anywhere, any way he wants to."

He was putting another meaning on the word, one that had her cheeks flaming, which he was quick to note. "Ah, it must be a fever," he continued, coming slowly toward the bed. "And no wonder, with that mountain of nightclothes you're wearing. Or is it a cold? No, you haven't bothered to redden your nose with a little pinching. A headache, then, of course. You don't need to produce visible symptoms to claim one, do you?"

His baiting enraged her beyond good sense. "Beast! If I did have one, you wouldn't care, would you?"

"Oh, I don't know." He sat down on the bed, fingering the tie of her robe. His smile was more humorous now that she had given up her ruse. "Do you have one?"

"Yes!"

"Liar."

"I'm learning from a master."

He laughed. "Very good, my dear. I was wondering how I was going to introduce the subject, but you've done it for me."

"What subject?"

"What indeed. Are we going to play dumb now?"

"*We* aren't going to play anything. *You're* going to leave this room."

Of course he didn't. That would have been too much to hope for. He sat back, leaning on one elbow, infuriating her with his quiet scrutiny.

Suddenly he leaned forward and snatched her nightcap away. "That's better." He twirled the cap on his finger as he gazed at the red-gold locks scattered about her shoulders. "You know how I love your hair. I suppose you hid it just to annoy me?"

"You flatter yourself."

"Maybe," he said softly. "And maybe I've known enough women to know how their minds work when they turn vindictive for some supposed wrong. Cold food, cold shoulders, and cold beds. Well, you've served me up all but the food, but I suppose that will come."

She threw the book at him. He dodged it handily.

"If you want to get violent, sweetheart, you've certainly caught me in the right mood for it. In fact, if I had found Cameron today, I think I'd have shot the bastard first and asked questions later. So don't press your luck."

He said it too quietly for her to take him seriously. She was too caught up in her own enraged passions to realize that she'd never seen Anthony like this. He was calm. He was in control. He was furious. She just didn't know it.

"Will you just get out?" she demanded shrilly. "I'm no' ready to talk to you yet, mon!"

"So I see." He threw her nightcap across the room. "But I don't particularly care whether you're ready or not, my dear."

She gasped when he reached for her. Her hands flew up to hold him back. Her action worked only because he allowed it—for the moment.

"Recall the first condition of this marriage, Roslynn. I'm to get you with child, at your own insistence. I agreed to do just that."

"You also agreed to the second condition, and

you've done that too. It's the lying that came after that has changed things, mon.''

She didn't doubt that he was angry now. It was there in the hard glint of his eyes, the clenched jaw. He was a different man, a frightening man—a fascinating man. He stirred something in her that was primitive, unrecognizable. Shouting she could have dealt with. But this? She didn't know what he would do, what he was capable of, but a part of her wanted to find out.

But Anthony was angry, not crazy. And that spark of desire that flashed in her eyes as she pushed away from him mollified him to a degree. She still wanted him. Even in her fury, she still wanted him. Assured of that, he found he could wait until she got over her pique. It wouldn't be a pleasant wait, but he wasn't about to have her crying rape come morning, putting him right back where he started, only with another grudge for her to hold against him.

''You really should have pinched your nose, my dear. I might have believed that.''

Roslynn blinked, doubting her ears. ''Oh!''

She shoved against him with all her might. He obliged her by leaving the bed. But his smile was tight as he stared down at her.

''I've been patient, but I give you fair warning. A man's patience is a fickle thing. It shouldn't be tested too often, especially when he's got nothing to apologize for and nothing to feel guilty about—yet.''

''Hah!''

Anthony ignored that as he walked to the door. ''It might help if you told me how long you intend to punish me.''

''I'm not punishing you,'' she insisted stonily.

''Aren't you, sweetheart?'' He turned to chill her

with a parting shot. "Well, just remember that two can play this game."

What he might have meant by that bothered Roslynn for the rest of the night.

Chapter Twenty-nine

A jab. Another jab. A left hook, followed by a right cross. The man was down, out cold, and Anthony stood back, swearing because it was over too quickly.

Knighton tossed a towel in his face, swearing too as he jumped into the ring to examine Anthony's partner. "Jesus, Malory! No wonder Billy tried to beg off today after he got one look at you. I always say the ring's a nice place to work out frustrations, but not for you."

"Shut up, Knighton," Anthony snapped as he tore off his gloves.

"The hell I will," the older man shot back angrily. "I'd like to know where I'm going to find another bloke stupid enough to step into the ring with you. But I'll tell you this. I ain't even going to bother looking until you've bedded the wench and got it out of your system. Stay out of my ring until you do."

Anthony had laid men flat for less, but Knighton was a friend. He nearly laid him flat anyway for his bloody insight in calling it too close to the mark. He stood there, the urge overpowering. It was James' voice, breaking into the haze of his rage, that checked him.

"Having trouble finding partners again, Tony?"

"Not if you're still willing to oblige me."

"Do I look like a fool?" James glanced down at his apparel in mock surprise. "And here I thought I was done up quite smartly today."

Anthony laughed, feeling some of his tension drain

253

away. "As if you didn't think you could make short work of me."

"Well, of course I could. No doubt a-tall. Just don't want to."

Anthony snorted, started to remind James of the going-over Montieth had given him, even if James did come out the winner, but changed his mind. No point in putting it to the test when he had no quarrel with his brother.

"I get the impression you're following me, old man. Any particular reason?"

"As a matter of fact, I've a bone to pick—outside of the ring, of course."

Anthony jumped down, reaching for his coat. "Mind if we get out of here first?"

"Come on. I'll buy you a drink."

"Make it more than one and you're on."

The afternoon atmosphere in White's was quiet, soothing, a place to relax, read the dailies, conduct business, discuss politics, gossip, or get drunk, as Anthony contemplated doing, all without the disruptive presence of women, who were not allowed. The lunch crowd was gone, leaving only the regulars, who lived more at the club than at home. The dinner crowd and serious gamblers had yet to arrive, though there were a few games of whist in progress.

"Who kept up my membership all these years?" James asked as they took seats away from the bow window before which the fashionable set would soon be gathering.

"You mean you're still a member? And here I thought you were getting in as my guest."

"Very amusing, dear boy. But I know bloody well Jason and Eddie boy wouldn't have bothered."

Anthony frowned at being cornered. "So I'm a

sentimental ass. It's only a few guineas a year, for God's sake. I just didn't want to see your name stricken from the list.''

"Or you were certain I'd come back into the fold eventually?''

Anthony shrugged. "There was that, not to mention a bloody long waiting list to get in. Didn't want to see you deserting us for Brook's.''

"Malory!'' Anthony was hailed and descended upon by a red-cheeked fellow of his acquaintance. "Stopped by your house yesterday, but Dobson said you were out. Wanted to clear up a little wager I have with Hilary. She saw this notice in the paper. You'll never believe it, Malory. It said you'd married. 'Course I knew it couldn't be you. Had to be some other chap, same name. I'm right, aren't I? Tell me it's a bloody coincidence.''

Anthony's fingers tightened around his glass, but other than that, there was no inkling that he was bothered by the question. "It's a bloody coincidence,'' he replied.

"I knew it!'' the fellow crowed. "Wait till I tell Hilary. The easiest five pounds I've won from her in a long time.''

"Was that wise?'' James asked as soon as red-cheeks drifted away. "Imagine the disagreements it's going to cause when he claims to have it from your own lips that you're not married. There'll be fights with those who know better.''

"What the hell do I care?'' Anthony snarled. "When I feel like I'm married, I'll admit I'm married.''

James sat back, a small smile playing about his lips. "So the 'bemoanment' has begun, has it?''

"Oh, shut up.'' Anthony downed his drink and

left to get another. He came back with a bottle. "I thought you had a bone to pick with me. Pick away. It seems to be becoming a habit."

James let the more interesting discovery pass for the moment. "Very well. Jeremy tells me Vauxhall was your idea, not his. If you'd wanted to be rid of us for the evening, why go through the lad?"

"Didn't you enjoy yourselves?"

"That's beside the point. I don't like being manipulated, Tony."

"But that's precisely why I sent the message to the lad." Anthony grinned. "You've admitted how hard it is for you to deny him anything, now that you've become such a doting parent."

"Bloody hell. You could have just asked me. Am I so insensitive that I can't appreciate that you might want to spend an evening alone with your new wife?"

"Come off it, James. You're about as sensitive as a dead tree. If I had asked you to leave last night, you'd have stayed just to see why I wanted you gone."

"Would I?" James' smile came grudgingly. "Yes, I suppose I would. I'd have envisioned you and the little Scot running about the house bare-ass naked, and you'd never have been able to get rid of me. Wouldn't have missed that for the world. So what was it, actually, that you wanted privacy for?"

Anthony poured another drink. "It doesn't matter now. The evening didn't end as I had hoped."

"So there *is* trouble in paradise?"

Anthony slammed the bottle down on the small table next to his chair, exploding. "You wouldn't believe what she's accused me of! Bedding that little twit of a barmaid we met the other night!"

"Careful, lad. I've fond memories of Margie."

"Then you did meet her later?"

"Did you doubt I would, a pretty piece like that? Though the little vixen in breeches would have done . . . never mind." James poured himself another drink, disturbed by the regret he felt at losing that one. "Why didn't you just tell your lady I'd marked the girl for myself? I mean, we've shared women before, but there's something unsavory about sharing in the same day, don't you think?"

"True, but my dear wife wouldn't put any unsavory deed beyond my capabilities. And I resent being put in a position of having to explain that I've done nothing wrong. I shouldn't have to do that. A little trust wouldn't be amiss."

James sighed. "Tony, lad, you've a lot to learn about new brides."

"You've had one, have you, which makes you an expert?" Anthony sneered.

"Of course not," James retorted. "But common sense would tell you it's got to be a very delicate time for a woman. She's feeling her way, adjusting. She's devilish insecure, nervous. Trust? Hah! First impressions are more likely to be the lasting ones. Stands to reason, don't it?"

"It stands to reason you don't know what the deuce you're talking about. When's the last time you even bumped elbows with a lady of quality? Captain Hawke's tastes lean toward a different sort entirely."

"Not *entirely*, lad. Leading a band of brigands does have its drawbacks, mainly in the lower class of establishments one is limited to frequenting. And acquired habits are hard to break. But my tastes, as you put it, are no different from yours. Duchess or whore, as long as she's comely and willing, she'll do. And it hasn't been *that* many years that I can't remember the idiosyncrasies of the duchess. Besides, they're all the same in one respect, dear boy. Jealousy turns them into shrews.''

''Jealousy?'' Anthony said blankly.

''Well, good God, man, isn't that the problem?''

''I hadn't thought . . . well, now that you mention it, that could be why she's so unreasonable. She's so bloody angry, she won't even talk about it.''

''So Knighton was right.'' James' chuckle turned into an outright laugh. ''Where's your finesse gone, dear boy? You've had enough practice in these matters to know how to get around—''

''Look who's talking,'' Anthony cut in irritably. ''The same man who got his shin kicked the other night. Where was the Hawke's finesse—''

''Blister it, Tony,'' James growled. ''If you keep bandying that name about, I'm going to end up with a rope around my neck yet. Hawke's dead. Kindly remember that.''

Anthony's mood improved, now that his brother's had taken a turn for the worse. ''Relax, old man. These chaps wouldn't know a hawk from a Hawke. But point taken. Since you've gone to the trouble of killing him off, we may as well let him rest in peace. But you never said, you know. What happened to the rest of your brigands?''

''Some went their own way. Some formed an attachment for the *Maiden Anne,* even though she's changed her colors. They're landlocked only till we sail.''

''And when, pray tell, will that be?''

''Relax, old man.'' James tossed the phrase back at him. ''I'm having too much fun watching you make a mess of your life to leave just yet.''

Chapter Thirty

*I*t was five o'clock in the afternoon when George Amherst assisted the two Malory brothers out of the carriage in front of the brownstone-faced house on Piccadilly, and they did need assistance. George was smiling and had been ever since he came upon the two in White's and smoothed over the disturbance they'd caused. He couldn't help it. He'd never seen Anthony so foxed he didn't know if he was coming or going. And James, well, it was utterly comical to see this intimidating Malory laughing his head off over Anthony's condition when his own was anything but sober.

"She's not going to like this," James was saying as he hooked an arm around Anthony's shoulders, nearly unbalancing them both.

"Who?" Anthony demanded belligerently.

"Your wife."

"Wife?"

George grabbed Anthony as the brothers began to sway and steered them to the door. "Splendid!" He chuckled. "You nearly get yourself kicked out of White's for decking Billings when all he did was offer felicitations on your marriage, and here you can't remember you've got a wife."

George was still getting used to the idea himself. He had been rendered speechless when Anthony had come by his house yesterday morning to tell him personally, before he read about it in the papers.

"One laugh, George . . . one little chuckle . . .

and I'll rearrange your nose for you," Anthony had told him with appalling sincerity. "I was out of my mind. That's the only excuse for it. So no congratulations, if you please. Condolences are more in order."

Then he had refused to say another word about it, not who she was or why he'd married her, nor a hint about why he was already regretting it. But George wasn't so sure he was actually regretting it, not when Anthony had dragged him off on a search for this cousin of hers who was some sort of danger to her. The desire to protect her was obvious. The desire not to talk about her was equally as obvious. Most obvious was Anthony's anger, simmering just below the surface all day. George was bloody well relieved they hadn't found the chap Anthony was looking for. He would have hated to see the result if they had.

But a chance remark from James as George was hustling them out of White's put some perspective on the thing. "You've just found a temper to match your own, Tony. Can't say as it's a bad thing in a wife. It'll keep you on your toes, if nothing else." And he had laughed, even when Anthony snarled back, "When you get one of your own, brother, I hope she's as sweet as that little viper who kicked you instead of thanking you for your help the other night."

The door opened just as George was about to pound on it. A wooden-faced Dobson stood there, but the butler's expression relaxed into aggrieved surprise as James abandoned Anthony for a steadier handhold—Dobson.

"Where's Willis, dear fellow? I'm going to need help with my boots, I think."

That wasn't all he would need help with, George thought, grinning, as the skinny Dobson, saying nothing, tried to get the much larger man to the stairs. George was having trouble holding Anthony up as well.

"You'd better call some footmen, Dobson," George suggested.

"I'm afraid," Dobson puffed without looking back, "they're on errands for the mistress, my lord."

"Bloody hell." Anthony perked up, hearing that. "What's she doing dispatching—"

George poked him in the ribs to shut him up. The lady in question had come out of the parlor and stood with hands on hips and an unpleasant gleam in her hazel eyes, which moved over them all. George swallowed hard. *This* was Anthony's wife? Gad, she was breathtaking—and furious.

"Beg pardon, Lady Malory," George offered hesitantly. "I found these two rather deep in their cups. Thought it prudent to get them home to sleep it off."

"And who are you, sir?" Roslynn asked stonily.

George didn't get a chance to answer. Anthony, fixing his gaze on his wife, sneered, "Oh, come now, my dear, you must know old George. He's the very chap responsible for your distrust of the male gender."

George flushed hotly as her eyes narrowed with a distinct golden glow on him. "Blister it, Malory," he hissed, throwing Anthony's arm off his shoulder. "I'll leave you to the tender mercies of your wife. No more than you deserve after that crack." Not that he understood it, but that was no way to introduce one's best friend to one's wife.

To Roslynn, George nodded. "Another time, Lady Malory, hopefully under better circumstances." And he departed angrily, not even bothering to close the door.

Anthony stared after him, bemused and unsuccessfully trying to keep his balance in the middle of the hall. "Was it something I said, George?"

James laughed so hard at that, he and Dobson fell back two steps on the stairs. "You're amazing, Tony. Either you don't remember at all, or you remember more than you should."

Anthony rounded about to stare at James, halfway up the stairs now. His "What the deuce does that mean?" got only another laugh.

When it looked as if Anthony was going to fall flat on his face, Roslynn rushed forward, dragging his arm about her neck, and putting her own around his waist. "I canna believe you've done this, mon," she gritted out, maneuvering him carefully across the hall. "Do you ken what time of day it is, to be coming home like this?"

"Certainly," he replied indignantly. "It's—it's . . . well, whatever time it is, where else would I come home to, except to my own home?"

He tripped on the bottom step, pulling Roslynn down with him to sprawl at the foot of the stairs. "Hell's teeth! I ought to leave you here!"

Anthony misunderstood in his befuddled state. His arm whipped around her, holding her so tight against his chest she couldn't breathe. "You're not leaving me, Roslynn. I won't allow it."

She stared at him incredulously. "You . . . oh, God, save me from drunks and imbeciles," she said in exasperation, pushing away from him. "Come on, you foolish man. Get up."

Somehow, she got him upstairs and into his bedroom. When Dobson appeared at the door a moment later, she waved him away, why, she wasn't sure. She could have used his assistance. But it was a unique

situation, having Anthony helpless and unable to do
for himself. She was rather enjoying it, now that the
first irritation had passed. That she was likely the
cause of his condition was satisfying too. Or was she?

"Do you mind telling me why you've come home
drunk in the middle of the day?" she asked as she
straddled his leg to remove the first boot.

"Drunk? Good God, woman, that's a disgusting
word. Gentlemen do not get drunk."

"Oh? Then what do they get?"

He shoved against her backside with his other foot
until the boot popped off. "The word is . . . it's . . .
what the deuce is it?"

"Drunk," she repeated smugly.

He grunted, and when she came for the second
boot, his shove was a bit harder, sending her nearly
toppling when the boot came off in her hands. She
swung around, eyes narrowed, only to find him grinning innocently at her.

She threw the boot down, coming back to the bed
to tackle his coat. "You didn't answer my question,
Anthony."

"What question was that?"

"Why are you in this disgusting condition?"

He didn't take offense this time. "Come now, my
dear. Why else would a man tip one too many? Either
he's lost his wealth, a relative's died, or his bed's
empty."

It was her turn to look deliberately innocent. "Did
someone die?"

He placed his hands on her hips, pulling her a touch
closer between his legs. He was smiling, but there
was nothing humorous about it. "Play with fire,
sweetheart, and you'll get burned," he warned
thickly.

Roslynn yanked hard on his cravat before she pushed him back on the bed. "Sleep it off, *sweetheart.*" And she turned on her heel.

"You're a cruel woman, Roslynn Malory," he called after her.

She closed the door with a decisive bang.

Chapter Thirty-one

Anthony woke with a splitting head and a curse on his lips. He sat up to light the lamp by his bed, cursing again. The clock on the mantel said a few minutes after two. It was dark outside his window, so that told him which two o'clock it was. He cursed again, realizing he was wide awake now in the middle of the night, with his head coming off and too damn many hours till dawn.

What the hell had possessed him? Ah, well, he knew what possessed him, but he shouldn't have let it. He vaguely remembered old George bringing them home and something about his having belted Billings—bloody hell. Wished he hadn't done that. Billings was a good sort. He'd have to apologize, probably more than once. Hadn't George left angry? Anthony couldn't quite remember.

Uncomfortable, he glanced down at himself and grimaced. Mean-tempered wife. She could at least have undressed him and tucked him in proper, since it was her fault he'd got foxed to begin with. And hadn't she got snippy there, rubbing it in? He couldn't remember that clearly either.

Anthony leaned forward, gently massaging his temples. Well, he had his options, even at this hour. He could try to get back to sleep, which was doubtful. He'd slept more than his customary hours already. He could change and go back to White's for some whist—that is, if he hadn't behaved too abominably earlier and they'd let him in. Or he could be as mean-tempered as his wife and wake her up to see what might come of it. No, he felt too bloody rotten to want to do anything about it if she did prove amenable suddenly.

He laughed, which made him grimace. Best to just work on getting rid of this hangover before morning. A bath would be nice, but he'd have to wait for a decent hour to rouse the servants. Some food, then.

Slowly, because each step reverberated through his head, Anthony left his room. He stopped just down the hall, seeing the light under his brother's door. He knocked once but entered without waiting for permission, to find James sitting naked on the edge of his bed, holding his head in his hands. Anthony almost laughed but caught himself in time. It hurt too much to indulge.

James didn't glance up to see who had intruded. Softly, ominously, he grated out, "Not above a whisper if you value your life."

"Got a little man hammering in your head too, old man?"

James raised his head slowly. His scowl was murderous. "A dozen at least, and I owe every bloody one to you, you miserable——"

"The devil you do. You're the one who offered to buy me a drink, so if anyone has a right to complain——"

"One drink, not several bottles, you ass!"

They both winced at the raised tone. "Well, I suppose you have me there."

"Good of you to admit it," James snorted as he massaged his temples again.

Anthony's lips began to twitch. It was ludicrous, the punishment they put their bodies through, though James' body didn't look any the worse for wear. Anthony had been surprised for a moment on first entering, not having seen his brother naked since the time he had burst into that countess' bedroom, he couldn't even remember her name now, to warn James that her husband was on his way upstairs. James had changed since that night more than ten years ago. He was broader, more solid. In fact, he fairly bulged with thick muscles running across his chest and arms, down his legs. Must be from climbing all that rigging in ten years of pirating.

"You know, James, you're an incredible brute specimen."

James shook his head at that sudden remark, looking down at himself, then back at Anthony. He finally grinned at his brother's surprise. "The ladies don't seem to mind."

"No, I don't imagine they do." Anthony chuckled. "Care for a few hands at cards? I can't get back to sleep to save my soul."

"As long as you don't break out the brandy."

"God, no! I had coffee in mind, and I seem to recall we missed our dinner."

"Give me a few minutes and I'll meet you in the kitchen."

When Roslynn sat down to breakfast, she was still bleary-eyed, having spent another restless, sleepless night. This time it was her own fault. She felt rather guilty about her treatment of Anthony yesterday afternoon. She could have at least undressed him and made him more comfortable instead of leaving him as she had, not even bothering to see he got under the covers. After all, he was her husband. She was familiar with his body. Nothing to be embarrassed about.

Half a dozen times she had nearly gone up to rectify the matter but changed her mind, afraid he might wake and misconstrue her concern. And after she had gone to bed, well, she wasn't about to enter his bedroom in her nightclothes. *That* would certainly be misconstrued.

It bothered her that she felt guilty at all. She wasn't sympathetic to his plight. If he wanted to get drunk and blame it on her, well, that was his problem. And if he suffered for it this morning with a gruesome hangover, that was also too bad. One had to pay for excesses, didn't one? So why had she lost half a night's sleep thinking about him sprawled helpless on his bed?

"If the food's so bad that you must scowl at it, perhaps I'll eat at my club this morning."

Roslynn glanced up, Anthony's sudden appearance surprising her enough that she replied simply, "There's nothing wrong with the food."

"Splendid!" he said cheerfully. "Then you won't mind if I join you?"

He didn't wait for her to answer, but moved to the sideboard and began piling a mountain of food on his plate. Roslynn stared at his tall frame, immaculately encased in a coat of dark brown superfine, buckskin breeches, and gleaming Hessians. He had no right to look so magnificent, to be so chipper this morning. He should be moaning and groaning and damning his folly.

"You slept late," Roslynn said tersely, stabbing a plump sausage on her plate.

"I've just come back from my morning ride, actually." He took the seat opposite her, his brows raised slightly in inquiry. "Did you only just rise yourself, my dear?"

It was a good thing the sausage hadn't entered her mouth yet, or she would have choked on that seemingly innocent question. How dared he deny her the satisfaction of taking him to task for yesterday's disgraceful behavior? And that was exactly what he was doing, sitting there looking as if he had just had the most wonderful night's sleep of his life.

Anthony didn't expect an answer to his last question, nor did he get one. With an amused glimmer in his cobalt eyes, he watched Roslynn attack her food, determined to ignore him. Perversely, he wouldn't let her.

"I noticed a new rug in the hall."

She didn't spare him a glance, even though it was an insult to call the expensive piece woven to resemble the figured Aubusson tapestry a rug. "Strange you didn't notice it yesterday."

Bravo, sweetheart. He smiled to himself. She was going to get her licks in one way or another.

"And a new Gainsborough too," he went on conversationally, his eyes briefly touching the magnificent painting that now dominated the wall to his left.

"The new rosewood china cabinet and dining table should arrive today."

She still had her eyes fastened on her plate, but Anthony didn't miss the sudden change in her. No longer was she sitting there seething with suppressed anger. Her smug satisfaction was palpable.

Anthony nearly laughed aloud. She was so transparent, his sweet wife. Considering her present antipathy toward him and the subject they were discussing, it wasn't hard to figure out what she was up to. It was an old trick, a wife making her husband pay for her displeasure through his pocketbook. And from various remarks Roslynn had made in the past, he knew she didn't think his pocketbook could bear too much displeasure.

"So you're doing a little redecorating, are you?"

A barely perceptible shrug, but a too-sweet tone. "I knew you wouldn't mind."

"Not at all, my dear. I meant to suggest it myself."

Her head snapped up at those words, but she was quick to reply. "Good, because I've only just begun. And you will be glad to know it isn't going to cost as much as I thought when I first toured the house. Why, I've spent only four thousand pounds so far."

"That's nice."

Roslynn gaped at him, disbelieving her ears. His blatantly bored response was the last thing she had expected. Was it possible he thought she was spending her own money? Well, the wretch would find out differently when the bills started coming in.

She stood up, throwing her napkin down on the table, too chagrined with his reaction, or lack of it, to remain in his company. But she couldn't make the dramatic exit she would have liked. After yesterday, it was imperative that she insist there not be a repeat performance today when she was expecting company.

"Frances is coming for dinner this evening. If you should happen to change your habit of returning late and show up to join us, kindly do so soberly."

It was all Anthony could do to keep his lips from twitching. "Bringing in reinforcements again, my dear?"

"I resent that," she said with icy hauteur before she stalked away, only to whip around at the door, glowering at him. "And for your information, my lord, I don't distrust all men, as you so boorishly pointed out yesterday while introducing me to your friend—only rakes and bounders!"

Chapter Thirty-two

"*T*hat be 'im, m'lord."

Geordie Cameron turned to the short, bewhiskered man next to him and could have crowned him. "Which one, ye idiot? There are two of them!"

Wilbert Stow didn't blink an eye at the Scot's abrasive tone. He was used to it by now, used to his impatience, his short temper, his arrogance. If Cameron didn't pay so well, he'd tell him where he could stuff this job. Probably slice his gullet too, just for good measure. But he was paying well, thirty English pounds, a fortune to Wilbert Stow. So he held his tongue as always, letting the insults pass over him.

"The dark one," Wilbert clarified, keeping his tone servile. " 'E's the one what owns the 'ouse. Sir Anthony Malory be 'is name."

Geordie trained a spyglass across the street, bringing Malory's features into sharp relief as he turned at the door to say something to the blond chap with him. So this was the Englishman who had been combing the slums for Geordie these past few days, the one who was hiding Roslynn? Oh, Geordie knew she was in there, even if she hadn't shown her face outside the door since he had ordered Wilbert and his brother, Thomas, to keep a constant watch on the house. She had to be in there. This was where her clothes had been sent. And this was where that Grenfell woman had come twice now to visit.

Roslynn thought she was so smart, secreting herself inside that house and not coming out. But it was easier here, keeping watch, what with Green Park just across the street. Plenty of trees for concealment, not like having to sit in a carriage that might draw suspicion, as had been the case on South Audley Street. She couldn't make a move without Wilbert or Thomas knowing it, and they kept an empty coach up the street just waiting to follow her in. It was just a matter of time.

But in the meantime, he would take care of the English fop who was hiding her and who had twice forced Geordie to change location in the last five days because of his infernal snooping. Now that he knew what the dandy looked like, it would be an easy task to settle.

Geordie lowered the spyglass, smiling to himself. *Soon, lass. Soon I'll make ye pay for all this trouble. Ye'll be wishing ye hadna turned against me like yer stupid mother and the auld mon did, may they both be rotting in hell now.*

"Would you care for another sherry, Frances?"

Frances looked at her glass, still nearly full, then back at Roslynn, who was already refilling her glass with the amber liquid. "Will you relax, Ros. If he hasn't shown up by now, it's rather doubtful that he will, don't you think?"

Roslynn glanced over her shoulder at her friend, but she couldn't quite manage the smile she tried for. "I've come to the conclusion that Anthony shows up when least expected, just to keep me nervous."

"*Are* you nervous?"

Roslynn gave a little half laugh, half groan, and took a large swallow of her second sherry before returning to join Frances on the new Adams sofa. "I shouldn't be, should I? After all, he wouldn't do anything outrageous with you here, and I did warn him you were coming.''

"But?''

Roslynn finally did smile, though it was more a grimace. "He amazes me, Fran, with his many different moods. I never know which one to expect."

"There's nothing unusual in that, m'dear. We have our moods too, don't we? Now, stop fretting. Tell me what he thought of this new room instead."

Roslynn's deep chuckle was infectious. "He hasn't seen it yet.''

Frances' eyes widened. "You mean he didn't approve your choices first? But these pieces are so—so—''

"Delicate and feminine?''

Frances gasped at the twinkle in Roslynn's hazel eyes. "Good God, you did it on purpose! You're hoping he'll hate it, aren't you?''

Roslynn glanced about the once-masculine room that had been drastically transformed with the lovely satinwood furnishings. Now it looked the way a parlor should look, for a parlor was really a woman's domain. Adams might be known for his excessively refined style in delicacy of structure and ornament, but she liked the carved and gilded framework on the two sofas and chairs, and especially the satin brocade upholstery of silver flowers on an olive-green background. The colors weren't really feminine. She had compromised there. But the ornamentation was. Then there was the new wall papering that she hadn't made a decision on yet . . .

"I doubt Anthony will hate it, Frances, and if he does, it's unlikely he would say so. He's like that.'' Here she shrugged. "But of course, if he does, I'll just get rid of these pieces and buy something else.''

Frances frowned. "I think you're too used to spending money without thought to price. You're forgetting your husband isn't quite as rich as you are."

"No, that's the one thing I'm not forgetting."

At that bald statement, Frances sighed. "So that's it. Well, I hope you know what you're doing. Men can have funny reactions where money is concerned, you know. Some can lose twenty thousand pounds and not care. Others would go out and kill themselves for such a loss."

"Don't worry, Frances. Anthony is bound to fall into the not caring category. Now, can I make you another drink before dinner?"

Frances looked at her glass, still half full, then at Roslynn's, empty again. She shook her head, but not in answer to the question. "Go ahead and make light of it, Ros, but you can't tell me you're not anxious over his reaction. Was he very . . . unpleasant when you had this argument you don't want to talk about?"

"It wasn't an argument," Roslynn replied stiffly. "And he's been unpleasant since I married him."

"You weren't exactly gushing over with charm yourself the last time I saw you two together. I would guess that his moods are directly related to yours, m'dear."

Roslynn made a face at this sage observation. "Since he's obviously not going to join us for dinner, and his brother and nephew are out for the evening, it's just the two of us. Surely we can find a more pleasant topic to discuss."

Frances gave in and grinned. "Surely we can if we try hard enough."

Roslynn grinned too, feeling some of her tension drain away. Frances was good for her, even if some of the advice she offered Roslynn didn't want to hear.

She set her glass down and stood up. "Come on. Another drink will spoil the excellent fair cook has prepared, and Dobson has only been waiting for us to adjourn to the dining room to commence serving. And wait until you see the new table that was delivered this afternoon. It is sheer elegance, quite suitable to anyone's taste."

"And no doubt devilish expensive?"

Roslynn chuckled. "That too."

They linked arms and left the parlor to cross over to the small dining room, which had previously been no more than a breakfast room, since Anthony had rarely dined at home before he married and still didn't, for that matter. But Roslynn stopped, noticing Dobson in the process of opening the front door, and then stiffened as Anthony walked in. However, she lost her breath entirely on seeing who was with him. He wouldn't dare! He *had* dared! He had deliberately brought George Amherst home with him, knowing full well that Frances would be here. And from the look of George, who had come to a dead standstill on seeing Frances, he hadn't been warned either.

"Splendid," Anthony said drolly as he handed his hat and gloves to the wooden-faced butler. "I see we're just in time for dinner, George."

Roslynn's fingers curled into fists. Frances' reaction was a bit more dramatic. Ashen-faced, and with a small squeal of horror, she tore away from Roslynn's side and ran back into the parlor.

Anthony clapped his friend on the back, bringing him out of his bemusement. "Well, what are you standing there like an ass for, George? Go after her."

"No!" Roslynn snapped before George could take a step. "Havena you done enough?"

Her contempt sliced into the poor man, but he

didn't hesitate another moment in starting toward the parlor. Aghast, Roslynn turned to beat him there, intending to slam the door in his face. But she hadn't counted on Anthony's intervention. Somehow he crossed ten feet of space before she had reached the parlor door, and with a band of steel locking firmly about her waist, he steered her toward the stairs instead.

She was outraged beyond belief by his highhandedness. "Let go of me, you—"

"Now, now, my dear, have a care, if you please," he told her glibly. "I believe we've had quite enough distasteful scenes in that hall for the delectation of the servants. We don't need another."

He was absolutely right, so her voice was lowered, but no less furious. "If you dinna—"

His finger pressed to her lips this time. "Pay attention, sweetheart. She refuses to listen to him. It's time she was forced to, and George can do that here—and without interruption." Then he paused, grinning at her. "Sounds awfully familiar, doesn't it?"

"Not at all," she gritted out beneath her breath. "I listened to you. I just didna believe you!"

"Stubborn chit," he gently chided. "But no matter. You're coming along with me while I change for dinner."

She didn't have any choice but to go along with him, since he practically carried her up the stairs. But once in his room, she jerked away, not even noticing that Willis stood beside the bed.

"That is the most loathsome thing you have ever done!" she exploded.

"Glad to hear it," he replied blithely. "Here I was under the impression that the most loathsome thing I had—"

"Shut up! Just shut up!"

She pushed past him to get to the door. He caught her up about the waist and deposited her in the chaise longue by the mantel. And then with a hand on each side of it, he leaned over, until she had to press back in the chair to keep a distance between them. There was no longer a trace of humor in his expression. He was now deadly serious.

"You're going to stay put, my dear wife, or I will tie you to that chair to see that you do." With just the barest crook of his brow, he added, "Is that perfectly clear?"

"You wouldna do that!"

"You may be absolutely certain that I would."

Her lips set mutinously while their eyes did battle. But when Anthony wouldn't move away and stayed there hovering over her, she thought it prudent to give in for now.

Her agreement was offered by lowering her eyes and drawing her legs up into the chair to get comfortable. Anthony accepted these signs of surrender and straightened, but his humor did not return. He was aware that in helping George, he had thoroughly damaged his own cause. Whatever progress had been made toward the diminishing of Roslynn's anger by the sheer passage of time was now destroyed. So be it. After all these years, George deserved his chance. What were a few more weeks of Roslynn's renewed bad temper? Torture.

He turned away from the chair, his scowl so black his valet took an involuntary step backward upon seeing it, which finally brought him to Anthony's attention. "Thank you, Willis." His voice was deliberately colorless to sheathe the inner turmoil of his thoughts. "Your choice is superb as usual."

Roslynn's head snapped around upon hearing that, her eyes first lighting on Willis, then on the clothes carefully laid out on the bed. "Do you mean to be saying he knew you'd be home for dinner?"

"Of course, my dear," Anthony replied as he shrugged out of his coat. "I always let Willis know when to expect me if I am reasonably certain of my schedule."

She gave Willis an accusatory look that brought hot color to his already ruddy cheeks. "He could have told me," she said to Anthony.

"That is not his responsibility."

"*You* could have told me!"

Anthony glanced over his shoulder at her, wondering if it would do any good to risk turning her anger onto this lesser subject. "Quite true, sweetheart. And if you hadn't flounced off in a pout this morning, I would have."

Her eyes flared. Her feet hit the floor. She came half out of the chair before she remembered his threat and dropped back into it.

But she hadn't lost her voice. "I did no such thing! And how dare you say so?"

"Oh?" Anthony faced her again, his lips slightly curled. "Then what would you call it?"

His shirt dropped into Willis' waiting hand before she could answer. Roslynn turned around so fast, Anthony nearly laughed aloud. At least the new subject was improving his temper, if not hers. And that she was reluctant to watch him undress was most interesting.

He sat down on the bed so Willis could tackle his boots, but he kept his eyes on his wife. She was wearing her hair differently tonight, more frivolously, with dainty curls dangling from a high-swept coiffure. It had been too long since his hands had been in those glorious red-gold tresses, too long since his lips had tasted the smooth skin along her neck. Her head was turned away, but her body was in profile, the sharp thrust of her breasts particularly drawing his attention.

Anthony was forced to look away before it became an embarrassment to both him and Willis to go any further in his undressing. "You know, my dear, it quite escapes me, the cause of your ill humor this morning."

"You provoked me."

He had to strain to hear her, since she wouldn't face him. "Now how could I have done that when I was so exceedingly well behaved?"

"You called Frances my reinforcements!"

That he heard well enough. "I suppose it will be boorish of me to point this out, sweetheart, but you were in a sulk long before your friend was mentioned."

"You're right," she hissed. "It's boorish of you to be saying so."

He stole another glance at her to see her fingers worrying at the arms of the chair. He had pushed her into a corner. That had not been his intention.

Even-toned, he said, "By the by, Roslynn, until I locate your cousin, I would appreciate it if you wouldn't leave the house without me."

The abrupt change of subject floored her. At any other time she would have retorted that she had already concluded for herself that it was wisest to stay at home for a while. But at the moment she was too grateful that he had given up pressing her about this morning.

"Of course," she agreed simply.

"*Is* there any place you would like to go in the next few days?"

And be forced to endure his company the whole while? "No," she assured him.

"Very well." She sensed his shrug. "But if you change your mind, don't hesitate to tell me."

Did he have to be so bloody reasonable and accommodating? "Aren't you finished yet?"

"As a matter of fact—"

"Malory!" The shout was muffled on the other side of the door, but then George Amherst burst into the room. "Tony! You'll—"

Roslynn shot out of the chair, Amherst's presence canceling Anthony's threat in her mind. She didn't wait to hear what he was so eager to impart to her husband, but rushed past him and out the door, offering up a little prayer that Anthony wouldn't make another scene by trying to stop her.

She didn't look back, either, as she ran down the stairs and straight into the parlor. She came to an abrupt halt on finding Frances still there, standing in front of the white marble fireplace with her back to the room. She turned, and Roslynn felt a lump of misery rise in her throat, seeing the great tears swimming in her friend's eyes.

"Och, Frances, I'm so sorry," Roslynn lamented as she swiftly closed the space between them, catching up Frances in her arms. "I'll never forgive Anthony for interfering. He had no right—"

Frances stepped back to interrupt. "I'm getting married, Ros."

Roslynn just stood there, rendered speechless. Not even the brilliant smile Frances gave her, a smile like one she hadn't seen for years, could make her believe what she had just heard. The tears denied it. The tears . . .

"Then why are you crying?"

Frances laughed shakily. "I can't seem to help it. I've been such a fool, Ros. George says he loves me, that he always has."

"You—you believe him?"

"Yes." And then with more force, "Yes!"

"But, Fran—"

"You're not trying to change her mind, are you, Lady Malory?"

Roslynn started and turned to see the most unfriendly look she had ever received from a man on George Amherst's handsome face as he sauntered forward. And his tone had been rife with menace too, the gray eyes positively frigid.

"No," she said uneasily. "I wouldn't dream—"

"Good!" The transformation was immediate, the smile blinding. "Because now that I know she still loves me, there isn't anyone I would let come between us."

The implication was there, as plain as the warmth now generating from his eyes, that "anyone" also included Frances. And it was also plain to see that Frances was thrilled by the subtle warning.

She hugged a bemused Roslynn, whispering happily in her ear, "You see now why I don't doubt his sincerity? Isn't he wonderful?"

Wonderful? Roslynn wanted to choke. The man was a rake, a libertine. It was Frances herself who had warned her about trusting such men, and here was her friend, willing to marry the very one who had broken her heart.

"I hope you'll forgive us for running off, m'dear," Frances was saying as she stepped back, a becoming blush staining her cheeks as she finished. "But George and I have so much to talk about."

"I'm sure she understands how we'd like to be alone just now, Franny," George added as he put an arm about Frances' waist, drawing her indecently close. "After all, she's newly married herself."

Roslynn did choke this time, but fortunately, neither of them heard, too involved with gazing into each other's adoring eyes to pay attention to much else. And somehow she must have said the appropriate thing in reply, for less than a minute later she found herself alone in the parlor, staring dazedly at the floor, bombarded with so many conflicting emotions that not one of them could dominate to eliminate her bewilderment.

"I see you've received the good news."

Roslynn turned slowly toward the door, and for a moment every single thought in her head deserted her at the sight of her husband. He had done himself up fancy in a dark emerald coat of satin, with an abundance of snowy lace spilling from his throat. And he had combed his hair back in defiance of the current favored style, but it was so soft it refused discipline, already falling forward over each temple in thick ebony waves. He was stunning, there was no other word for it, so handsome she felt her heart trip over.

But then she noticed the stance, one very familiar to her now, the shoulder braced against the doorjamb, the arms crossed over his chest—and the smugness. Hell's teeth, it fairly dripped from him, the self-satisfied smirk, the laughter in his cobalt eyes, made so much bluer in contrast to the dark green of his coat. He was peacock-proud of himself, the scoundrel, and flaunting it with his usual male arrogance.

"Nothing to say, sweetheart, after you made so much fuss over nothing?"

Now he was taunting her, rubbing it in. Her teeth slammed together, her fingers curling into fists on her hips. Her emotions had found their channel. Fury. But he wasn't finished. He had to go for blood.

"It must be disconcerting to have the very woman who fostered your distrust of men turn traitor and trust one. Rather puts a new light on things, doesn't it?"

"You—" No, she wouldn't do it. She refused to yell like a fishwife again for the servants' amusement. "Actually," she gritted out between clenched teeth, "there's no comparison between my case and hers." And then she hissed, "She'll come to her senses in the morning."

"Knowing old George, I doubt it. The only thing your friend will have on her mind in the morning is how she spent the night. Sound familiar?"

She tried to fight it, to hold it back, but her cheeks bloomed with color despite her effort. "You're disgusting, Anthony. They left here to talk."

"If you say so, sweetheart."

The condescending tone infuriated her. He was right, of course. She knew it. He knew it. It had been so embarrassingly obvious why George and Frances were in such a hurry to leave. But damned if she'd acknowledge it to him!

Tightly, she said, "I believe I've developed a headache. If you'll excuse me . . ." But she had to stop when she reached the door, the space still blocked by his casual pose. "Do you mind?" she asked scathingly.

Anthony straightened up slowly, amused when she gave him her back by twisting to squeeze past him without touching. "Coward," he said softly and grinned when she stopped halfway across the hall, shoulders stiffening. "And I believe I owe you a lesson in a chair, don't I?" He heard her gasp just before she broke into a run for the stairs. His laughter followed her. "Another time, sweetheart."

Chapter Thirty-three

Approaching the wide double-door entrance of Edward Malory's grand ballroom two nights after Frances' defection to the enemy camp, as Roslynn had come to think of her reunion with Amherst, Roslynn was brought up short, dragging her two escorts to a halt as well. The many carriages in front of the Malory mansion should have given some indication, but even so, they wouldn't have accounted for the nearly two hundred people gathered in the large room before her.

"I thought this was only to be a quiet affair of friends and family," Roslynn remarked to Anthony, unable to keep the stiffness from her tone. After all, this party was for them. She should have been given some kind of warning. " 'Nothing too big,' I recall were your brother's very words."

"Actually, this is small for one of Charlotte's entertainments."

"And I suppose these are all *your* friends?"

"I hate to disillusion you, sweetheart, but I'm not that popular." Anthony grinned. "When Eddie boy said friends of the family, I believe he meant friends of each individual member of the family, or so it appears. You're dressed accordingly, my dear."

She wasn't worried about how she was dressed. The moss-green gown of silk crepe, with black lace over satin bandings around the cap sleeves, the deep-scooped neckline, and the high waist and hem, was suitable for any ball, and that was certainly what this had turned out to be. Black evening gloves and satin slippers completed the outfit, but it was the diamonds, dripping from ears, neck, wrists, and several fingers, that made her presentable in her mind, even for a presentation to the Prince Regent.

She said no more. Anthony wasn't exactly paying attention anyway, leisurely scanning the room, which gave her a moment to gaze at him, but only a moment. She forced her eyes away, gritting her teeth.

Arriving with Anthony and James, two of the most handsome men in London, she should have been immeasurably proud, and would have been if she had considered it. But the only thing on Roslynn's mind was how soon she could escape her husband's presence. After the intolerable ride over here, during which she had been forced to sit next to him in the carriage, she was now a mass of screaming nerves.

The ride wouldn't have been so bad, the seats were certainly wide enough, but Anthony had deliberately pulled her close, draping an arm firmly about her shoulders, and she couldn't do anything about that with James sitting across from them, quietly observing them with his misplaced humor. But then that was why Anthony had done it. Because he knew very well she wouldn't make a scene in front of his brother.

But it had been hell, tortured bliss, feeling his thigh burning against hers, his hips, his side pressed so close. And his cursed hand wouldn't be still for a minute, the fingers constantly caressing her bare arm between the short sleeve of her gown and her elbow-length glove. And he knew exactly what it did to her. Even though she was as stiff as a board, she couldn't stop the quickened breath, the hammering of her heart, or the telltale gooseflesh that appeared again and again under his fingers, bringing one shiver after another to tell him how effective was his *innocent* touch.

The ride had seemed to take forever, when it was no more than a few blocks around the corner from Piccadilly to Grosvenor Square, where Edward Malory lived with his wife and five children. And even though they had arrived and Roslynn could breathe normally again by putting a distance between herself and Anthony, she still knew it would be a while yet before she could escape him entirely. With the party in their honor, they would be forced by etiquette to remain together for introductions, and now she saw how long that was going to take, with so many guests to meet. But the very moment she had met the last one . . .

All the Malorys were present. She saw Regina and Nicholas standing with several of Edward's offspring; Jason and his son Derek by the refreshment table, along with Jeremy, who had come over earlier to help his aunt Charlotte with the last-minute decorations, which by the looks of them had entailed raiding Charlotte's garden of every single flower in bloom. She noticed Frances and George, and several other people she had met since arriving in London.

And then she realized the hush falling over the room. They had themselves been noticed, and she groaned inwardly, feeling Anthony's arm slip around her waist to present a very loving picture. Was there to be no end to the liberties he was going to take tonight? It seemed not, for he didn't release her when Edward and Charlotte appeared at their side with a small group of people in tow, and the introductions began. The only interruption was when they had to start off the dancing together as the guests of honor, and that was another excuse for Anthony to torment her with his closeness.

She soon met *his* friends, the sorriest bunch of lecherous rakes imaginable. There wasn't one who didn't ogle her shamelessly, flirt with her, or banter with wicked insinuations. They were amusing. They were outrageous. And they managed to get her away from Anthony's side with one dance after another, until when she finally begged for a moment's respite, Anthony was no longer in sight. At last, Roslynn felt she could relax and enjoy herself.

"See here, Malory, either you're going to play cards or you're not," the Honorable John Willhurst said in exasperation as Anthony rose from the table for the third time in less than an hour.

The two other players tensed as Anthony placed both hands on the table and leaned toward Willhurst. "I'm going to stretch my legs, John. But if you've a problem with that, you know what you can do."

"No—not at all," John Willhurst got out. He was a neighbor of Jason's and so knew from past experience the explosive tempers of the Malory brothers, having grown up with them. What *had* he been thinking of? "Could use a new drink myself."

Willhurst hurried away from the table himself while Anthony shot the other players a look to see if there would be any more objections. There weren't.

Calmly, as if he hadn't just been on the brink of challenging an old family friend, Anthony picked up his drink and left the card room. He stopped at the place he had stopped at previously, the entrance to the ballroom, his eyes scanning the crowd until he found what was repeatedly drawing him back here.

Damnation take her, he couldn't even play a simple

game of cards with Roslynn in the same vicinity. Just knowing she was near, but where he couldn't keep his eye on her, destroyed his concentration, so much so that he had already lost nearly a thousand pounds. It was no good. He couldn't stay near her without touching her, but he couldn't stay away from her either.

Across the room, Conrad Sharp nudged James in the ribs. "He's back again."

James glanced in the direction Connie had indicated and chuckled to see Anthony scowling at his wife as she whirled by on the dance floor. "A face worth a thousand words, that. I would say my dear brother is not at all happy."

"You could remedy that by having a little talk with the lady and enlightening her to the truth."

"I suppose I could."

"But you're not going to?"

"And make it easy for Tony? Come now, Connie. It's so much more fun watching him muddle through this on his own. He hasn't the temperament for rejection. He's bound to dig the hole deeper before he finally crawls out."

"If he can crawl out."

"Where's your faith, man? Malorys always win in the end." And here James grinned. "Besides, she's already weakening, if you haven't noticed. Can't keep her eyes from searching the room for him either. If ever there was a woman smitten, it's Lady Roslynn."

"She just doesn't know it, I suppose?"

"Quite so."

"And what are you two grinning about?" Regina asked as she and Nicholas joined them.

James gave her a brief hug. "The foibles of man, sweet. We can be such asses sometimes."

"Speak for yourself, old man," Nicholas retorted.

"I was excluding myself, actually," James replied, a quirk to his lips as his eyes moved over his nephew by marriage. "But then you're a prime example, Montieth."

"Famous." Regina sighed in exasperation, glaring at both before she ignored them to hook her arm through Conrad's. "Connie, would you rescue me with a dance? I'm tired of getting splattered with the blood from their slashes."

"Love to, squirt." Connie grinned.

James snorted as he watched them twirl away. "She puts it rather plain, don't she?"

"You don't know the half of it," Nicholas grumbled, more to himself. "Try sleeping on the sofa when you have a wife annoyed with you."

James couldn't help it. He burst out laughing. "Good God, you too? That's rich, lad. Damn me if it ain't. And what have you done to merit—"

"I haven't forgiven you, that's what." Nicholas scowled at this amusement at his expense. "And well she knows it. Every time you and I have words, she lays into me later. When the devil are you leaving London, anyway?"

"My, but that's becoming a source of keen interest." James continued to chuckle. "If it'll keep you on the sofa, dear boy, I may never leave."

"You're all heart, Malory."

"I like to think so. If it's any consolation, I forgave you a long time ago."

"How magnanimous, when you were at fault to begin with. All I did was best you on the high seas—"

"And land me in gaol," James replied, no longer quite so amused.

"Hah! That was after you landed me in my bed to recover from your thrashing, nearly making me miss my own wedding."

"Which you had to be dragged to," James pointed out sourly.

"That's a bloody lie!"

"Is it? Well, you can't deny my brothers had to do a little arm twisting to get you there. Would that I'd been here at the time—"

"But you were, old man—skulking around alleys trying to waylay me."

"Skulking? Skulking!" James blustered.

Nicholas groaned. "Now you've done it with your bloody shouting."

James followed the direction of his gaze to see that Regina was no longer dancing. She was standing in the middle of the dance floor watching them and looking none too pleased, with Connie next to her, trying to look as if he hadn't heard their raised voices too.

"I believe I could use another drink," James said abruptly, grinning. "Enjoy your sofa, lad." And he deserted Nicholas for the refreshment table. Passing Anthony on the way, he couldn't resist commenting, "You and Montieth ought to compare notes, dear boy. He suffers from the same complaint as you, don't you know."

"Does he?" Anthony scanned the room until his eyes lit on Nicholas. Dryly, he added, "If he does, he's obviously discovered how to correct it."

James chuckled, seeing Nicholas kissing his wife with flagrant disregard for the audience they were attracting. "Damn me if he hasn't got something there.

Regan can't very well rail at him if she can't get her lips free.''

But Anthony wasn't there to hear this comment. He had heard once again, and one time too many, Roslynn's throaty laugh at some sally her present partner had made. Weaving his way through the dancers until he came to the pair, he tapped Justin Warton on the shoulder none too gently, bringing them to a sudden halt.

"Is something amiss, Malory?" Lord Warton asked cautiously, sensing the underlying menace in Anthony's stance and expression.

"Not at all." Anthony smiled tightly, but his arm shot out to catch Roslynn as she started to edge away. "Just retrieving what's mine." And with a curt nod, he whirled his wife into the waltz that was still in progress. "Enjoying yourself, sweetheart?"

"I was," Roslynn retorted, keeping her eyes averted from his.

The only indication that the insinuation had struck home was a slight tightening of his fingers on her waist. "Shall we leave, then?"

"No," she said too quickly.

"But if you're having no fun . . ."

"I'm—having—fun," she gritted out.

He smiled down at her, watching her eyes dart about the room, anywhere but up at him. He drew her closer, and saw the pulse beat quicken at her throat, and wondered what she would do if he followed Montieth's strategy.

He asked her. "What would you do, sweetheart, were I to end this dance with a kiss?"

"What?"

He had her eyes locked fast to his now. "That sends you into a panic, does it? Why is that?"

"I'm no' panicked, mon."

"Ah, and there's the brogue, a sure sign—"

"Will you shush!" she hissed, his teasing alarming her so, she missed a step in the dance.

Anthony grinned delightedly and decided to let her off the hook for now. Starting something in a ballroom was not only in bad taste but would get him nowhere.

Noting the fortune in diamonds that sparkled on her with each turn into the light, he said in an impersonal tone, "What does a man give a woman who has everything?"

"Something that canna be bought," Roslynn replied absently, for she was still thinking about what *might* happen when this dance ended.

"His heart, perhaps?"

"Perhaps—no—I mean—" she stammered to a halt, glaring up at him, her tone bitter as she continued. "I'm no' wanting *your* heart, mon, no' anymore."

One hand disturbed the curls along her temple. "But what if it's already yours?" he asked softly.

For a moment, Roslynn lost herself in the vivid blue of his eyes. She actually drifted closer to him, was about to offer him her lips, heedless of the crowded room and what was between them. But she came to her senses with a gasp and drew back, glaring at him again.

Furious at herself, she said, "If your heart's mine, then it's mine to do with as I choose, and I'd be choosing to cut it into wee pieces afore I give it back."

"Heartless wench."

"Not so." She smiled wryly, amusing him though she didn't know it. "My heart's right where it's supposed to be, and that's where it'll be staying."

With that, she jerked loose of his hold and flounced off in the direction of his elder brothers. In their presence was the only place she felt safe from Anthony's bold taunts and the supposedly innocent touches of his caressing hands.

Chapter Thirty-four

George gave the door knocker a few sharp raps, then stood back, whistling a jaunty tune as he waited. It was Dobson who answered.

"You've just missed him, my lord, by five minutes," Dobson informed him before George even started his business.

"The devil, and here I thought I had time to spare," George replied, but he was undaunted. "Right you are, then. He'll be easy enough to find."

George remounted his bay stallion and headed for Hyde Park. He knew the paths Anthony favored, those well away from Rotten Row, where the ladies turned out. He had joined him several times on his morning rides, but then those times had been after a night of carousing, when neither of them had yet to go to bed. Never had he actually gotten up at this ungodly hour to ride or do anything else, for that matter—until recently.

George continued to whistle, his spirits so high he could have been floating along. His habits had changed in the past three days, drastically, but he couldn't have been happier. Early to bed, early to rise, and each day spent with Franny. No, he couldn't be happier, and he owed it all to Anthony. But he had yet to have an opportunity to thank his friend, which was why he had thought to ride with him this morning.

Entering the park, he picked up his pace to catch up with Anthony, but it was a while before he finally spotted him a good distance ahead, and that only because Anthony had stopped at the start of the long run that he usually used for his all-out gallop. George raised his arm, but before he could shout to be heard, a shot was fired.

He heard it, he just didn't believe it. He saw Anthony's horse rear up so far that nearly both rider and horse tumbled over backward, but he still didn't believe it. Anthony did tumble over. The horse found his footing, but he was obviously spooked, shying away, tossing his head, backing into a bush that further spooked him. And a redheaded gent about twenty yards away from Anthony mounted a horse concealed in the brush and took off at an instant gallop.

Anthony had yet to rise, and although it had all happened in the space of only a few seconds, the pieces finally came together in George's mind with heart-stopping clarity. And then Anthony sat up, running a hand through his hair, and the blood rushed back into George's ashen face. He glanced between the fleeing redhead and Anthony pushing himself to his feet, apparently not wounded at all, and made his decision. He turned his horse to follow the redhead.

Anthony had just handed his mount over to the waiting footman to return him to the stable when George cantered up behind him. Bloody hell. He was in no mood for George and his ''everything going right'' ebullience. Not that Anthony begrudged him his good fortune. He just didn't need to be reminded how opposite was his own state of affairs.

''So you made it home under your own steam,'' George remarked, grinning at the instant scowl that darkened Anthony's features. ''No broken bones, then?''

"I take it you witnessed my unseating? Nice of you to lend a hand in retrieving that bloody nag of mine."

George chuckled at the deliberate sarcasm. "Thought you might rather have this, old man." He tossed a scrap of paper at Anthony.

Anthony's brow rose just a smidgen as he read the address, which meant nothing to him. "Doctor? Or butcher?" he snarled.

George laughed outright, knowing very well he wouldn't consign his favorite mount to the butcher's block. "Neither. You'll find the red-haired chap who used you for target practice there. Strange fellow. He didn't even wait around to see if you were down and out for the count. Probably thinks he's a crack shot."

Anthony's eyes were gleaming now. "So you followed him to this address?"

"After I saw you dragging your bruised bones off the ground, of course."

"Of course." Anthony finally smiled. "My thanks, George. His trail was cold by the time I'd mounted up again."

"He the one you've been looking for?"

"I'd say it's a safe bet."

"You going to pay him a call?"

"You may depend upon it."

George wasn't too sure he liked the cold sparkle in his friend's eyes. "Need some company?"

"Not this time, old man," Anthony replied. "This meeting's long overdue."

Roslynn opened the door to the study but was brought up short to find Anthony seated behind his desk, cleaning a pair of dueling pistols. She hadn't heard him return from his morning ride. She had purposely stayed in her room until she heard him leave, not wanting to face him after having made a fool of herself last night.

Anthony had been so amused when she dragged Jeremy home with them from the ball, against the lad's protests too. He knew exactly why she didn't trust herself alone with him, even for such a short ride. But James had left the ball early with his friend, Conrad Sharp. Jeremy was her only buffer. It had been inconceivable for her to think of being alone with Anthony after the way he had taunted her all evening.

Now here she was alone with him, having come to exchange one book for another from his small library. But he hadn't glanced up when she entered. Perhaps if she left quietly . . .

"Did you want something, my dear?"

He still hadn't glanced up. Roslynn gritted her teeth. "Nothing that can't wait."

Anthony finally gave her his attention, his eyes flitting to the book she was grasping so tightly in her hands. "Ah, the companion of spinsters and widows. There's nothing like a good book to while away an evening when you've nothing else to do, is there?"

She felt like throwing the book at him. Would he always allude to their estrangement every time they encountered each other? Couldn't he back off long enough for her to come to terms with his unfaithfulness? He acted as if *she* were the guilty party.

Her hackles rose with the unfairness of it, and she attacked. "Preparing for a duel, my lord? I've heard it's one of your more favorite pastimes. Which unfortunate husband is it to be this time?"

"Husband?" Anthony smiled tightly. "Not at all, sweetheart. I thought I'd challenge you. Perhaps if I

let you draw some of my blood, you might be moved
to sympathy, and our little war can end.''

Her mouth dropped open for at least five seconds
before she snapped it shut. ''Be serious!''

He shrugged. ''Your dear cousin has decided that
if he can get rid of your current husband, he will have
another chance at you.''

''No!'' Roslynn gasped, her eyes flaring wide. ''I
never considered—''

''Didn't you?'' he cut in dryly. ''Well, don't let it
concern you, sweetheart. I did.''

''You mean you married me knowing you were putting your life in danger?''

''Some things are worth putting one's life in jeop-
ardy for—at least I used to think so.''

The dig stung, so much so that she couldn't bear
to face him another moment and ran from the study,
up to her room, where she felt safe to burst into tears.
Oh, God, she had thought it would be over once she
married. She never dreamed Geordie would try to kill
her husband. And her husband was Anthony. She
couldn't bear it if anything happened to him because
of her.

She had to do something. She had to find Geordie
and talk to him herself, give him her fortune, anything. Nothing must happen to Anthony.

Having made up her mind, Roslynn dried her eyes
and went back downstairs to tell Anthony what she
had decided to do. They would buy Geordie off. All
he wanted was the money anyway. But Anthony was
gone.

Chapter Thirty-five

Anthony saw now why neither he nor his agents had had any luck in locating Cameron. The Scot had moved away from the docks, letting a flat in a better part of town, which was amazing when such accommodations were at a high premium during the season. The landlord, a congenial chap, admitted that Cameron had been there only a few days, and yes, he was in at present. Whether he was alone, the landlord couldn't say. It made no difference to Anthony.

Campbell was the name Cameron was assuming, and Anthony had little doubt it was assumed. He had found his man. He felt it. His blood pumped with that certainty, the adrenaline flowing through his veins. And once he had settled with Cameron, he would settle with Roslynn. Letting her dictate the rules had gone on long enough.

The room was on the second floor, third door on the left. Anthony knocked softly and had only a few seconds to wait before the door swung open, giving him his first look at Geordie Cameron. The eyes were the giveaway, sky-blue, and bright with recognition.

It took the Scot several moments before his wits returned and panic took over, enough for him to try slamming the door in Anthony's face. A single hand was all it took to prevent the door from closing. A forceful shove and Geordie lost his hold on the handle, cringing as the door slammed into the wall.

Fury and anxiety mixed sickeningly in Geordie's gut. The Englishman hadn't looked this strong from a distance. He hadn't looked this dangerous either. And he was supposed to be dead, or at least seriously wounded, at the very least intimidated by knowing he had a deadly enemy in Geordie Cameron. Roslynn was supposed to have panicked and left the protection of the house on Piccadilly, and Wilbert and Thomas Stow would be there to grab her. The Englishman was *not* supposed to show up at his door, looking disgustingly healthy, lips turned up in an ominous smile that did more to shake Geordie than anything else.

"I'm glad we don't have to waste time introducing ourselves, Cameron," Anthony said as he stepped into the room, forcing Geordie to back up. "I would have been disappointed to have to explain why I'm here. And I'll give you a sporting chance, which is more than you gave me this morning. Are you gentleman enough to accept my challenge?"

The quiet, nonchalant tone gave Geordie back some of his belligerence. "Hah! I'm no' a bloody fool, mon."

"That's debatable, but I didn't think we'd do this in the usual way. So be it, then."

Geordie didn't see the punch coming. It caught him square on the chin and sent him careening into his small dining table, breaking the spindly legs, and knocking over both straight-backed chairs as the table collapsed, Geordie on top of it. He leaped to his feet instantly, to see the Englishman calmly removing his coat, in no hurry. Geordie wiggled his jaw, found it still intact, and eyed his own coat on the foot of his bed across the room. He wondered how much chance he had of reaching the pistol in its pocket.

None at all, he discovered as he turned toward the bed, only to be spun back around. A fist slammed into his midsection; another connected with his cheek.

He was on the floor again, not so quick to rise this time. He couldn't breathe either. The bloody bastard had rocks for fists.

Anthony came to stand at his feet. "That was for this morning. Now we'll get down to the real issue."

"I'm no' going tae fight ye, mon," Geordie spat out, tasting blood where his teeth had cut into his cheek.

"But of course you are, dear boy," Anthony replied in the lightest tone. "It's the only choice you have, you see. Whether you defend yourself or not, I'm going to wipe the floor with your blood."

"Ye're crazy!"

"No." Anthony's tone changed, all humor gone. "I'm deadly serious."

He bent over to lift Geordie to his feet. Geordie kicked out to keep him away, but Anthony blocked with his knee, yanking him up anyway. And then he felt those rocks slammed against his jaw again. He only staggered back this time, and had time to raise his own fists before Anthony reached him. Geordie threw a right and struck nothing. He doubled over as two successive punches sank into his stomach. Before he regained his breath this time, his lips were smashed against his teeth.

"En-ough," he tried to get out.

"Not even close, Cameron," Anthony replied, not at all winded from his exertions.

Geordie groaned, and groaned again with the next two punches. He went a little crazy then from the numbing pain. He'd never experienced a beating before in his life. He didn't have the character to take it like a man. He started screaming, throwing wild punches. He laughed when one finally struck, only to find, when he squinted his eyes open, he had hit the wall, breaking three of his own knuckles. Anthony spun him around, and this punch cracked his head back into the wall. His nose was also broken, he realized as he slowly slid to the floor.

He thought that would be the end of it. He was beaten. He knew it. He hurt all over. He was bleeding profusely. It wasn't the end. Anthony pulled him up by his shirtfront, stood him against the wall, and simply pounded away at him. And no matter how Geordie tried warding off the punches, they kept coming, kept landing unerringly.

Finally he didn't feel them anymore. Finally they had stopped. He was slumped on the floor again, sitting up only because the wall was supporting his back. Blood was splattered all around him from his mouth, nose, and several cuts on his face. Two ribs were broken. The little finger on his left hand was broken too, from one of his attempted blocks. He could see out of only one eye, and what he saw was Anthony staring down at him in disgust.

"Bloody hell. You give a man no satisfaction at all, Cameron."

That was funny. Geordie tried to smile, but he had no feeling in his lips, couldn't tell if he had managed it or not. But he did manage a single word.

"Bastard."

Anthony grunted and hunkered down in front of him. "You want some more?"

Geordie moaned. "No—no more."

"Then pay attention, Scotsman. Your life may very well depend upon it, because if I have to come looking for you again, I won't use my fists next time. She's mine now, and so's her inheritance. I married her a week ago."

That penetrated Geordie's fuzziness. "Ye're lying!

She'd no' have wed ye unless ye signed that stupid contract of hers, and nae mon in his right mind would've done that.''

"There you're wrong, dear boy. I did sign it, and in front of witnesses, then promptly burned it after the ceremony.''

"Ye couldna. No' wi' witnesses.''

"Did I neglect to say the witnesses were related to me?'' Anthony taunted.

Geordie tried to sit up farther, but couldn't. "Sae what? She'll still be having it all back when I make her a widow.''

"You just don't learn, do you?'' Anthony said, grabbing hold of Geordie's shirtfront again.

Geordie quickly grasped his wrists. "I didna mean that, mon, I didna, I swear!''

Anthony let him go this time, deciding to further the lie instead of using more force. "It won't matter to you, Scotsman, whether I die or not. According to my new will, everything I possess, including my wife's inheritance, goes to my family. They'll of course see that my widow doesn't want for anything, but other than that, she gets nothing. She lost it all the day she married me—and so did you.''

Geordie's one good eye narrowed furiously. "She mun hate ye fer tricking her!''

"That's my problem, isn't it?'' Anthony remarked as he stood up. "Your problem is getting out of London today in your present condition. If you're still here tomorrow, Scotsman, I'll have you arrested for that little stunt you pulled in the park this morning.''

"Ye've nae proof, mon.''

"No?'' Anthony grinned at last. "The Earl of Sherfield witnessed the whole thing and followed you here. How else do you think I finally found you? If my testimony won't put you in prison, his will.''

Anthony left him mumbling about how Anthony expected him to leave London when he couldn't even get up off the floor.

Chapter Thirty-six

Fortunately, Roslynn didn't see Anthony when he returned home, and by the time he had bathed and changed, there was no evidence left of the fight. His knuckles might be tender, but thanks to the gloves he had worn, there were no cuts or abrasions from Cameron's teeth. Still, he was disgusted with the whole affair. The man had offered him no challenge at all. It put him in a foul mood, one that wasn't conducive to tackling his next challenge—Roslynn.

He didn't even care to see her at the moment, but, as his luck would have it, she came out of the parlor as he was on his way out again.

"Anthony?"

He frowned at her hesitant tone, so unlike her. "What is it?"

"Did you—challenge Geordie?"

He grunted. "He wouldn't accept."

"Then you saw him?"

"I saw him. And you can relax your guard, my dear. He won't be bothering you again."

"Did you—"

"I did no more than persuade him to leave London. He might have to be carried out, but he'll go. And don't wait dinner on me. I'm going to my club."

Roslynn stared at the closed door after he left, wondering why his terseness upset her so. She should be feeling relief, delight over Geordie's thrashing, for she was sure that was the persuasion Anthony had used; but instead she felt deflated, depressed. It was Anthony's curtness, his cold indifference. He had been in many different moods this past week, but this was a new one she didn't like at all.

She had procrastinated too long, she realized. It was time she reached a decision about her relationship with Anthony, before the decision was no longer hers to make. And it must be done now, today, before he returned.

"Well, Nettie?"

Nettie paused in pulling the brush through Roslynn's fiery hair to stare at her in the mirror. "Is that what ye really mean tae do, lass?"

Roslynn nodded. She had finally told Nettie everything, about Anthony's seduction of her in this very house, about the conditions she had placed on their marrying, even about his lies that he would be faithful, only to have the truth come out the very next day. Nettie had been both furious with and aghast at the two of them. But Roslynn had left nothing out, and had ended by telling Nettie what she had decided to do. She wanted her abigail's opinion, her support.

"I think ye're making a big mistake, lass."

She didn't want *that* opinion. "Why?"

"Ye'll be using him. Ye mark me, he'll no' be liking that one bit."

"I'll be sharing his bed," Roslynn pointed out. "How is that using him?"

"Ye'll be sharing his bed only fer a time."

"He agreed to give me a child!"

"Sae he did. But he didna agree tae leave ye alone once that child is conceived, did he now."

Roslynn's eyes narrowed in a frown. "I'm only protecting myself, Nettie. Constant intimacy with him . . . I don't want to love him."

"Ye already do."

"I dinna!" Roslynn gasped, swinging around to glare at the older woman. "And I willna. I refuse! And I'll be letting him decide. I dinna ken why I told you anyway."

Nettie snorted, not at all perturbed by this outburst. "Then go and put it tae him. I saw him enter his room afore I came in here."

Roslynn looked away, a cold knot of nervousness tightening in her belly. "Maybe I should wait until tomorrow. He wasn't exactly pleasant when he left today."

"The mon's no' been pleasant since ye moved oout of his room," Nettie reminded her. "But perhaps ye're seeing how silly is yer notion—"

"No," Roslynn replied, determination back in her voice. "And it's not silly. It's self-preservation."

"If ye say sae, hinny." Nettie sighed. "But remember I did warn ye—"

"Good *night*, Nettie."

Roslynn sat there at her new vanity another ten minutes after Nettie left, staring at her reflection in the mirror. She had made the right decision. She wasn't forgiving Anthony. Not in the least. But she had come to the conclusion that she was only thwarting herself with the stand she had taken. Either she could go on hugging her anger to her breast and keeping Anthony at arm's length, or she could get a child. She wanted the child. It was that simple.

But it meant swallowing her pride and going to Anthony. After his coldness today, she had little doubt that she would have to make the first move. But it was only temporary, she reminded herself. He would have to agree to that. She still couldn't convince herself to accept him the way he was, even if she had agreed to

when they married. The truth was, she didn't want
him as he was anymore. She found she was exceedingly selfish in wanting him all to herself. But since
that wasn't to be, she had to remain detached, to keep
in mind that she would never be the only woman in
his life.

Before she lost her nerve, Roslynn abruptly left her
room. Across the hall, she knocked sharply on Anthony's door. The deed done, her presence known,
her apprehension returned. Her second knock was so
soft only she could have heard it. But the first knock
had done it.

Willis opened the door, took one look at her, and
silently left the room, leaving the door open for her
to enter. She did, hesitantly, closing the door behind
her. But she was reluctant to find Anthony in there.
She stared at the bed instead, empty but turned down.
Her cheeks flushed with color; her palms began to
sweat. And then it hit her suddenly what she had come
for—to make love to Anthony. Her heart began to
pound, and she hadn't even looked at him yet.

He was looking at her. His breath had caught and
held at the sight of her in her white silk negligee, the
material clinging provocatively to the soft curves of
her body, the robe she wore open, of the same thin
silk except for the long sleeves, which were transparent, revealing her bare arms beneath. Her hair was
loose and flowing in red-gold waves down her back,
making his fingers itch to get into it. And she was
barefoot.

It was the bare feet that made Anthony consider
why she had come to him. Only two reasons came to
mind. Either Roslynn was a fool to think she could
torture him with her scanty attire and escape back to

her room untouched, or she was here to end his torture.

Whatever her reason for seeking him in the privacy of his room and giving him this tantalizing view of what she had been withholding from him all week, he wasn't about to let her leave now. Whether she had set her own trap or was here to end their estrangement, his days of celibacy were over.

"Roslynn?"

There was a question in his voice. He wanted to know why she was here. Hell's teeth, was she going to have to spell it out? Wasn't it obvious? Willis had understood just by her presence, dressed as she was, and that was embarrassing enough. But Anthony was going to make her say it. She should have known this wouldn't be easy.

She finally turned toward the sound of his voice. He was sitting in the overstuffed lounge chair that he had once threatened to tie her down in. She was embarrassed further, remembering that, and remembering that he had forced her to sit there while he had changed clothes that day. Staring at him, watching the way his inscrutable eyes moved over her, she couldn't get any words out.

But her heart continued to pound, harder now that she'd seen him. He was wearing the same silver-blue robe over loose trousers that he'd worn the night they'd first made love, which brought more memories to heat her cheeks and turned that nervous knot in her belly to something entirely different.

"Well, my dear?"

Roslynn cleared her throat, but it did little good. "I—I thought that we might . . ."

She couldn't finish, not with his eyes locked to hers.

They were no longer inscrutable, but quite intense, though with what emotion she couldn't tell.

Anthony lost patience, waiting to hear what he wanted to hear. "Might *what?* There are numerous things you and I might do. What exactly did you have in mind?"

"You promised me a child!" she blurted out, then sighed with relief to have it out in the open.

"You're moving back in here?"

Hell's teeth, she'd forgotten about the rest. "No, I . . . when I conceive, there won't be any reason—"

"For you to share my bed?"

The sudden anger in his expression gave her pause, but she had made her decision. She had to stick with it.

"Exactly."

"I see."

Those two words had such an ominous ring to them, Roslynn actually shivered. Nettie had warned her he wouldn't like it, but she could see by the tight set of his jaw and the frigid blue of his eyes that he was quite furious. And yet he didn't move from the chair. His grip might be a little tighter on the brandy snifter he held in one hand, but his voice remained soft as he continued—soft and menacing.

"This was not our original agreement."

"Everything has changed since then," she reminded him.

"Nothing has changed, except what you imagine in your suspicious little mind."

She cringed. "If you won't agree—"

"Stay right where you are, Roslynn," he cut in harshly. "I haven't finished analyzing this newest condition of yours." He set his glass down on the table next to him and clasped his hands over his waist, all the while never taking his eyes off her. And then calmly again, or at least with self-restraint: "So what you want is the temporary use of my body for breeding purposes?"

"You needn't be vulgar about it."

"We'll treat the subject as it deserves, my dear. You want a stud, nothing more. The question is whether I can be detached enough to give you only what you want. It would be a new experience for me, you see. I'm not sure I'm capable of performing in a purely perfunctory manner."

At the moment, he was. He was so angry with her he wanted nothing more than to turn her over his knee and thrash some sense into her. But he would give her exactly what she was requesting and see how long it took her to admit it wasn't what she wanted at all.

Roslynn was already having doubts. He made it sound so—so animalistic. And perfunctory? What the devil did he mean by that? If he was going to be indifferent about it, then how could he make love to her? He himself had said that it couldn't be done unless desire was involved. Of course, that was when he had told her he wanted no other woman but her, and that had all been lies. But even now he said he wasn't sure he could do it. Hell's teeth! He had been after her from the beginning. How could he *not* do it?

He broke into her thoughts with a quiet command. "Come here, Roslynn."

"Anthony, perhaps—"

"You want a child?"

"Yes," she answered in a small voice.

"Then come here."

She approached him, but slowly, and a little fearfully now. She didn't like him this way, so controlled, so cold. And she knew his anger was still simmering just below the surface. Yet her heart was accelerating with each step that brought her closer to him. They were going to make love. How didn't matter. Where didn't matter, though she spared a glance at the empty bed before looking back at the chair. And then suddenly she remembered Anthony's threat the night George and Frances had been here, that he owed her a lesson in a chair. Roslynn stopped cold.

Unfortunately, she stopped too late. She was close enough to Anthony for him to reach out and drag her down onto his lap. She turned to sit sideways, to face him, but he wouldn't let her, maneuvering her the way he wanted, which was sitting straight, with her back to him. The position only made her more nervous because she couldn't see his face behind her. But perhaps that was his intention. She just didn't know what to think at this point.

"You're stiff as a board, my dear. Need I remind you this was your idea?"

"Not in a chair."

"I haven't said we'll do it here . . . but then I haven't said we won't. What does it matter where? The priority is to first discover if I'm up to this endeavor."

In the position he had placed her, sitting forward on his thighs, she had no way of knowing that he was already up to any endeavor, and had been since she'd walked into the room. She felt him gather her hair in his hands, but again, she didn't know he pressed the silken locks to his lips, to his cheek, couldn't see his eyes close as he savored the feel of her hair against his skin.

"Anthony, I don't think—"

"Shh." He pulled her head back by her hair as he leaned forward to whisper into her ear. "You do entirely too much thinking as it is, my dear. Try a little spontaneity for a change. You might like it."

She held her tongue as he slipped her robe off her shoulders, his hands traveling down her arms, pushing the sleeves down to her wrists and then off, then retracing the path back to her shoulders. He continued touching her, on her shoulders, her neck, but she quickly became aware of the difference between this time and the last time. Even last night in the carriage when he had caressed her bare arm was different from this. Then she had felt his ardor like a hot brand. Now she sensed nothing, only complete indifference, as if touching her were simply a matter of course. Perfunctory—oh, God!

She couldn't bear it, not like this. She started to get up, only to have a hand grip each of her breasts, pulling her back against him.

"You're not going anywhere, my dear. You came here with your damnable conditions, and I agreed to them. It's too late to change your mind—again."

Roslynn's head fell back against his chest. His hands hadn't remained still while he spoke. They had begun kneading, squeezing, drawing a fullness into her breasts. *He* might not be feeling anything, but she certainly was. And she couldn't seem to help it, to stop the warmth from uncoiling in her belly, making her limbs grow languorous one moment, tensed in anticipation the next.

She no longer cared if he was lacking ardor. Her own senses had taken over. It was too late to change her mind. He said it was too late. And it was a means to an end, wasn't it? She had to keep that in mind.

Moments later, she had very little in mind. His hands were roaming the front of her body, stroking gently, roughly, but in no way indifferently now,

though she had ceased to notice the difference. Even
the silk of her negligee gliding up her legs was a
heady caress. And then one hand touched the triangle
of hair he had bared and became still.

"Open your legs for me," he commanded, his
breath filling her ear with warmth.

Roslynn stiffened for a brief moment, but the words
had sent a thrill clear down to her toes. Breathlessly,
heart slamming against her chest now, she parted her
knees the barest fraction. His hand remained motion-
less on her titian curls, though the other one slipped
up under her negligee, raising it even higher as he
sought her breasts, this time without the silk to separate her from his teasing fingers.

His command came again. "Wider, Roslynn."

Her breath caught in her throat, but she obeyed him
to the letter this time, moving her knees across his
own, until her legs dropped down of their own accord
along his outer thighs. That still wasn't enough for
him. He parted his own knees, forcing her legs open
even wider, and only then did his hand glide lower to
insert a single finger inside her.

Roslynn moaned deep in her throat, her back arch-
ing away from him, her fingers digging into his jacket
behind her head. She wasn't aware of what she was
doing, but he was. Each gasp of pleasure she emitted
was like a flame licking at his soul. That he was still
in control of his own raging passions at this point was
beyond his understanding, but he wouldn't be for
much longer.

"It doesn't matter, does it?" His question was cal-
culatedly cruel, to keep his anger alive. "Here? On
the bed? On the floor?"

She heard the question. All she could do was shake
her head no.

"At this moment, I could make you break all your bloody conditions. You know that, don't you, sweetheart?" She was incapable of answering, except with a whimper. "But I won't. I want you to remember this was your choice."

Roslynn didn't care anymore. All that mattered now was the fire he had ignited in her. Anthony didn't care anymore either. She had pushed him past his limits.

Without warning, he moved her forward on his legs to ready himself, then lifted her, positioned himself, and dropped her hard. Her soft cry was ambrosia to his ears. Her hands moved up to grasp his head, the only part of him within her reach. He still had her entire torso at his disposal, and he caressed every inch while she lay back against him, savoring the fullness inside her.

He gave them that brief moment, before recalling that this was not an act of love, but one for a specific purpose only. Damnation take her and her bloody conditions. He wanted to kiss her, to turn her around and take her with all the tenderness and passion he felt for her. But he wouldn't. She had to look back on this with disgust, to admit that she wanted more from him than a child.

With that in mind, he took her hands and placed them on the arms of the chair, leaned forward until she was sitting straight up, then leaned back himself, leaving her astride him, her hair cascading down across his belly. She glanced around, expectant. He knew she was waiting for him to begin, to lead her, that she didn't know the first thing about the many positions available for lovemaking, or that in this one she was in command.

Deliberately, he said, "You wanted the use of my

body. You have it. Now ride me.'' Her eyes widened, but he didn't give her a chance to protest. ''Do it!''

She turned back to face forward, her cheeks flaming. But there was that fullness inside her that had to be answered. And if he wouldn't do it . . .

It was easy, once she found her rhythm. It was easy because it felt so wonderful, and she was in control, able to set her own pace. She could rock gently back and forth, or she could lift herself up, to slam down hard if she wanted, or to glide down with exquisite slowness. Her whims, her control—until Anthony took over.

He had no choice. She had caught on too quickly, was doing too good a job on him, and he knew damn well he wouldn't be able to wait for her to climax. He shouldn't wait. He should leave her wanting. After all, it wasn't necessary for her to experience pleasure to get with child. But he couldn't do that to her, whether she deserved it or not.

He sat up, locking an arm around her waist to keep her still while his other hand slid into the soft folds of her lower lips to find the little nub of her pleasure. He brought her to the very pinnacle, then let her go to finish on her own, and she did, riding him so hard and fast that the rolling spasms enveloped them both within mere seconds of one another.

She collapsed back on him in the chair, exhausted, blissful, and he allowed her a few moments, allowed himself the pleasure of wrapping his arms around her—for those few moments. But then he sat up and helped her to her feet.

''Get into bed—my bed. Until you conceive, you will sleep there.''

The cold tone broke into her euphoria, shocking her. She turned around to see his expression was bland, his cobalt eyes opaque, making her wonder if her ears had deceived her. Then he looked away, as if he had dismissed her from his mind, while he calmly closed his trousers. And it finally dawned on her that he hadn't removed them. He hadn't even unbelted his robe. For that matter, she was still wearing her negligee.

Tears gathered in her eyes. Anthony looked up to see them, and his face transformed with fury.

"Don't!" he snarled. "Or so help me, I'll blister your backside. You got exactly what you came in here for."

"That's no' true!" she cried.

"Isn't it? Did you expect more when you put desire on a time schedule?"

She turned her back on him so he wouldn't see the tears fall and took refuge in his bed. Much as she wanted to return to her own room at that moment, she didn't dare put it to the test, not in his present mood. But shame washed over her, keeping the tears pouring. He was right. She had come in here thinking he would make love to her as he had before. That she got something entirely different was no more than she deserved. And to her further shame, she had actually experienced pleasure from it.

She had been so sure she had made the right decision. Ah, God, why hadn't she listened to Nettie? Why was she always so self-centered, never considering anyone else's feelings but her own? If Anthony had come to her with the same proposal, that she share his bed only until she conceived, then he wanted nothing more to do with her, she would have been destroyed and thought him the most callous, cruel . . . ah, God, what must he think of her now? *She* wouldn't have agreed to such an outrageous suggestion. She would have been horribly insulted, and yes, furious, just as he was.

At least he didn't love her. She would hate to think what he would be feeling now if he did. But he did feel other things for her, desire, jealousy, possessiveness . . .

Roslynn's eyes rounded with the startling realization that those particular feelings all accompanied love. But he had said he didn't love her! No, he had said it was too soon to speak of love. But he'd never corrected her when she'd mentioned that he didn't love her. He couldn't love her. But what if he did? For that matter, what if he were telling the truth and he hadn't been unfaithful? If that were so, then her actions since they had married would be unforgivable. No—no! She couldn't be wrong about everything!

She sat up to see him still in the chair, his brandy snifter in hand again. "Anthony?"

He didn't glance her way, but his voice was terse, bitter. "Go to sleep, Roslynn. We will breed again at my convenience, not yours."

She flinched, lying back down again. Did he really think she had called him to invite him to "breed" again? No, he was just being nasty, and she couldn't blame him. She would undoubtedly have to put up with a lot more nastiness too, because she couldn't think for the moment how to get out of this latest bargain she had struck with him.

But she didn't sleep. And Anthony didn't come to bed.

Chapter Thirty-seven

It was only half past seven when Roslynn hurried downstairs the next morning. Her cheeks were still blooming with color from the mortifying experience of having come face-to-face with James as she sneaked out of Anthony's room earlier, wearing only her revealing negligee. Still wearing his evening clothes, and still looking impeccable for that matter, he had obviously just come home from a night's carousing and was just opening the door to his room down the corridor when Roslynn saw him and he saw her. And his eyes made sure that he saw *all* of her, moving slowly down her frame, then maddeningly back up, before one infuriating brow crooked in amused inquiry.

Hell's teeth, she had been embarrassed, and, face flaming, she had shot immediately into her own room and soundly closed the door, cringing to hear James' hearty laughter before he entered his own room. She had wanted nothing more than to crawl under the covers on her bed and never come out. It was one thing for James to think that she had made up with Anthony and was sharing his bed again, but quite another for him to see that that wasn't the case, that she was still keeping her own quarters, separate from his. What must James think? She shouldn't care. She had too many other problems on her mind to worry about what Anthony's brother thought of her curious behavior.

One of those problems was finding the bills from

all her recent purchases before Anthony did. She realized now how childish was her desire to cause him penury just for spite. It was utterly contemptible for a woman her age to resort to such ploys. And besides, he was too angry with her now for her to risk antagonizing him further if he discovered the enormous amount of money she had spent, all in his name.

She didn't have much time. Though she had left Anthony still sleeping in the chair he had never left last night, he always rose early for his morning ride. She wanted to be out of the house before he came down. Now that it was safe to leave, with Geordie no longer a worry, she could go to the bank and then personally take care of each of those bills. By the time she had to face Anthony again, she would at least have a clear conscience about that. Then she could consider how to get out of the horrible bargain she had made with him without sacrificing her pride or revealing that she still hadn't forgiven him for his lies. As far as she could see, it was going to be impossible to make amends to him without her pride suffering in some way. She had already spent half the night on the problem, with no solution forthcoming.

She carried her reticule and bonnet still in her hands and dropped them into a chair in Anthony's study as she went to search his desk. Her short spencer jacket in brown with a gold weave and the sorrel-brown dress she wore were sedate enough for doing business, and for her mood, which was bordering on depression, and desperation, to see her way out of the hole she was afraid she had dug too deep.

The first drawer contained ledgers and account books, the second personal correspondence she didn't even glance through. In the third drawer she found what she was looking for, more than what she was looking for. It was stuffed full of bills, some opened, some not. Typical of the gentry, and what she had been counting on. Bills tended to be ignored, sometimes for months, sometimes indefinitely, usually at least until they were ready to be paid. Hers hadn't even been opened, as she found to her relief when she recognized the names of the five merchants she had dealt with.

But this time Røslynn couldn't resist glancing through the contents of the drawer. A bill for five hundred pounds from a tailor didn't surprise her; one for two thousand from a jeweler made her brows rise. Another for thirty thousand to a Squire Simmons fairly boggled her eyes, and it didn't even say what it was for! And those were only three creditors of at least twenty bills that she could see piled in the drawer!

Was Anthony already in debt? Hell's teeth, and she had planned to add to it substantially. He would have gone through the roof if he had opened her bills. Thank God he was typical of his class and had just stuffed the things away to be ignored until a later day.

While she was at the bank, she would have to see about having the funds due him from her marriage contract transferred to an account for him and arrange to have the allotted amount added each month. Then she would have to go through the unpleasant task of explaining about the money, for if she didn't tell him, he would never know it was available. And this was *not* the time to talk of money to him. Another cursed problem to worry about.

"Hello, there!"

Roslynn jumped and hastily crumpled the bills in her hand and stuffed them in her skirt pocket, which was, fortunately, below the level of the desk, so Jeremy couldn't see what she was doing. At least it was only he. If it had been Anthony who had caught her behind his desk, she would have had no excuse. With Jeremy, she didn't need one, but was still nervous from the start he had given her.

"You're up early," she pointed out, coming around the desk to get her bonnet and tie it on.

"Derek's picking me up. We're off to a wild party in the country that could last for days."

His excitement fairly bubbled over. God, how she wished she had known Anthony when he was this young and probably looked exactly as Jeremy did now, they were so close in resemblance. But she doubted Anthony had ever been this transparent, even at the tender age of seventeen.

"Does your father know?"

" 'Course he does."

This was said too quickly, and Roslynn felt her maternal instincts rise unexpectedly. "Just what do you mean, wild?"

Jeremy winked at her, full of high spirits. "There's to be no ladies, if you get my drift, but lots of women."

"Does your father know about *that?*"

He laughed at her look of censure. "Said he might stop by himself."

Roslynn felt another blush coming on. If it was all right with his father, who was she to say otherwise? The lad was certainly old enough to . . . well, James must think him old enough. But no son of hers would be cavorting with women at seventeen. She would see to that—if she ever had a son.

She sighed, picking up her reticule. "Well, have a—" No, she wouldn't wish him a good time. She just couldn't condone what he was off to do at his age, even if he did look a full-grown man already. "I'll see you when you return, I suppose."

"You're going out?" he asked in sudden concern, her bonnet making that obvious. "Is it safe?"

"Perfectly." She smiled. "Your uncle took care of everything."

"You need a ride, then? Derek will be here shortly."

"No, I have a carriage waiting and one of the footmen is accompanying me, though I'm only going to the bank. Be good, Jeremy," she said in parting, to his chagrin.

It wasn't that short a ride to the bank, but to Roslynn's irritation, she was still too early. She hadn't even thought of the time in her impatience to be out of the house. Rather than just sit there, she had the driver slowly round the block several times, until the bank was finally open.

Her business took just under an hour, longer than she had expected because of opening the account for Anthony. A hundred thousand pounds' lump sum, plus another twenty each month as per her contract, ought to help if he was as deep in debt as she thought. Whether he would appreciate this dowry of hers was another matter. Most men would. She just wasn't sure Anthony was one of them.

Coming out of the bank, Roslynn was distracted, as her driver and the accompanying footman were, by the sight of two men engaged in fisticuffs up the street, something one might expect to see down by the waterfront, not here . . .

She didn't finish the thought. An arm came around her waist from behind, cutting off her breath, and something hard and sharp poked in her side.

"No funny stuff this time, m'lady, or I'll let ye see just 'ow sharp this 'ere sticker be."

She said not a word. She was at first too surprised to, then too afraid when she realized what his "sticker" was. In broad daylight, right in front of a bank—this was incredible. And her carriage was right there, not five feet away. But she was being led behind it while the fight in front of it was still claiming everyone's attention. Had that been planned as a distraction? Hell's teeth, if this was Geordie's doing— but it couldn't be. He had been warned off, violently. He wouldn't dare—would he?

She was shoved into an old coach, one with dark shades over the windows, and the fellow closed the door behind them after following her in. She started to get up off the floor, but a rough hand shoved her back down.

"Give me no trouble, m'lady, an' this'll go real easy fer ye," he said as he stuffed a cloth in her mouth, then quickly tied her hands behind her back. He looked down at his handiwork, noticed her feet, and decided to take no chances, whipping a rope around her ankles. His chuckle was ugly as he plucked her dirk out of her boot. "Ye won't be gettin' another chance to use this on me brother."

Roslynn groaned inwardly, hearing that. So he was one of the men from her last attempted abduction, Geordie's men. Her cousin must be insane to still try and take her. He knew she was married. What the devil did he think he was doing? She stiffened, the answer coming to her. The only thing he could want with her now was revenge for her having eluded his well-planned trap.

The fellow left the coach, left her lying on the floor. A few moments later the old vehicle started to move.

Roslynn turned over on her side to try and sit up. The gag in her mouth hadn't been secured, and she frantically worked with her tongue to push it out. She had almost succeeded when the coach slowed down and she heard the driver shout, "That's enough, Tom!"

A second later the door opened and another fellow jumped inside the coach. She recognized this one as the footpad she had taken a chunk out of with her dirk. His lip was bleeding, and he was out of breath. So the distraction *had* been arranged. This was one of the pugilists, who had probably picked a fight with a stranger just so no one would notice when the other fellow led her away. And she had gone along willy-nilly, with a knife pricking her side, not making a single protest.

The fellow, Tom, was grinning at her as he lifted her up and set her on the seat across from him. He tucked her gag back in her mouth too, shaking his head at her in an amused way. At least he wasn't vengeful for the hurt she had caused him the last time, or he didn't seem to be. He was studying her and continued grinning. Finally he laughed.

"God, ye're a bleedin' beauty close up, ye are. Too good fer the likes o' that bastard what's payin' us, I'd say." She tried to speak through the gag, uselessly. "None o' that, now. Thought we'd never get ye, but 'ere ye are. Be good, and there'll be no cause to get rough wi' ye."

Her second warning not to cause trouble. So what would happen if she did? Stupid question, when she was bound up hand and foot and couldn't make a sound louder than a squeak.

Chapter Thirty-eight

*T*hey brought her into the building tossed over Tom's shoulder. They had waited first, however, until Wil, as the other, shorter man was called, had said that all was clear. Roslynn's hopes picked up immediately. They were taking her somewhere where someone might stop and question them for treating her in this horrid manner. One good scream, if she got the chance, was all she might need to be rescued.

From her upside-down position, she saw little of the building before they entered it and she was being hurried up some stairs. But across the street were dwellings faced with brownstone, looking as if they belonged in a normal residential area, and one of fair quality. A boarding house, then? Likely, if no one was about at this time of the morning.

So this was where Geordie had moved, to a finer part of town? No wonder Anthony had so much trouble finding him when all he had to go by was that waterfront hovel where she had been taken last time. But little good it had done, his finding Geordie. And she had walked right into the trap, thinking herself safe at last. Hell's teeth, but she despised Geordie for his Scot's stubbornness in refusing to give up.

There was a brief stop while a door was pounded on. Then a few more steps and Roslynn was dumped into a chair. She groaned as she sat back on her bound arms, terribly sore now after the slow, long ride getting here. But she spared only a moment for the dis-

comfort before glancing furiously about the room for
a sight of Geordie.

When she saw him standing next to the bed, a
folded shirt in hand, his valise open on the bed in the
process of being packed, she simply stared, wondering who he was. But the carrot thatch of hair . . .

Roslynn grimaced, unable to help herself. If not
for the hair, she wouldn't have recognized him. He
looked horrible. He looked as if he belonged in bed,
not packing to leave. Good God, what Anthony had
done to him! His whole face was discolored and
puffed to twice its size, it seemed, one eye black and
completely closed, the other bluish-purple and just
able to open a mere slit. His nose was swollen and
off center. His lips were caked with bloody crusts.
There were other ugly scabs on his cheeks and above
his eyes where the skin had cracked on bone.

He wasn't looking at her, at least not now. He was
staring at the two miscreants responsible for her presence, who were staring at him as if they'd never seen
him before. Hadn't they known he'd taken a beating?
Hell's teeth, had a mistake been made?

It had been. Geordie threw down his shirt in a rage,
then groaned, grabbing his rib cage, the sharp movement ripping him apart with pain. Wilbert and
Thomas Stow just stood there, not knowing what to
think.

Geordie told them what to think, in a voice choked
with rage, the words slurred because of puffed lips.
"Ye idiots! Didna the lad I sent tae find ye give ye
my note?"

"This?" Tom took out a scrap of paper from his
pocket. "We can't read, m'lord," he stated with a
shrug, letting the note drop to the floor.

Geordie made an ugly sound in his throat. " 'Tis

what I get fer hiring English dolts!" He pointed a stiff finger at Roslynn. "I dinna want her now. She married the bloody Englishmon!"

Wilbert and Thomas apparently thought that was funny. They started laughing, and Roslynn watched what wasn't black-and-blue on Geordie's face turn bright red. If what she had gone through to get here wasn't so infuriating, she might have found the situation as it was amusing too.

Geordie didn't. "Get oout, the both of ye!"

The pair stopped laughing. "When ye pay us, m'lord."

Wilbert might have given him the title of respect, but there was no respect in his tone. In fact, the short, thickly bearded fellow looked absolutely menacing as he stared at Geordie. So did the bigger chap beside him. And Geordie had gone quiet, his rage replaced by something else. Roslynn's eyes widened. He was afraid! Didn't he have the money to pay them?

Geordie in fact had only enough money to get back to Scotland. He had counted on Roslynn's money to pay his hirelings off. All that money, gone to the Englishman. It wasn't fair. And now these two would probably kill him. And in his condition, he couldn't even defend himself.

Working her gag while no one was watching, Roslynn finally managed to spit it out. "Untie me, and I'll give you your money—in exchange for my dirk."

"Dinna touch her!" Geordie commanded.

Roslynn turned on him furiously. "Shut up, Geordie! Do you ken what my husband will do to you when he finds out about this? You'd look bonny right now by comparison if he gets his hands on you again."

Wilbert and Thomas didn't miss the significance of

that "again," but they were done listening to Geordie anyway. They might have killed a few men in their time, but they had never harmed a woman before. They hadn't liked this job to begin with, and wouldn't have taken it if the Scot hadn't offered what was a bleeding fortune to them.

Wilbert stepped forward and cut Roslynn's bonds with her own dirk. Flipping the blade over in his hand, he handed it to her, but was quick to step back out of her way.

Roslynn was amazed it had been so easy, since she hadn't been at all sure the two ruffians would obey her. But they had, and she felt infinitely better already. And she had obviously guessed right, or Geordie would have gotten them their money before she was cut loose. Instead, he had sat down on the bed, holding his ribs, warily watching all three.

"How much?" she demanded as she stood up.

"Thirty pounds, m'lady."

She spared a contemptuous glance for her cousin. "You're cheap, Geordie. It seems you could have offered a bit more to two such dependable fellows."

"I might have, if they'd have gotten ye afore that bastard married ye!" he spat out.

She clucked her tongue, feeling rather good about having miraculously gotten the upper hand in the confrontation she had so dreaded. Reaching into the reticule that was still tied to her wrist, she took out a handful of money.

"This will do, I believe, gentlemen." She handed the notes to Wilbert.

Both brothers' eyes gleamed at what amounted to nearly fifty pounds. Wilbert glanced at her reticule. Roslynn intercepted his look, stiffening.

"Don't even think about it," she warned. "And if

you don't want to end up looking like him''—she
nodded toward Geordie—''you'll never let me see you
again.''

They both grinned at the little woman threatening
them. But they had been paid enough. If the Scot
hadn't been mashed to a pulp, they would have gotten
in a few licks themselves for all his insults. As it was,
they were satisfied and, with grinning nods, left.

They stopped grinning, however, at the top of the
stairs. Coming up them was the same gent whose
house they had been watching for the past ten days,
the same gent who was undoubtedly now the lady's
husband. He didn't look menacing, didn't even spare
them a glance as he slowly mounted the stairs, and
yet neither brother could get out of his mind the Scot's
condition that this man was responsible for.

Wilbert pulled his knife, just to feel safe, though
he palmed it close to his thigh. That would have been
the end of it if the nabob wasn't deceptive in his nonchalance. He had in fact noticed the knife and
stopped. They both heard him sigh before he spoke.

''Bloody hell. Come along, then, and let's get this
over with.''

Wilbert glanced once at Thomas before they both
charged as one. Their attack didn't turn out as they
had expected, however. The nobleman stepped out of
the way at the last second, putting his back to the
wall, and with one foot extended, Thomas went tumbling down the rest of the stairs. And before Wilbert
knew what was happening, he had lost his knife. Seeing it in the noble's hand, he tore down the stairs
himself, collected a groaning Thomas up from the
floor, and dragged them both out of the building.

Upstairs in the room, Roslynn was pacing furiously
before an embittered Geordie. ''There are no' enough

dirty, loathsome, vile names for what you are, Geordie Cameron. It's shamed I am, you carry that name. You've never brought anything good to it, have you now?''

''And ye have, have ye?''

''Shut up, mon! Because of you I'm married now. Because of you I *had* to get married, when that was no' what I was wanting, at least no' this way!''

''And ye've lost it all, havena ye. ye stupid fool!'' he shot back at her. ''And I'm glad, do ye hear? If I canna have the Cameron wealth, at least I'm knowing he's tricked ye oout of it as well!''

Roslynn stopped short, glaring at him. ''What are you blathering about?''

''He told me he burned yer marriage contract,'' Geordie replied in what passed for a laugh. ''The wily bastard's got it all now, and ye wouldna even be getting it back if he died, 'cause he's leaving it all tae his own kin. Nice husband ye've shackled yerself wi', cousin.''

She almost laughed, but if Anthony had gone to the trouble to tell Geordie that lie, she wouldn't take it back. It was brilliant, really, in making Geordie think his chance was forever lost.

''I'd still rather have him than you, *cousin.*''

He tried getting up at that slur. He moaned loudly, falling back on the bed. Roslynn goaded him further, not in the least sympathetic.

''You should have left when you had the chance, Geordie. There willna be much left of you if my husband finds out you're still here. He's no' a man to trifle wi', as you've found out. But you deserve it for trying to kill him.''

''I was only trying tae scare him into forsaking ye. I didna know then ye'd married the mon. But he only hit me a few times fer shooting at him. The rest was all fer ye. And I'll have ye know, I couldna even get up off the floor where he'd left me until this morning.'' This was said in what sounded very much like a whine. "But ye can see fer yerself that I was leaving, sae ye've nae tales tae take tae that bloody Spartan.''

Spartan? Yes, she supposed Anthony could at times be likened to that austere race known for its strict discipline and military prowess, but only in the lightest sense. His self-control might be absolutely maddening when he chose to use it, but when he didn't, he was as hot-tempered as any Scot. And look at what he had done to Geordie, without getting even a scratch in the process. Poor Geordie looked like he had been trampled by a horse, not merely beaten by a man's fists.

"I wasn't going to tell Anthony, not if you really are leaving,'' she conceded.

"Ye're all heart, lass.''

It was impossible to mistake the bitter sarcasm, and her outrage shot to the fore again. "If you're expecting me to feel sorry for you, Geordie, I mun disappoint you. I just canna do it, no' after all you've done. You tried to hurt me!''

"I loved ye!''

The words were like a rope around her throat, choking off her breath. Was it possible? He had said that often enough over the years, but she had never believed him. Why did it have a ring of truth to it this time? Or had he deluded himself into thinking it was so?

Quietly, actually afraid of the answer, she demanded, "If that's true, Geordie, then tell me about my mother. Did you put a hole in her boat?''

His head came off the bed, followed more slowly by the rest of his body. "Why did ye no' ask me when it mattered, Ros, when it happened? Why did the auld mon never ask? Nae, I never tampered wi' her boat. I was down by the loch finding worms tae put in cook's stew. That was as close as I ever came tae those boats."

"But your face when you were told? We all saw you were horrified."

"Aye, because I'd wished her dead, fer boxing my ears that morning. I didna mean it, but I thought my wish had been granted. I *felt* I was tae blame."

Roslynn felt sick to her stomach. All these years, they'd blamed him for something he didn't do. And he knew what they thought but never spoke up to defend himself, just harbored his resentment unto himself. It didn't make him a nicer person in her eyes, but it made him innocent of any real crime.

"I'm sorry, Geordie, I really am."

"But ye still wouldna have married me, would ye, knowing the truth?"

"No. And you shouldn't have tried to force me."

"A mon will do anything when he's desperate."

For love or money? She didn't ask. But she wondered if her grandfather's will might have been different if he had known the truth. Somehow, she didn't think so. He had always despised Geordie's weakness, an unforgivable trait for a man of Duncan's strength of character. She wasn't that uncharitable. And she had to salve her conscience for blaming Geordie for her mother's death, which she now realized must have been no more than a freak accident.

She would leave him the money in her reticule that had been intended to pay her bills. Ten thousand pounds wasn't much compared with what she had, but it would be a start for Geordie. And maybe he could do something with it to make his own way, instead of always looking for the easy road that cost him nothing and made him weaker.

Roslynn turned around to remove the money without his seeing. She would leave it where he wouldn't find it until she had gone.

"I'll help you pack, Geordie."

"Dinna do me any favors."

She ignored the bitterness and moved to the bureau, where several articles of clothing still remained in an open drawer. She gathered them up and slipped the money between the clothes before dropping the pile in his valise. It was a mistake to have gotten that close. His hand snaked out, wrapping around her wrist.

"Ros—"

The door opened and she was freed, never to know what Geordie had been about to say. She would like to think it might have been an apology for all he'd put her through. It didn't matter at the moment, not with Anthony's presence filling the room.

"With as quiet as it got, I was afraid you might have killed each other."

She didn't question why he was there, not just then. "Eavesdropping at doors seems to be a habit of yours, my lord."

He didn't deny it. "A useful one, and most times fascinating."

That "most times" referred to his eavesdropping on her and Frances, she knew, and he didn't like what he had overheard then. But there wasn't much he could have overheard this time to annoy him. He might look stern, but by now she knew the difference.

He was angry, but not *that* angry. In fact, it could just be a carryover from last night.

"He's leaving, as you can see," she said, walking toward her husband.

"And you came to say good-bye?" Anthony replied dryly. "How thoughtful of you, my dear."

She wasn't going to be baited. "If you've come to take me home, I thank you. I find myself without a ride."

She hoped that that would do it, that he wouldn't direct his attention to Geordie now and start a scene that she would be forced to witness. She didn't particularly want to see Anthony in the mood that could have brought about what he'd already done to Geordie. His level stare made her hold her breath. And then he directed that intense look to Geordie. Roslynn knew her cousin must be trembling in mortal fear.

"I'll be gone wi'in the hour," Geordie volunteered.

Anthony's nerve-racking stare lasted a moment longer. Then he nodded curtly and led Roslynn out the door. His hand on her elbow was impossible to break loose from, so she gave up after one try. Outside, there was no carriage, just his horse being held by a street urchin.

Roslynn decided to attack before he could. "What were you doing back here?"

"Come to see you home, of course."

"Making sure he was gone, you mean, since you couldn't possibly know I'd be here."

"That too."

She gritted her teeth. *"Did* you know?"

"Not until I heard you tearing into the poor man with all the vile, loathsome, and despicable names you never got around to calling him."

So he had been outside the door from the beginning. Had she said anything he shouldn't have heard?
No, she didn't think so—not this time. But she was
still annoyed.

"You would have been better served to have fer-
reted out his men, who had still been watching the
house—from the park, no doubt. They followed me
to the bank and—"

"Yes, Jeremy did mention that was your destination. Imagine my surprise to find you here instead."

He said it as if he didn't believe her. "Hell's teeth,
Anthony! I didn't know where he was, so how could
I have found him even if I'd wanted to, which I didn't?
Those dolts he hired hadn't been told yet that he'd
given up."

"Plausible," was all he said as he tossed the youth
a coin and mounted his stallion.

She glared at the hand he leaned over to offer her.
Sitting next to him all the way home was not very
enticing at the moment. She would have preferred to
find a hack but saw none on the street.

She took his hand and found herself sitting between
his legs, her own draped over his thigh. Color rose
swiftly to her cheeks as she was forced to put her
arms around him. It was a disconcerting ride, one that
brought vividly to mind her main dilemma. Surrounded by his warmth, her nostrils filled with his
scent, she could think only about how to get out of
the bargain she had struck with him and back into his
bed without any stipulations at all.

Chapter Thirty-nine

*T*he ride to Piccadilly seemed to take forever, and yet it wasn't nearly long enough. A hazy kind of euphoria had settled over Roslynn. With no words to distract her, just the steady gait of the horse, the steady beat of Anthony's heart next to her ear, it was easy to forget reality and float in a cocoon of contentment.

So it was quite jarring to be placed on her feet and have her plaguey problems recalled. The suddenness of it left Roslynn disoriented for a moment. In fact, she stared at the crumpled envelope lying at her feet for a good fifteen seconds before she realized what it was and reached for it. Anthony's hand came up the victor.

Roslynn groaned inwardly, having forgotten all about those stupid bills. To have one fall out of her skirt pocket was bad enough. To have Anthony retrieve it was the worst luck. And it was too much to hope he would just hand it back to her. He didn't. He opened it!

"Anthony!"

He shot her a glance with one dark, winged brow arched. "It's addressed to me," was all he said.

She started to walk into the house, as if that would end the matter. His hand on her arm detained her while he still perused the paper in his other hand.

When he spoke, his voice sounded merely curious. "Might I ask what you're doing with this?"

She could see no way out and turned to face him. "It's for some of the furniture I bought."

"I can see what it's for, my dear. I asked what you're doing with it."

"I was going to pay it. That's why . . ."

Her words trailed off as she saw his eyes drift down to her pocket. She followed his gaze and saw another envelope poking out. The bloody ride had worked them loose. And before she could say another word, Anthony's hand was in her pocket and pulling out the rest of the bills.

"You were going to pay these too?"

She nodded, but he wasn't looking at her, so she choked the word out. "Yes."

"Then wouldn't it have been appropriate to have them billed to you instead of me?"

She didn't understand why he was being so calm about this. "I—I meant to, but I forgot."

"No, you didn't," he replied, making her heart sink, only to confuse her by adding, in what was unmistakable amusement, "You're not very good at bargaining, my dear. I could have found these items for half the price you paid for them."

He stuffed the bills into his own pocket, annoying her, because it was just what she would have expected him to do. "Those are *my* purchases," she reminded him.

"They grace *my* house."

"I bought them," she insisted. "I'll bloody well pay for them."

"No, you won't. You had no intention of paying for them to begin with, so let's just leave it as it is, shall we?"

He was smiling at her. Smiling! "Don't be stubborn about this, Anthony. You have enough creditors already. I want to pay for what I—"

"Be quiet, sweetheart," he interrupted, his hands resting on her shoulders. "I suppose I shouldn't have let you go on thinking I was just struggling by, but you were having so much fun trying to put me in debt, I didn't want to spoil it." He chuckled when she lowered her eyes guiltily, and lifted her chin back up. "The truth is, you could have redecorated a hundred households, and I wouldn't have raised a brow."

"But you can't be rich!"

He laughed delightedly. "It pays to have a brother who is a genius where money is concerned. Edward has a golden touch, you might say. And he handles the family's finances with our blessings. If the town house still doesn't suit you after all the trouble you've gone through to redo it, I have several estates in the outlying vicinity, as well as in Kent, Northampton, Norfolk, York, Lincoln, Wiltshire, Devon—"

"Enough!"

"Are you so disappointed I didn't marry you for your money, my dear?"

"You've still got some of it, as per the marriage contract. I put the money into an account for you this morning." There, at least that was out of the way.

So was his amusement. "You'll take yourself back to the bank and put it in a trust for our children. And as long as we're on this subject, I support you, Roslynn. Your clothes, your jewels, anything that adorns your body, I pay for."

"And what am I supposed to do with *my* money?" she demanded sharply.

"Anything you like, as long as it's nothing to do with clothing, food, or shelter, or what is my prerogative to buy you. You might do well to discuss with me first what you decide to spend your money on. We just might avoid future arguments in that way.''

Her independent spirit was infuriated. Her woman's heart was delighted. And that word ''children'' kept buzzing in her head. It implied an eventual end to their difficulties, though she couldn't see that end in sight.

''If this discussion is going to continue, shouldn't we take it inside?''

Anthony grinned at her neutral tone. He had made his point, and his earlier pleasure that she had given up her spite against him returned. For whatever reason, it was a peace offering, and he could make one too. That what he had in mind was more of a necessity after that close ride with her was just plain luck.

''This subject has run its course,'' Anthony said, leading her inside the house. ''But there is another that needs immediate attention.''

Roslynn's heart skipped a beat, but she couldn't be sure she had grasped his meaning correctly. So she didn't allow herself to hope until he took her arm and escorted her upstairs to his room. Even then, as he closed the door behind them, she still wasn't certain of his intentions. He crossed the room, removed his coat, and tossed it into that cursed chair they had occupied last night.

She frowned at the chair. Oh, she had learned her lesson in it, as he had promised she would. Resentment bubbled up in her chest, to fight with the powerful arousal she felt just by being in this room again.

''Come here, Roslynn.''

He had moved to the bed, was sitting on it, was slowly unbuttoning his white cambric shirt. Her heart picked up double time. He was a temptation beyond imagining, but she didn't think she could bear it if he was going to be "perfunctory" with her once more.

"You—you feel capable of simulating desire, I take it?"

"Simulate?" Both brows shot up. "Oh, I see. You still don't believe in spontaneity, do you, sweetheart? Come here and help me with my boots, will you?"

She did, only because he hadn't answered her question yet, and she didn't feel like running until she knew for sure. The nastiness she could take, but not the lack of passion.

"You're nervous," he noted when she wouldn't turn around after dropping his second boot on the floor. "You needn't be, my dear. You have to take advantage of me when the opportunity presents itself."

He saw her back stiffen and immediately regretted those words. He had made his point last night. She wouldn't forget it. But he couldn't go through that experience again to save his soul.

He reached forward to draw her between his legs, his hands sliding up her ribs to cup her breasts, his cheek pressed against her spencer. Her head fell back. She arched into his hands. Anthony ignited, dropping her down onto the bed, twisting so he leaned over her but kept her legs locked between his.

"Simulation, my dear? I don't believe you and I are capable of such a feat."

His mouth covered hers with a scorching passion that singed all her nerve ends, taking her breath away. It was exquisite. It was what she remembered, this consuming fire between them that defied all reason. Last night was forgotten. He was kissing her now as if he would die if he didn't, hiding nothing from her, and the soul of the woman came alive in his arms.

Chapter Forty

"*I*'ll be leaving in two days, Tony," was the first thing James said as he entered the dining room.

"Need help packing?"

"Don't be tedious, puppy. You know you've loved having me."

Anthony grunted and resumed eating his breakfast. "When did you finally decide to be on your way?"

"When I saw how hopeless your situation has become. It's simply no fun to watch anymore."

Anthony tossed down his fork, glaring at his brother's back as James walked casually to the sideboard after that remark and heaped food on a plate. Actually, he thought he'd made a great deal of progress in the past two weeks. He had only to touch Roslynn now and she turned into his arms. He failed to see what was hopeless about that. Soon she would admit that she needed him as much as he needed her. She would admit her folly and damn her own rules. But until she did, he would abide by them, to the bloody letter.

"Would you mind explaining that remark?"

James sat down across from him and said maddeningly, "I like this room now. What'd it cost you?"

"Blister it, James!"

A shrug. "It's obvious, dear boy. Here she is sharing your room, at all hours of the day, I've noticed, yet when you two aren't ensconced behind that door, you're bloody strangers. Where's the finesse you're known for that has women eating out of the palm of your hand? Is she immune?''

''This is none of your business, you know.''

''I know.''

Anthony answered him anyway. ''She's not immune, but she's not like other women either. She has these infernal notions . . . the point is, I want her to come to me of her own will, not with senses drugged and giving her no choice.''

''You mean she won't—come to you, that is?'' When Anthony simply scowled at him, James chuckled. ''Don't tell me you haven't straightened up that little misunderstanding about sweet Margie?''

''You still remember her name?''

The sneer was obvious, but James chose to ignore his brother's testiness. ''Actually, I've been back to see her quite often. She was a delectable piece.'' But that vixen in breeches hadn't shown up at the tavern again, the real reason he had gone back there. ''Did you never think to explain?''

''I did. I won't do it twice.''

James sighed at such stubbornness, never mind that his own was just as irksome to friend and foe. ''Pride is the advent of fools, dear boy. You've been married nearly a month. If I had known what a bloody mess you were going to make of it, I would have pursued the lady in earnest.''

''Over my dead body,'' Anthony snarled.

''Touchy, aren't we?'' James grinned. ''But it doesn't matter. You won her. What you've done with the prize, however, is deplorable. A little romancing wouldn't be amiss. She did melt for you in the moonlight, didn't she?''

Anthony just managed to keep his seat when the urge to clobber his brother was overwhelming. ''The last thing I need from you is advice, James. I have my own strategy where my wife is concerned, and although it may not appear to be working, it is.''

"Strangest bit of strategy I've ever witnessed, enemies by day, lovers by moonlight. I wouldn't have the patience myself. If they don't succumb by the first effort—''

"They're not worth it?''

"Some are. But there are just too many other sweet consolations to be bothered.''

"But I've got Roslynn.''

James laughed. "Point taken, I suppose. *Is* she worth it?''

Anthony's answer was a slow smile, his first, and James sobered. Yes, he supposed the little Scot was worth a bit a patience. But as for Anthony's strategy, it was obvious to James he was only digging his hole even deeper. James wouldn't be at all surprised if, when he returned to England, Anthony's wife had much in common with Jason's, who used any excuse available to avoid her husband.

Nettie appeared in the doorway. "Excuse me, Sir Anthony, but Lady Roslynn would be liking a word wi' ye.''

"Where is she?''

"In her room, my lord. She's no' feeling up tae snuff.''

Anthony waved the woman away before growling, "Bloody hell!''

James shook his head in disgust. "There, you see? You hear your wife's ill, and instead of being concerned—''

"Confound you, James, you don't know what the bloody hell's going on, so stay out of it! If she's ill, it's what she's been praying for. I noticed it the other morning when—'' Anthony stopped at James' quirked brow. "Damnation. She's going to tell me I'm going to be a father.''

"A—but that's splendid!'' James said in delight, only to notice Anthony's scowl grow even blacker and add hesitantly, "Isn't it?''

"No, it bloody well isn't!''

"For God's sake, Tony, children usually do follow marriage—''

"I know that, you dolt! I want the child. I just don't want the conditions that come with it.''

James started to laugh, misunderstanding. "The price of fatherhood, don't you know. Good God, it's only a few months you'll have to stay out of the lady's bed. You can always find relief elsewhere.''

Anthony stood up, his voice calm, but cold enough to freeze. "*If* I wanted relief elsewhere, and *if* it were only for a few months, you might be right, brother. But my celibacy begins the moment my dear wife announces her condition to me.''

James was surprised enough to reply, "Whose ridiculous idea was *that?*''

"It bloody well wasn't mine.''

"You mean the only reason she came to you was to get a child?''

"None other.''

James snorted. "I hate to say it, dear boy, but it sounds like your wife needs her backside treated to a good thrashing.''

"No, what she needs is to admit she's wrong, and she will. How soon is the question that's going to drive me crazy.''

Chapter Forty-one

*W*eak tea and dry toast, at Nettie's insistence. Not a very appetizing breakfast, but better than the hot chocolate and pastries that had sent Roslynn flying toward the chamber pot earlier. She had suspected her condition for the past week, after her monthly time was late. She had been sure three days ago, when the most ghastly queasiness had started in the morning, only to vanish come noon. And each day it had gotten a little worse. This morning she had had to stay near the chamber pot for nearly an hour, had heaved her stomach dry. She dreaded what tomorrow would bring, and tomorrow morning was Frances' wedding. She wasn't at all sure she would be able to make it, which was just one more thing to depress her at the moment, when she should have been nothing but overjoyed by her condition.

Her stomach still wasn't settled completely, even with the bland toast she had nibbled on. It was hard for her to remember, considering how she was feeling, that a baby was what she wanted more than anything. Why couldn't she be one of those lucky women who suffered not a day of morning sickness? And to have started so soon! Why, she had made her infamous bargain with Anthony just two weeks ago. And she had suspected she was pregnant one week later, which told her plainly she hadn't needed to make that bargain at all, that she had in all likelihood conceived the very first time they made love.

Roslynn very gently set the teacup back on the table

beside the chaise longue on which she was reclining.
Undue movement, as she had discovered to her horror
the other morning when Anthony made love to her,
started her stomach rolling. Extreme concentration
had enabled her not to embarrass herself and have to
make her confession right then. And she had selfishly
gone to him for two more nights without telling him
the truth. But she couldn't put it off any longer. This
morning she had just barely made it out of his room
before he woke up and called her back to bed. And
with the nausea getting worse, there was no way she
could enjoy morning lovemaking anymore. She had
to tell him before he found out for himself and knew
she was ignoring their bargain.

Hell's teeth, how she hated that bloody bargain.
Anthony had been so wonderfully amorous these past
two weeks, at least in his bedroom. He made love to
her so often she knew very well he had nothing left
to give another woman, that she'd had him all to herself. It was as if each night were her wedding night,
with all the passion and tenderness he was capable
of, hers for the taking.

But outside his bedroom he was another man entirely, either indifferent or cold and sardonic, but
never pleasant. And Roslynn knew this could be
blamed on the bargain, his way of letting her know
his distaste for her conditions hadn't lessened.

And now it was over. But she didn't want it to be
over. Hell's teeth, she had become addicted to Anthony, but by her own idiotic decision, she was going
to lose him. Temporary, she had said. Two short
weeks was certainly that.

"You wanted to see me?"

He hadn't knocked, but had come right in. He

hadn't been in this room since the night she had pretended to be indisposed. There was no pretense now.

Anthony gave the new furnishings a cursory glance before his cobalt eyes settled on her. Roslynn could feel her stomach rioting from her nervousness.

"I'm going to have a baby," she blurted out.

He stood before her, his hands in his pockets. His expression didn't change. That was the worst. He could at least have shown some small pleasure about the child. If not that, then displeasure. She would have welcomed displeasure at the moment. She would have welcomed the fury he had shown the night she had given him her terms.

"How delightful for you," he said in the blandest tone. "So your sojourns to my room are at an end."

"Yes. Unless—"

"Unless?" he cut in deliberately. "Far be it from me to break your rules, sweetheart."

She bit her lip to keep from damning those rules in his presence. She didn't know what she had started to say anyway, before he interrupted. But he obviously hadn't wanted to hear it. And she had been hoping, praying, that *he* would insist she forget their bargain, that he would demand she move back to his room permanently. He wasn't going to. Didn't he care anymore?

She looked away toward the window, her voice toneless when it should have been filled with excitement, considering the subject. "I will need a room for the nursery."

"James is leaving in a few days. You can make over his room."

She had given him the opening. He could have suggested *this* room. It was certainly more convenient, directly across from his.

She continued to stare out the window. "This is your child too, Anthony. Have you any preferences for color—or anything?"

"Whatever pleases you, my dear. By the by, I won't be home for dinner tonight. We're celebrating old George's last night of sanity at the club."

His abrupt change of subject hurt. He obviously had no interest in the baby, nor in her, since he had turned to leave without another word.

Outside the room, Anthony's fist slammed into the wall. Inside, tears were streaming down Roslynn's cheeks. She started from the noise but didn't give it a thought.

She had never felt so miserable in her life, and it was all her own fault. She couldn't even remember the reason for the stupid bargain. Oh, yes. She had been afraid she'd fall in love with Anthony with constant intimacy. Well, it was too bloody late for that, wasn't it? Nettie had been right.

"Was it the news you were expecting?"

Anthony turned to find James standing outside his room. "It was."

"Strategy's not working, then, I take it?"

"Blister it, James. Two days from now isn't soon enough!"

Chapter Forty-two

"*W*hy don't you just tell him, Ros?"

"I can't," Roslynn replied, taking a sip of her second glass of champagne.

They stood away from the others at the party, which was just a small gathering of Frances' friends at her mother's house. The gentlemen weren't the only ones who could celebrate the night before the wedding. But Roslynn didn't feel like celebrating, though she had come to accept that Frances was ecstatic about this marriage, and she was happy for her friend. She just couldn't seem to show it.

Unfortunately, Frances had picked up on her depression and had taken her aside, afraid that Roslynn was still against the marriage. The only way she could convince her friend that she wasn't was to tell her the truth.

"If it were that simple—" Roslynn began, only to have Frances cut in.

"But it is that simple. All you do is say, I love you. Three little words, m'dear, and your problems will be over."

Roslynn shook her head. "The difference, Fran, is that those words are easy for you because you know George returns your love. But Anthony doesn't love me."

"Have you given him anything *to* love?"

Roslynn grimaced. "No. You might say I've been a royal bitch ever since we married."

"Well, you did have your reasons, didn't you? It

was really too bad of Sir Anthony, but you did say you're reasonably certain he strayed only that one time. It's up to you, m'dear. You can let him know you've forgiven him his one indiscretion and you want to start over, or you can go on as you are.''

Some choice, Roslynn thought, resentment still simmering just below the surface. Why did she have to make all the concessions? Anthony hadn't even apologized, and he wasn't likely to.

"A man like Sir Anthony won't wait forever, you know,'' Frances continued. ''You're going to send him right into the arms of another woman.''

"He doesn't need any sending for that,'' Roslynn replied bitterly.

But Frances had a point. If *she* wasn't sharing Anthony's bed, someone else would eventually. But then she had known that when she made her bargain. She just hadn't wanted to admit at that time that it would matter to her. But it did matter, terribly, because she loved him.

Returning home at eleven, Roslynn had only just removed her evening cloak and gloves when the door opened again and Anthony and George stumbled over the threshold. Dobson took one look at them and sighed. Roslynn felt she had played this scene before, and it had been no more amusing the last time, though this time it appeared Anthony was doing the supporting. George looked half asleep.

"You're home early,'' Roslynn remarked, keeping her tone neutral.

"The old boy got royally foxed and passed out. Thought I'd better get him to bed.''

"So you brought him here instead of taking him home?''

Anthony shrugged. "Habit, my dear. When we used to make a night of it, more times than not old George would end up here. Has his own room, don't you know. Though, actually, come to think of it, you have it now."

They stared at each other a long moment before George broke the contact. "What's that? Who has my room?"

"Don't worry about it, old man. My wife has a few of her things in it that she'll be happy to move for tonight. Won't you, my dear?"

Roslynn's heart turned over. Had he brought George home just so she *would* have to move? And the only place she could move to was his room.

"Don't go to any trouble on my account, Lady Malory."

She understood him perfectly, though his words were terribly slurred and he couldn't seem to locate her, his eyes settling on Dobson instead. "It's no trouble, George," Roslynn assured him. "If you'll just give me a moment—"

"Don't have a moment," Anthony interjected. "He's bloody well heavy, you know. And if I put him down, he'll never get back up. Just proceed us, my dear, and get what you need."

She did, quickly, rushing through the room to gather her things while Anthony dumped George on the bed. George's room? So those were George's sonnets she had found in here. She never would have thought it of such a rakehell, but then you never knew. Frances was luckier than she realized.

She left the room just as quickly, for Anthony hadn't waited to start undressing George. In the corridor, she stared at the door to Anthony's room. This was what he meant for her to do, wasn't it? But then where else could she sleep? Jeremy and James probably weren't home yet, but they would be. And there were only the four rooms upstairs.

She entered the room hesitantly, expecting to find Willis waiting there for Anthony, even though the valet had been scarce these past two weeks, coming only when Anthony summoned him. The room was empty, however. Either Anthony had planned this, or he hadn't yet told Willis to hold himself available again. Then, too, the hour *was* early, by London standards. Willis wouldn't expect Anthony home this soon.

Roslynn sighed, not knowing what to think. But she wasn't going to miss this opportunity. She couldn't have planned it better herself. She wouldn't have to sacrifice her pride and confess what a fool she'd been. She could simply show Anthony that she wasn't adverse to being here, that in fact she wanted to be here.

She began removing her evening apparel. She was down to her chemise when Anthony walked into the room. His gaze rested on her for several heartbeats before he went on into his dressing room. Roslynn hastily got into bed. She wished he had said something. God, how this reminded her of her wedding night. And she was just as nervous now as she had been then.

When he came out, he was wearing only a robe. She at least had thought to slip on a nightgown. She wasn't going to be *that* obvious about what she wanted.

But it was obvious. While he moved about the room to turn down the lamps, desire lit the golden flecks in her eyes as they followed his superb form. She had had too much of him lately. She had found that it wasn't nearly enough. It never would be.

It was dark now, with only a silver stream of moonlight spilling in through the windows. Before her eyes adjusted, her other senses came alive. She could smell him as he drew near. When the bed dipped, she held her breath, waiting. She was experiencing that same giddy feeling she always felt when he was near. He would lean toward her in a moment. His mouth would find hers in the dark, warm, demanding . . .

"Good night, my dear."

Her eyes flew open. Hell's teeth, he hadn't planned the eviction from her room, after all. He was holding to her own rules not to touch her once she had conceived. It wasn't fair. How *could* he, when she was lying right next to him, wanting him more than anything?

"Anthony—"

"Yes?"

His tone was sharp to her ears, killing her courage. "Nothing," she mumbled.

Roslynn lay there, counting her heartbeats, wishing she had drunk more than two glasses of champagne at Frances' party. But she had been thinking of tomorrow morning and the nausea she would have to fight to get to the wedding. She hadn't known sleep was going to be impossible. Just last night she had felt free to turn to Anthony, to rest her head on his chest, to count *his* heartbeats. What a world of difference a single day made. No, not the day. Her cursed bargain.

This just wouldn't do. She was going to have to . . .

She heard the groan just before Anthony's hands reached over and pulled her across his chest. His kiss was wild, full of unleashed passion that set them both aflame. Roslynn didn't question it, she just accepted, so delighted and relieved that she abandoned herself completely, wantonly, to the moment. Pride couldn't equal this. She loved him. She would have to tell him, but now was not the time. Later, when she could think clearly once again.

Chapter Forty-three

*I*t seemed anything and everything was conspiring against Roslynn to keep her from having a private word with Anthony, including herself. She had fallen blissfully asleep after they had made love the other night, and then the next morning Anthony had awakened her simply to tell her that George had left and she could have her room back. Just like that, as if the night had never been. And when she had been about to detain him, her stomach had erupted and she had made it to her room only in the nick of time.

Then there had been the wedding and the luncheon afterward that had taken most of the afternoon. But Anthony hadn't come home with her. He had gone off directly to spend this last evening with his brother, and Roslynn spent a tortuous night wondering what they were up to, because neither of them came home until the small hours of the morning.

And this morning she had been hurried out of bed for the ride to the docks to see the *Maiden Anne* off, with the whole family showing up for the occasion. She stood off to the side now with Jeremy while James' brothers each embraced him and bade him a fair voyage. She had kissed him good-bye herself, a brief peck, what with Anthony's close attention, which James couldn't resist commenting on.

"I suppose you'll miss him terribly, Jeremy?"

The boy grinned at her. "Hell's bells, he won't be gone *that* long. And I doubt I'll have time to miss him. He's laid the law down, don't you know. I'm to bury myself in studies, and get me no bast—ah, that is, I'm to stay out of trouble, mind Uncle Tony, and yourself, of course, and do him proud.''

"I'm sure you'll be up to it." Roslynn tried to smile, but the smells of the wharf were doing her in. She had to get to the carriage before she disgraced herself. "I believe it's your turn to tell your father good-bye, laddie."

Jeremy was crushed not only by James but by Conrad as well, and had to listen to another long list of dos and don'ts from the first mate. But he was saved by the tide. It wouldn't wait, and both men were forced to board.

James could blame Anthony for the hangover that nearly made him forget. He called Jeremy up the gangplank and handed him a note. "See your aunt Roslynn gets this, but not when Tony's around."

Jeremy pocketed the note. "It's not a love letter, is it?"

"A love letter?" James snorted. "Get out of here, puppy. And see you—"

"I know, I know." Jeremy threw up his hands, laughing. "I won't do anything you wouldn't."

He ran back down the gangplank before James could take him to task for his impudence. But he was smiling as he turned away, and came face-to-face with Conrad.

"What was that about?"

James shrugged, realizing Connie had seen him pass the note. "I decided to lend a hand after all. At the rate Tony's going, he'd be floundering forever."

"I thought you weren't going to interfere," Connie reminded him.

"Well, he is my brother, isn't he? Though why I bother after the dirty trick he played on me last night,

I don't know.'' At Connie's raised brow, he grinned, despite the slow throb in his head. ''Made sure I'd be feeling miserable today to cast off, the bloody sod.''

''But you went along with it, naturally?''

''Naturally. Couldn't have the lad drinking me under the table, now, could I? But you'll have to see us off, Connie. I'm afraid I'm done for. Report to me in my cabin after we're under way.''

An hour later, Connie poured a measure of rye from the well-stocked cabinet in the captain's cabin and joined James at his desk. ''You're not going to worry about the boy, are you?''

''That rascal?'' James shook his head, wincing slightly when his headache returned, and took another sip of the tonic Connie had had sent from the galley. ''Tony will see he doesn't get into any serious scrapes. If anyone will worry, it's you. You should have had one of your own, Connie.''

''I probably do. I just haven't found him yet like you did the lad. You've probably more yourself that you don't know about.''

''Good God, one's enough,'' James replied in mock horror, gaining a chuckle from his friend. ''Now what have you to report? How many of the old crew were available?''

''Eighteen. And there was no problem filling the ranks, except for the bos'n, as I told you before.''

''So we're sailing without one? That'll put a heavy load on yourself, Connie.''

''Aye, if I hadn't found a man yesterday, or rather, if he hadn't volunteered. Wanted to sign on as passengers, him and his brother. When I told him the *Maiden Anne* don't carry passengers, he offered to work his way across. A more persistent Scot I've never seen.''

"Another Scot? As if I ain't had enough to do with them lately. I'm bloody well glad your own Scot's ancestors are so far back you don't remember them, Connie. Between hunting down Lady Roslynn's cousin and running into that little vixen and her companion—"

"I thought you'd forgotten about that."

James' answer was a scowl. "How do you know this Scot knows the first thing about rigging?"

"I put him through the paces. I'd say he's had the job before. And he does claim to have sailed before, as quartermaster, ship's carpenter, and bos'n."

"If that's true, he'll come in right handy. Very well. Is there anything else?"

"Johnny got married."

"Johnny? My cabin boy, Johnny?" James' eyes flared. "Good God, he's only fifteen! What the devil does he think he's doing?"

Connie shrugged. "Says he fell in love and can't bear to leave the little woman."

"Little woman?" James sneered. "That cocky little twit needs a mother, not a wife." His head was pounding again, and he swilled down the rest of the tonic.

"I've found you another cabin boy. MacDonell's brother—"

Tonic spewed across James' desk. "Who?" he choked.

"Blister it, James, what's got into you?"

"You said MacDonell? Would his first name be Ian?"

"Aye." Now Connie's eyes flared. "Good God, he's not the Scot from that tavern, is he?"

James waved away the question. "Did you get a good look at the brother?"

"Come to think of it, no. He was a little chap, though, quiet, hiding behind his brother's coattails. I didn't have much choice in signing him on, what with Johnny only letting me know two days ago that he was staying in England. But you can't mean to think—"

"But I do." And suddenly James was laughing. "Oh, God, Connie, this is priceless. I went back to look for that little wench, you know, but she and her Scot had disappeared from the area. Now here she's fallen right into my lap."

Connie grunted. "Well, I can see you're going to have a pleasant crossing."

"You may depend upon it." James' grin was decidedly wolfish. "But we shan't unmask her disguise just yet. I've a mind to play with her first."

"You could be wrong, you know. She might be a boy after all."

"I doubt it," James replied. "But I'll find out when she begins her duties."

And as the *Maiden Anne* left England behind, James contemplated those duties and how he would add to them in the coming weeks. This was indeed going to be a pleasant voyage.

Chapter Forty-four

"You're not going out again, are you?"

Anthony stopped in the process of putting his gloves on. "I was."

Roslynn left the parlor doorway, stepping closer to him. They had been home only a little over an hour. It had taken her this long to get up the courage to approach him, but that courage was fast deserting her now that the opportunity was here. But she had to do it.

"I would like a word with you."

"Very well." He indicated the parlor.

"No, upstairs." At his sharply arched brow, she blushed and quickly added, "In my room." Jeremy was in the house somewhere, but this was one conversation she didn't want interrupted. "We can be private there—for what I have to say."

"Then lead on, my dear."

His tone implied indifference. God, he was not going to make this easy for her. And what if he didn't care? What if she succeeded only in making a fool of herself?

Roslynn hurried upstairs with Anthony slowly following. He was dragging his feet, afraid he wasn't going to like what she had to say. It was too soon for her to say what he wanted to hear. He had figured it would take at least several weeks before she would admit she didn't like sleeping alone. She wouldn't balk then when he put his foot down and demanded she honor her original agreement with him to be a wife in every way.

Roslynn was already seated on the chaise longue when Anthony entered her room. Since that seat was taken and the bed was out of the question, he sat down on the stool at her vanity only a few feet away. He fiddled with the perfume bottles there, waiting for her to begin. The piece of paper was just something else to touch, but when he opened it, James' handwriting caught his immediate attention.

"Anthony, could you at least look at me?" He did, his eyes narrowed now, and she lowered her own. "I don't know how else to say this except . . . I was wrong."

"Wrong?"

"To put limitations on our marriage. I—I would like to start over."

She glanced up then. The last thing she expected to see was anger, but there was no mistaking that he was angry.

"Could this have anything to do with your sudden change of heart?" The paper dangled from his fingers.

"What is it?" she asked warily.

"Don't play games with me, Roslynn! You know exactly what it is," he said tersely.

She matched her tone to his, forgetting for the moment all about reconciliation. "No, I don't! Where did you get it?"

"On your vanity."

"Impossible. I changed clothes when I returned from the docks, and that, whatever it is"—she pointed at the paper—"was *not* on my table."

"There's one way to prove that, isn't there?"

He was furious at James' interference, but mostly

at her. How dared she put him through hell, then, because of a simple note, admit she was wrong? He didn't want her bloody contrition. He wanted her to want him without exception. And she would have before long. Then, and only then, would he have convinced her that she had accused him falsely.

He stalked to the door and threw it open, bellowing for Jeremy. Either James had slipped her that note at the docks, which was doubtful since Anthony had been close to her the whole while, or James had given it to Jeremy to give to her. Whichever, he wasn't going to have her lying about it.

When the boy poked his head out of his room down the corridor, Anthony demanded, "Did your father entrust you with something to give to my wife?"

Jeremy groaned. "Hell's bells, Tony, I thought you'd left. I only just put it . . . you weren't supposed to see it," he finished lamely.

Anthony crumpled the paper in his hand. "That's all right, youngun. No harm done."

He closed the door again, frowning at his own stupid assumption. She hadn't seen the note. That meant . . . bloody hell, and he had just antagonized the hell out of her.

He found her on her feet, her hand outstretched, her eyes glittering with indignation. "I'll be taking that, if you please."

"I don't," he replied, wincing to hear her brogue, a sure sign of her temper. "Look, I'm sorry if I drew the wrong conclusion. The note isn't important. What—"

"I'll determine what's important. If that was on my vanity, then it was meant for me, no' for you."

"Then take it."

He held out his hand, palm up. When she came

forward and took the ball of paper, he didn't give her a chance to read it. His fingers closed over hers and he drew her into his arms.

"You can read that later," he said softly. "Tell me first what you meant by being wrong."

She forgot all about the note now crumpled in her fist. "I told you—about the limitations. I should never have—have placed conditions on our marrying."

"True. Is that all?"

He was smiling at her, that melting smile that turned her to honey. "I shouldna have come to you just for the bairn, but I was afraid I'd get so used to having you that nothing else would matter."

"Did you?" His lips brushed her cheek, the side of her mouth.

"What?"

"Get used to having me?"

He didn't let her answer, his lips slanting across hers, warm, beguiling, stealing her breath, her soul. She had to break the contact herself. "Och, mon, if you keep kissing me, I'll never say it all."

He chuckled, still holding her close. "But none of this was necessary, sweetheart. Your problem is, you've taken a bloody lot for granted. You assumed that I would have let this don't-touch-me stand of yours go on indefinitely. Not so. You also seem to think that I would have abided by any rules whatsoever that you set down for this relationship. Wrong again." He softened this news with another deep kiss before continuing. "I hate to disillusion you, sweetheart, but you get away with your outlandish demands for only as long as I allow you to. And I would have allowed you only a few more weeks, no more, to come to your senses."

"Or?"

"Or I would have moved in here."

"Would you, now?" she retorted, but her lips were twitching. "Without my permission, I suppose?"

"We'll never know, will we?" He grinned. "Now, what else did you want to tell me?"

She tried to shrug. It didn't work. Her senses were reeling with his body pressed to hers, his eyes warm, tender, his lips a breath away.

"I love you," she said simply, then squealed when he squeezed her so tight she couldn't breathe.

"Oh, God, Roslynn, I was afraid I'd never hear you say it! Do you really? Despite what an utter ass I've been half the time?"

"Yes." She laughed, giddy from his reaction.

"Then read that note from James."

It was the last thing she expected to hear at the moment. She glanced at him warily as he set her down on her feet and stepped back. But she opened the paper, too curious now not to. The message was brief, addressed to her.

Since Tony's too pigheaded to tell you, I thought you ought to know that the little tavern wench you assumed Tony dallied with was actually mine for the evening. Tony might have been her first choice, as he was yours, but she had no complaints in settling for me. You've been wrong about the lad, dear girl. I do think he loves you.

Roslynn's eyes were moist as they found his and he drew her gently back into his arms. "How can you ever forgive me, Anthony?"

"You forgave me, didn't you?"

"But you weren't guilty!"

"Shh, sweetheart. It doesn't matter now, does it? You're still the only woman I've wanted since I first saw you—bent over peeking in the Crandals' ballroom and presenting me with your sweet little derrière."

"Anthony!"

His laugh was rich and deep as he fastened his arms tighter around her so she couldn't hit him. "Well, it's true, my dear. I was utterly captivated."

"You were a rake!"

"I still am," he assured her. "You wouldn't want me to become morally proper, now, would you? You won't like making love only in the dark, suitably clothed so no skin touches except what is essential— ouch!" She had pinched him. "I'm not teasing you, my dear." He chuckled. "That's how Warton would probably have made love to you. 'Course, he would have died for it . . . now, now, no more pinches."

"Then be serious."

"But I am, my girl, most serious." His fingers slid into her hair, spilling pins this way and that, all the while his eyes remained locked to hers. "You became mine that first night, dashing toward me in the moonlight. You took my breath away. D'you know how much I wanted to make love to you then, right there in the Crandals' garden? What did you feel, sweetheart?"

"I—I was sorry I couldn't have you."

"Were you?" he asked softly, his thumbs caressing her cheeks, his lips just barely touching hers. "Do you want me now?"

"I've always wanted you, Anthony," she whispered, arms wrapping around his neck. "I didn't want it so. I was afraid I could never trust you."

"Do you trust me now?"

"I have to. I love you—even if you don't—"

He put a finger to her lips. "Oh, my beautiful, silly girl. Didn't you read all of my brother's note? My whole family knows I love you to distraction without my telling them. Why don't you?"

"You do?" she gasped.

"Would I have let you run rings around me if I didn't?"

"But why didn't you tell me?"

"You didn't want to marry me, sweetheart," he reminded her. "I practically had to twist your arm. And even when you agreed, you did everything possible to keep a distance between us. Would you have believed me then if I had told you I loved you? Roslynn, why else would I marry you?"

"But—" There were no but's. She kissed him, and kissed him again, her heart nearly bursting with joy. "Oh, Anthony, I'm so glad you did. And I'll never, ever be such a fool again, I swear—"

He told her, in between kisses, "You can be a fool . . . whenever you like . . . as long as you don't stop loving me."

"I couldn't, even if I wanted to. Will you?"

"Never, sweetheart. You may depend upon it."

Chapter Forty-five

"*I* understand congratulations are in order," Nicholas remarked as he joined Anthony for a smoke in the garden. Sunday dinner at Edward's had gathered the whole clan this time, minus James. "You don't think you're a bit old to be starting a family, Malory?"

"When are you going to visit Knighton's Hall, Montieth?" Anthony countered dryly.

Nicholas chuckled, ignoring the gibe. "Regina's been talking about nothing else since Roslynn told her. She wants another of her own now."

"That'll be a bit hard to do, won't it, dear boy? According to James, you're in the doghouse."

"Oh, I never stay there long, old man," Nicholas replied, his grin maddening. "Your niece might have the famous Malory temper, but she's not heartless. Besides, she doesn't like to sleep alone."

Anthony glowered. He still couldn't set it right in his mind that his little Reggie was a woman now—with a lusty rake for a husband. Seemed he ought to punch Montieth out for such a remark. 'Course, the whole family'd be down on his head if he did, Reggie in the lead.

"One of these days, Montieth, I'm going to like you. But don't hold your breath."

Nicholas' laughter followed him back into the house, rubbing him raw. Regina met up with him in the hall, however, to dispel the mood.

"Have you seen Nicholas, Tony?"

"Wish I hadn't, but he's in the garden."

"You didn't have words again, did you?" she asked, frowning.

"What can I say, puss?" He shrugged, then added deliberately, "But you'll notice I left. He goes for blood these days."

"Famous! Oh, when will you two *ever* get along?"

"We're too much alike, my girl, and we know it. But do me a favor and drag him back in the house, will you? I'd like to stroll with the wife, and a little privacy wouldn't be amiss."

Anthony was grinning when he left Regina. Hopefully Montieth would be back in the doghouse tonight, and the poor sod wouldn't even know what he'd done wrong. That thought brought a chuckle. One of these days Reggie was going to realize that he and Nicholas delighted in their verbal sparring. There'd be hell to pay then, but for now, Anthony counted himself the winner of this round.

He found Roslynn had been cornered by Edward, and he just caught her last words as he approached. "But I don't want to double my money. Hell's teeth, what would I do with more of it?"

"I should have warned you, sweetheart, that Eddie boy would be after you. He can't stand to see money just sitting around."

Edward defended himself. "Well, it's preposterous, Tony. No one ever has *too* much money, you know. There are the children to think of, and—"

"And I'm sure Roslynn will let you manage her estate, if she can ever get around to figuring out all it entails."

"That's not fair," Roslynn protested. "I know exactly what I own—I just can't be expected to remember it all." Both men laughed, to her chagrin. "Very well, I'll have my solicitor call on you, Edward. Perhaps this is something I should become interested in.''

"Good God, now see what you've done, Eddie," Anthony complained with mock horror. "I don't want her mind filled with figures."

"No, you just want it filled with you." Edward snorted.

"True." Anthony grinned unabashedly. "Now come along, my dear, and let me see if I can find something else for you to be interested in."

Anthony walked her away from the house, until there was only moonlight to light the way. He stopped near the rose bushes, his arms wrapping around her from behind, his chin resting on her shoulder.

"Do you really want to get involved in the empire your grandfather left you?"

"No, but I'm glad you at least asked." She smiled, her arms wrapped over his.

"Whatever makes you happy, Roslynn, since your happiness is mine."

She turned around in his arms, putting her cheek against his chest, loving him so much she could hardly contain it. One finger drew circles on the soft blue velvet of his jacket.

"There is something," she said in a small voice.

"Anything, sweetheart."

There was a long, shy silence before she asked, "Do you think we could try it again in the chair?"

Anthony's delighted laughter filled Grosvenor Square beyond the garden.

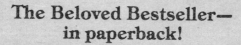